THE MOVIE

SECRETS OF THE JUNGLE

ANOTHER BEGINNING

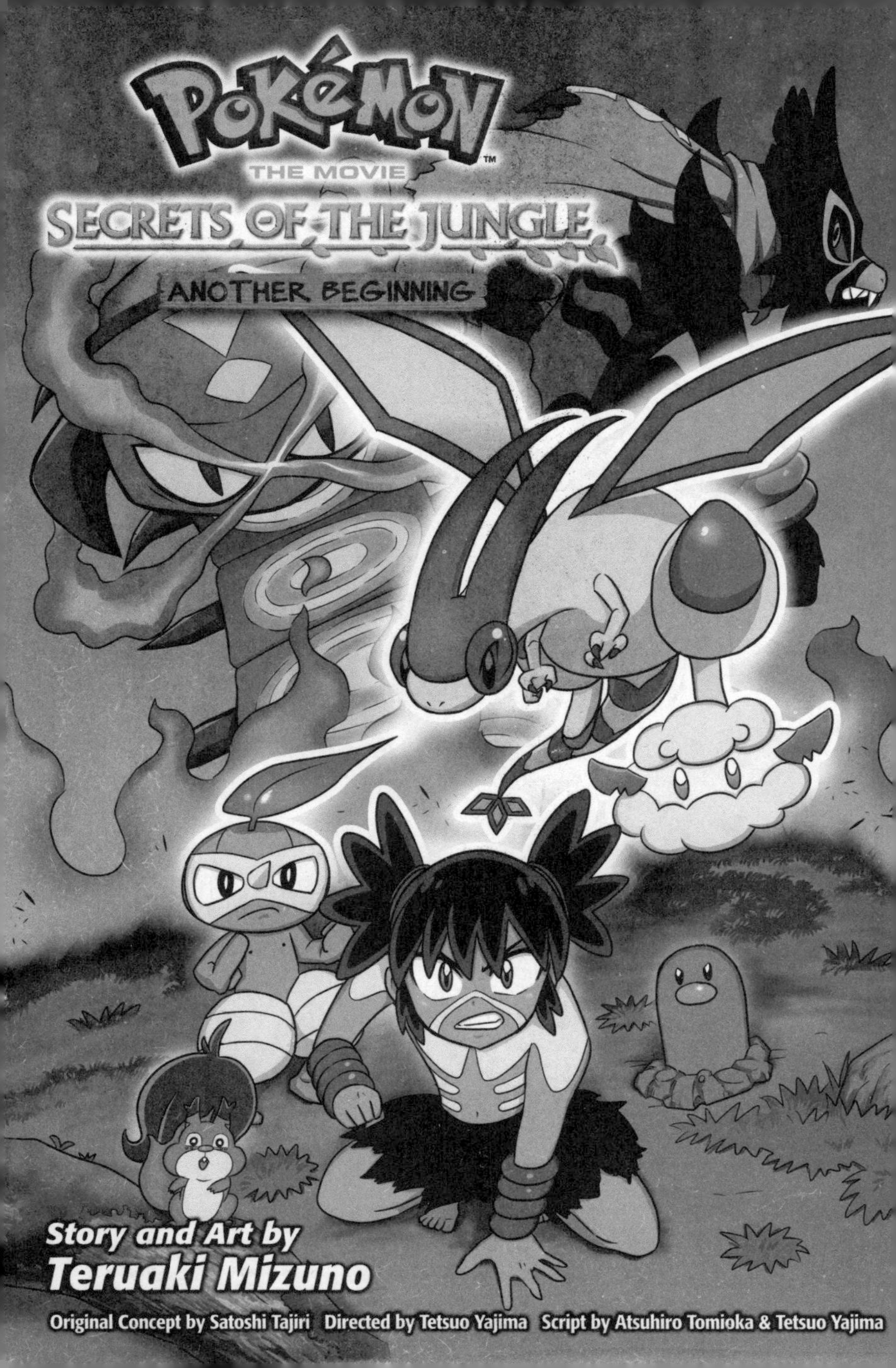

Pokémon The Movie
Secrets of the Jungle
Another Beginning

Story and Art by
Teruaki Mizuno

Original Concept by Satoshi Tajiri Directed by Tetsuo Yajima Script by Atsuhiro Tomioka & Tetsuo Yajima

CHARACTERS

Z.ARUDE

The Pokémon who raised Koko in okoya Forest.

KOKO

A human boy raised by Pokémon.

NUZLEAF

SKWOVET

COTTONEE

CONTENTS

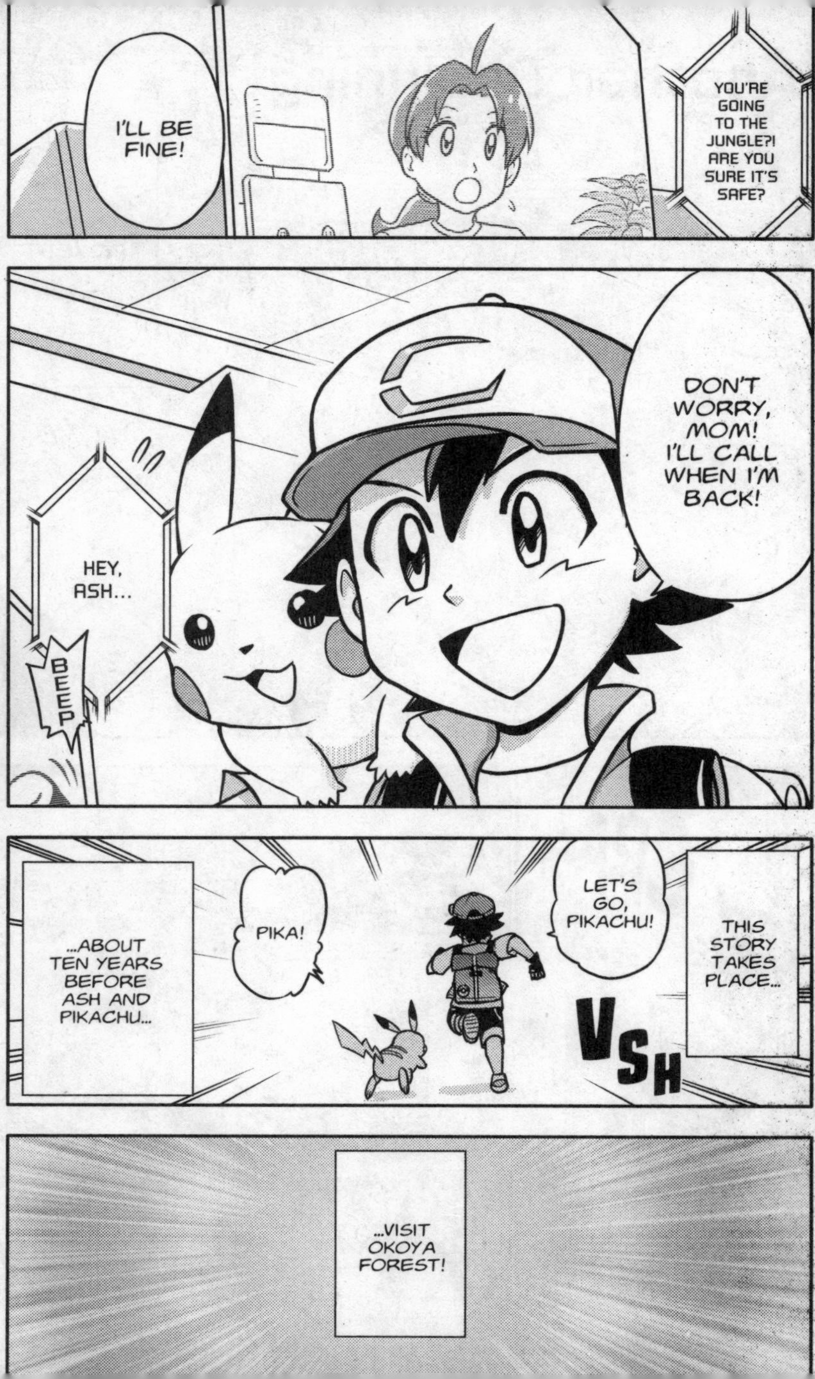
YOU'RE GOING TO THE JUNGLE?! ARE YOU SURE IT'S SAFE?
I'LL BE FINE!
DON'T WORRY, MOM! I'LL CALL WHEN I'M BACK!
HEY, ASH...
BEEP
THIS STORY TAKES PLACE...
VSH
LET'S GO, PIKACHU!
PIKA!
...ABOUT TEN YEARS BEFORE ASH AND PIKACHU...
...VISIT OKOYA FOREST!

Another Beginning

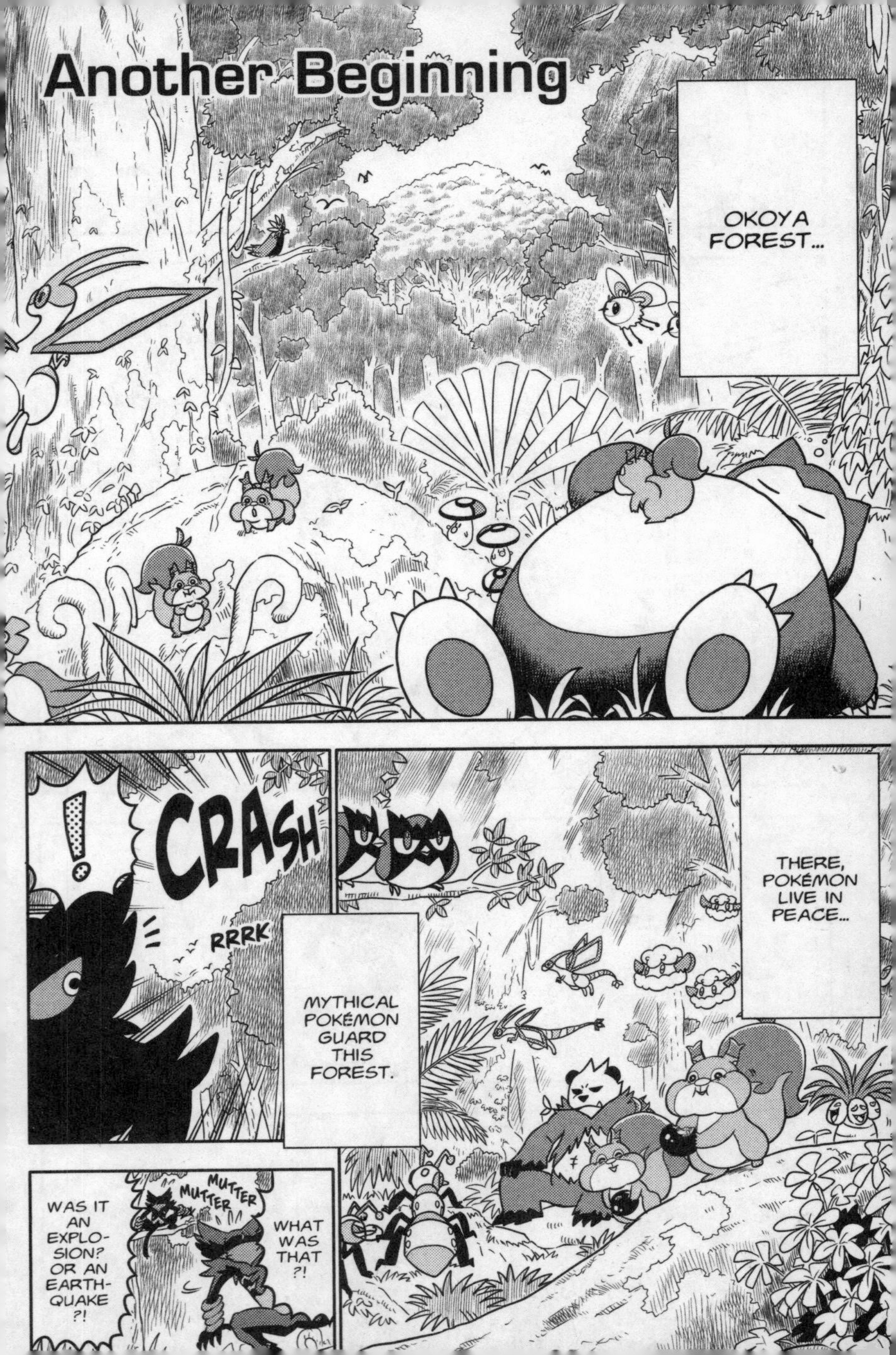
OKOYA FOREST...
THERE, POKÉMON LIVE IN PEACE...
MYTHICAL POKÉMON GUARD THIS FOREST.
CRASH
!
RRRK
WHAT WAS THAT ?!
MUTTER MUTTER
WAS IT AN EXPLO- SION? OR AN EARTH- QUAKE ?!

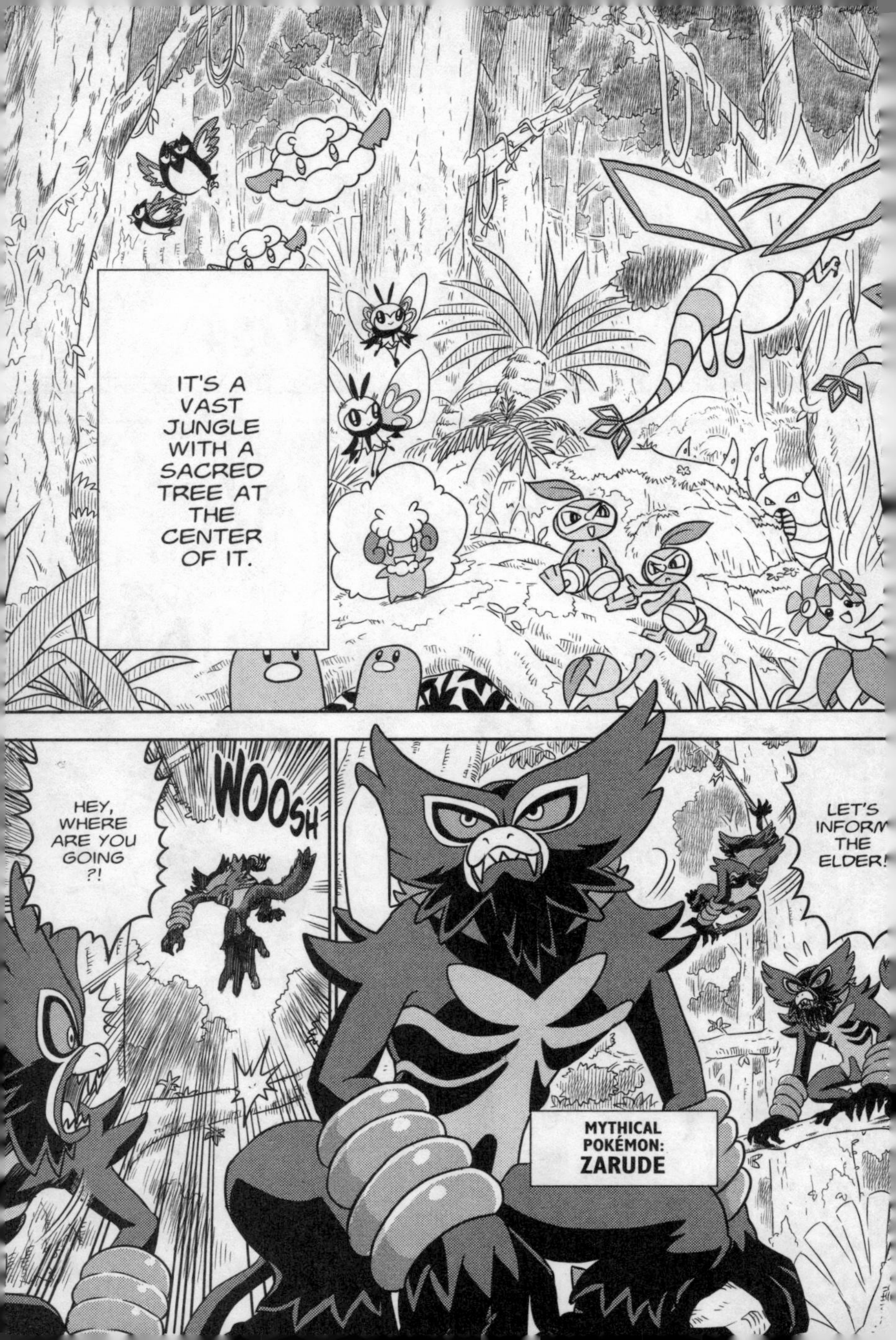
IT'S A VAST JUNGLE WITH A SACRED TREE AT THE CENTER OF IT.
LET'S INFORM THE ELDER!
MYTHICAL POKÉMON: ZARUDE
WOOSH
HEY, WHERE ARE YOU GOING ?!

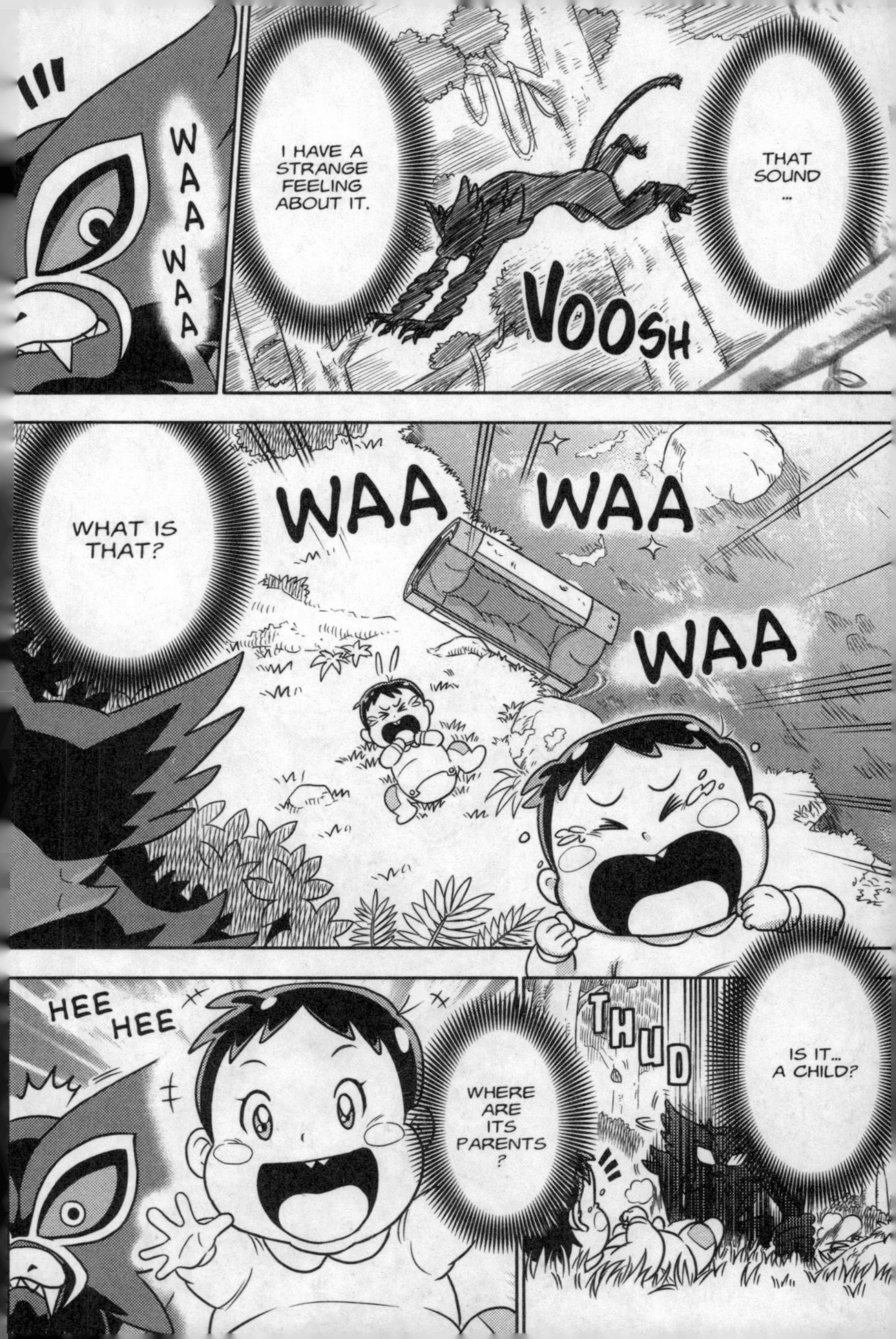
THAT SOUND ...
I HAVE A STRANGE FEELING ABOUT IT.
VOOSH
WAA WAA WAA
WAA WAA
WAA
WHAT IS THAT?
IS IT... A CHILD?
THUD
WHERE ARE ITS PARENTS?
HEE HEE

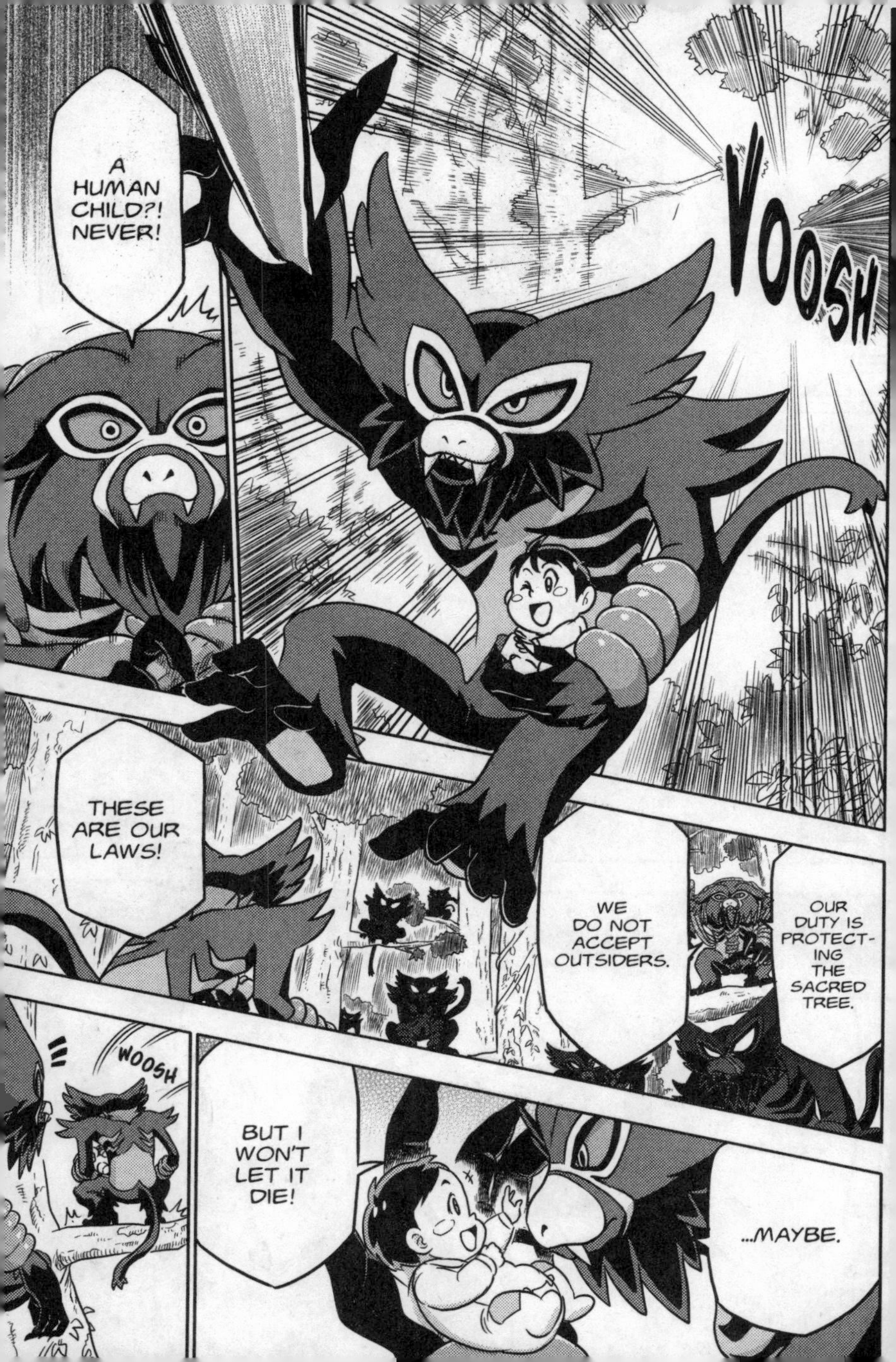
VOOSH
A HUMAN CHILD?! NEVER!
OUR DUTY IS PROTECTING THE SACRED TREE.
WE DO NOT ACCEPT OUTSIDERS.
THESE ARE OUR LAWS!
BUT I WON'T LET IT DIE!
...MAYBE.
WOOSH

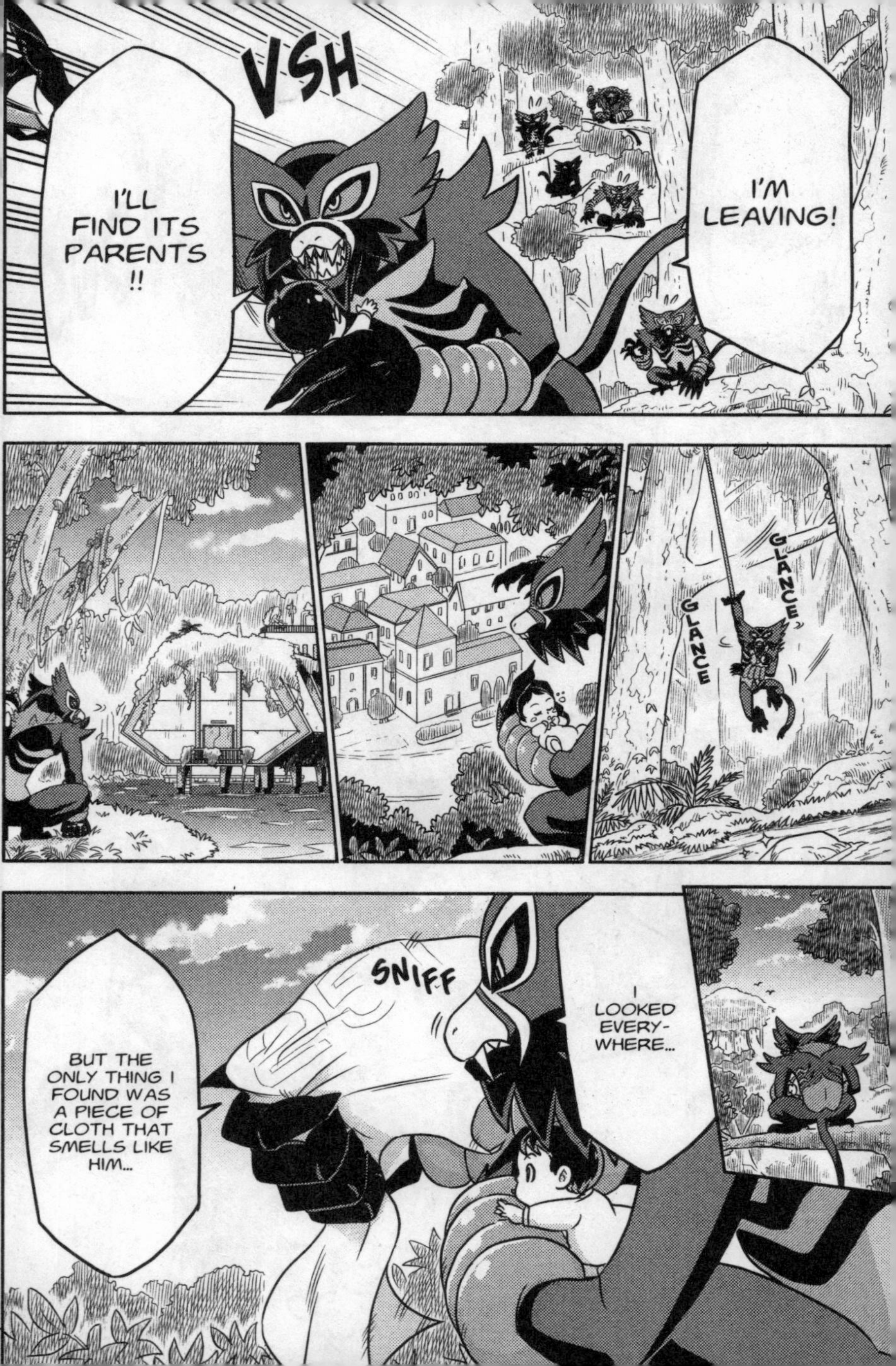
I'M LEAVING!
VSH
I'LL FIND ITS PARENTS !!
GLANCE
GLANCE
I LOOKED EVERY-WHERE...
SNIFF
BUT THE ONLY THING I FOUND WAS A PIECE OF CLOTH THAT SMELLS LIKE HIM...

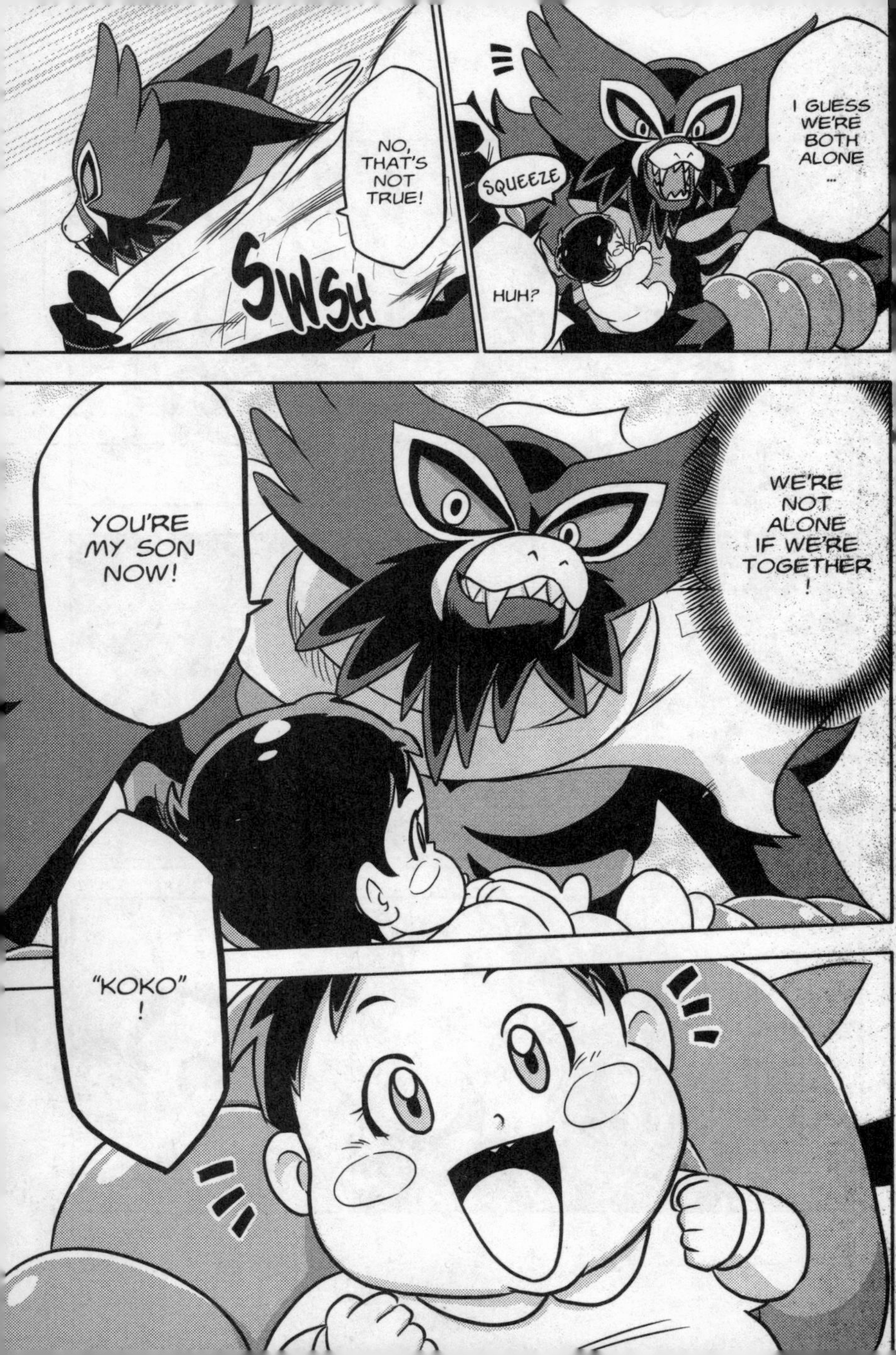
I GUESS WE'RE BOTH ALONE ...
SQUEEZE
HUH?
NO, THAT'S NOT TRUE!
SWSH
WE'RE NOT ALONE IF WE'RE TOGETHER!
YOU'RE MY SON NOW!
"KOKO"!

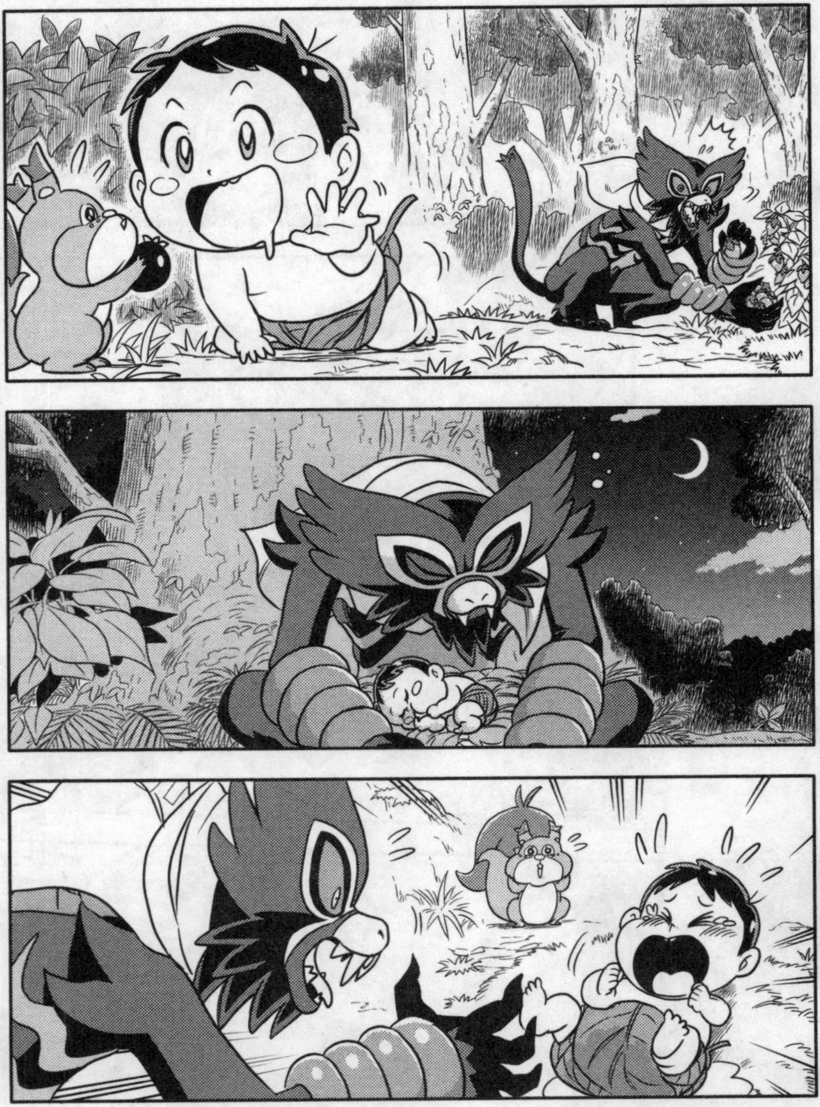

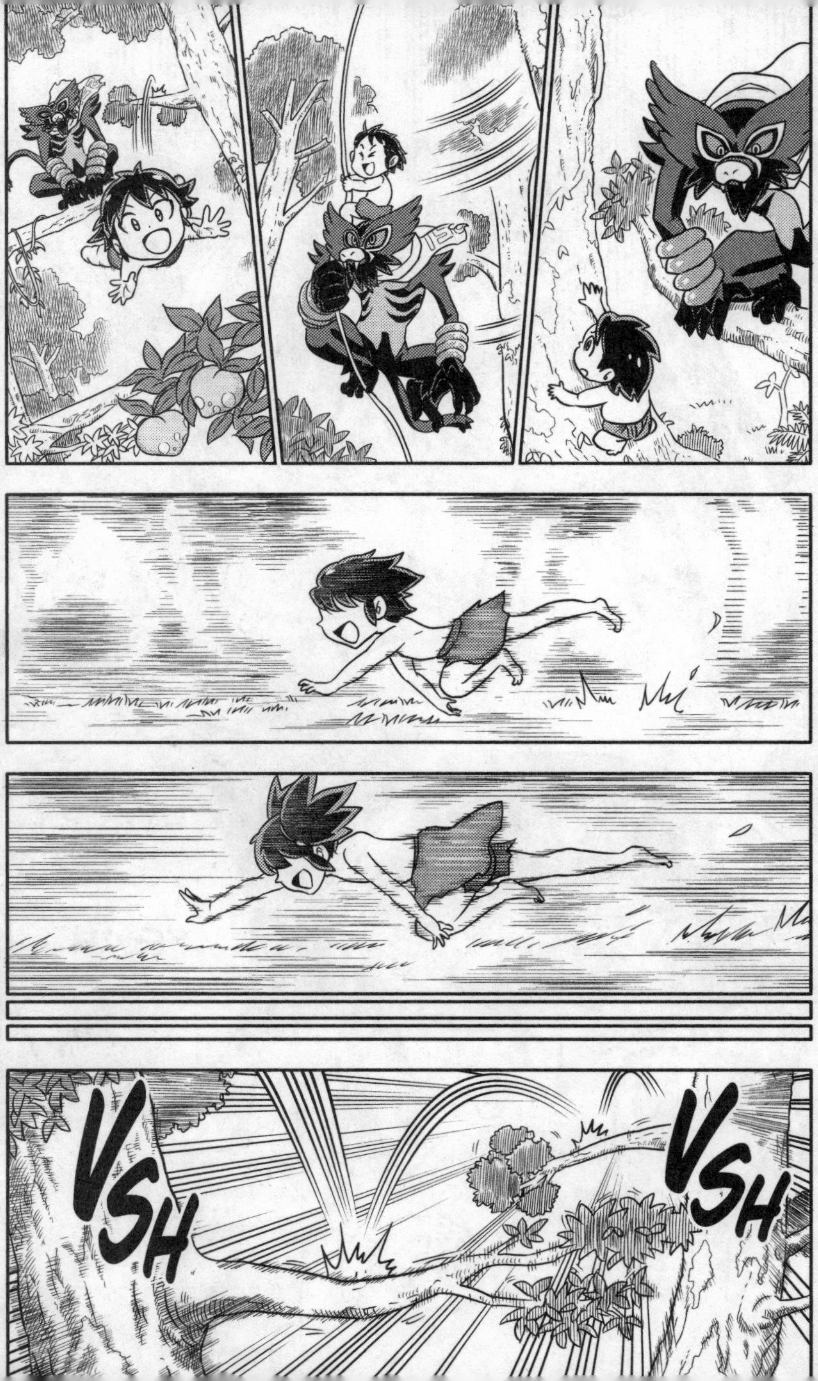
VSH
VSH

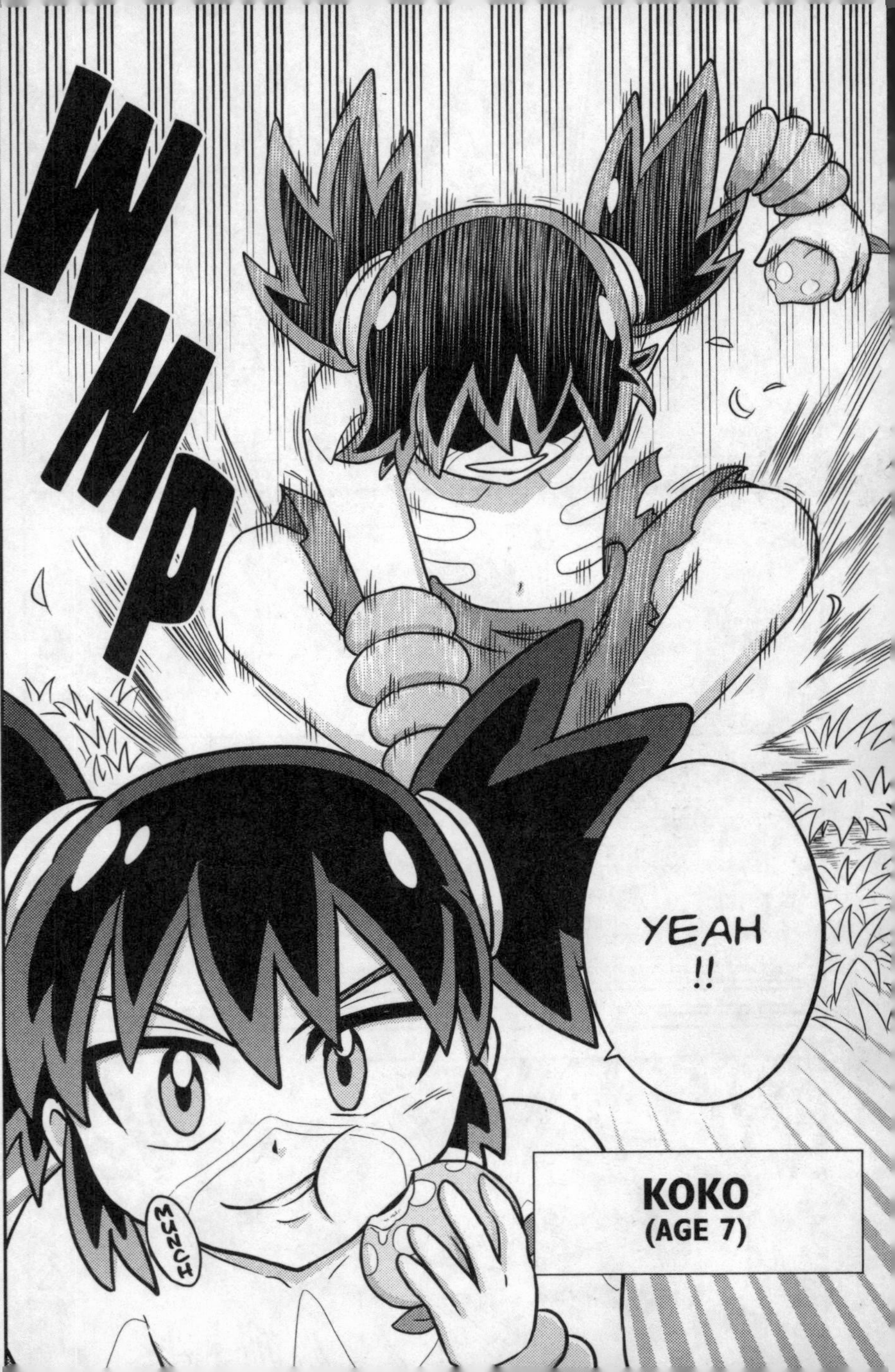
WHMP
YEAH !!
KOKO (AGE 7)
MUNCH

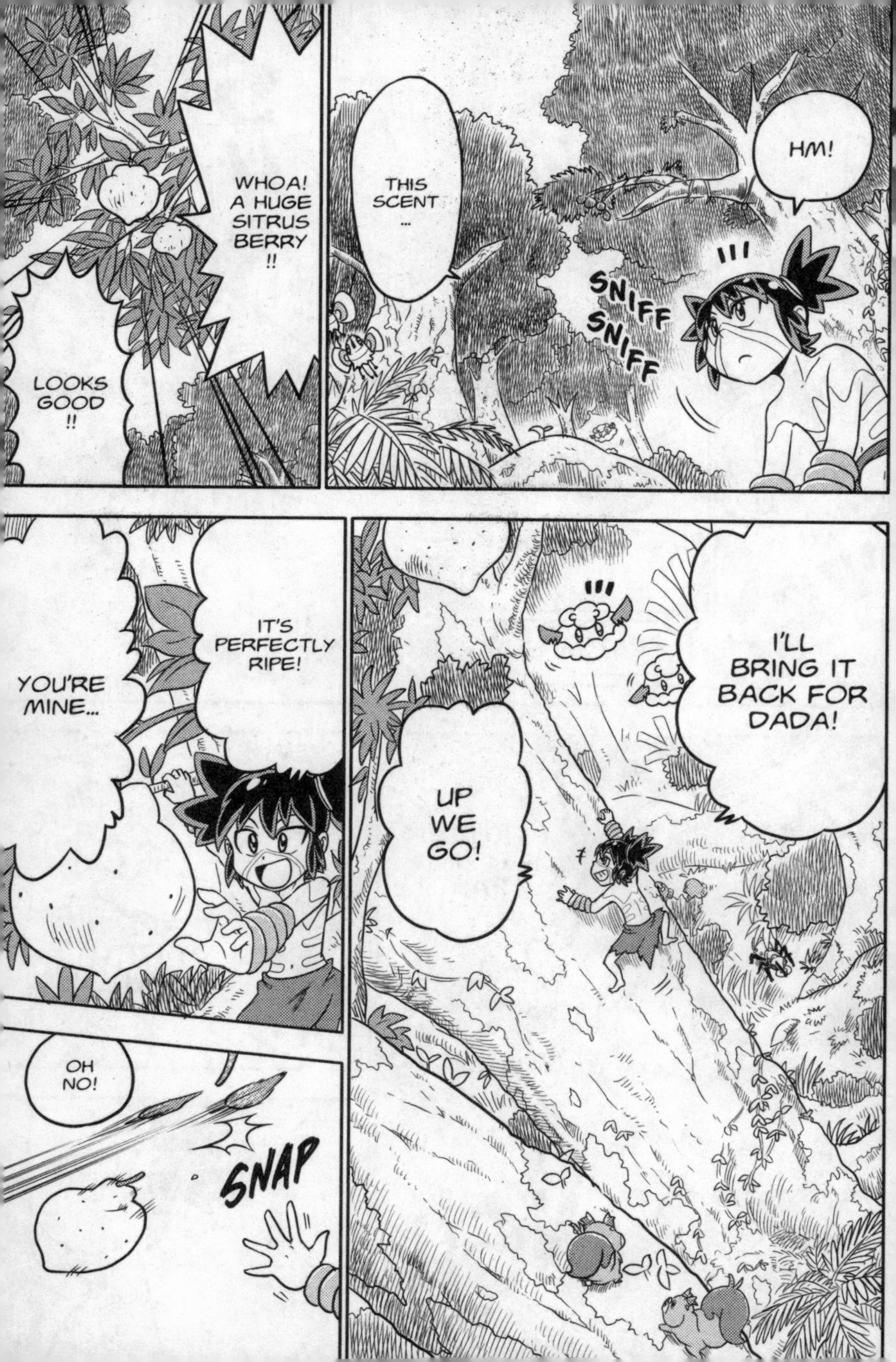
HM!
SNIFF SNIFF
THIS SCENT...
WHOA! A HUGE SITRUS BERRY!!
LOOKS GOOD!!
I'LL BRING IT BACK FOR DADA!
UP WE GO!
IT'S PERFECTLY RIPE!
YOU'RE MINE...
OH NO!
SNAP

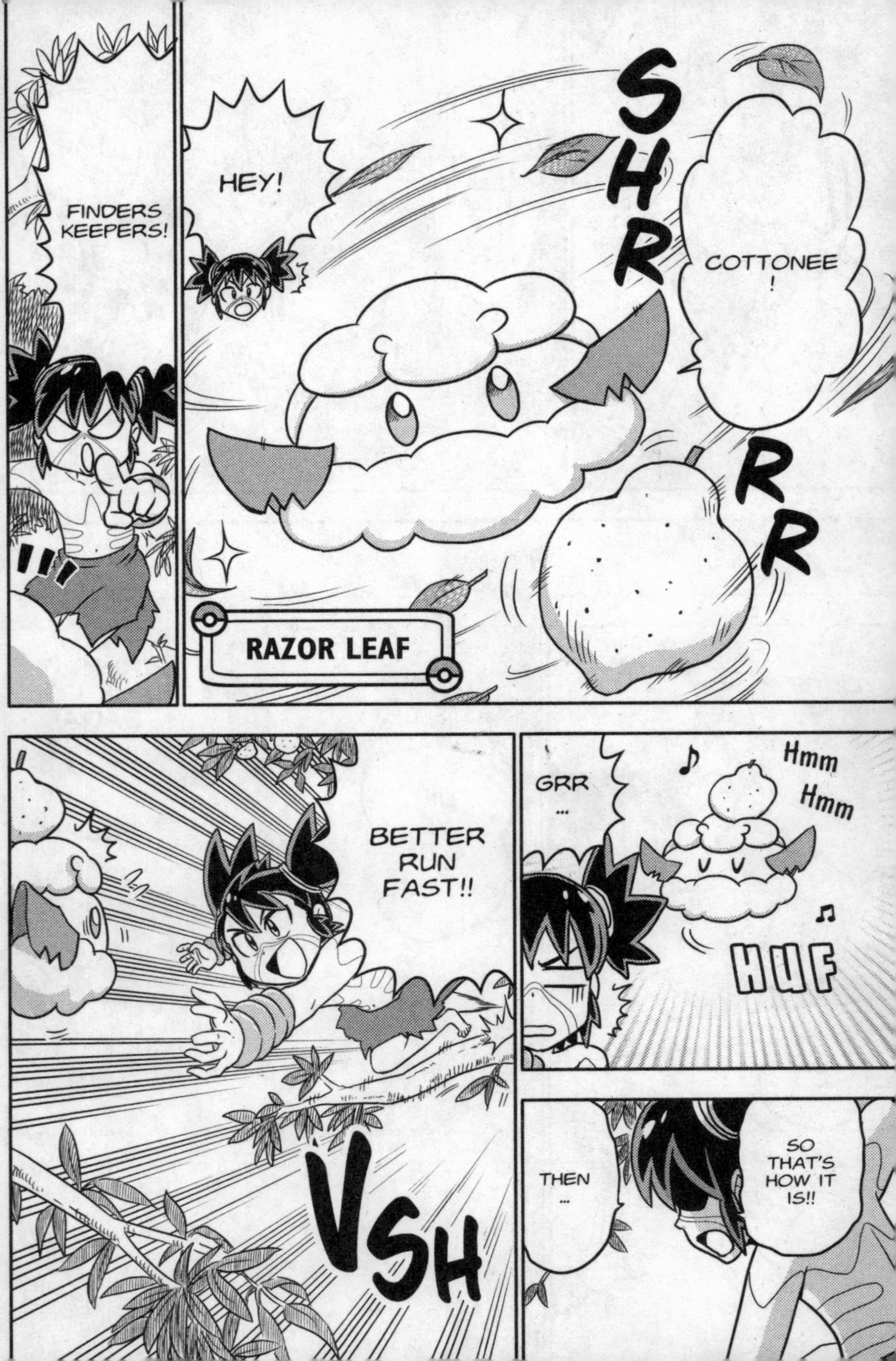
SHRRRR
COTTONEE!
HEY!
RAZOR LEAF
FINDERS KEEPERS!
Hmm Hmm
GRR ...
HUF
SO THAT'S HOW IT IS!!
THEN ...
BETTER RUN FAST!!
VSH

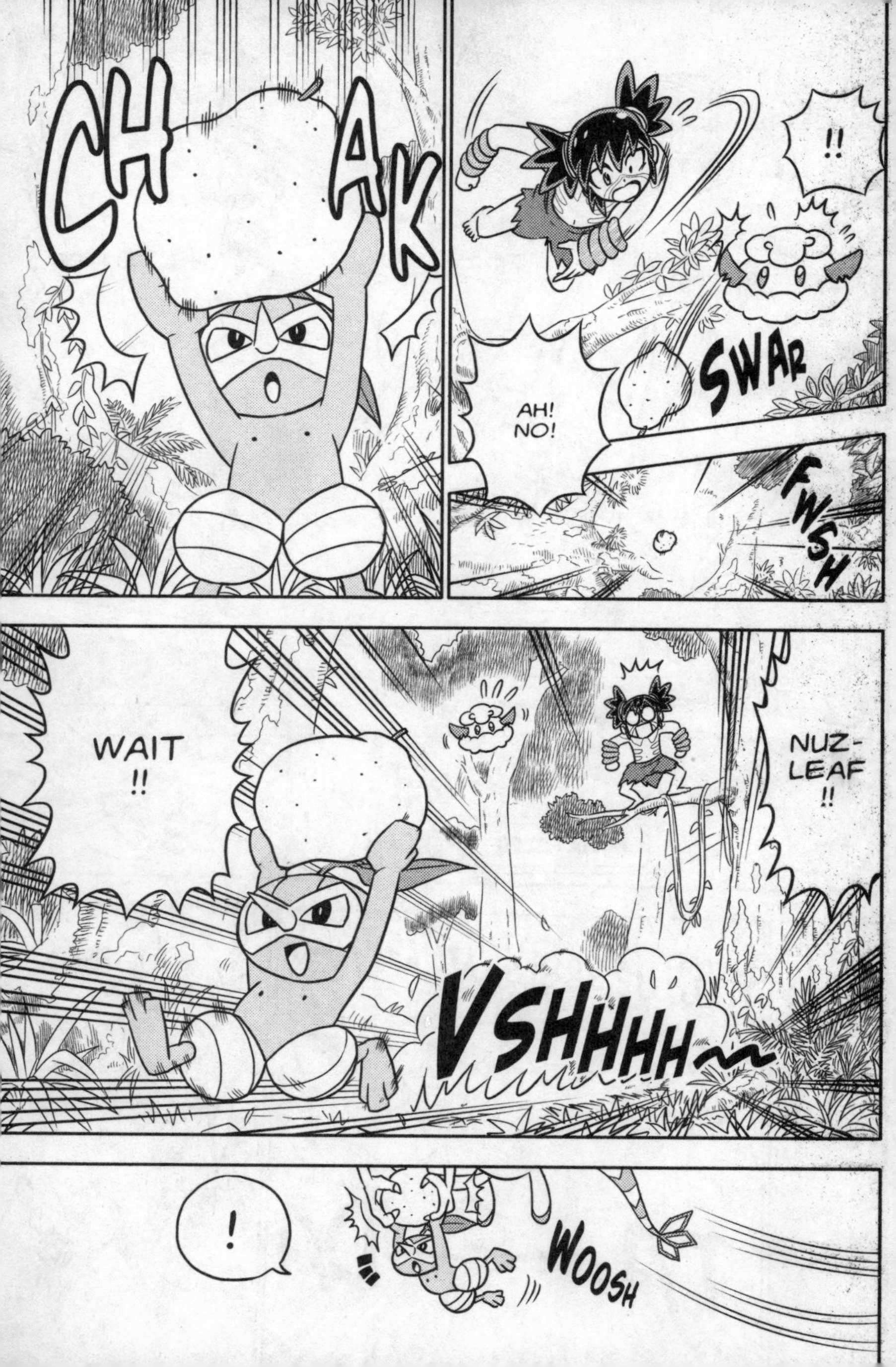
!!
AH! NO!
SWAR
FWSH
CHAK
NUZ-LEAF!!
WAIT!!
VSHHHH
WOOSH
!

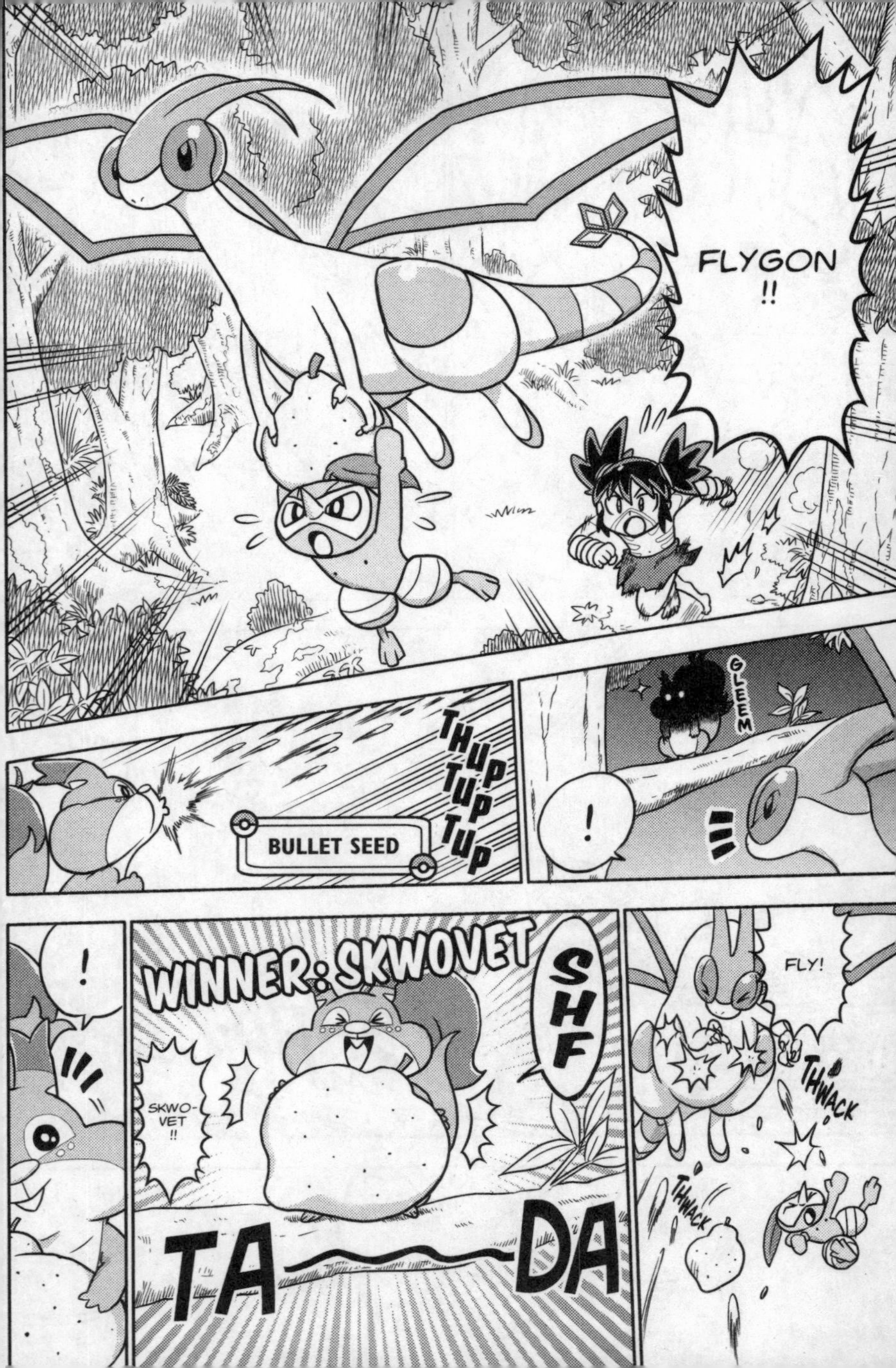
FLYGON !!
GLEEM
!
THUP TUP TUP
BULLET SEED
FLY!
THWACK
THWACK
WINNER: SKWOVET
SHF
SKWO-VET !!
TA——DA
!

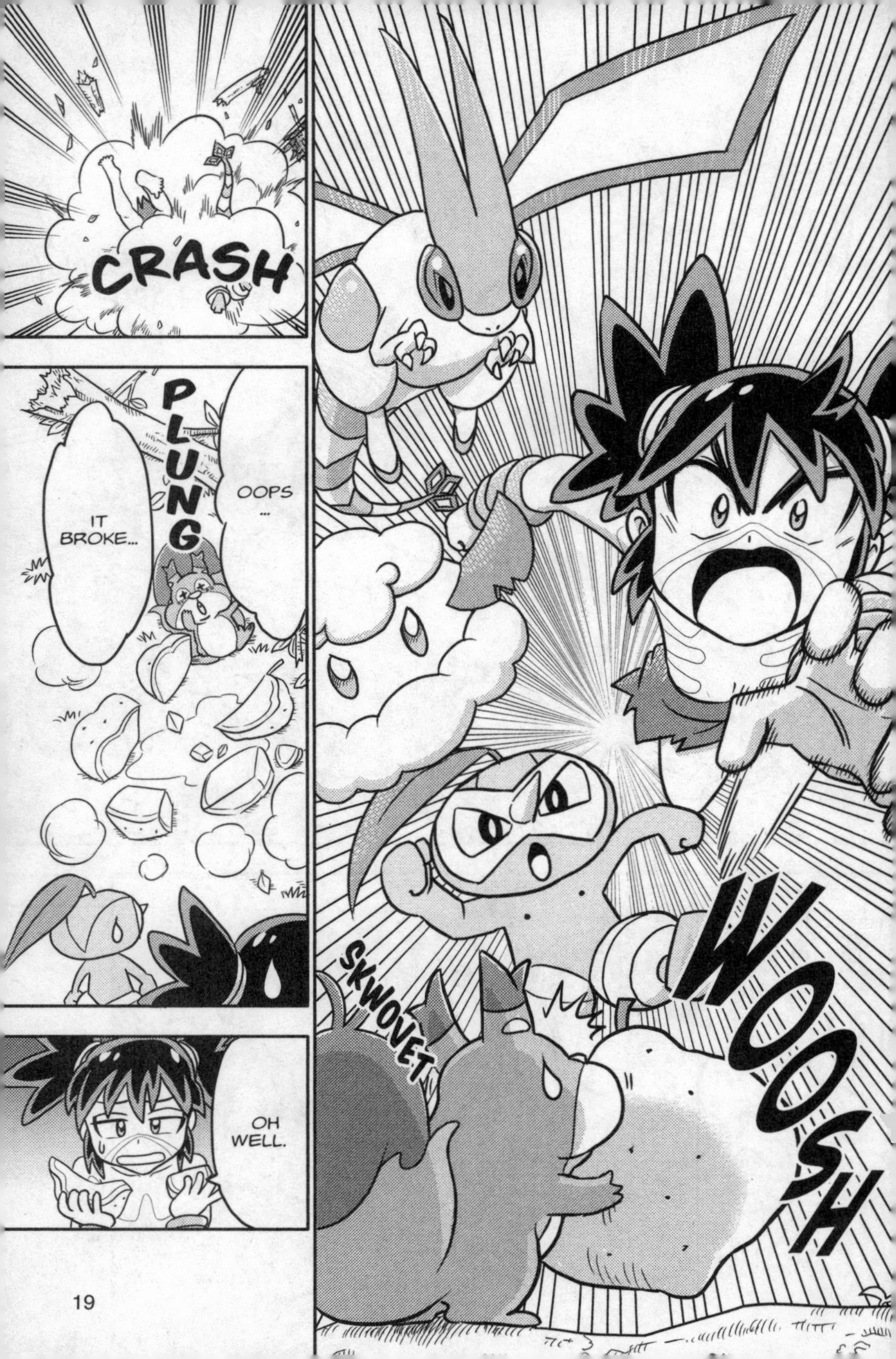
WOOSH
SKWOVET
CRASH
OOPS...
PLUNG
IT BROKE...
OH WELL.

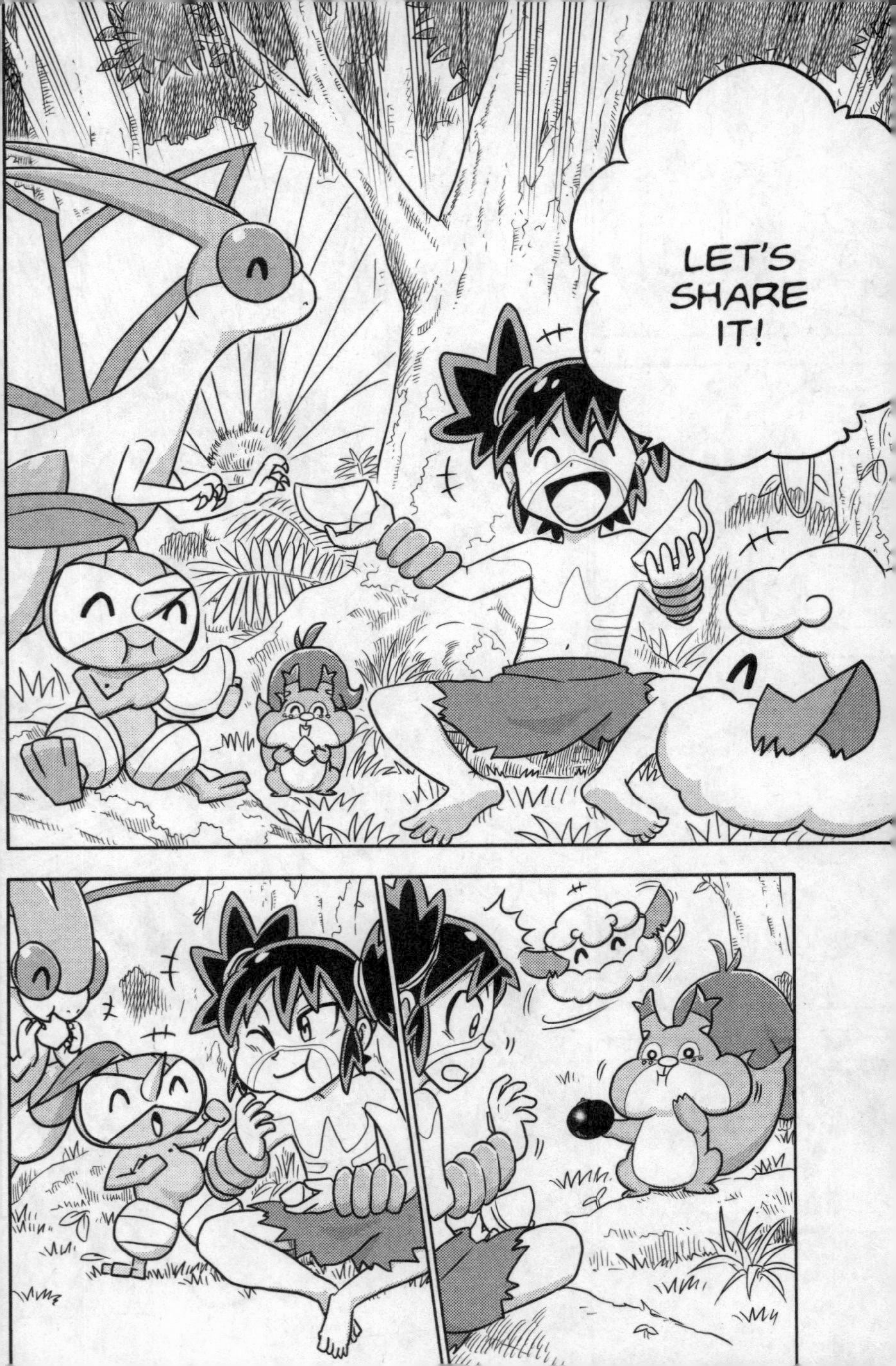
LET'S SHARE IT!

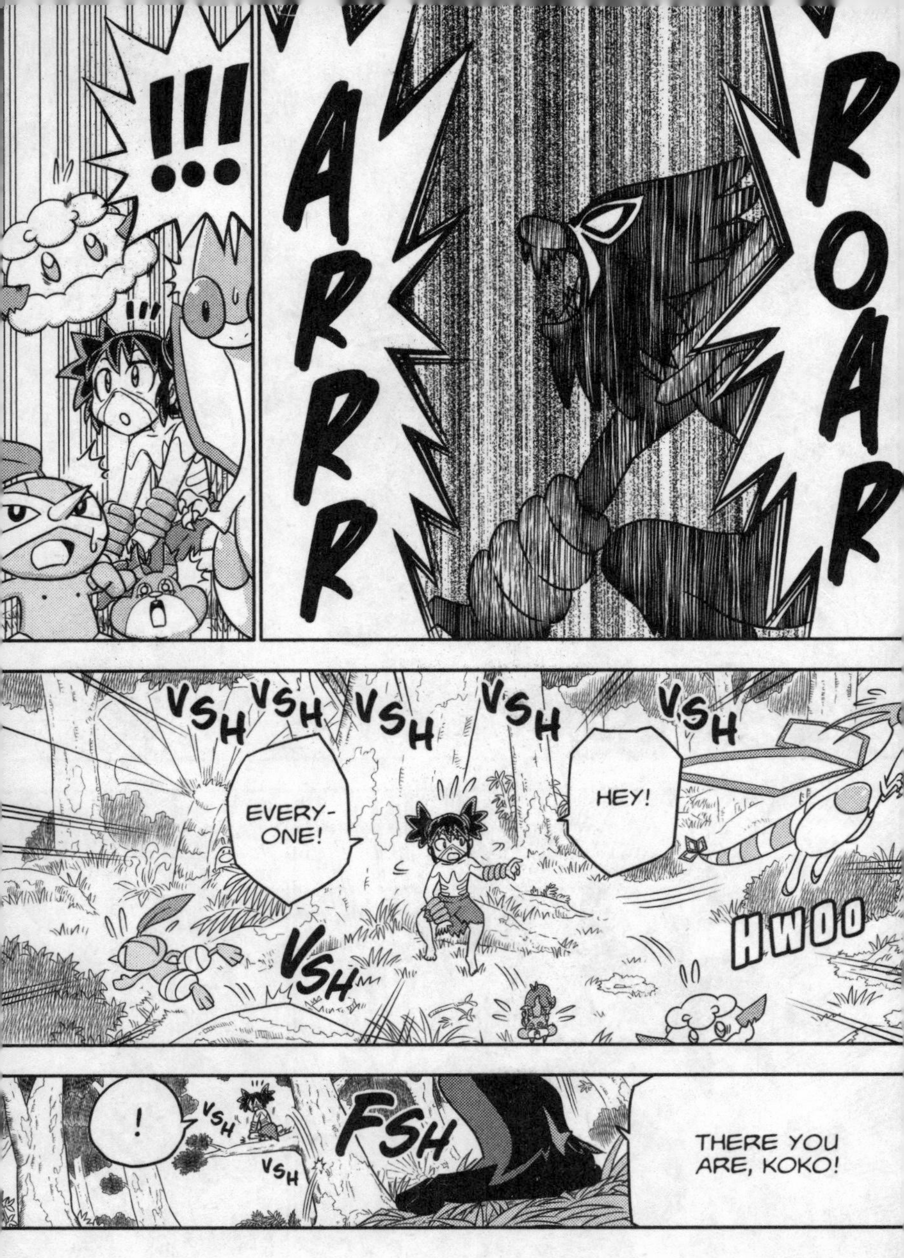
ROAR
ARRR
!!!...
VSH VSH VSH VSH VSH
HWOO
HEY!
EVERY-ONE!
VSH
THERE YOU ARE, KOKO!
FSH
!
VSH
VSH

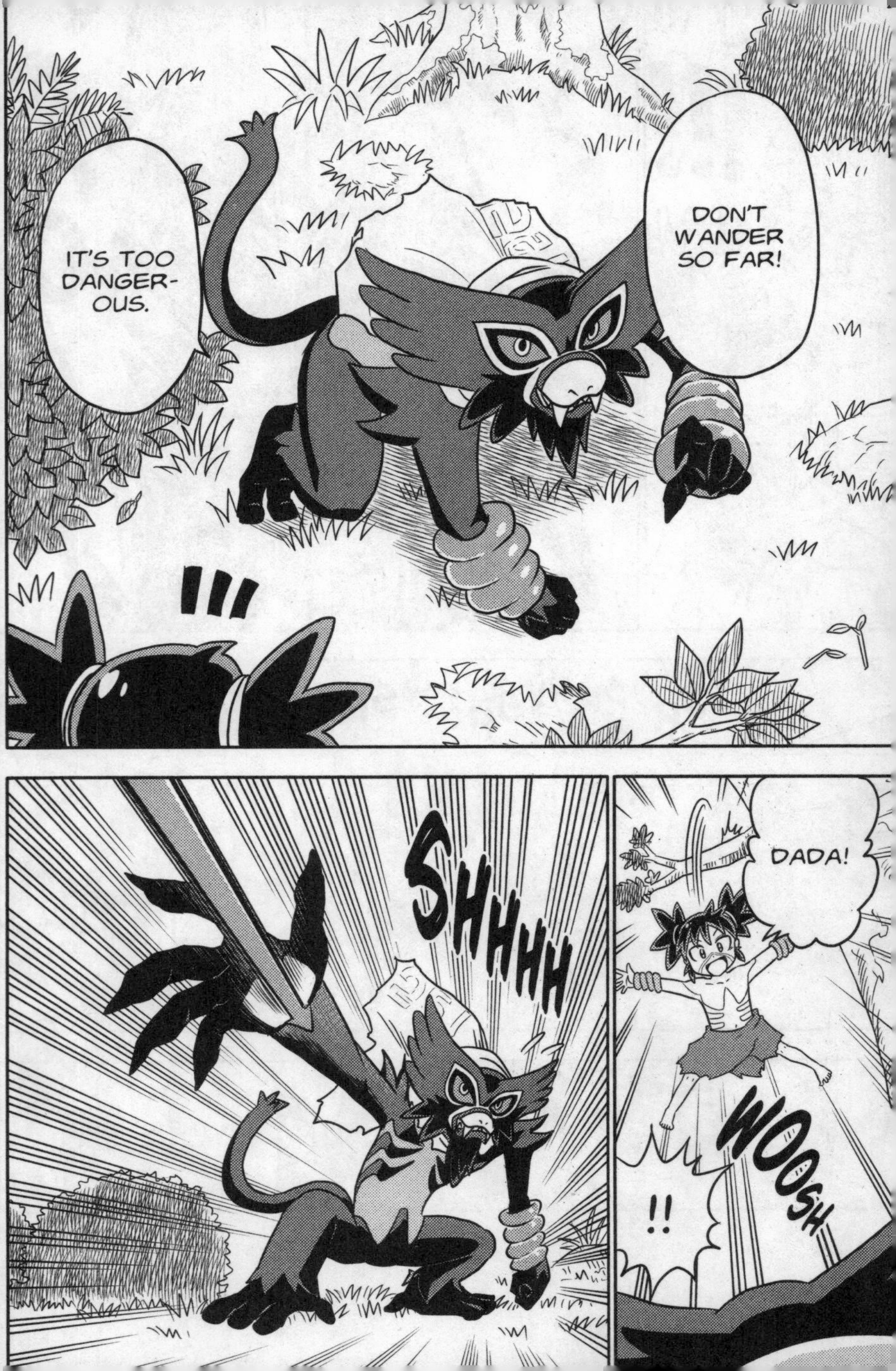
DON'T WANDER SO FAR!
IT'S TOO DANGER-OUS.
!!!
DADA!
WOOSH
!!
SHHHH

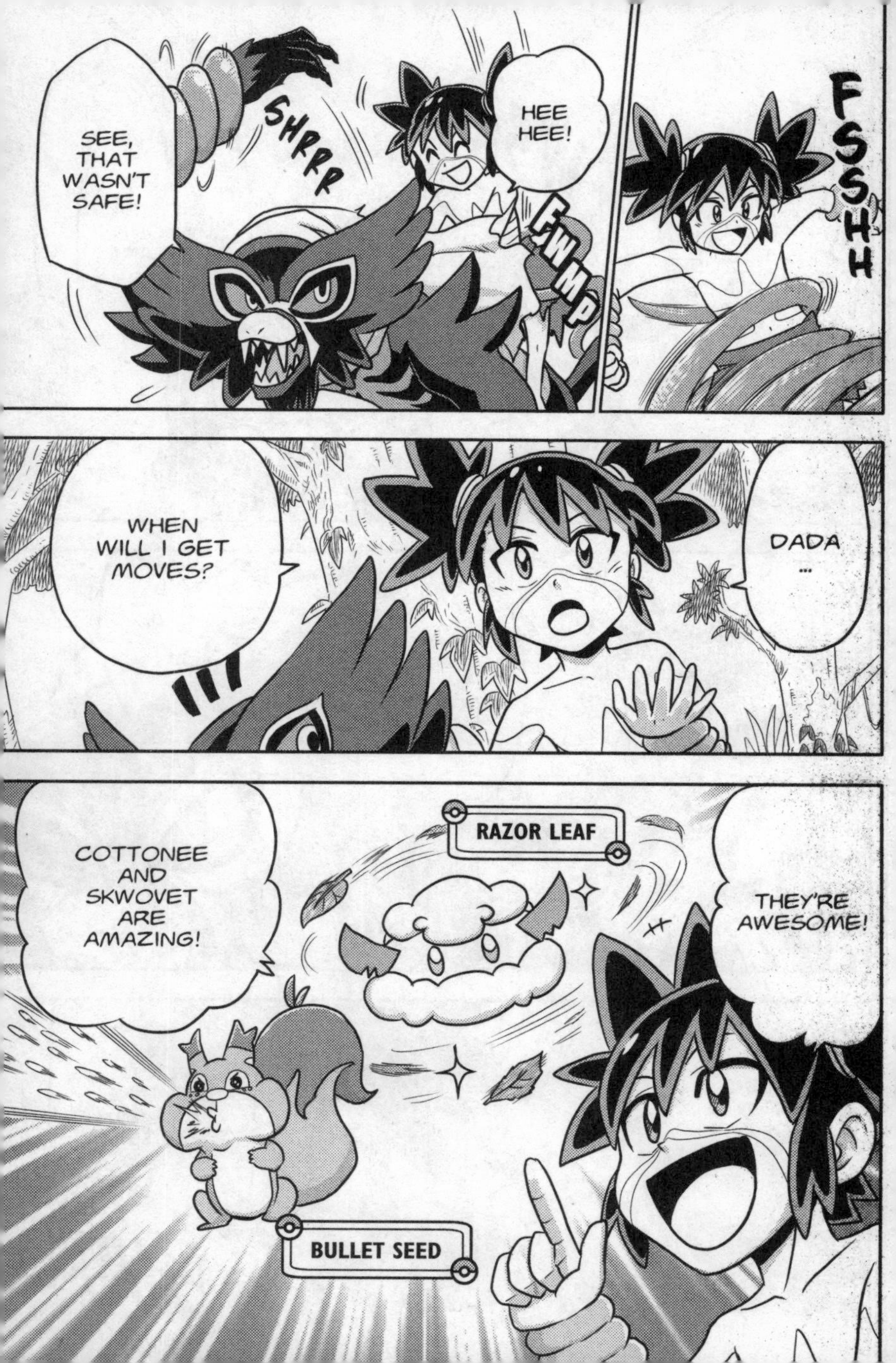
FSSHH
HEE HEE!
SEE, THAT WASN'T SAFE!
SHRRR
FWMP
DADA ...
WHEN WILL I GET MOVES?
THEY'RE AWESOME!
RAZOR LEAF
COTTONEE AND SKWOVET ARE AMAZING!
BULLET SEED

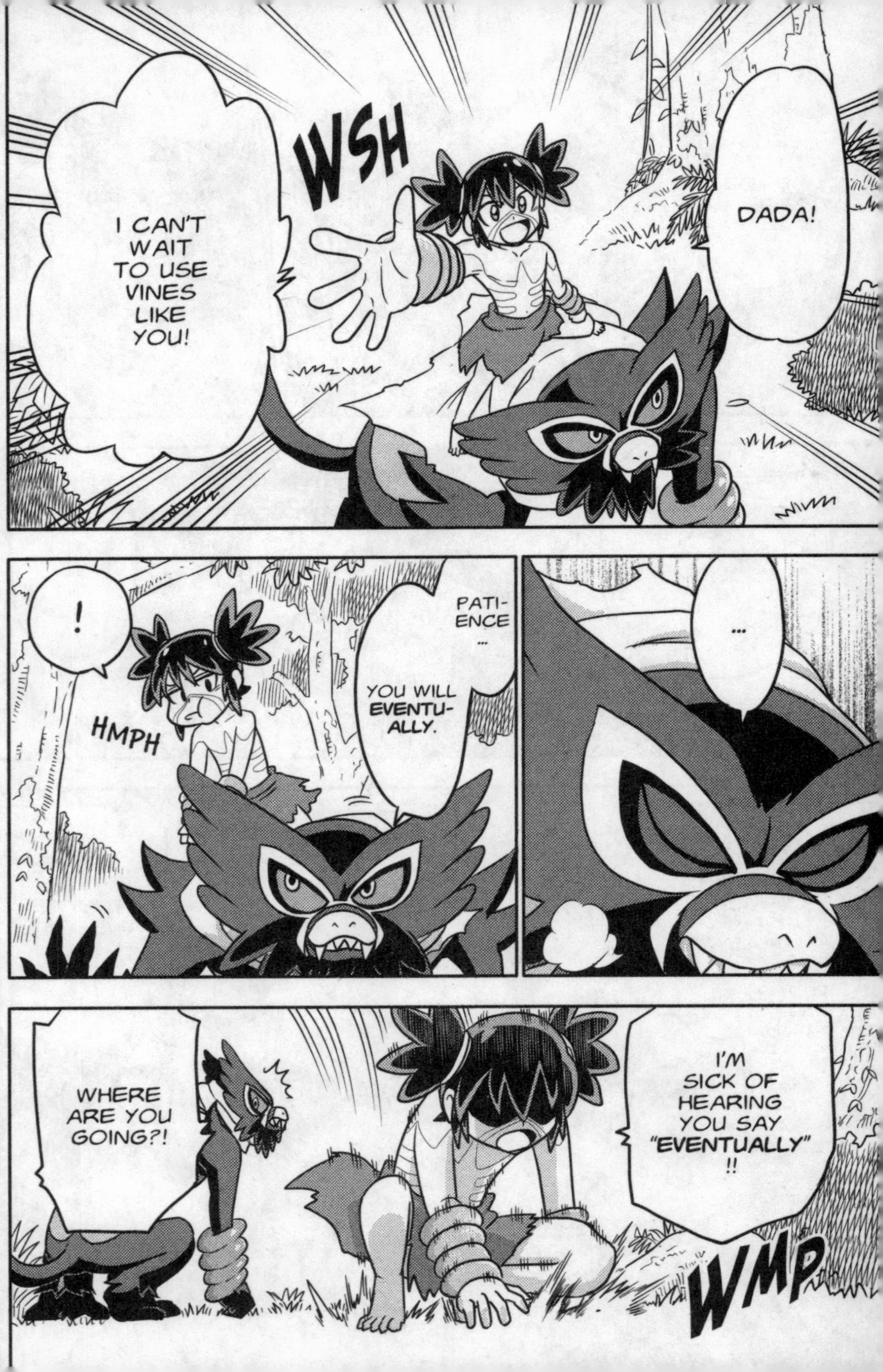
DADA!
WSH
I CAN'T WAIT TO USE VINES LIKE YOU!
...
PATI-ENCE ... YOU WILL EVENTU-ALLY.
!
HMPH
I'M SICK OF HEARING YOU SAY "EVENTUALLY" !!
WHERE ARE YOU GOING?!
WMP

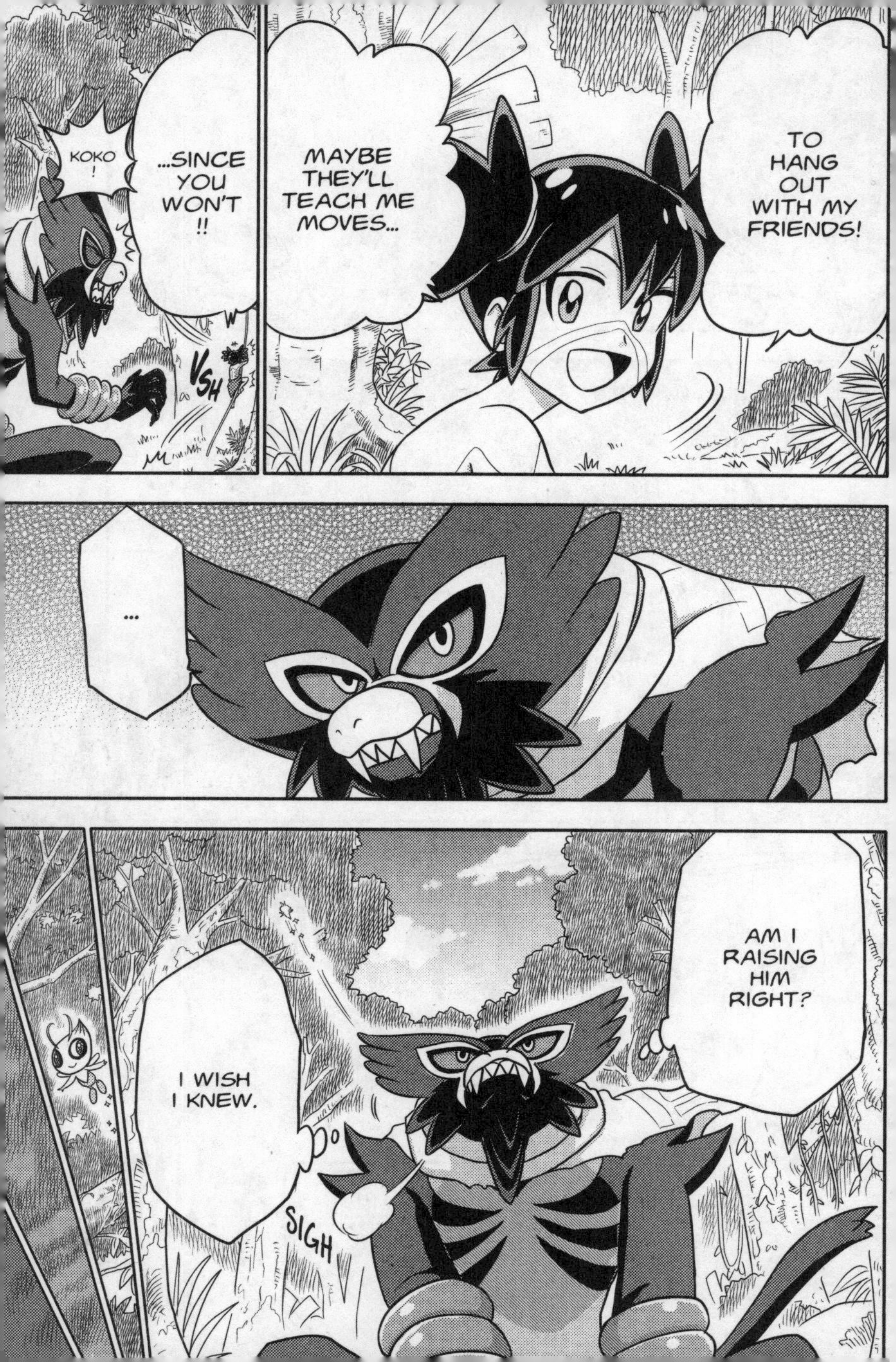
TO HANG OUT WITH MY FRIENDS!
MAYBE THEY'LL TEACH ME MOVES...
...SINCE YOU WON'T !!
KOKO !
VSH
...
AM I RAISING HIM RIGHT?
I WISH I KNEW.
SIGH

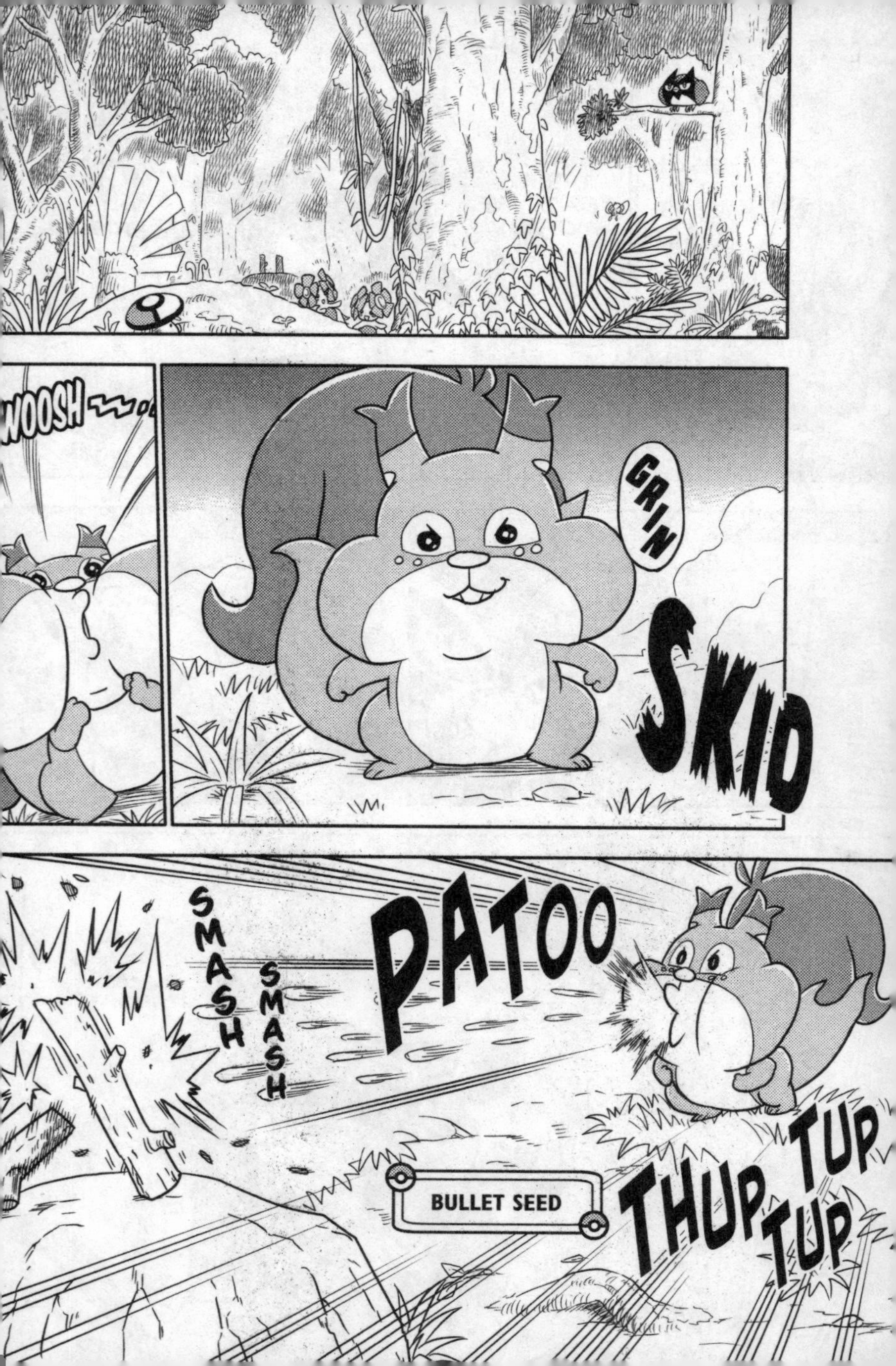
GRIN
SKID
WOOSH
PATOO
SMASH
SMASH
THUP TUP TUP
BULLET SEED

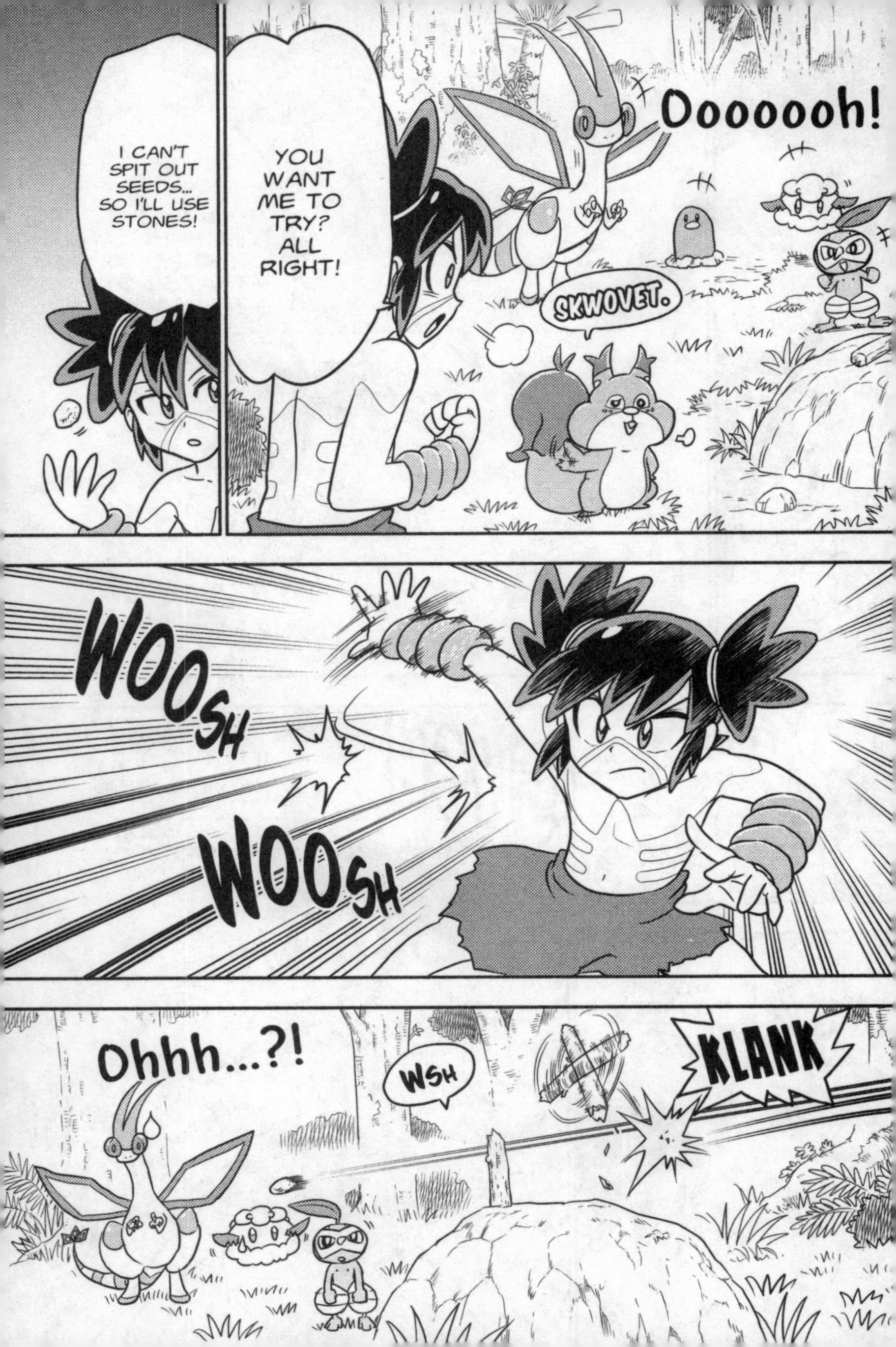
Oooooh!
SKWOVET.
YOU WANT ME TO TRY? ALL RIGHT!
I CAN'T SPIT OUT SEEDS... SO I'LL USE STONES!
WOOSH
WOOSH
KLANK
WSH
Ohhh...?!

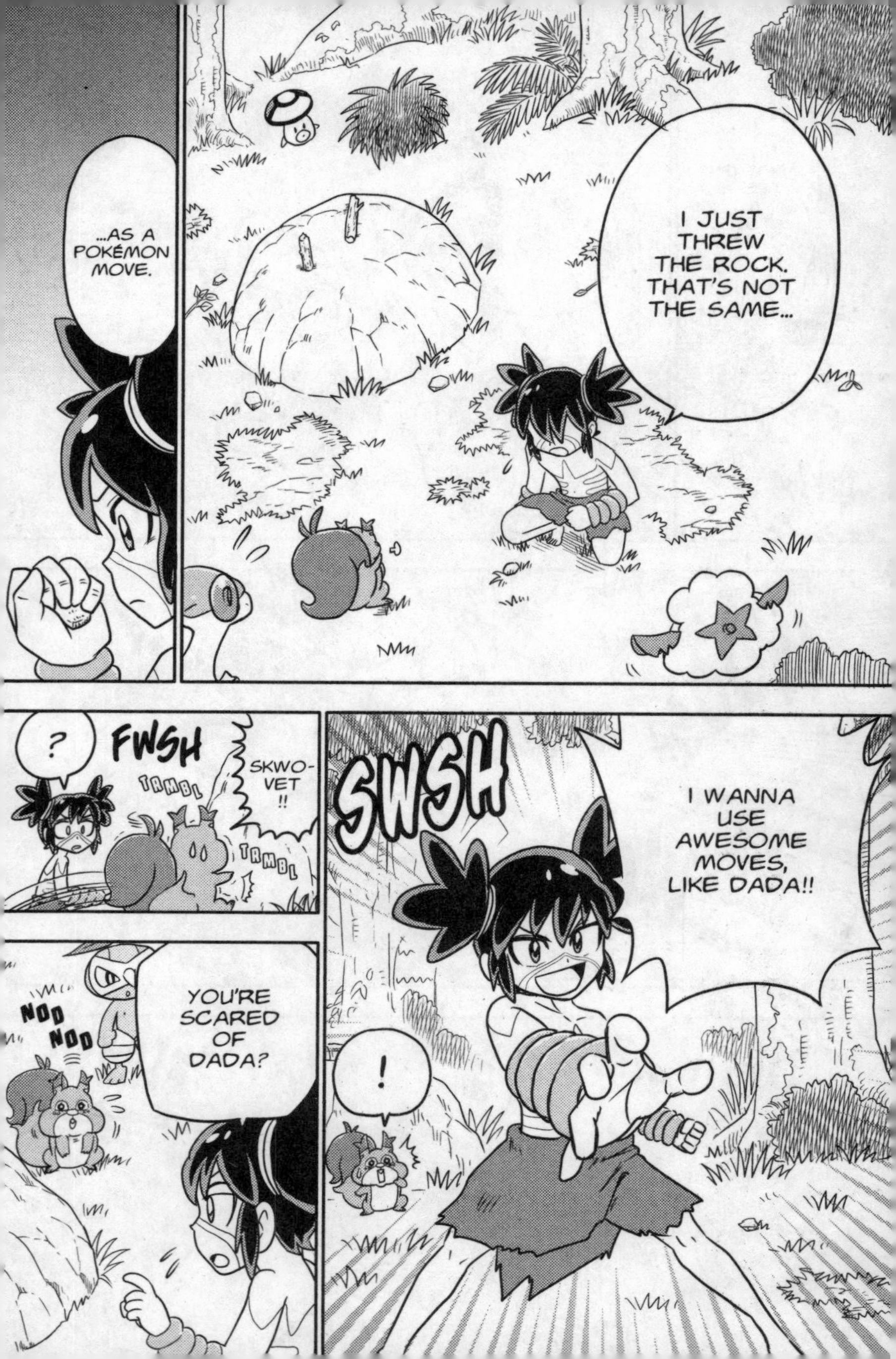
I JUST THREW THE ROCK. THAT'S NOT THE SAME...
...AS A POKÉMON MOVE.
I WANNA USE AWESOME MOVES, LIKE DADA!!
SWSH
!
?
FWSH
TAMBL
SKWO-VET !!
TAMBL
NOD NOD
YOU'RE SCARED OF DADA?

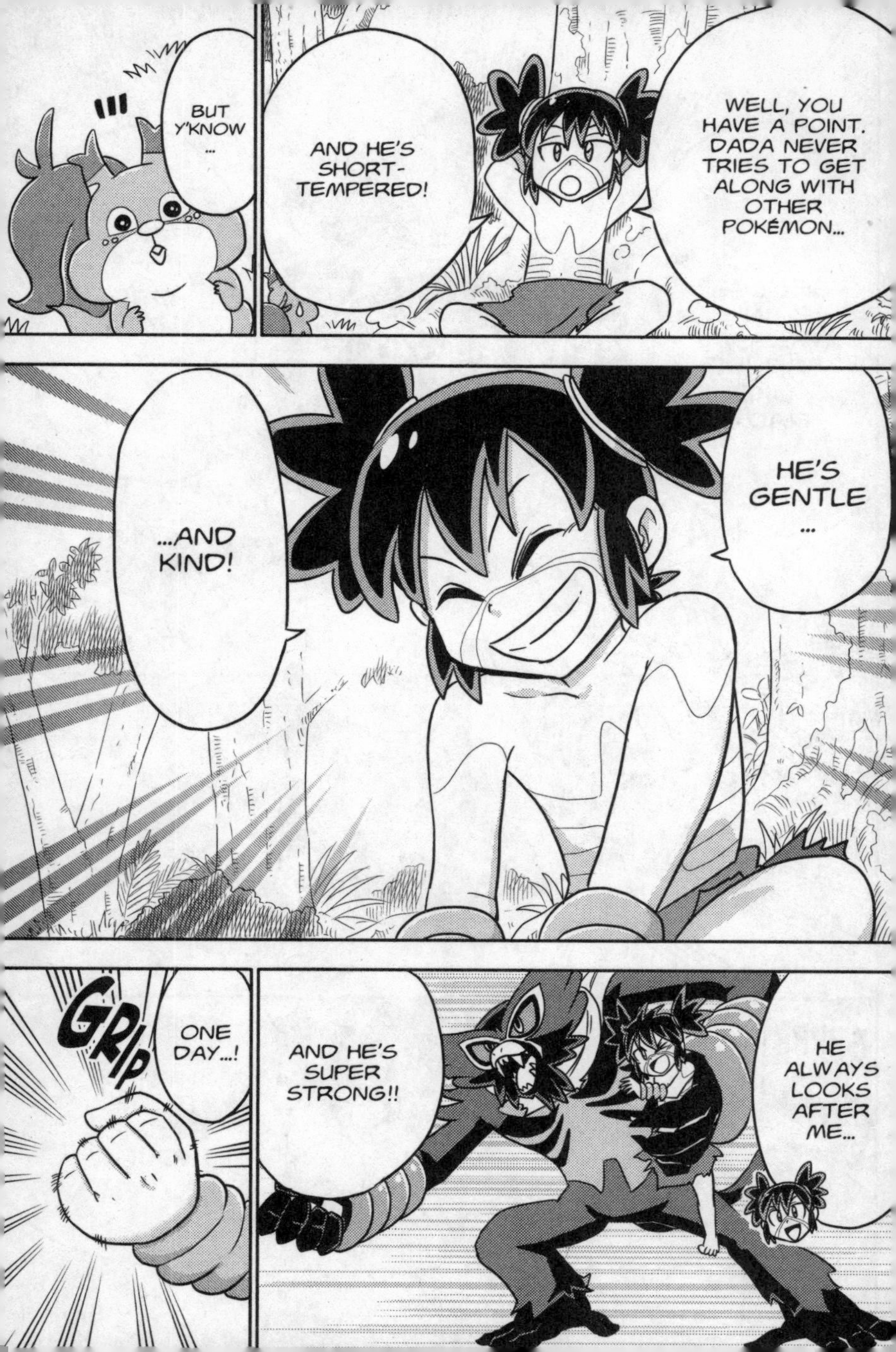
WELL, YOU HAVE A POINT. DADA NEVER TRIES TO GET ALONG WITH OTHER POKÉMON...
AND HE'S SHORT-TEMPERED!
BUT Y'KNOW ...
HE'S GENTLE ...
...AND KIND!
HE ALWAYS LOOKS AFTER ME...
AND HE'S SUPER STRONG!!
ONE DAY...!
GRIP

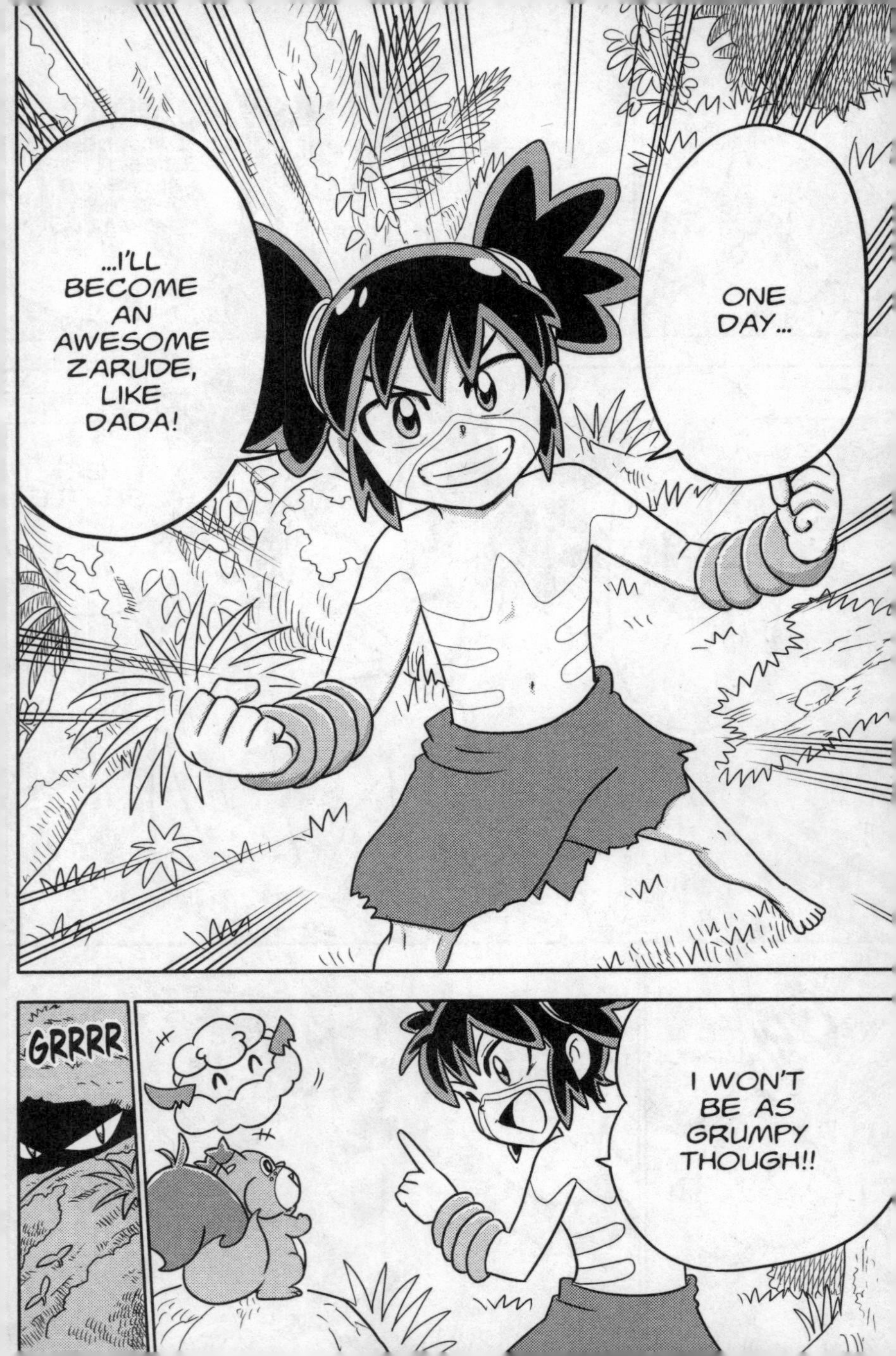
ONE DAY...
...I'LL BECOME AN AWESOME ZARUDE, LIKE DADA!
I WON'T BE AS GRUMPY THOUGH!!
GRRRR

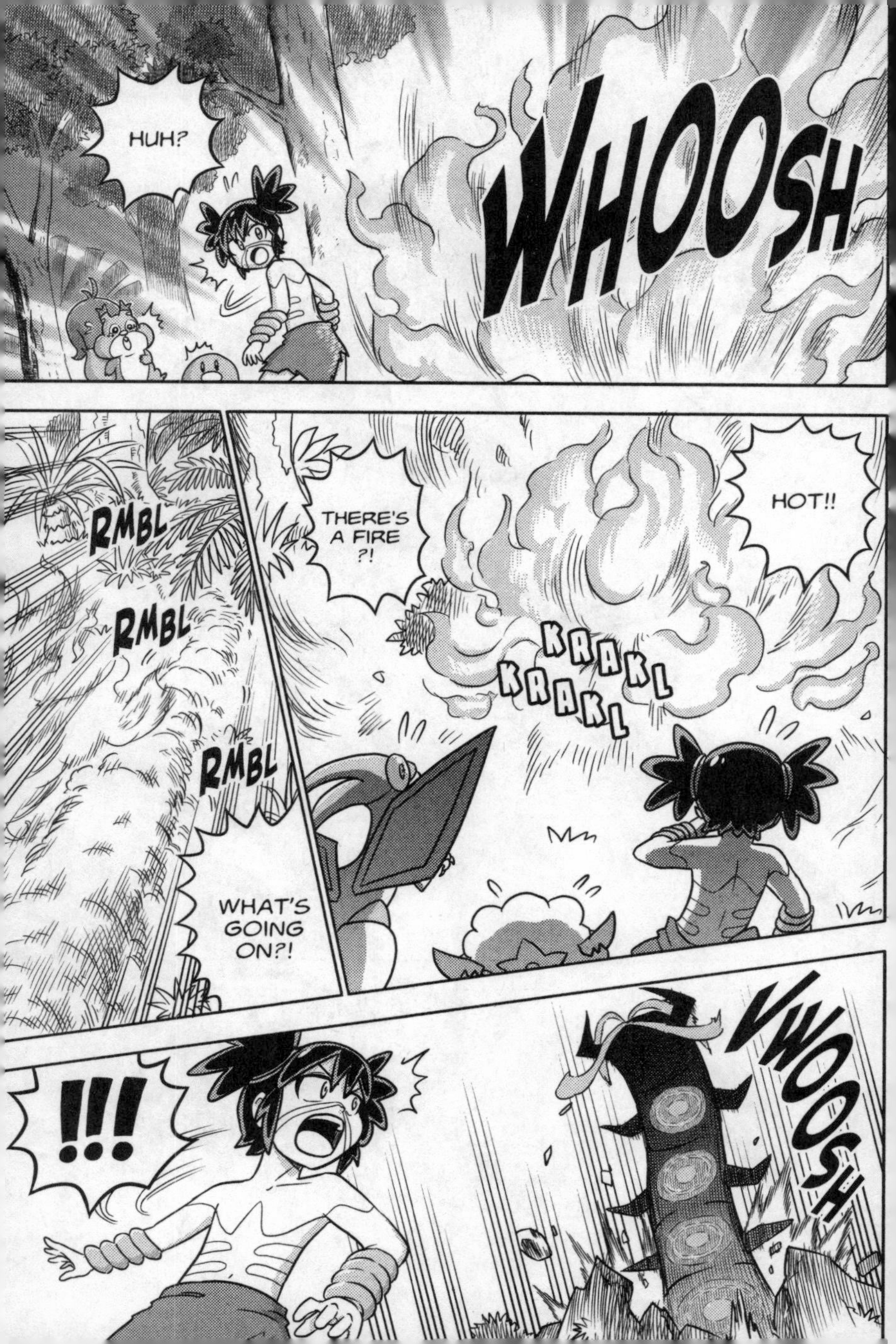
WHOOSH
HUH?
HOT!!
THERE'S A FIRE ?!
KRAKL KRAKL
RMBL
RMBL
RMBL
WHAT'S GOING ON?!
VWOOSH
!!!

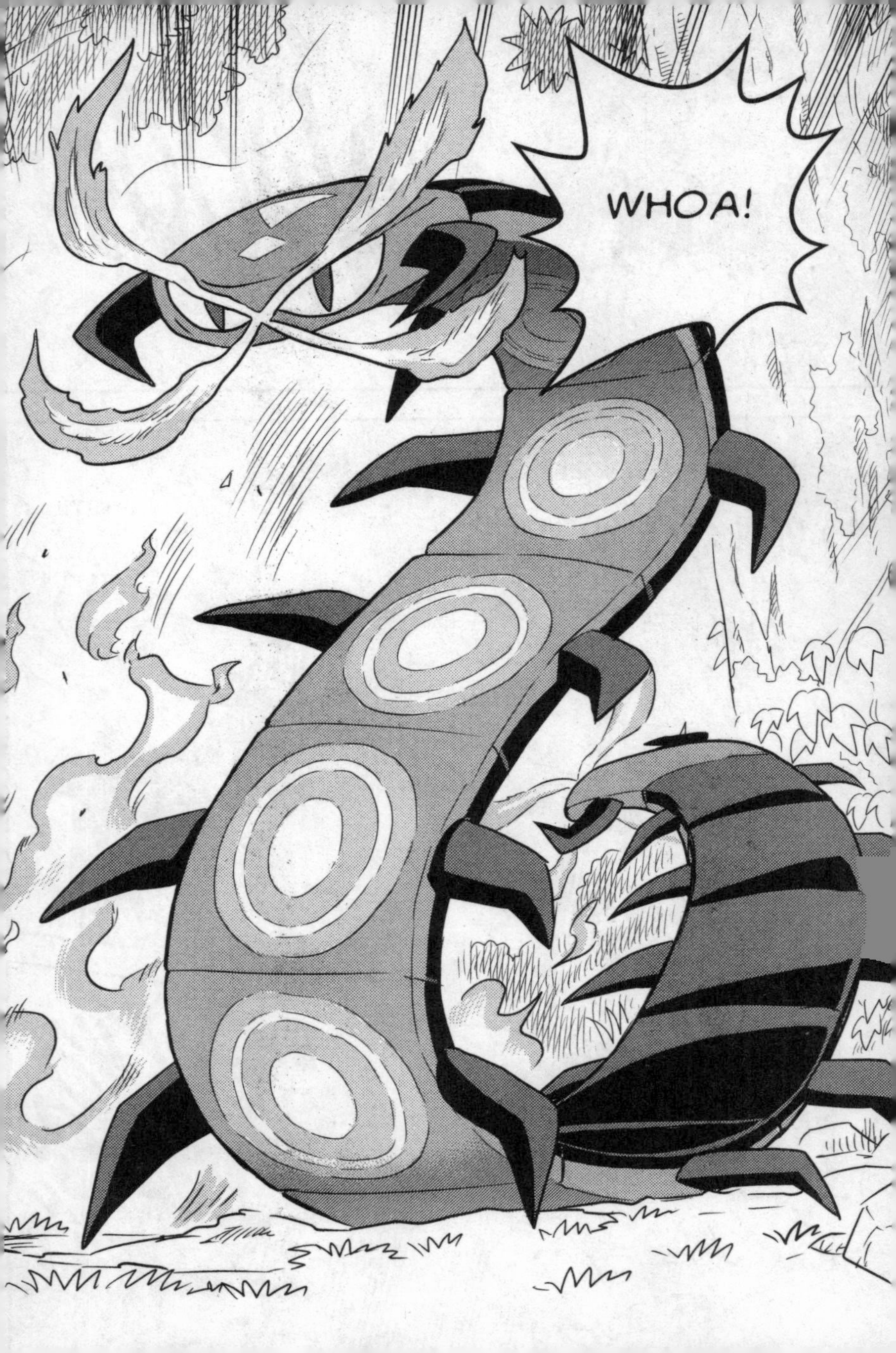
WHOA!

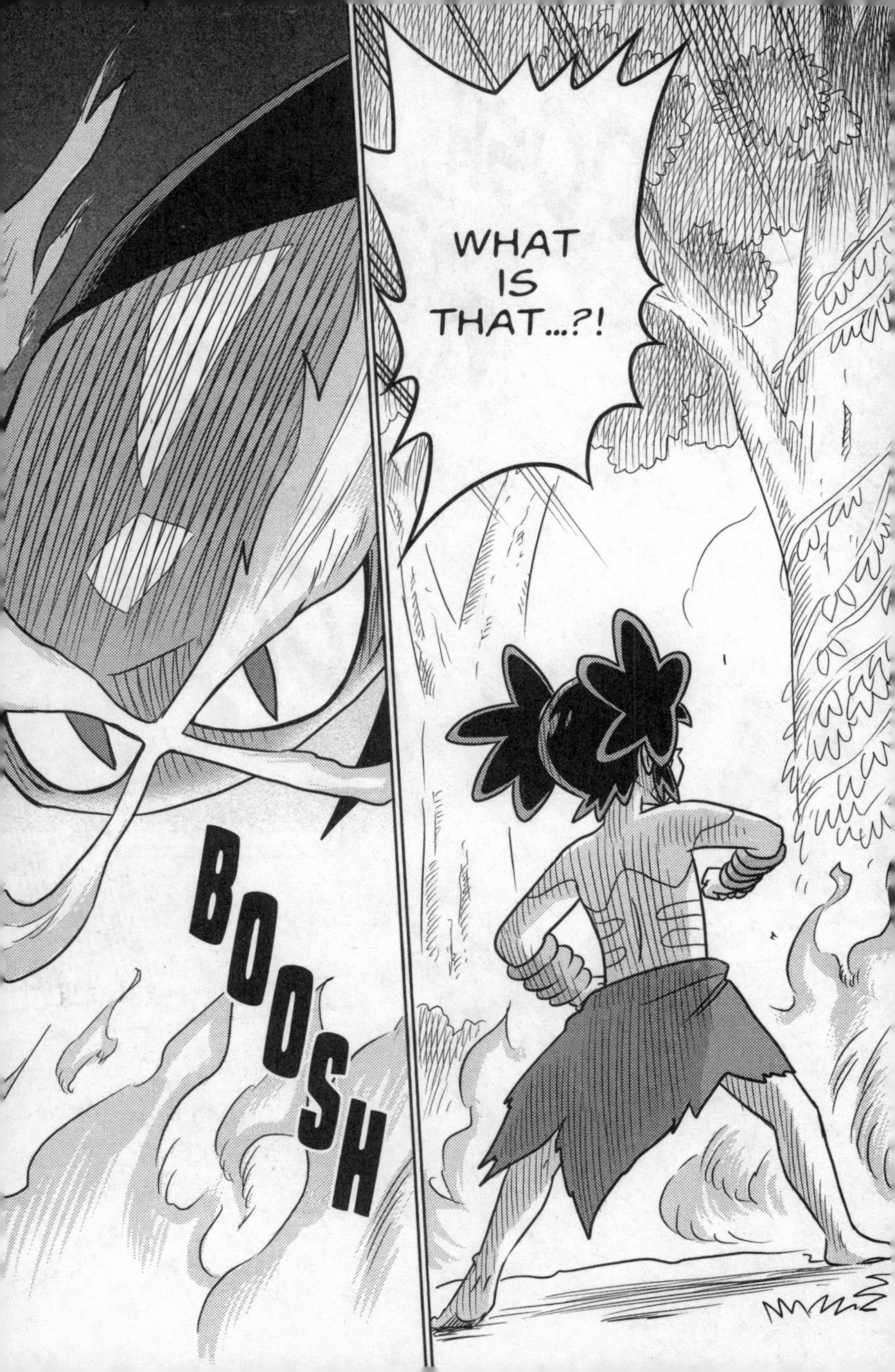
WHAT IS THAT...?!
BOOSH

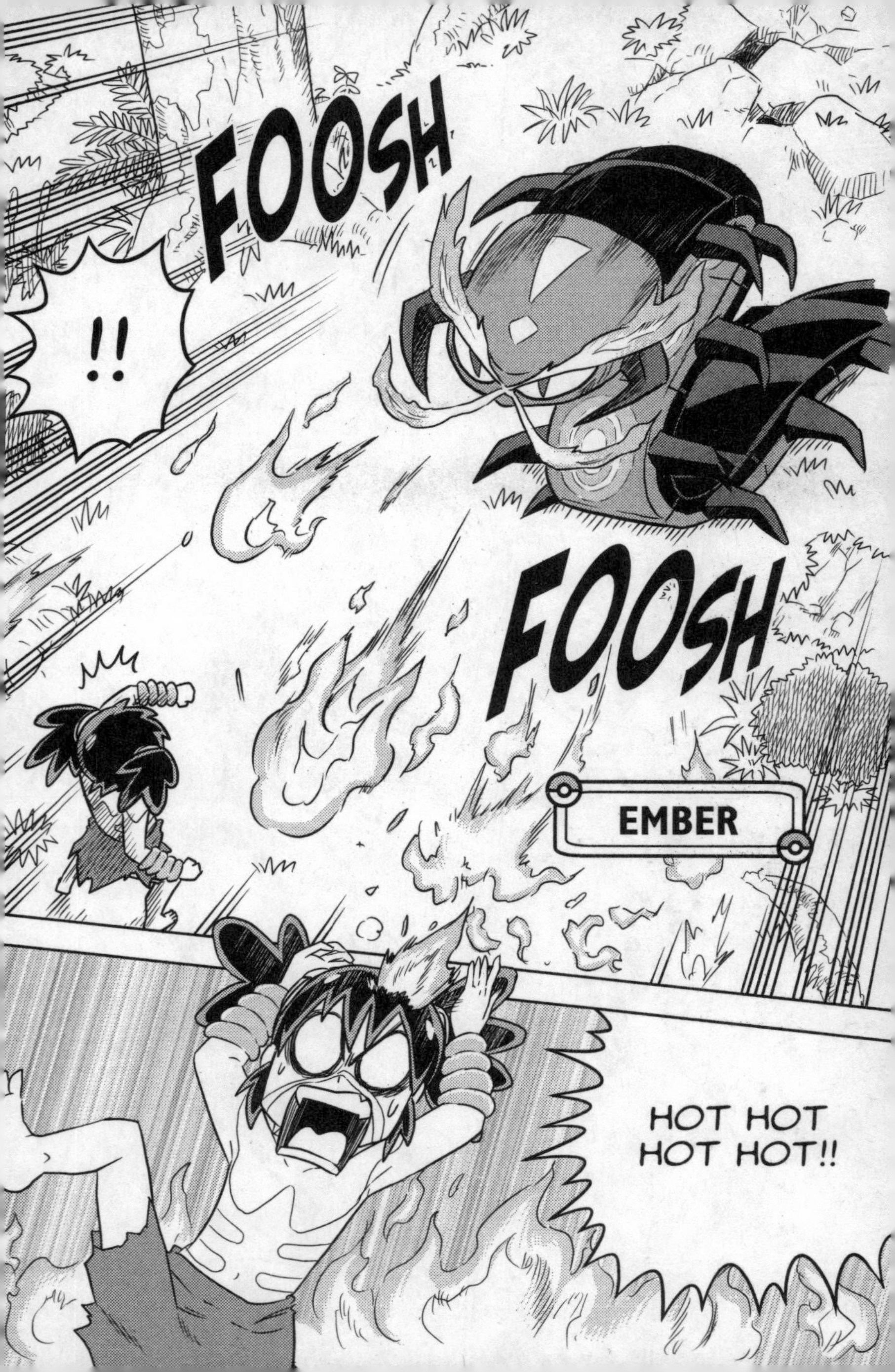
FOOSH
!!
FOOSH
EMBER
HOT HOT
HOT HOT!!

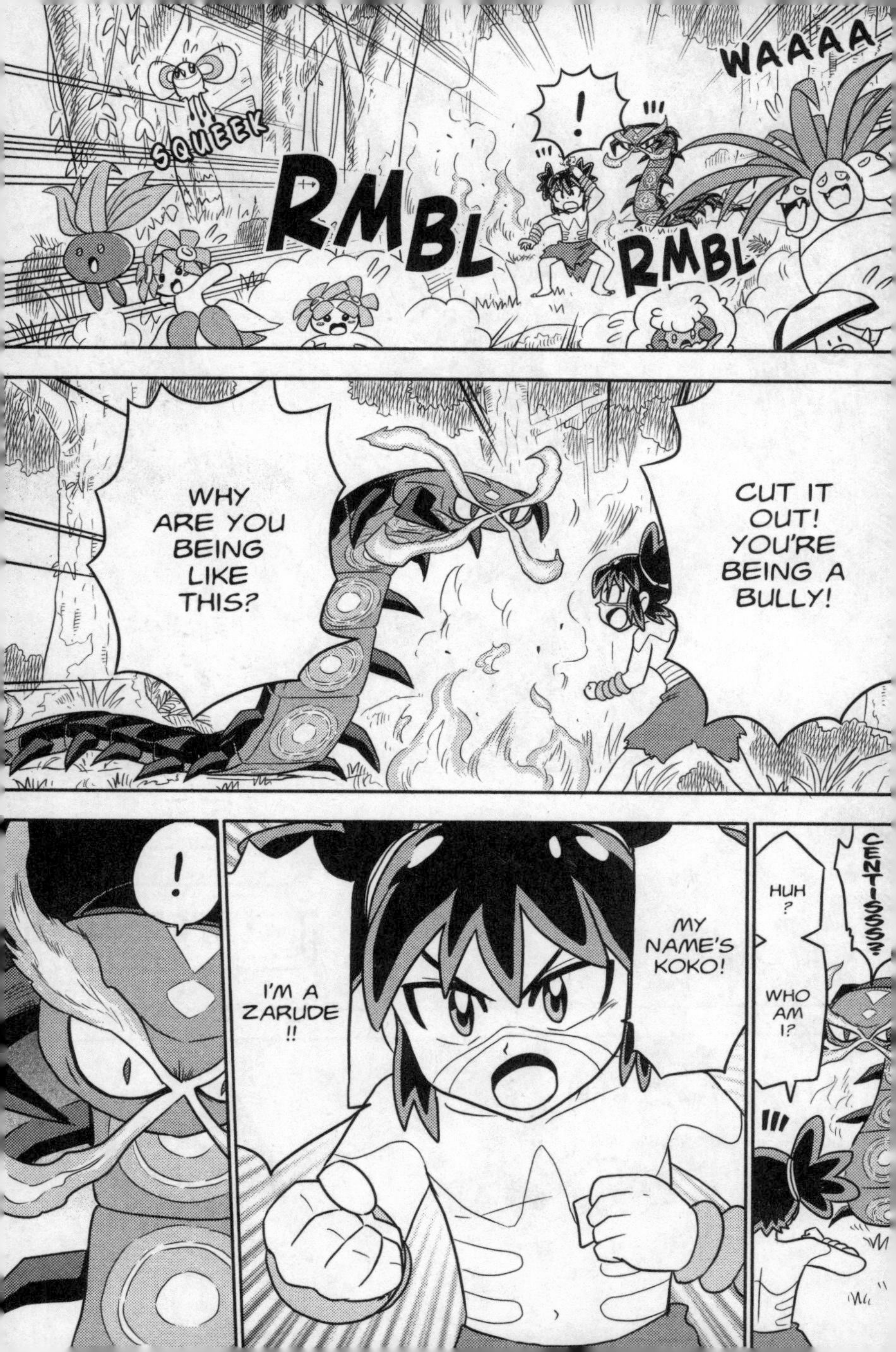
WAAAA
!
RMBL
RMBL
SQUEEEK
CUT IT OUT! YOU'RE BEING A BULLY!
WHY ARE YOU BEING LIKE THIS?
CENTISSS?
HUH?
WHO AM I!?
MY NAME'S KOKO!
I'M A ZARUDE!!
!

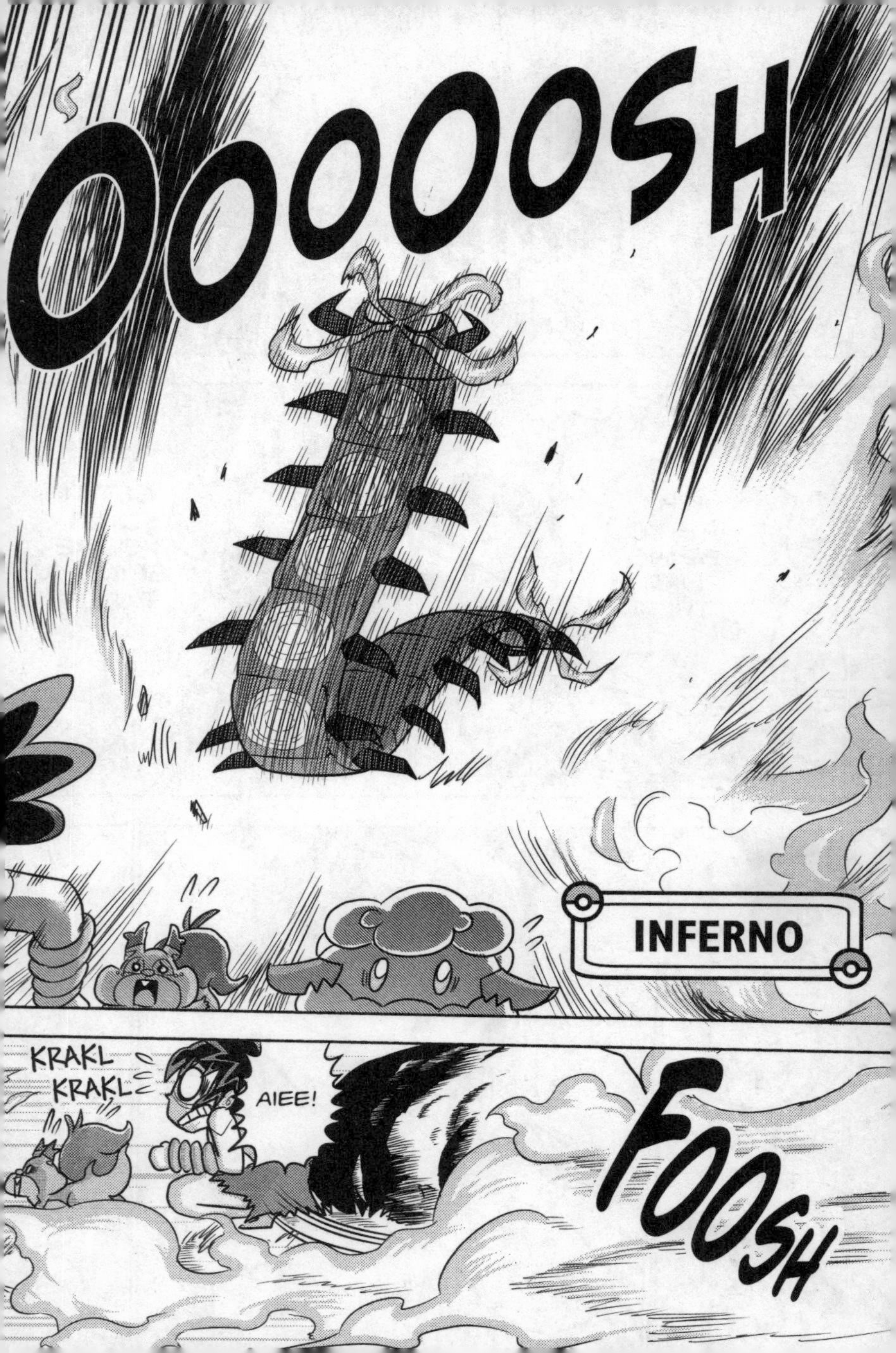
OOOOOSH
INFERNO
FOOSH
AIEE!
KRAKL
KRAKL

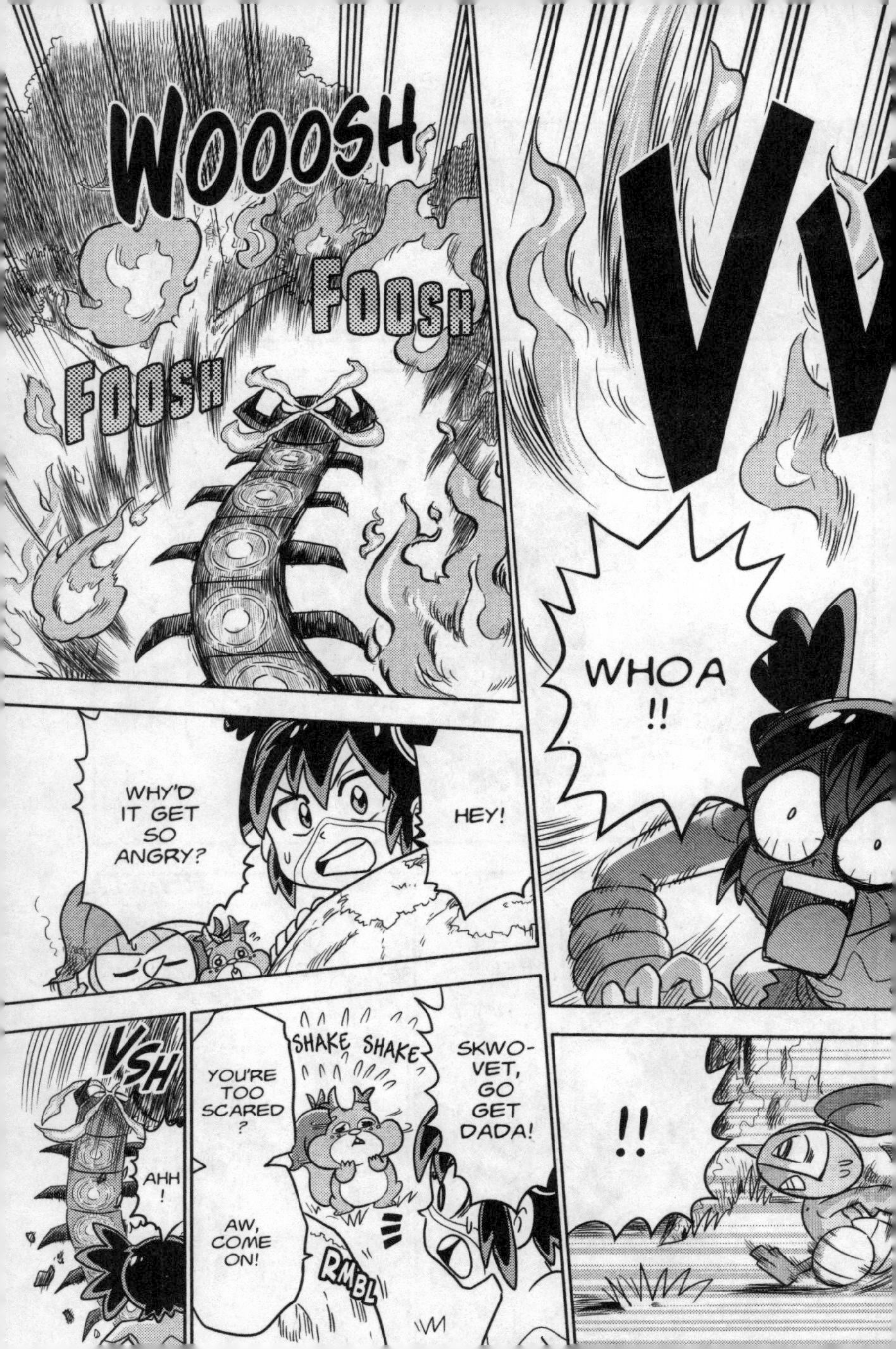

VV
WHOA !!
WOOOSH
FOOSH
FOOSH
HEY!
WHY'D IT GET SO ANGRY?
!!
SKWO-VET, GO GET DADA!
SHAKE SHAKE
YOU'RE TOO SCARED ?
AW, COME ON!
RMBL
VSH
AHH !

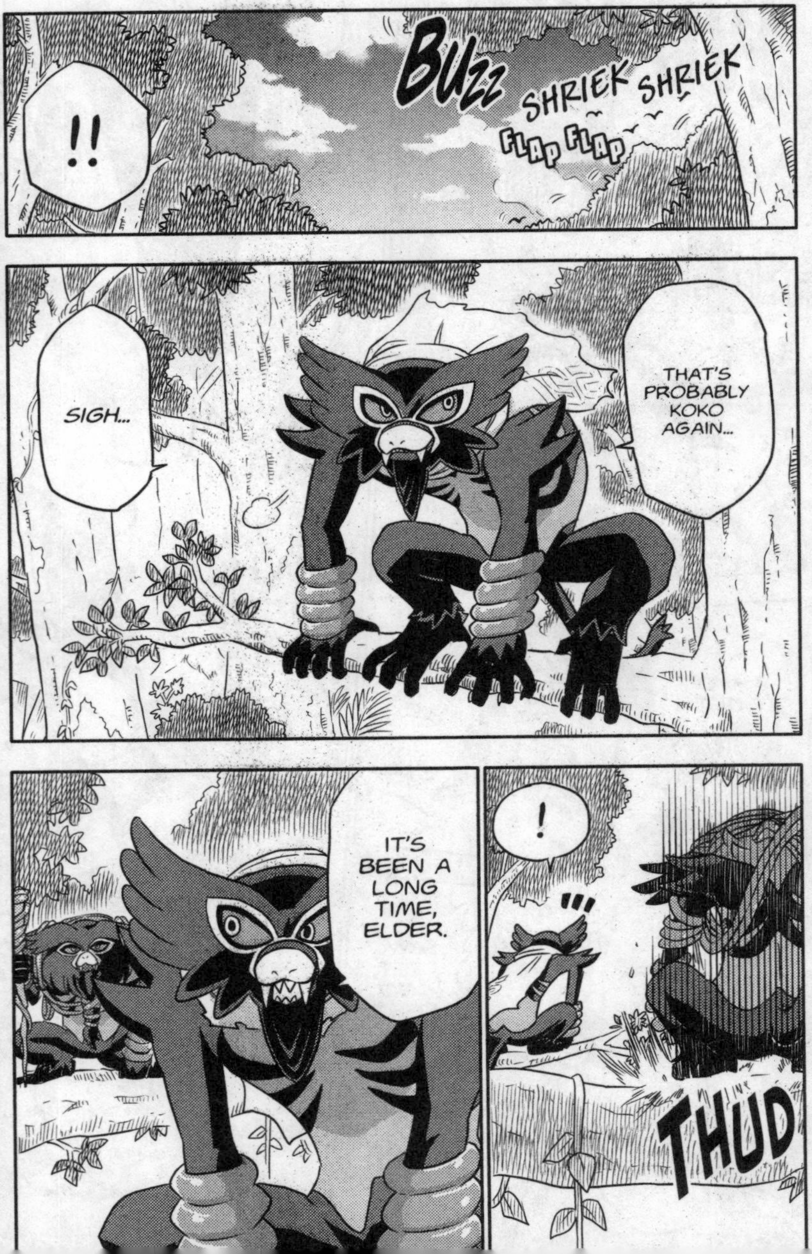
SHRIEK SHRIEK
BUZZ
FLAP FLAP
!!
THAT'S PROBABLY KOKO AGAIN...
SIGH...
!
THUD
IT'S BEEN A LONG TIME, ELDER.

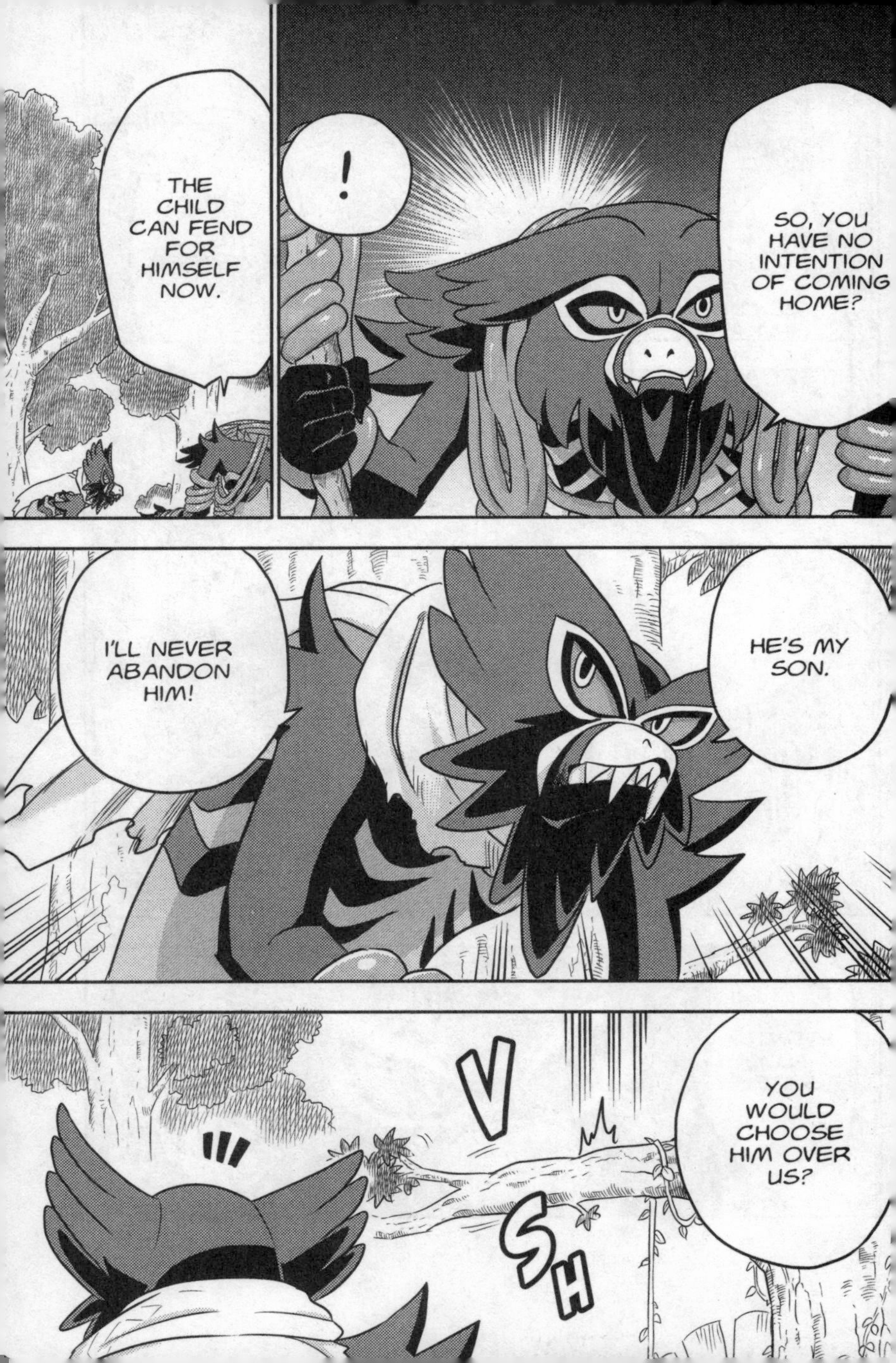
SO, YOU HAVE NO INTENTION OF COMING HOME?
!
THE CHILD CAN FEND FOR HIMSELF NOW.
HE'S MY SON.
I'LL NEVER ABANDON HIM!
YOU WOULD CHOOSE HIM OVER US?
VSSH
!!!

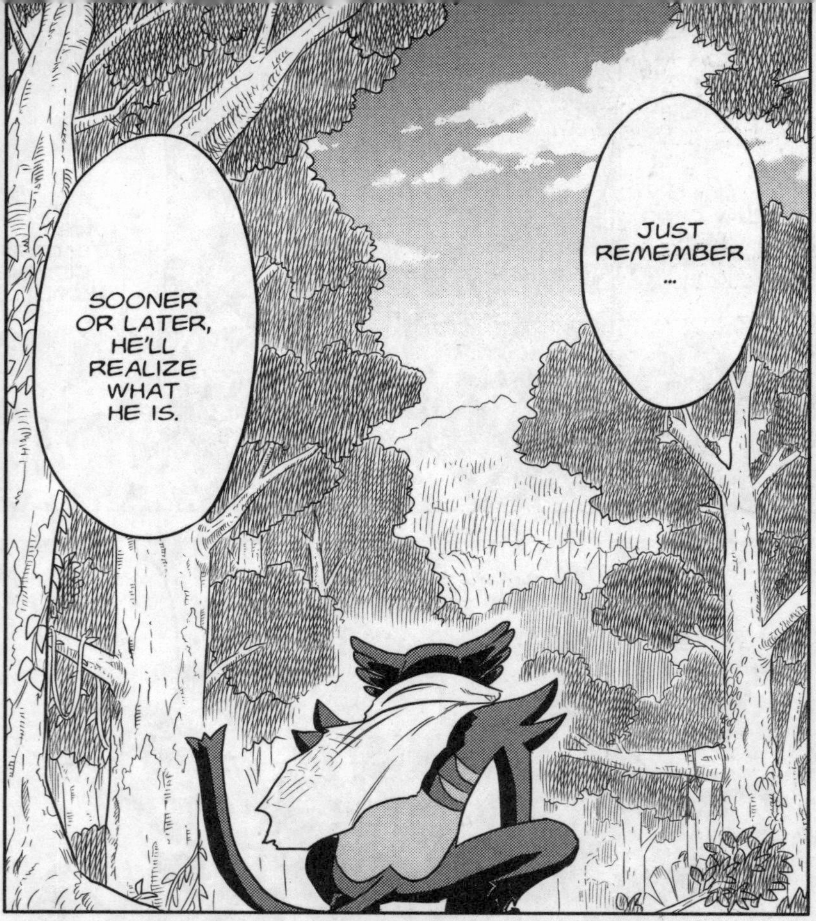
JUST REMEMBER ...
SOONER OR LATER, HE'LL REALIZE WHAT HE IS.

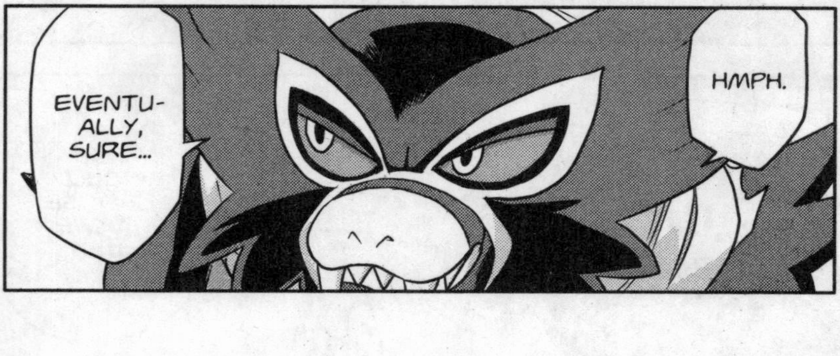
HMPH.
EVENTU-ALLY, SURE...

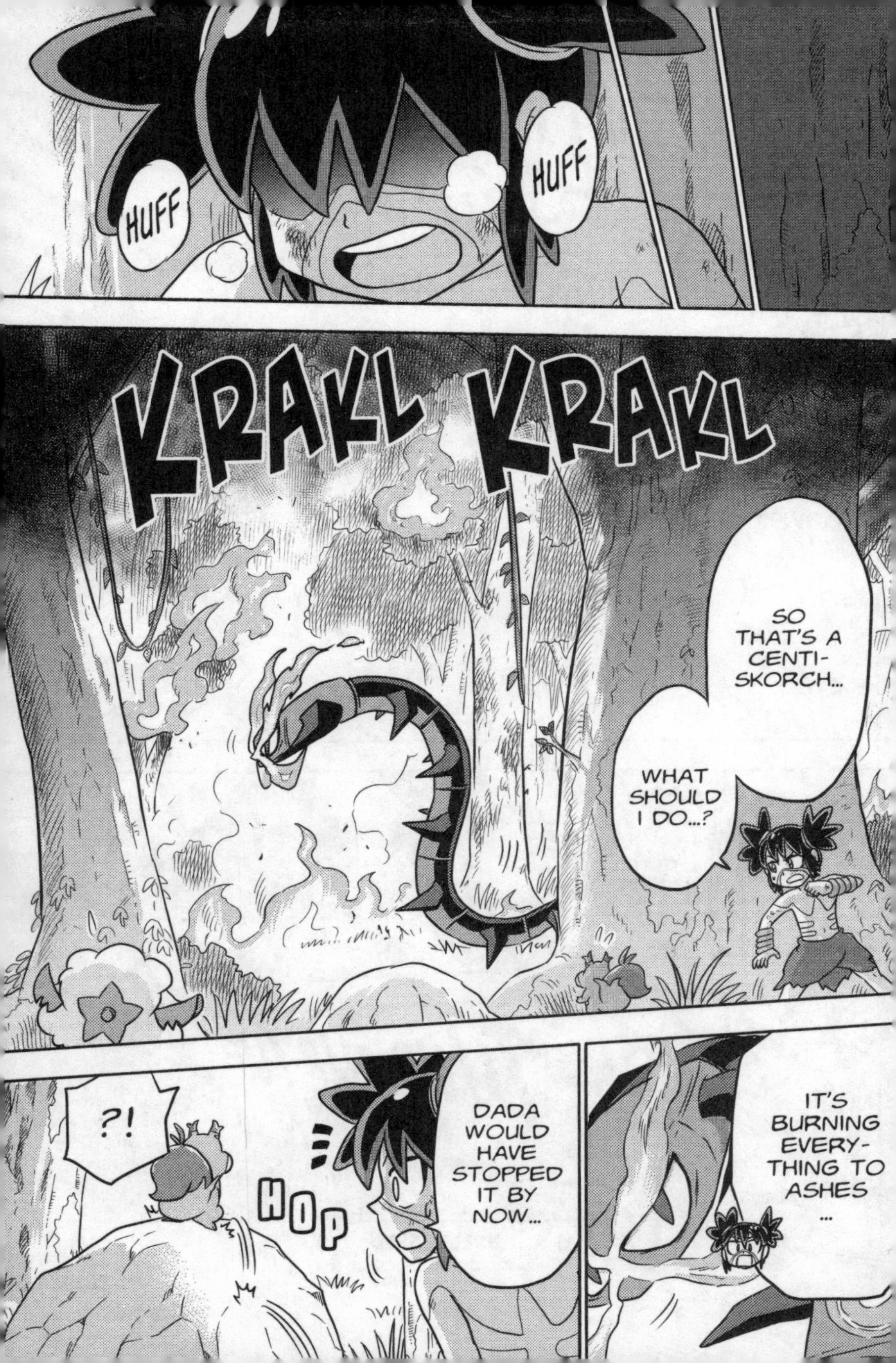
HUFF
HUFF
KRAKL KRAKL
SO THAT'S A CENTI-SKORCH...
WHAT SHOULD I DO...?
IT'S BURNING EVERY-THING TO ASHES ...
DADA WOULD HAVE STOPPED IT BY NOW...
HOP
?!

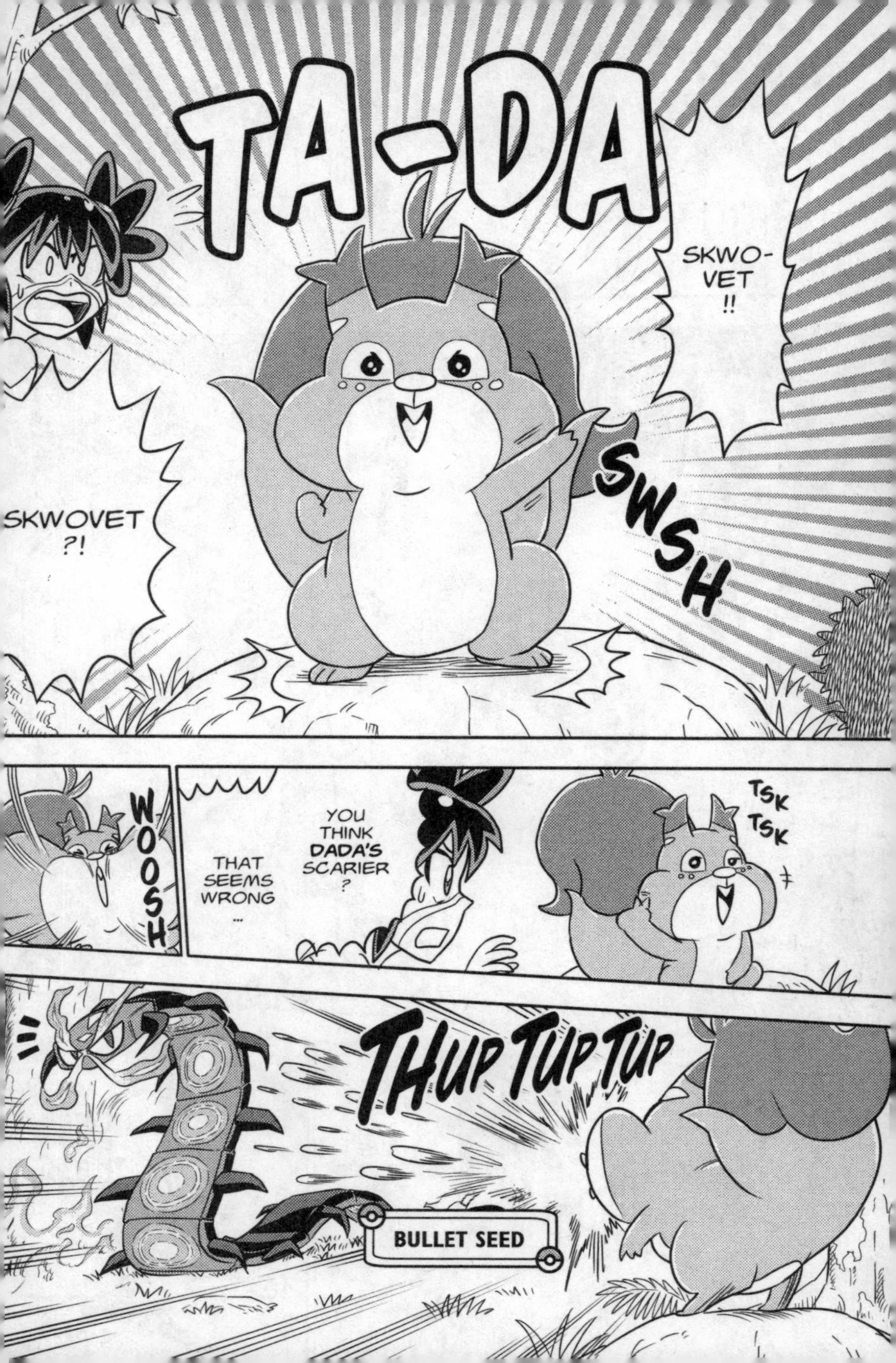
TA-DA
SKWO-VET!!
SWSH
SKWOVET?!
TSK TSK
YOU THINK DADA'S SCARIER?
THAT SEEMS WRONG...
WOOSH
THUP TUP TUP
BULLET SEED

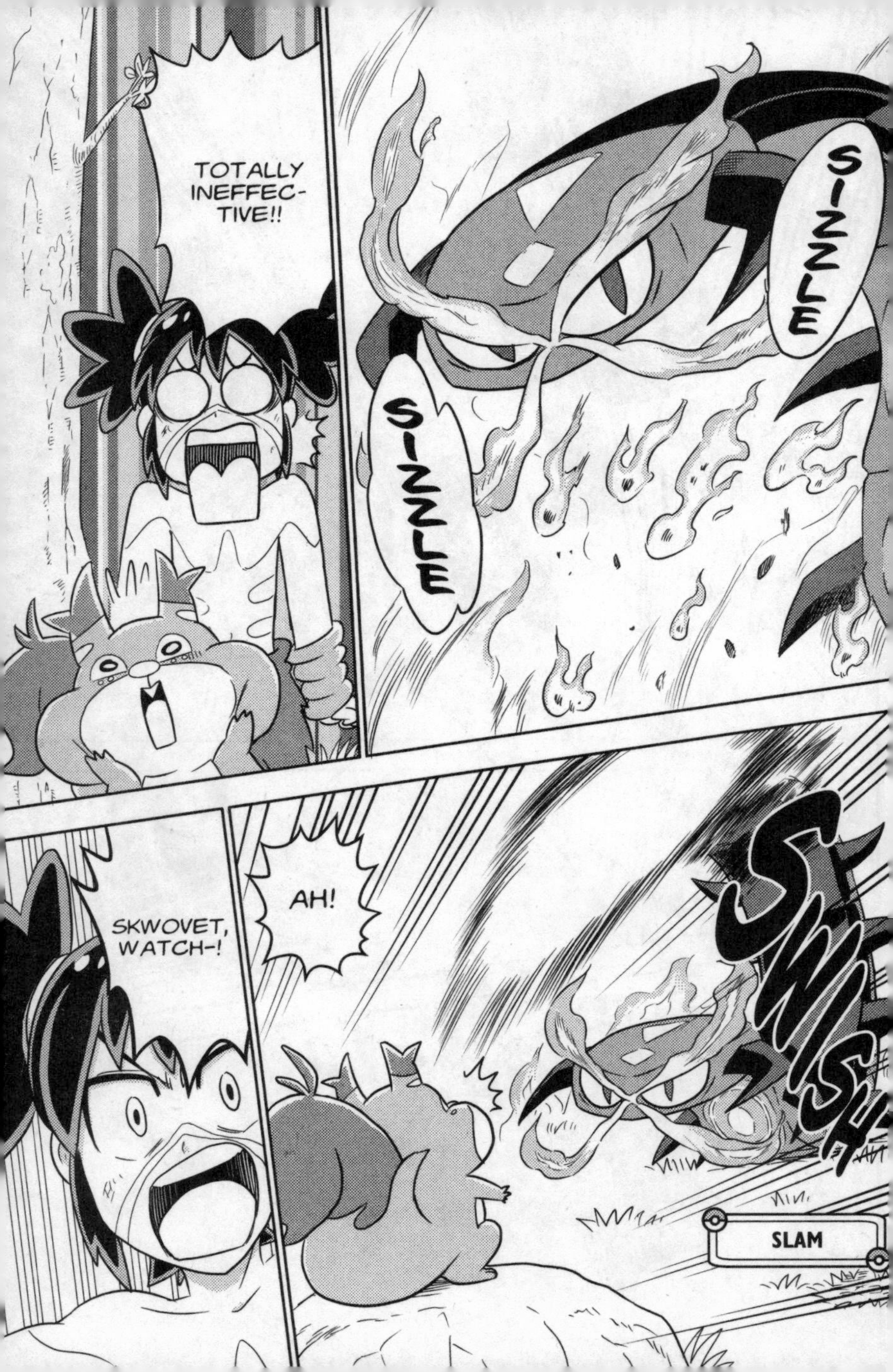
SIZZLE
SIZZLE
TOTALLY INEFFECTIVE!!
SWISH
AH!
SLAM
SKWOVET, WATCH-!

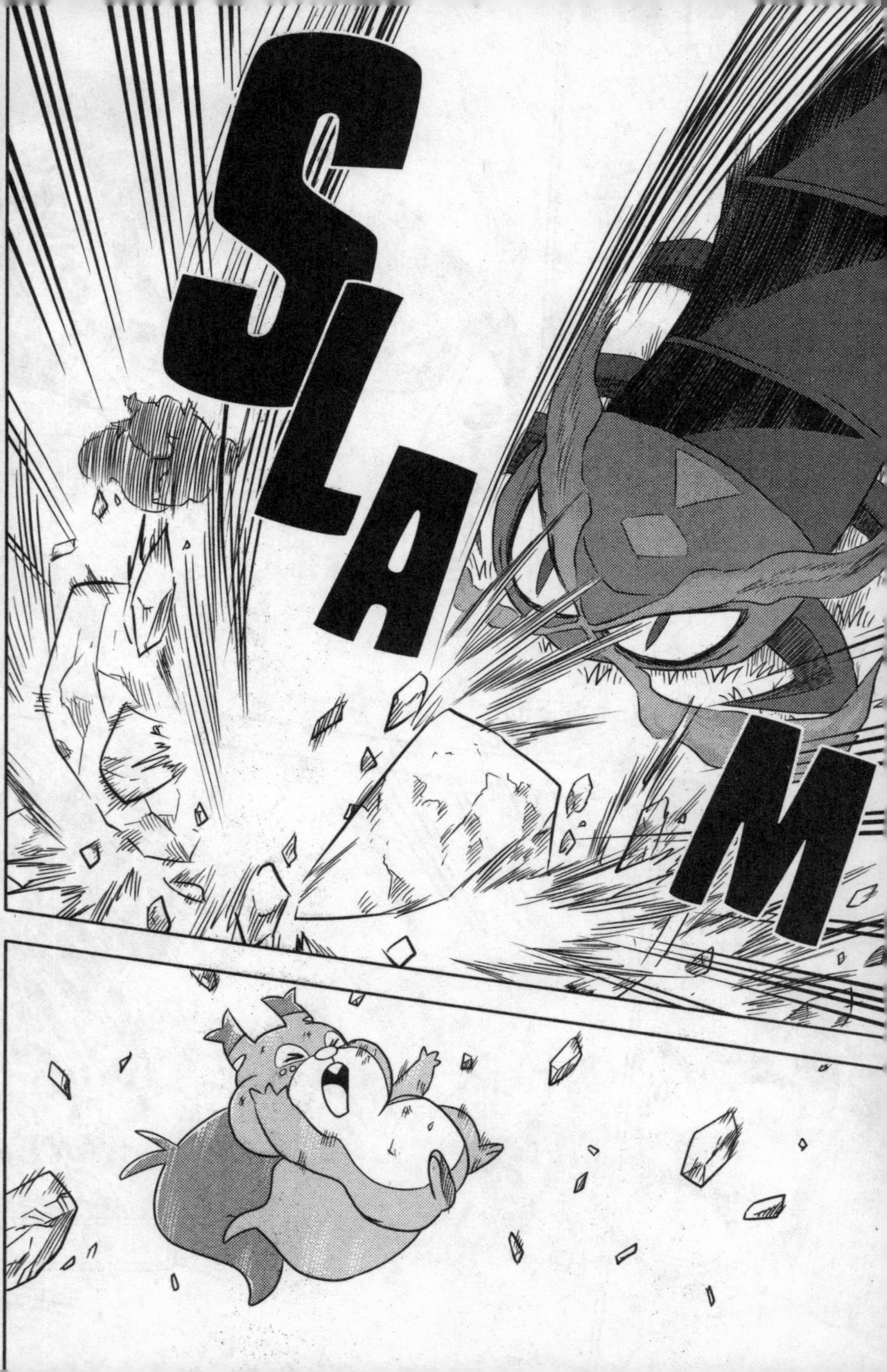
SLAM

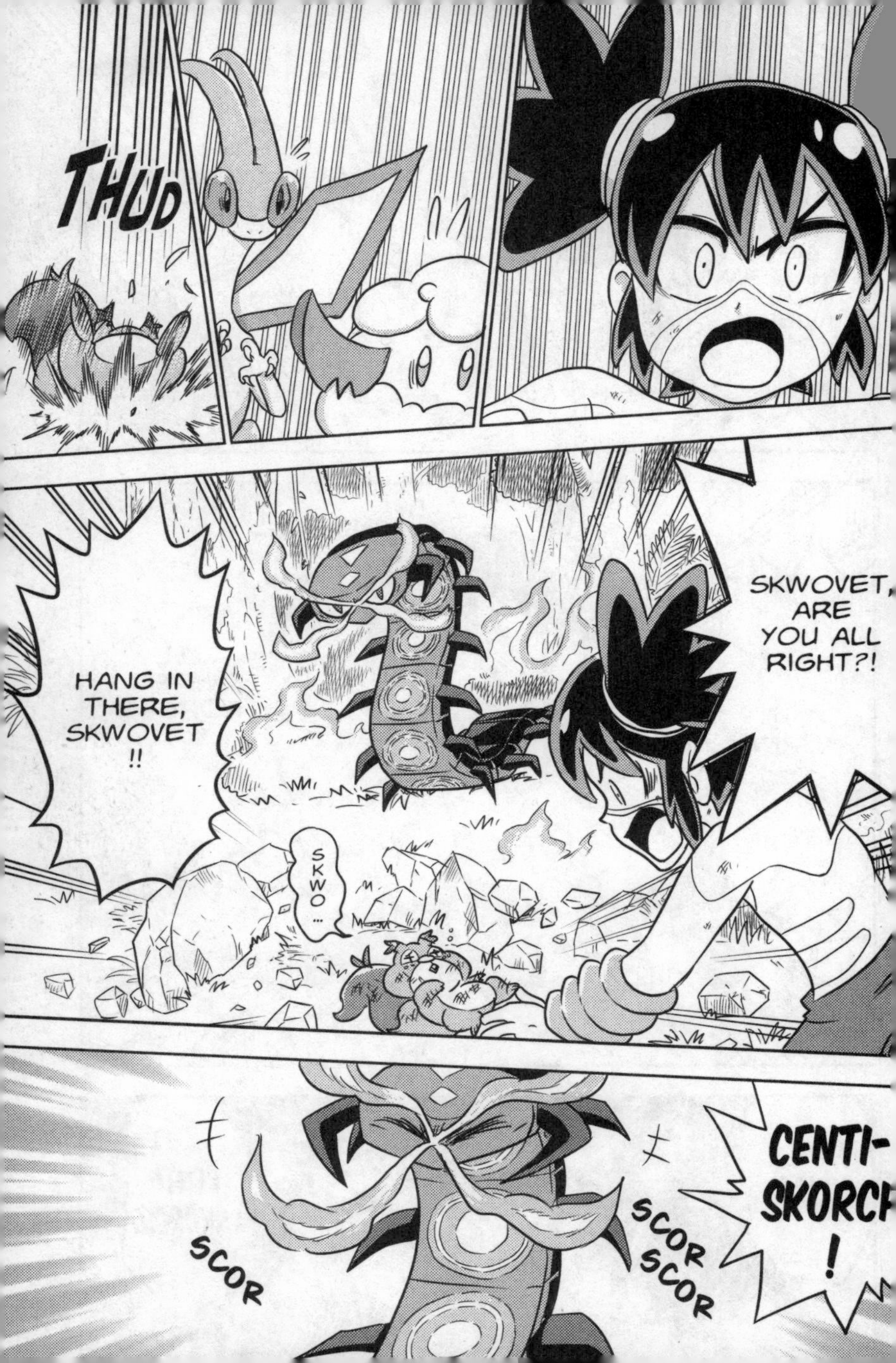
THUD
SKWOVET, ARE YOU ALL RIGHT?!
HANG IN THERE, SKWOVET!!
SKWO...
CENTI-SKORCH!
SCOR SCOR SCOR
SCOR

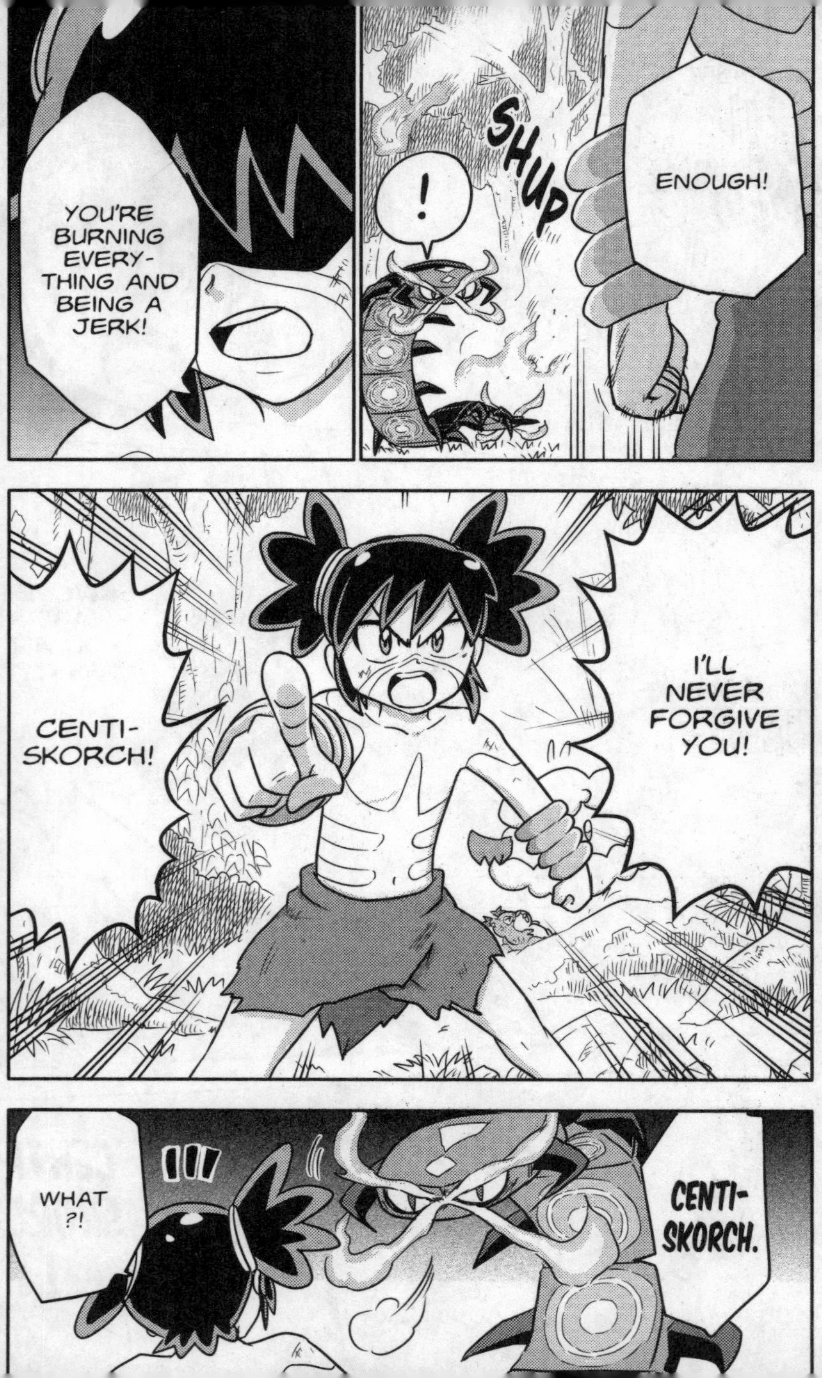
ENOUGH!
SHUP
!
YOU'RE BURNING EVERY-THING AND BEING A JERK!
I'LL NEVER FORGIVE YOU!
CENTI-SKORCH!
CENTI-SKORCH.
!!!
WHAT ?!

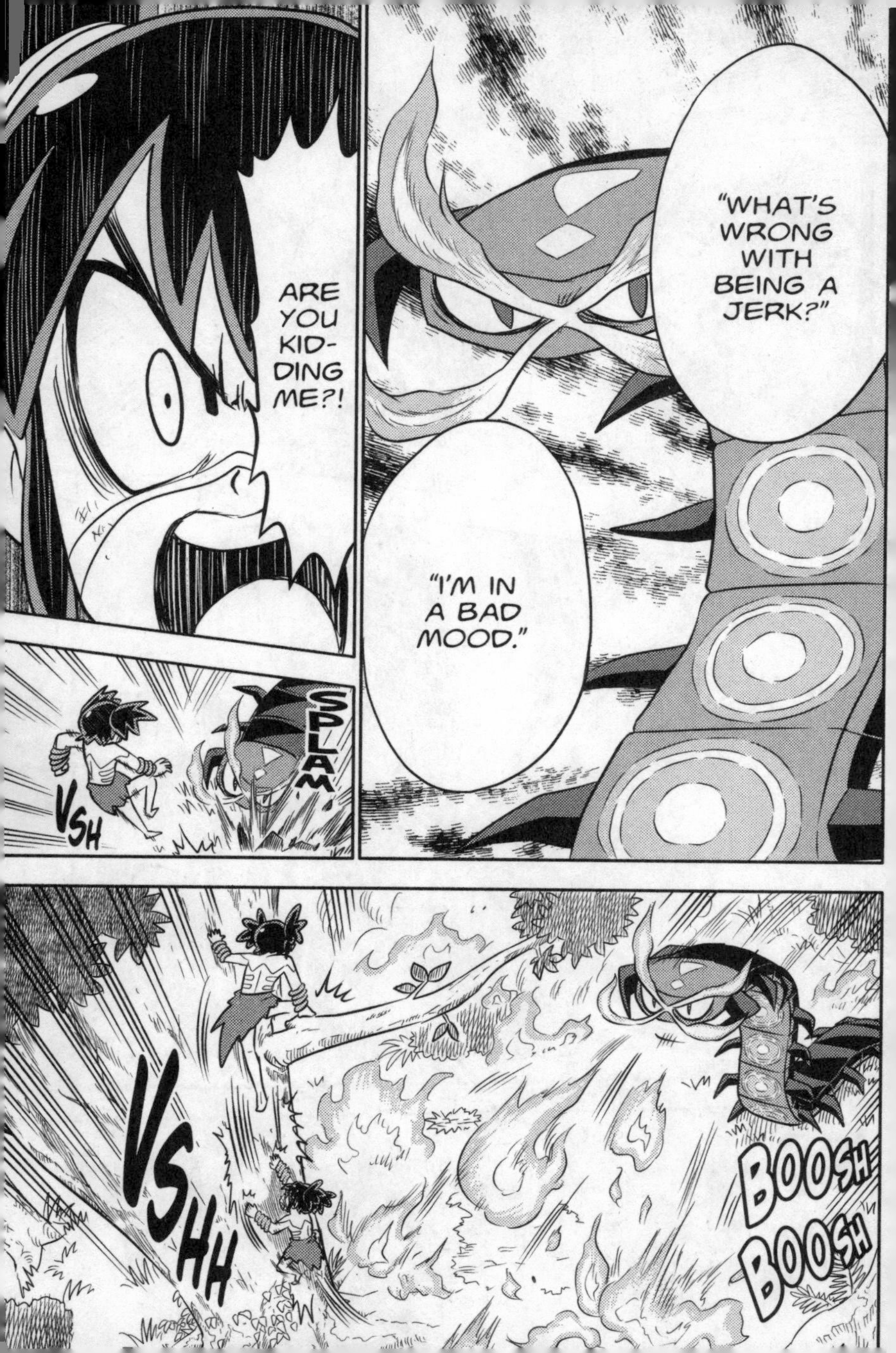
"WHAT'S WRONG WITH BEING A JERK?"
"I'M IN A BAD MOOD."
ARE YOU KID-DING ME?!
SPLAM
VSH
BOOSH
BOOSH
VSHH

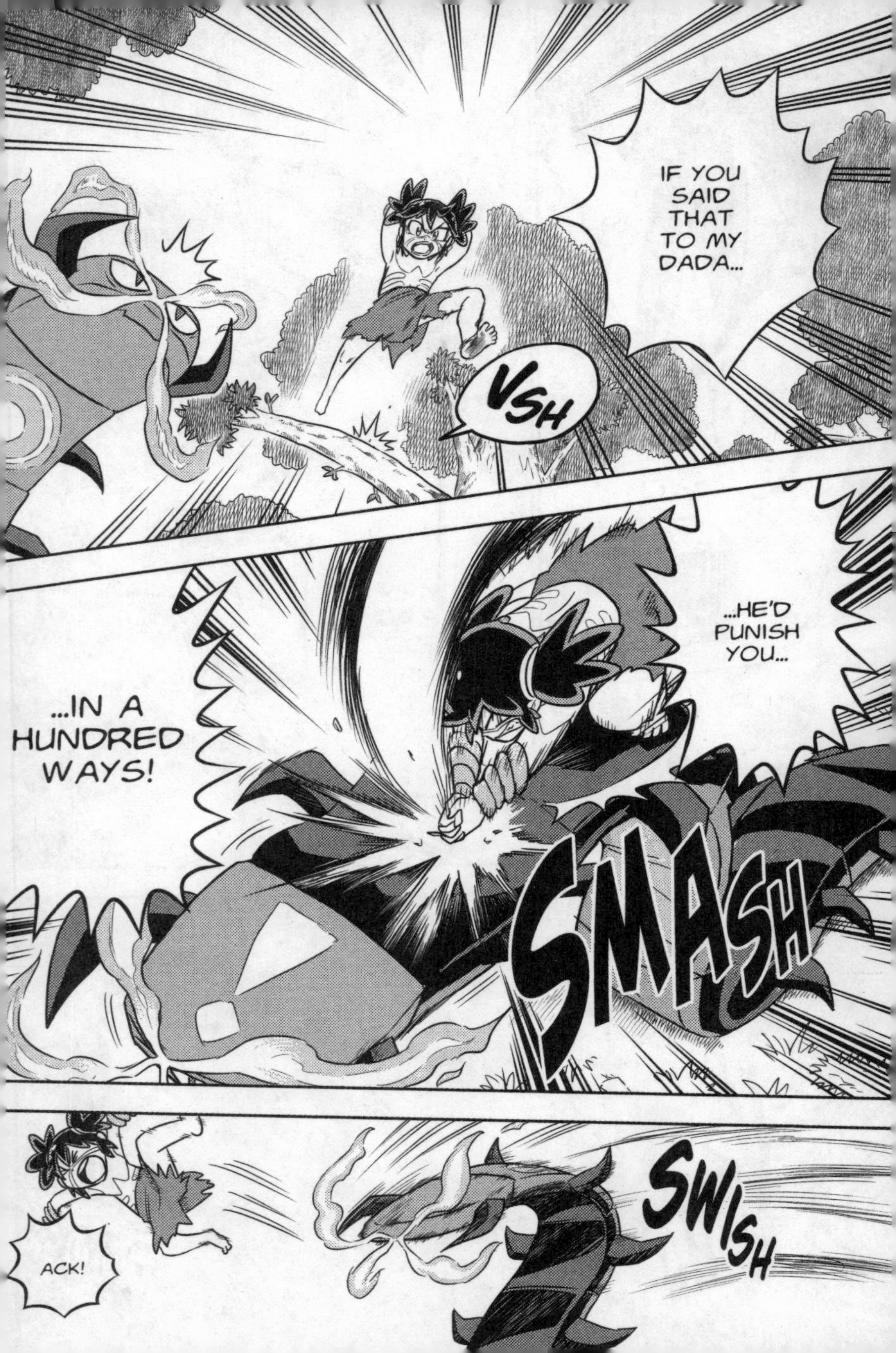
IF YOU SAID THAT TO MY DADA...
VSH
...HE'D PUNISH YOU...
...IN A HUNDRED WAYS!
SMASH
SWISH
ACK!

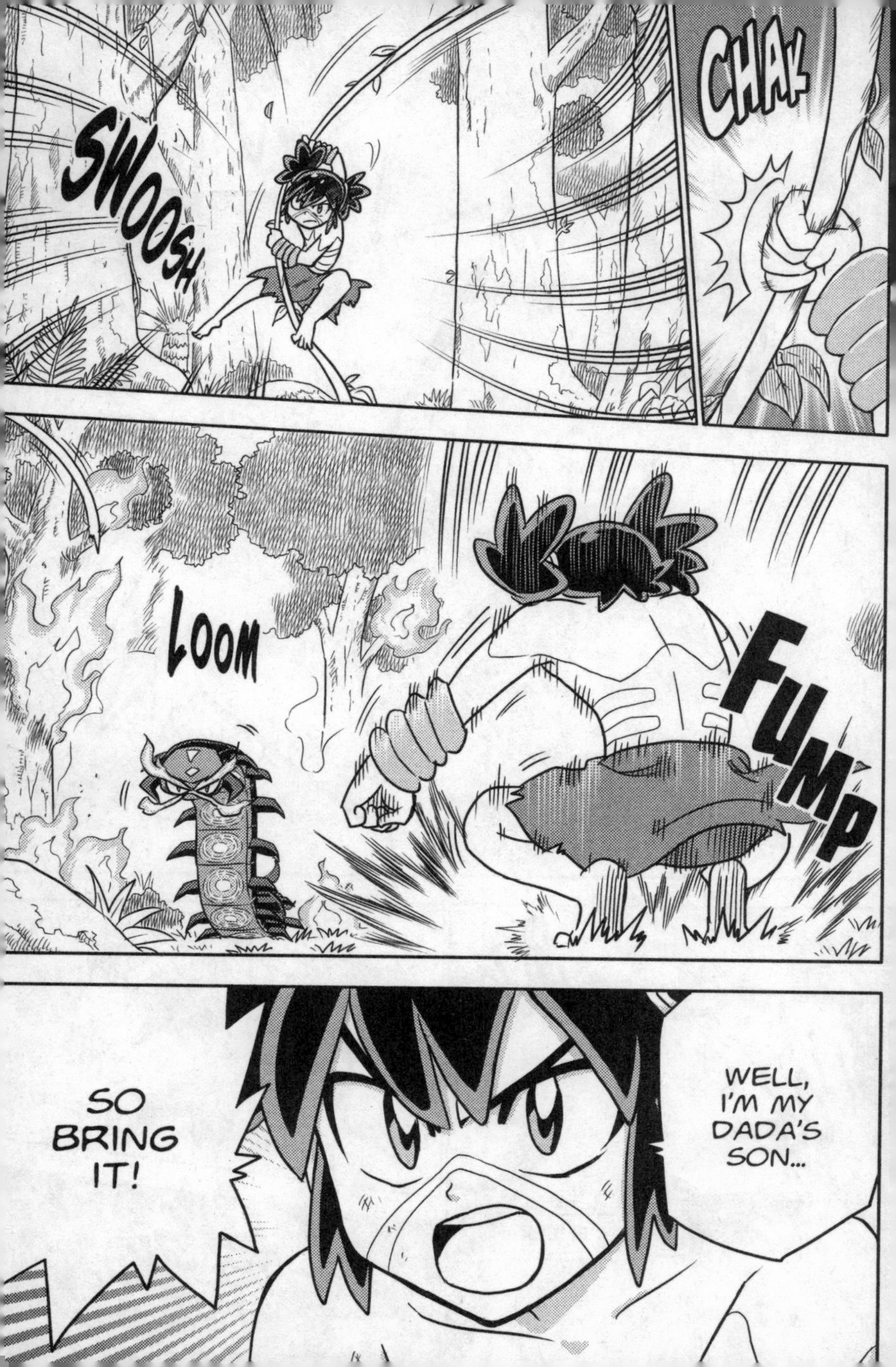
CHAK
SWOOSH
FUMP
LOOM
WELL, I'M MY DADA'S SON...
SO BRING IT!

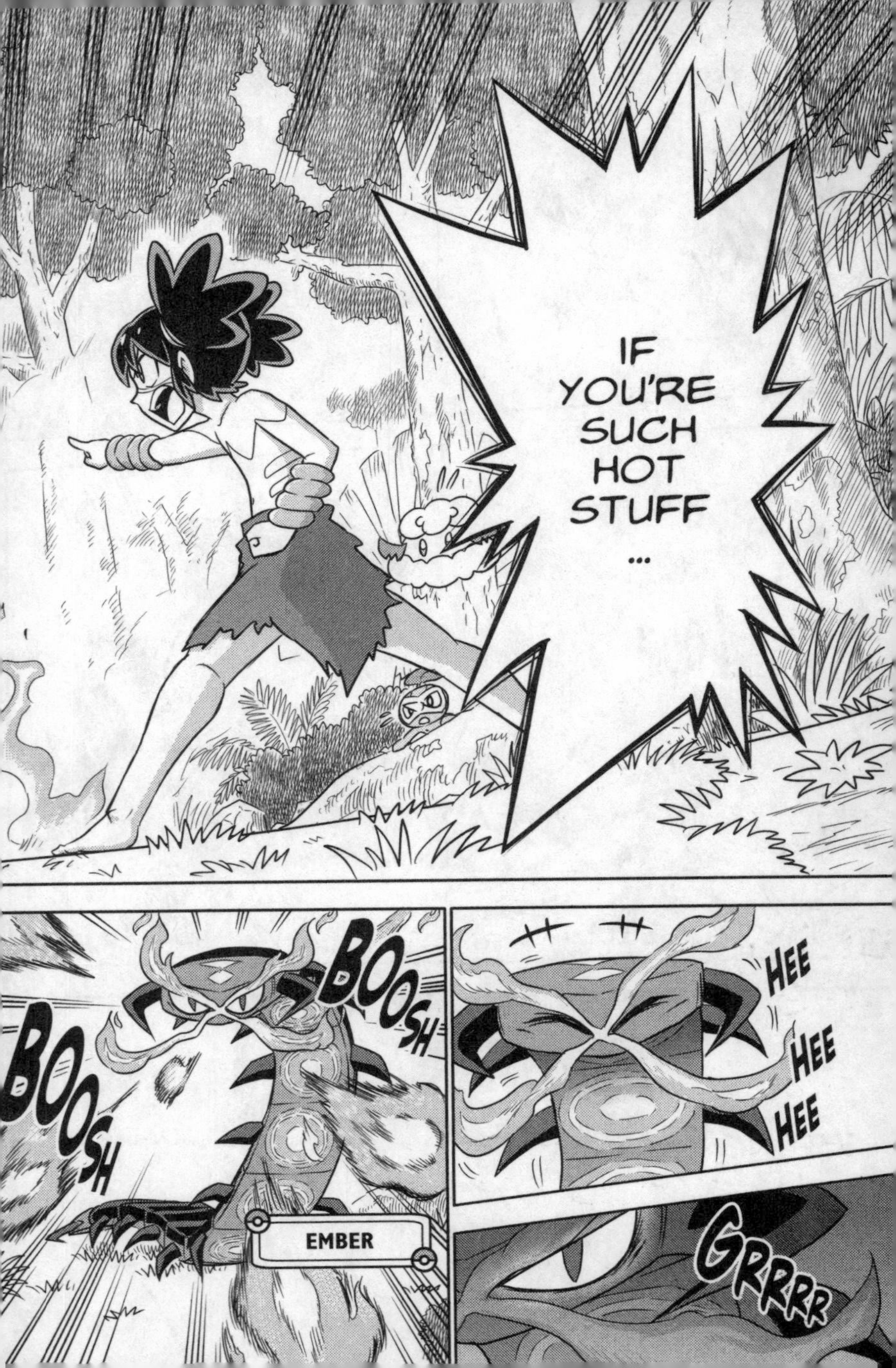
IF YOU'RE SUCH HOT STUFF ...
HEE HEE HEE
GRRRR
BOOSH
BOOSH
EMBER

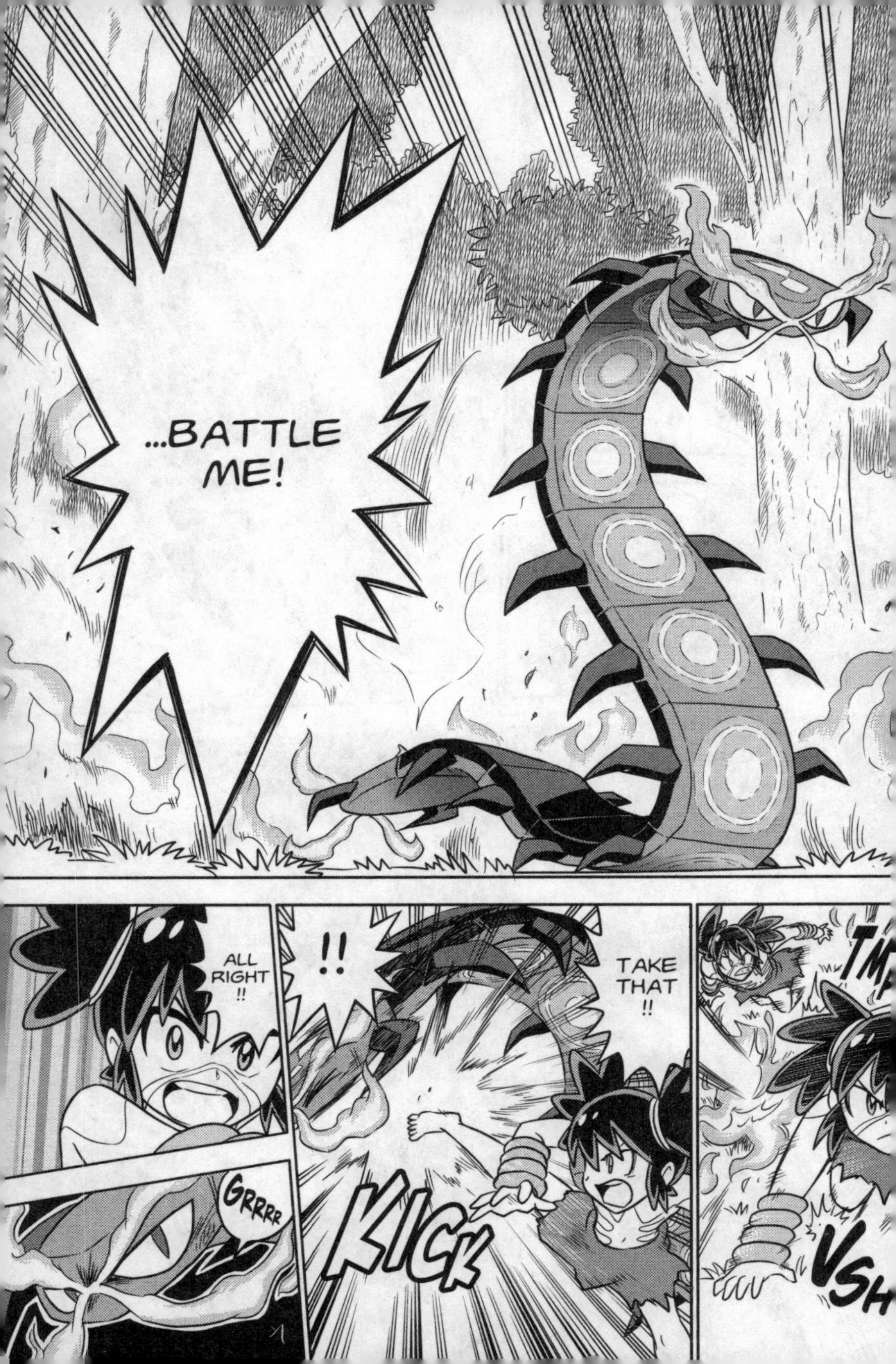
...BATTLE ME!
TMP
VSH
TAKE THAT !!
!!
KICK
ALL RIGHT !!
GRRRR

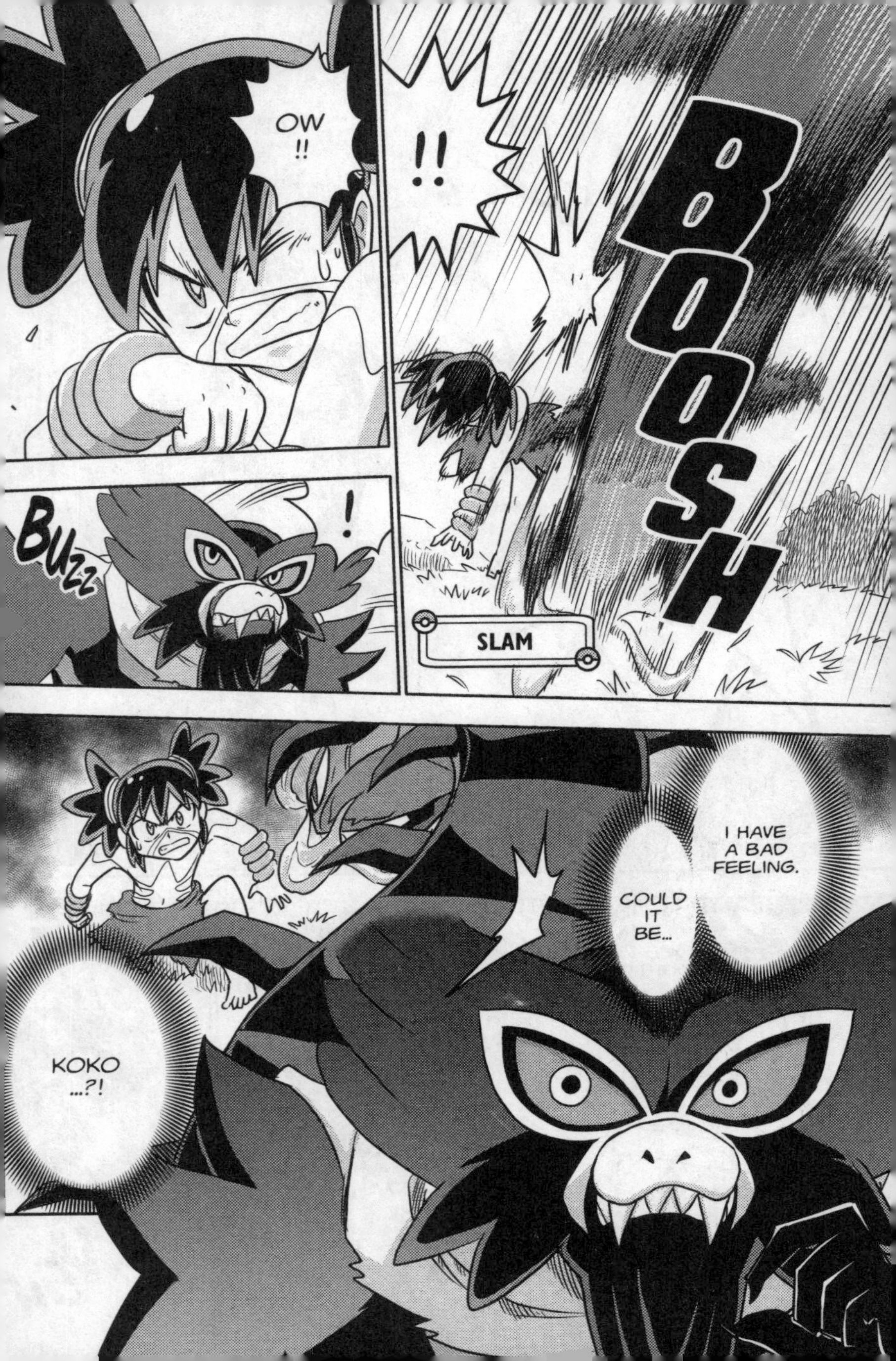
!!
BOOOSH
SLAM
OW !!
BUZZ
!
I HAVE A BAD FEELING.
COULD IT BE...
KOKO ...?!

Protect the Peace of the Forest!

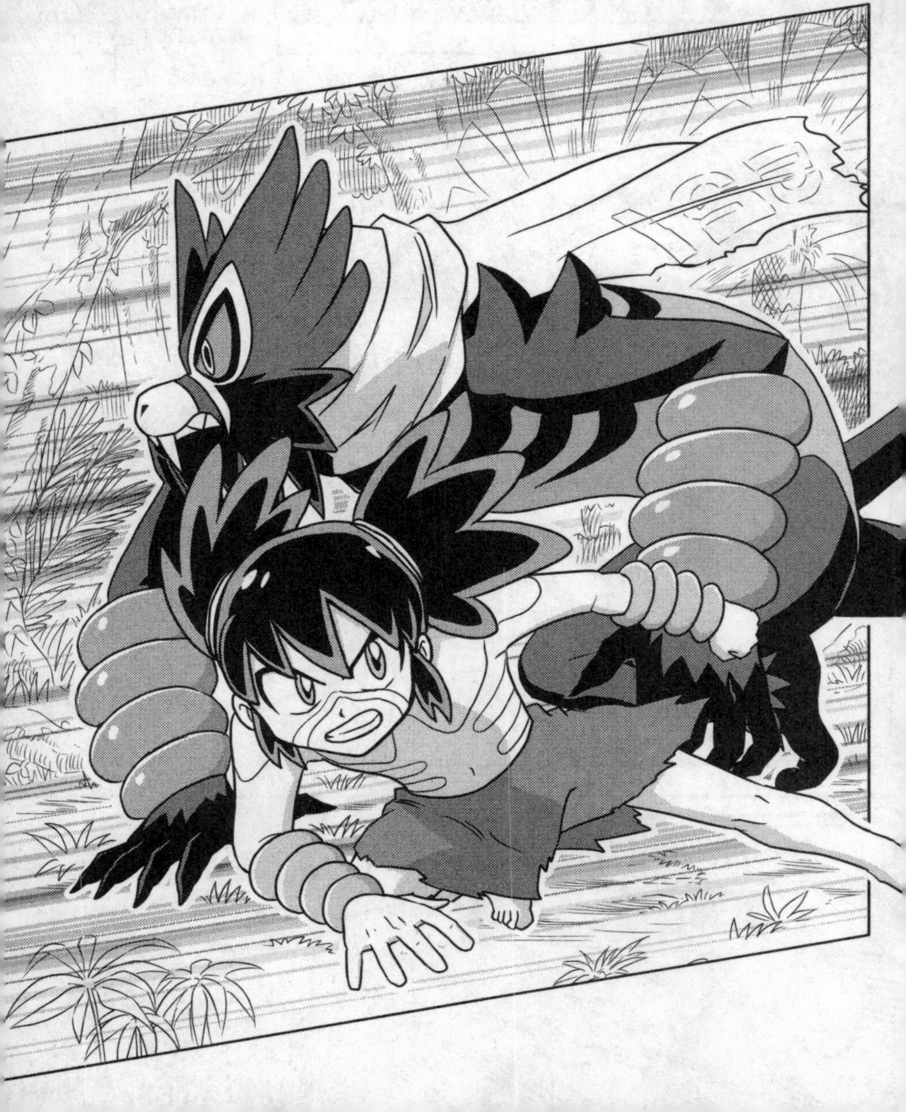

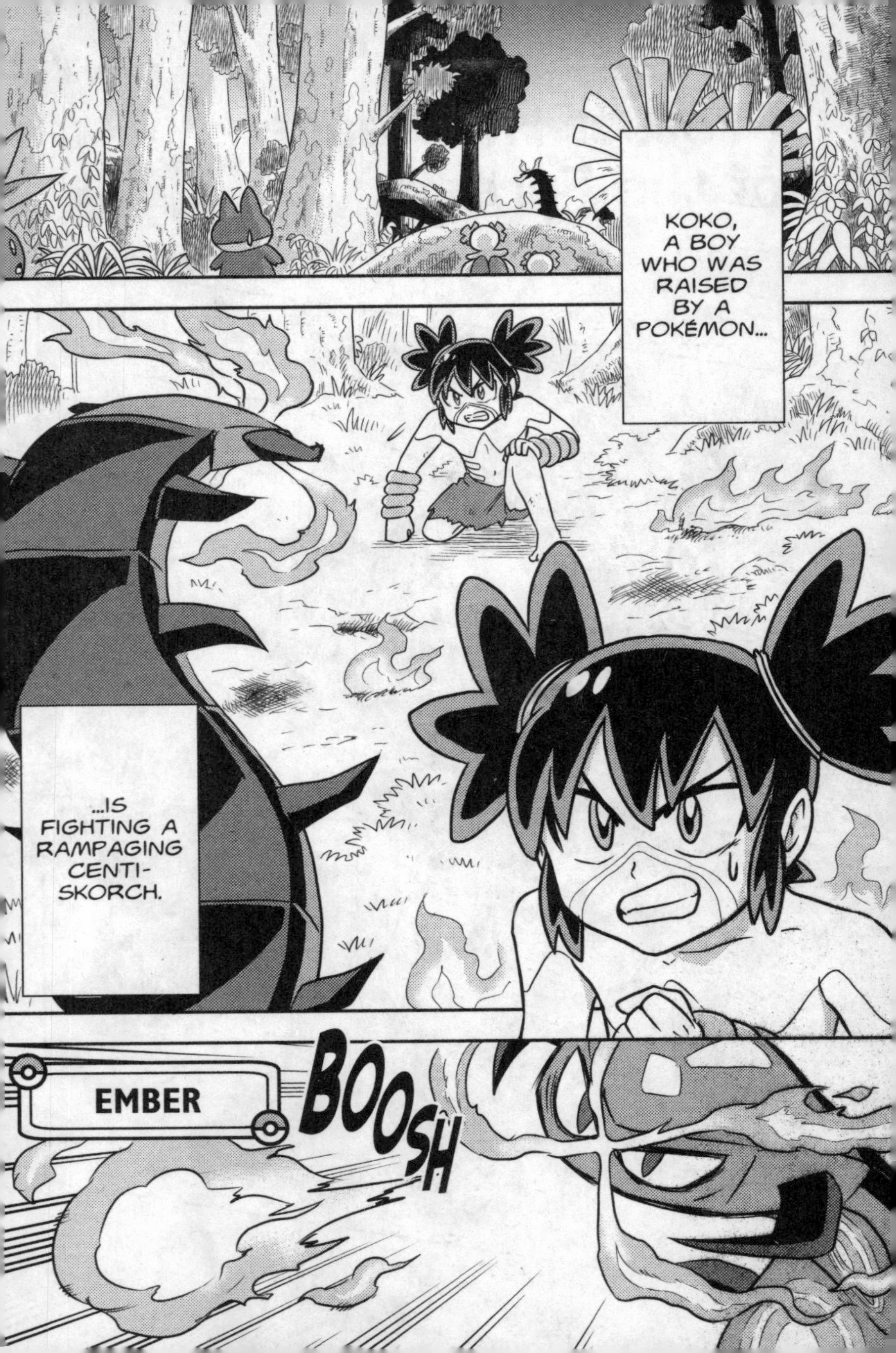
KOKO, A BOY WHO WAS RAISED BY A POKÉMON...
...IS FIGHTING A RAMPAGING CENTI-SKORCH.
BOOSH
EMBER

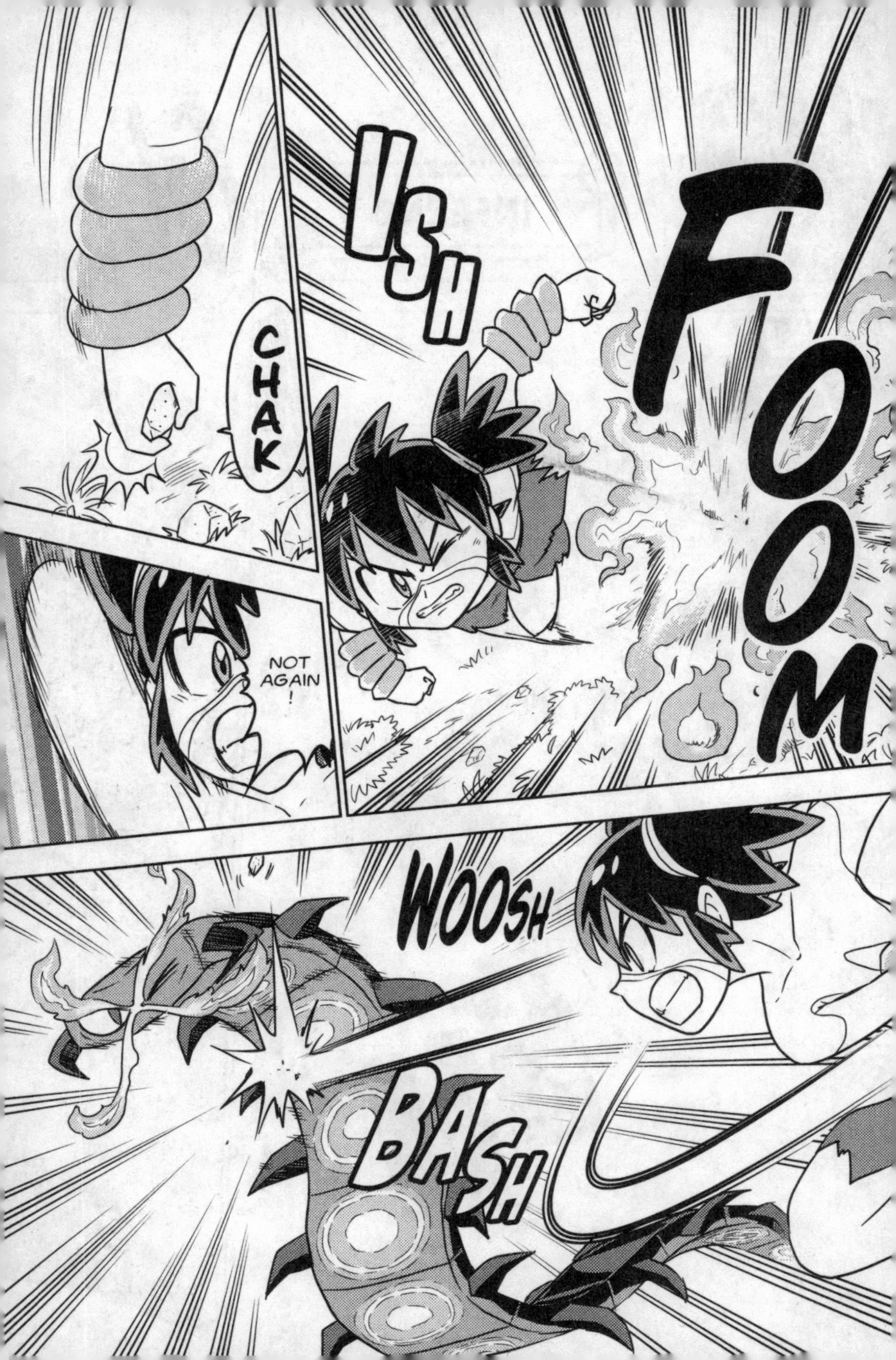

FOOOM
VSH
CHAK
NOT AGAIN!
WOOSH
BASH

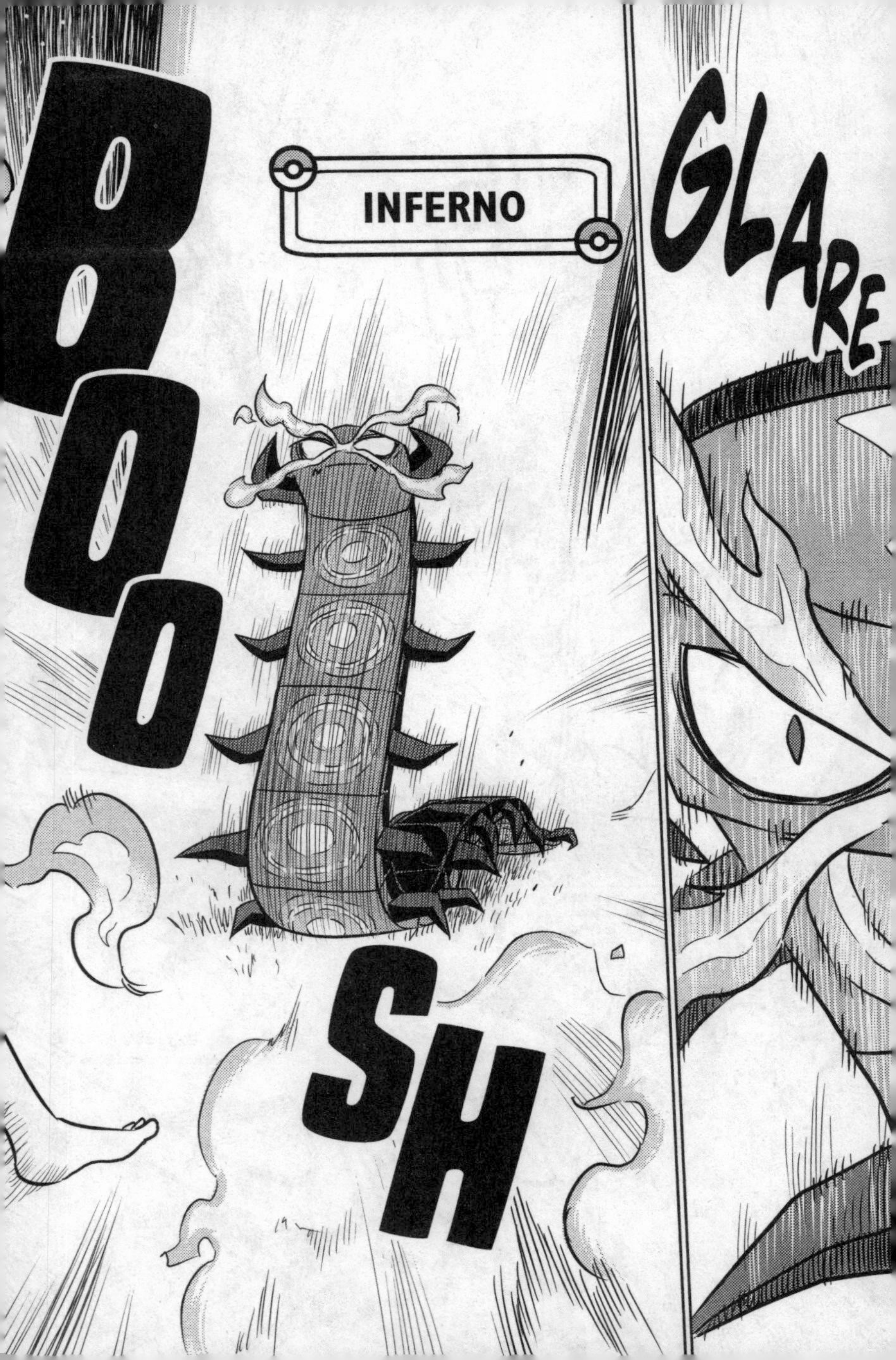
GLARE
INFERNO
BOOO
SH

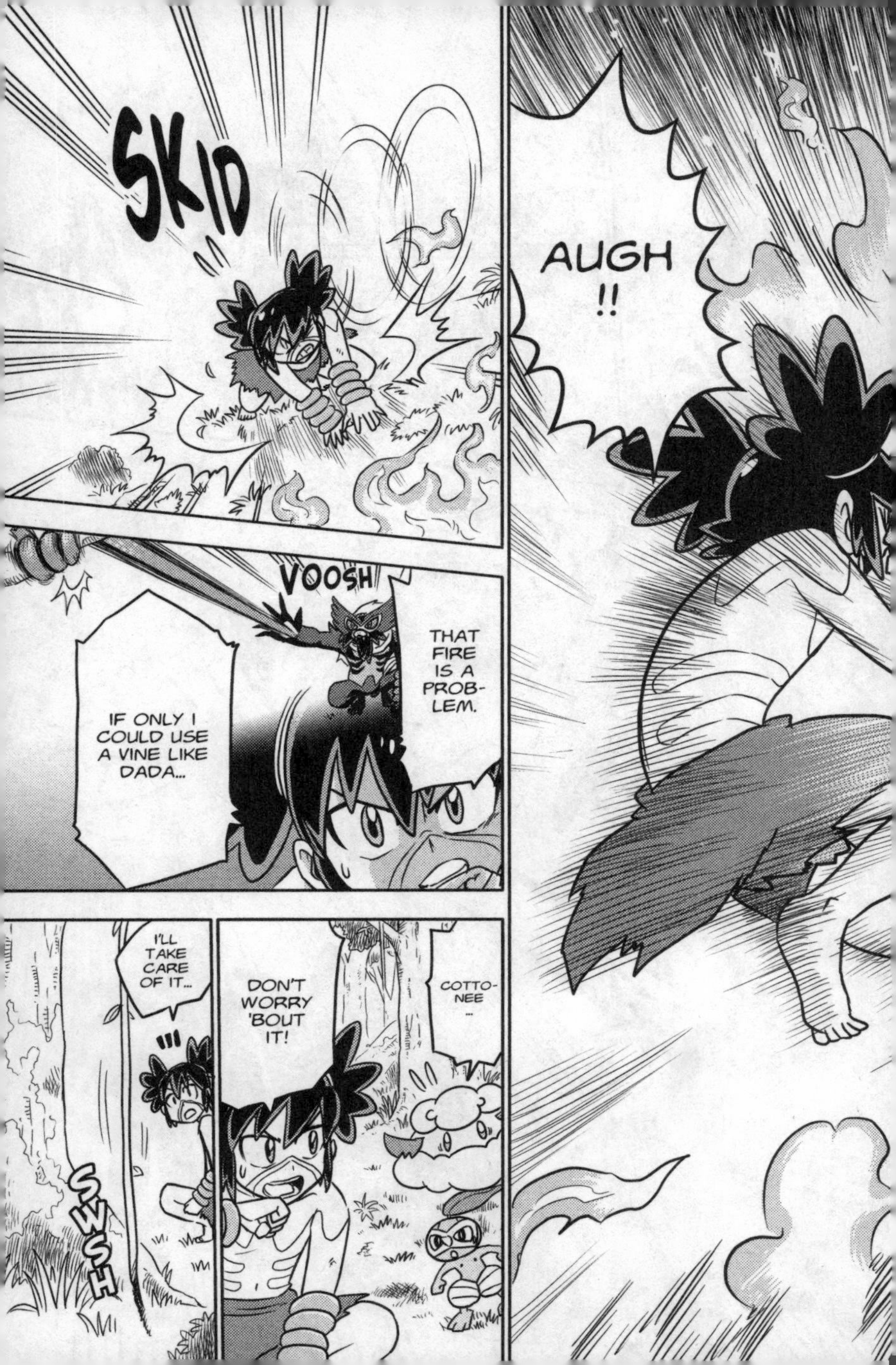
AUGH !!
SKID
VOOSH
THAT FIRE IS A PROB-LEM.
IF ONLY I COULD USE A VINE LIKE DADA...
COTTO-NEE ...
DON'T WORRY 'BOUT IT!
I'LL TAKE CARE OF IT...
!!!
SWSH

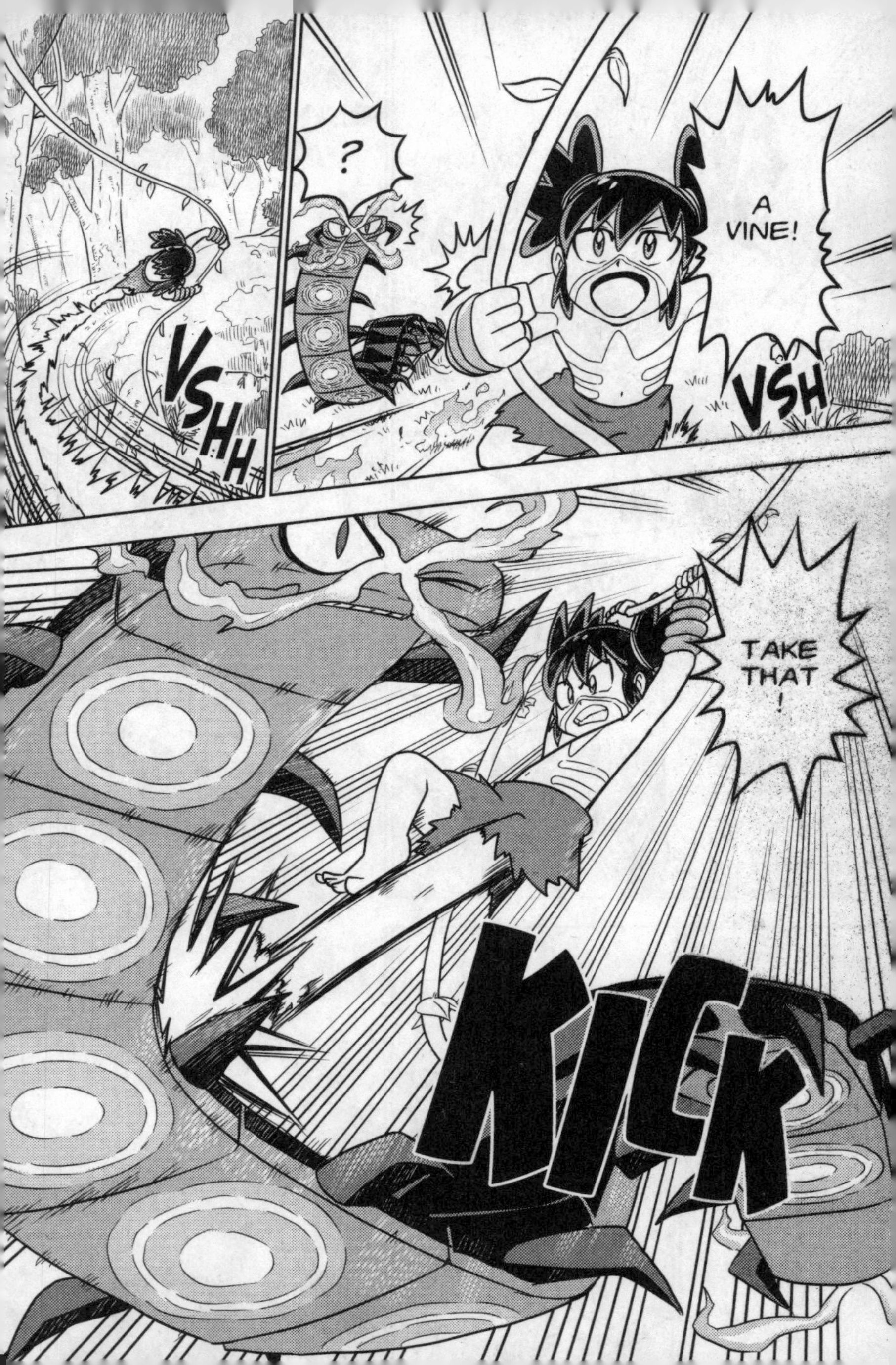

A VINE!
?
VSH
VSHH
TAKE THAT!
KICK

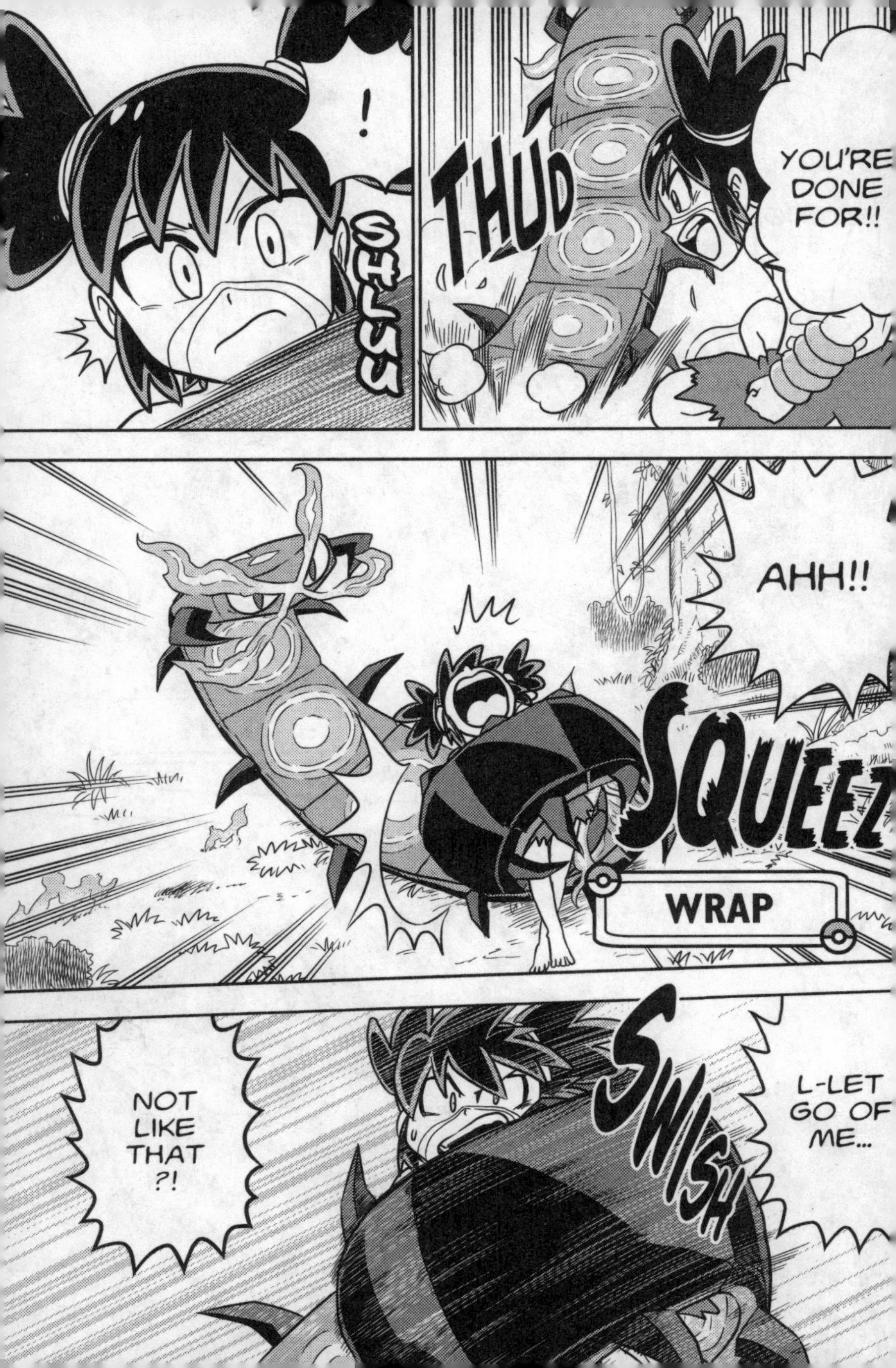
YOU'RE DONE FOR!!
THUD
!
SHLUUU
AHH!!
SQUEEZ
WRAP
L-LET GO OF ME...
SWISH
NOT LIKE THAT ?!

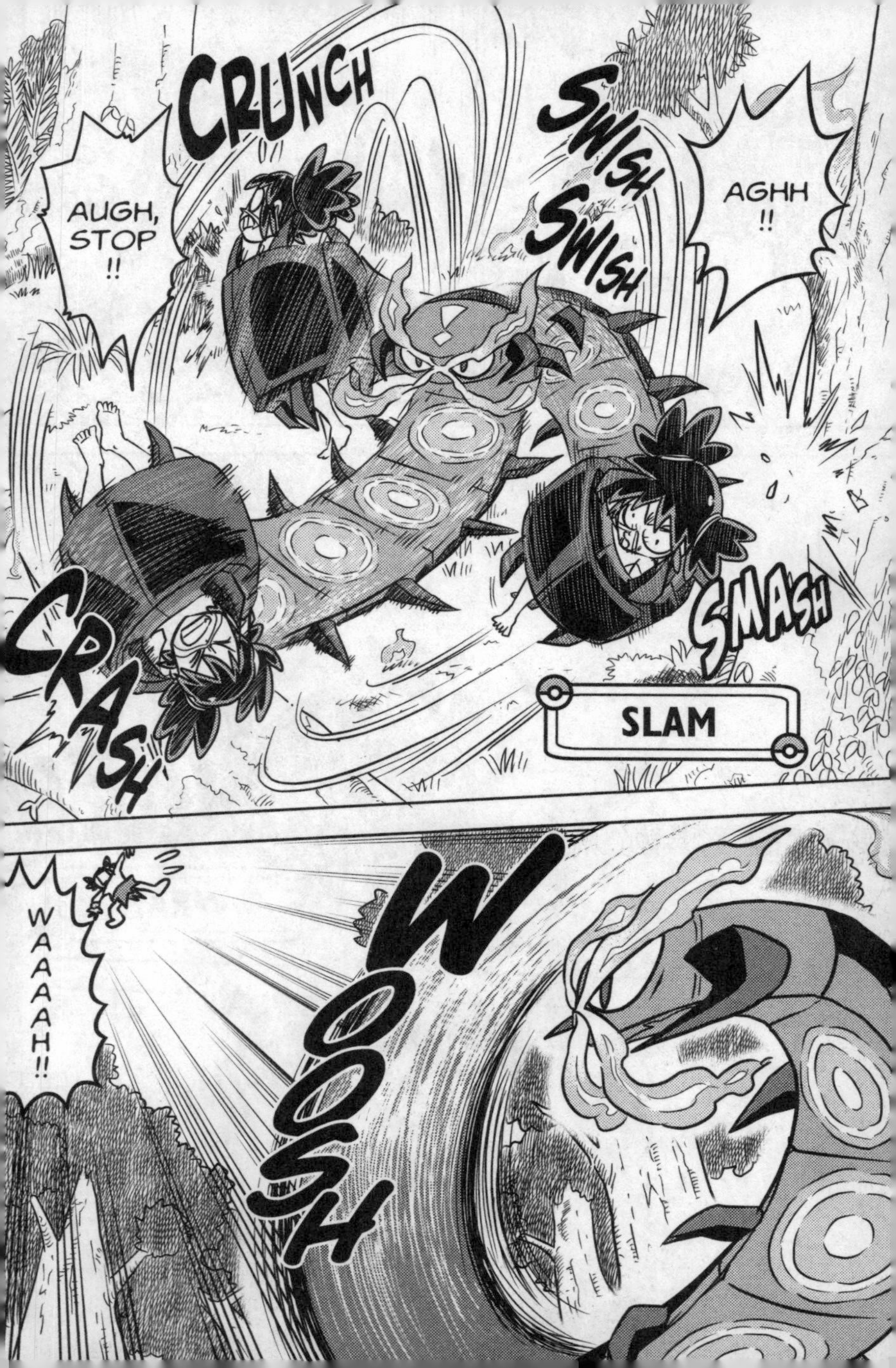
AGHH!!
SWISH
SWISH
CRUNCH
AUGH, STOP!!
SMASH
SLAM
CRASH
WOOSH
WAAAAAH!!

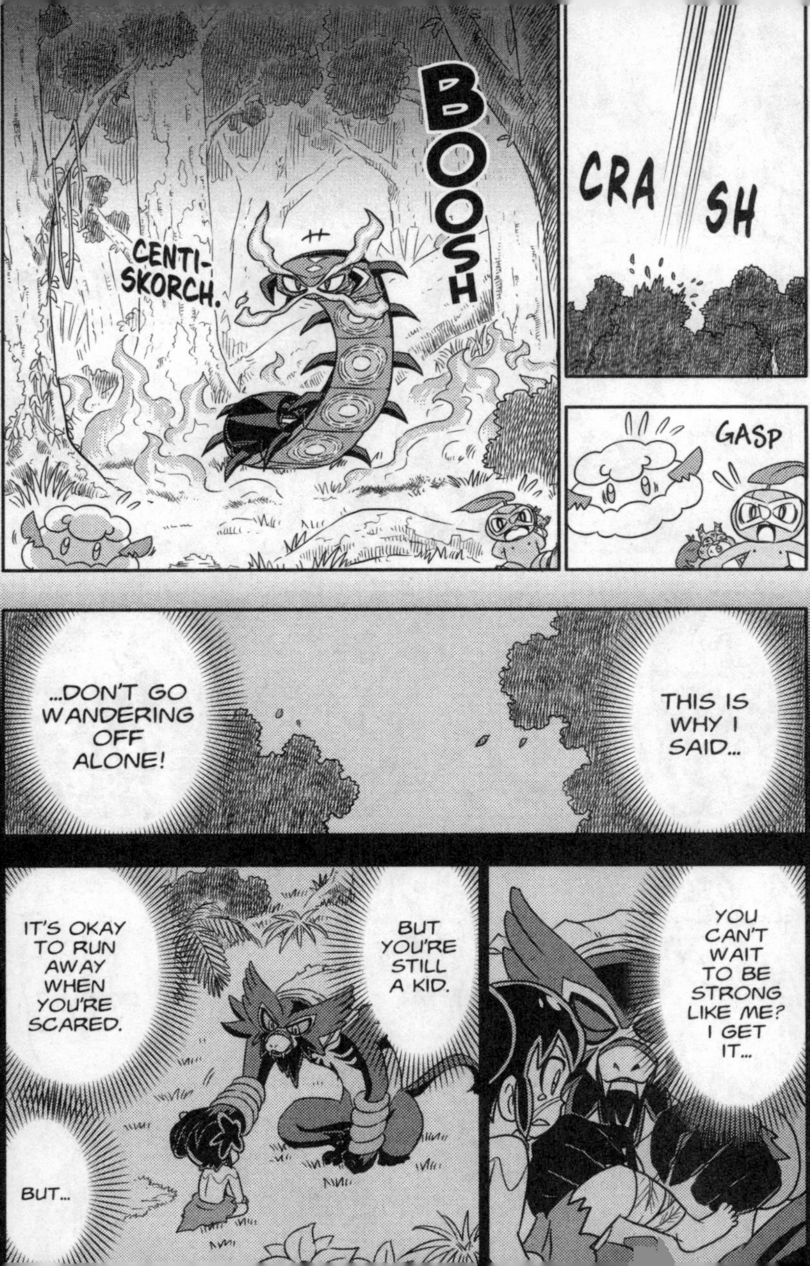
CRASH
GASP
BOOSH
CENTI-SKORCH.
THIS IS WHY I SAID...
...DON'T GO WANDERING OFF ALONE!
YOU CAN'T WAIT TO BE STRONG LIKE ME? I GET IT...
BUT YOU'RE STILL A KID.
IT'S OKAY TO RUN AWAY WHEN YOU'RE SCARED.
BUT...

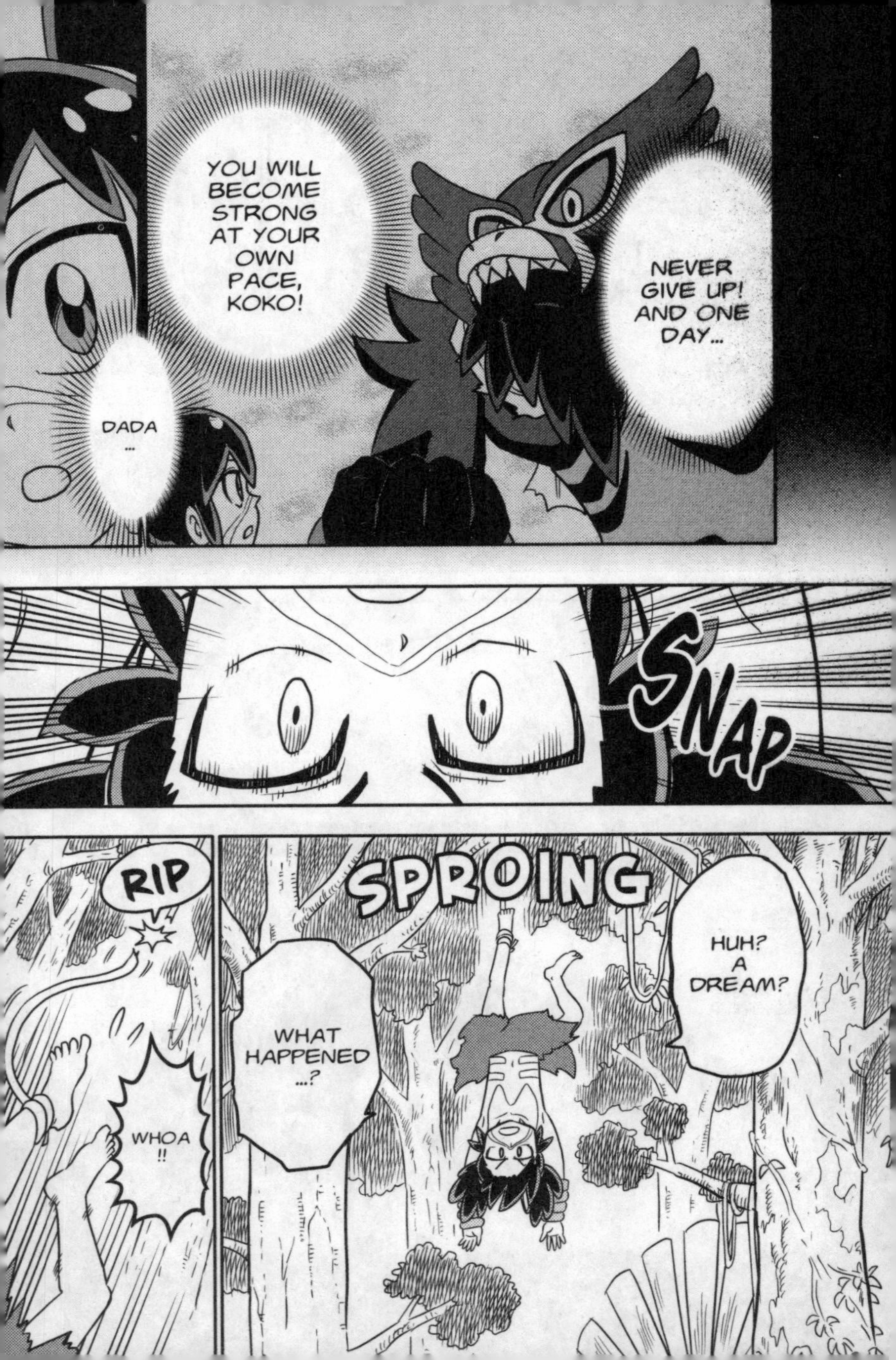

NEVER GIVE UP! AND ONE DAY...
YOU WILL BECOME STRONG AT YOUR OWN PACE, KOKO!
DADA ...
SNAP
SPROING
HUH? A DREAM?
WHAT HAPPENED ...?
RIP
WHOA !!

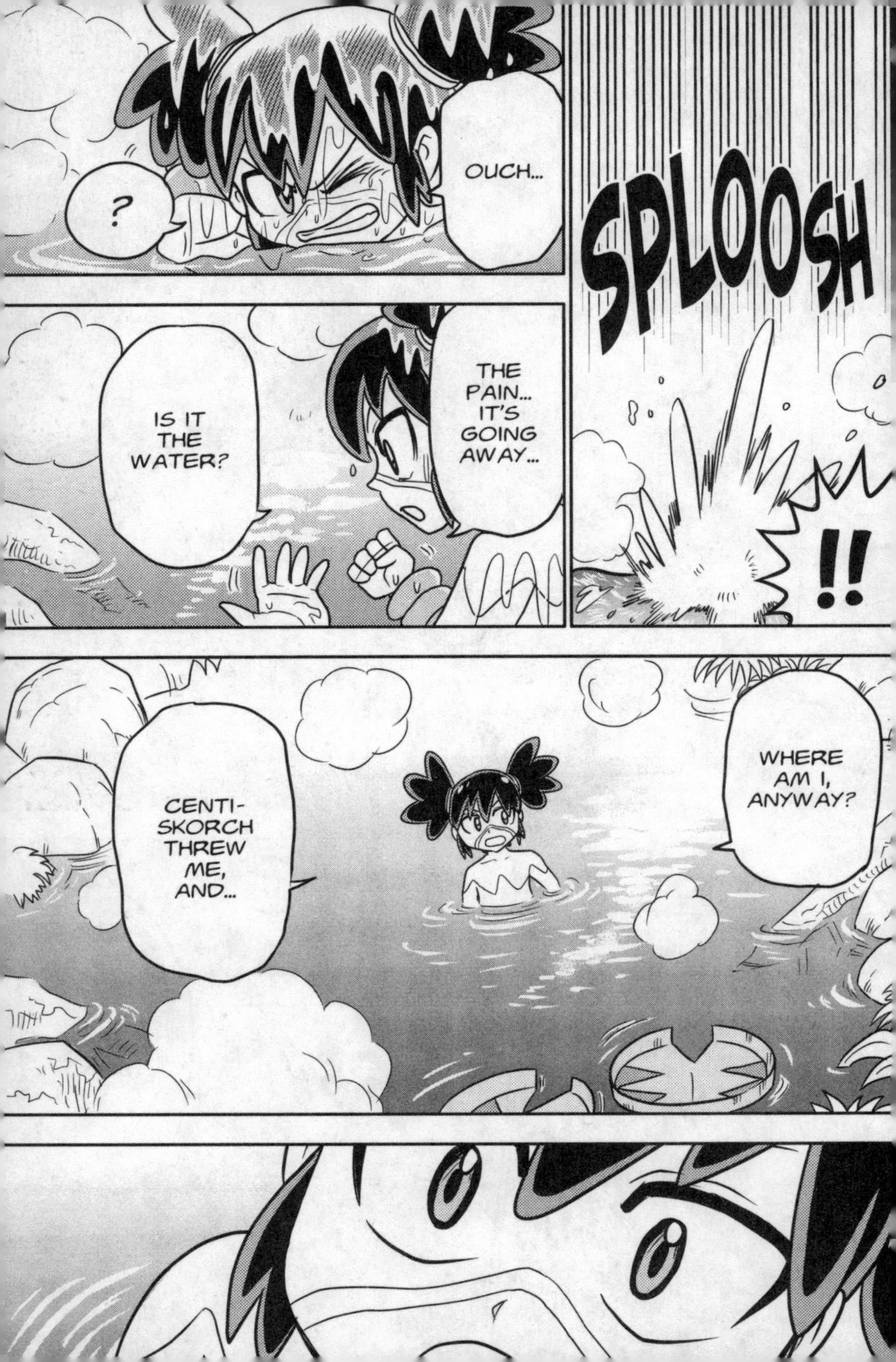
SPLOOSH
!!
OUCH...
?
THE PAIN... IT'S GOING AWAY...
IS IT THE WATER?
WHERE AM I, ANYWAY?
CENTI-SKORCH THREW ME, AND...

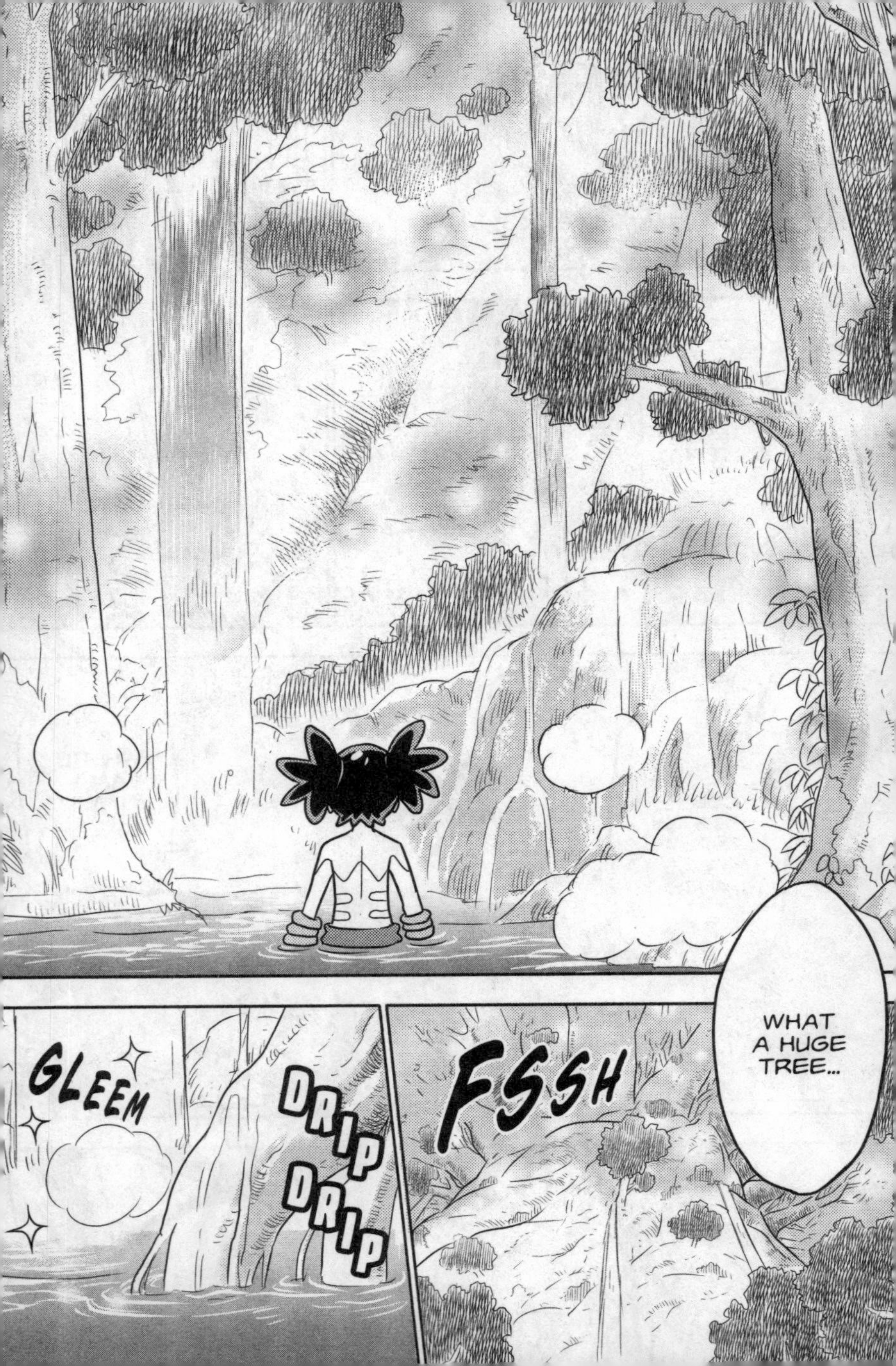
WHAT A HUGE TREE...
FSSH
DRIP DRIP
GLEEM

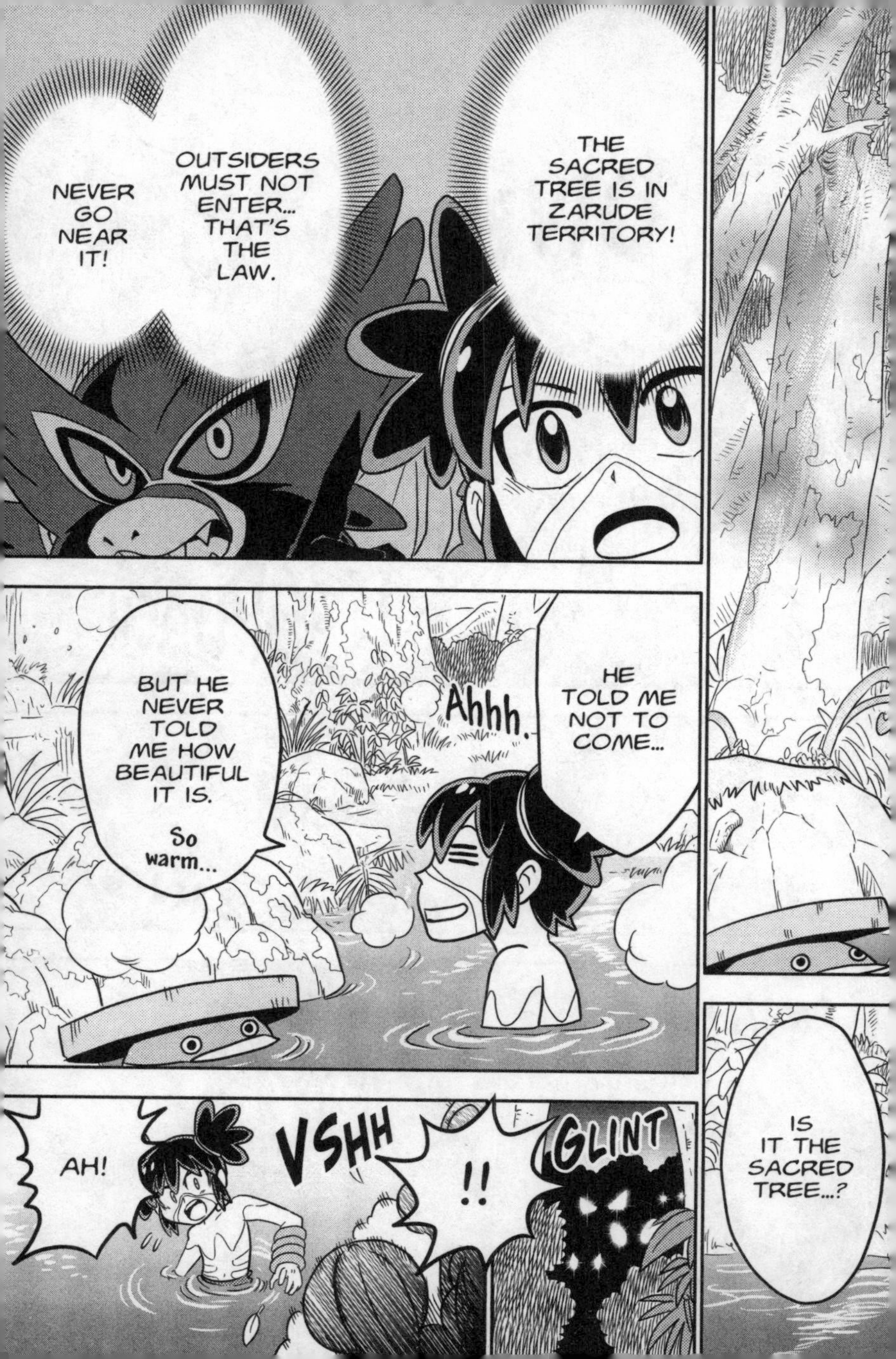
THE SACRED TREE IS IN ZARUDE TERRITORY!
OUTSIDERS MUST NOT ENTER... THAT'S THE LAW.
NEVER GO NEAR IT!
HE TOLD ME NOT TO COME...
Ahhh.
BUT HE NEVER TOLD ME HOW BEAUTIFUL IT IS.
So warm...
IS IT THE SACRED TREE...?
GLINT
!!
VSHH
AH!

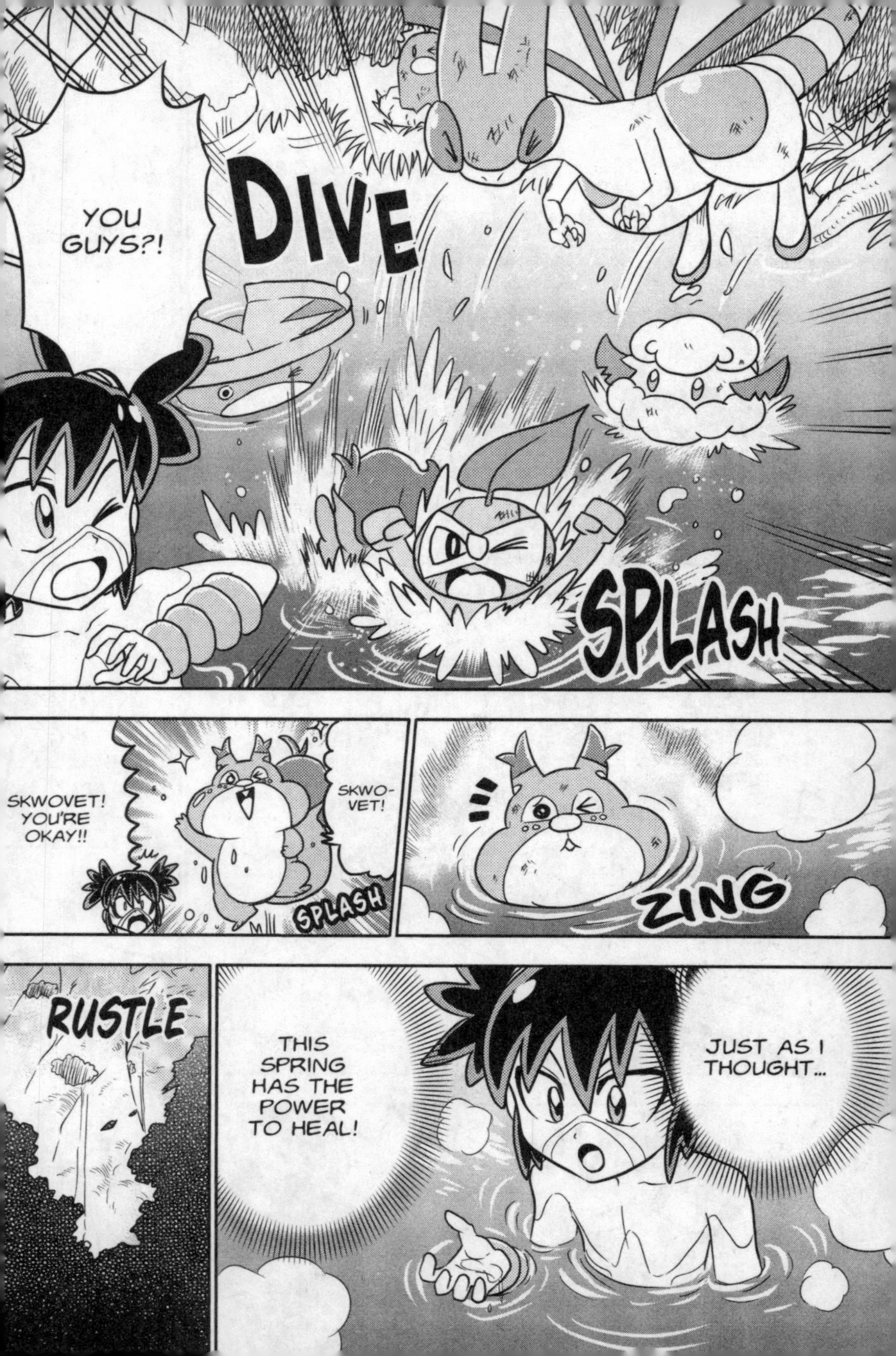
DIVE
YOU GUYS?!
SPLASH
ZING
SKWO-VET!
SKWOVET! YOU'RE OKAY!!
SPLASH
JUST AS I THOUGHT...
THIS SPRING HAS THE POWER TO HEAL!
RUSTLE

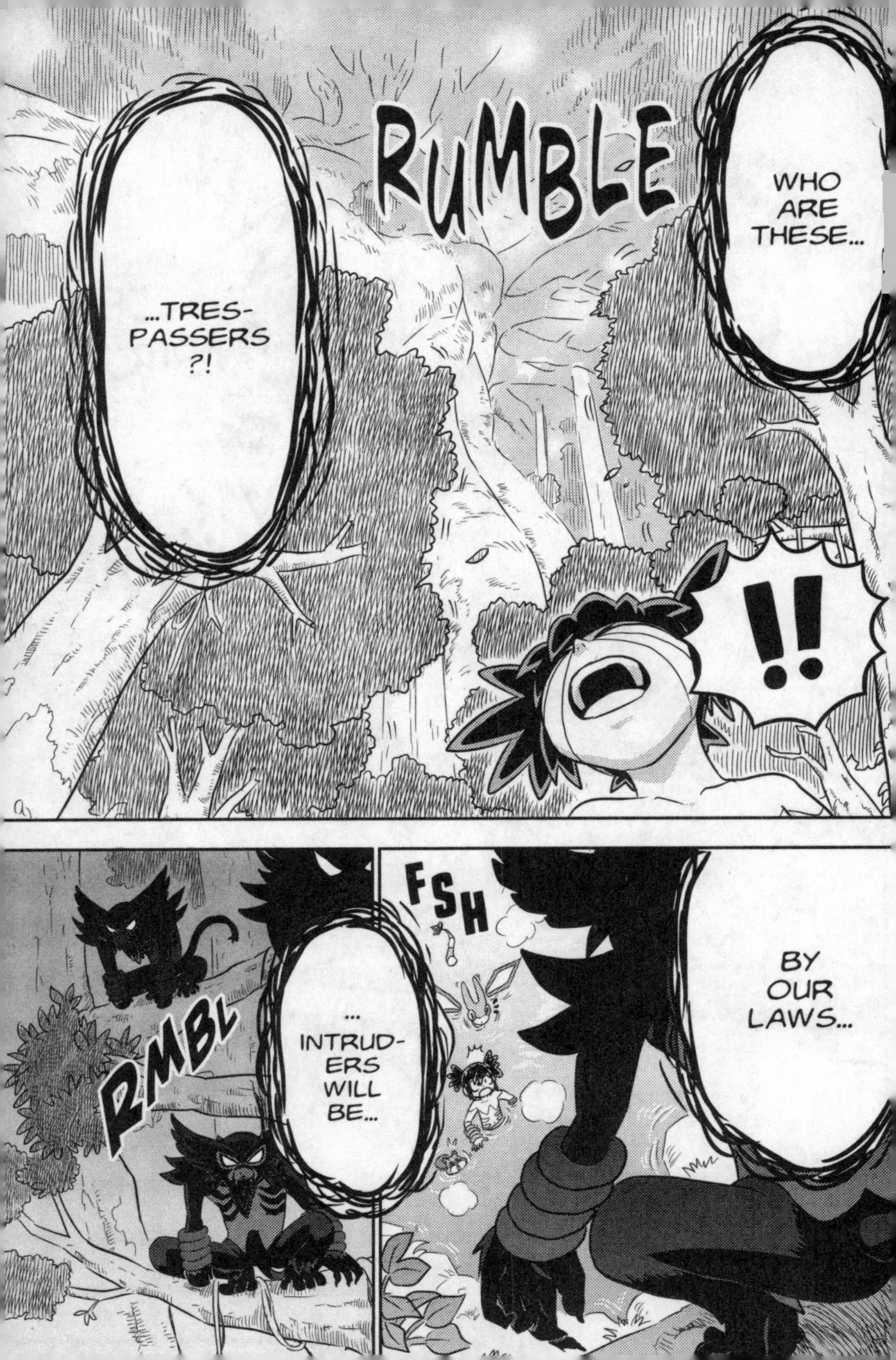
WHO ARE THESE...
RUMBLE
...TRES-PASSERS ?!
!!
BY OUR LAWS...
FSH
...INTRUD-ERS WILL BE...
RMBL

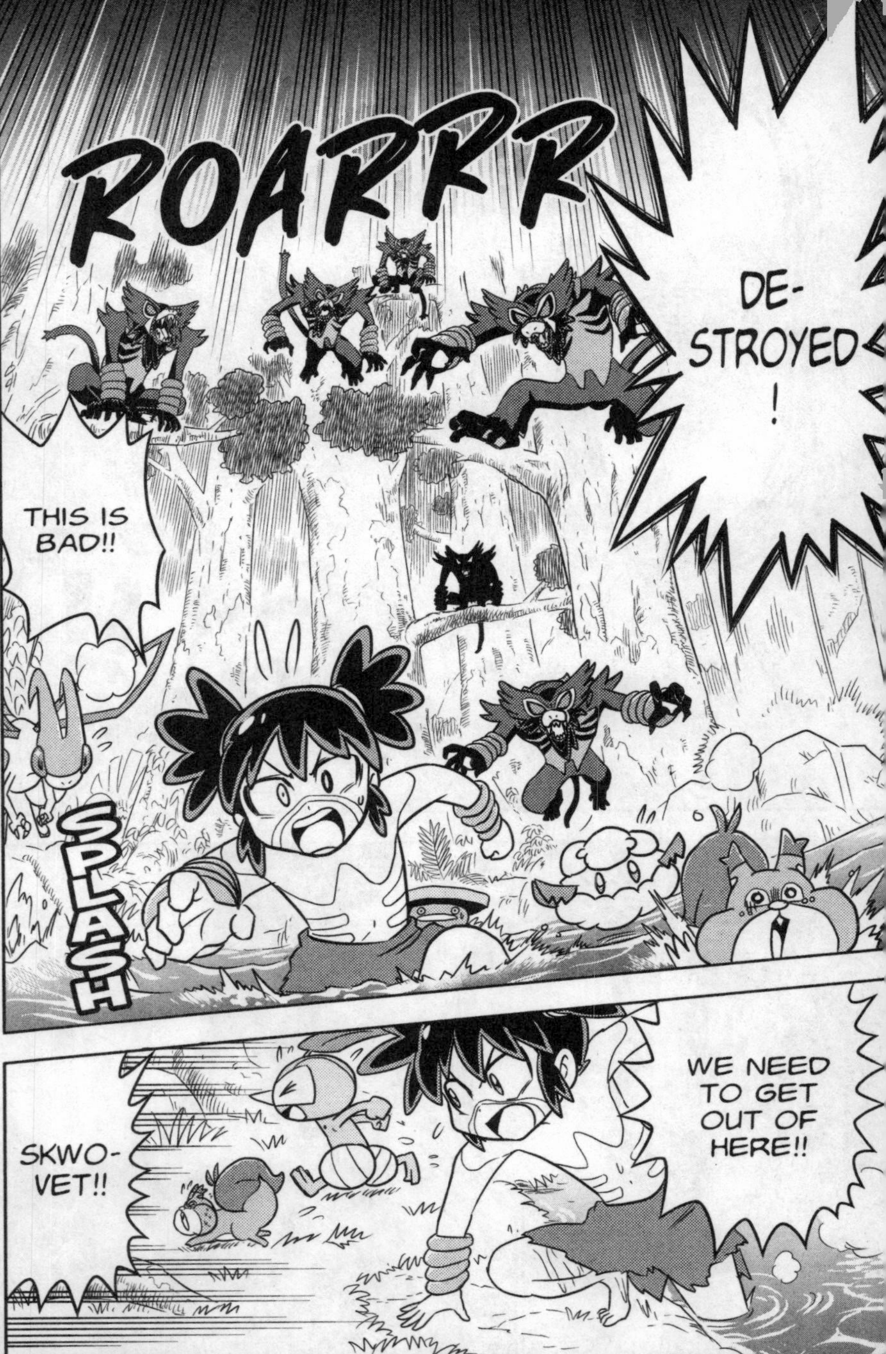
ROARRR
DE-STROYED!
THIS IS BAD!!
SPLASH
WE NEED TO GET OUT OF HERE!!
SKWO-VET!!

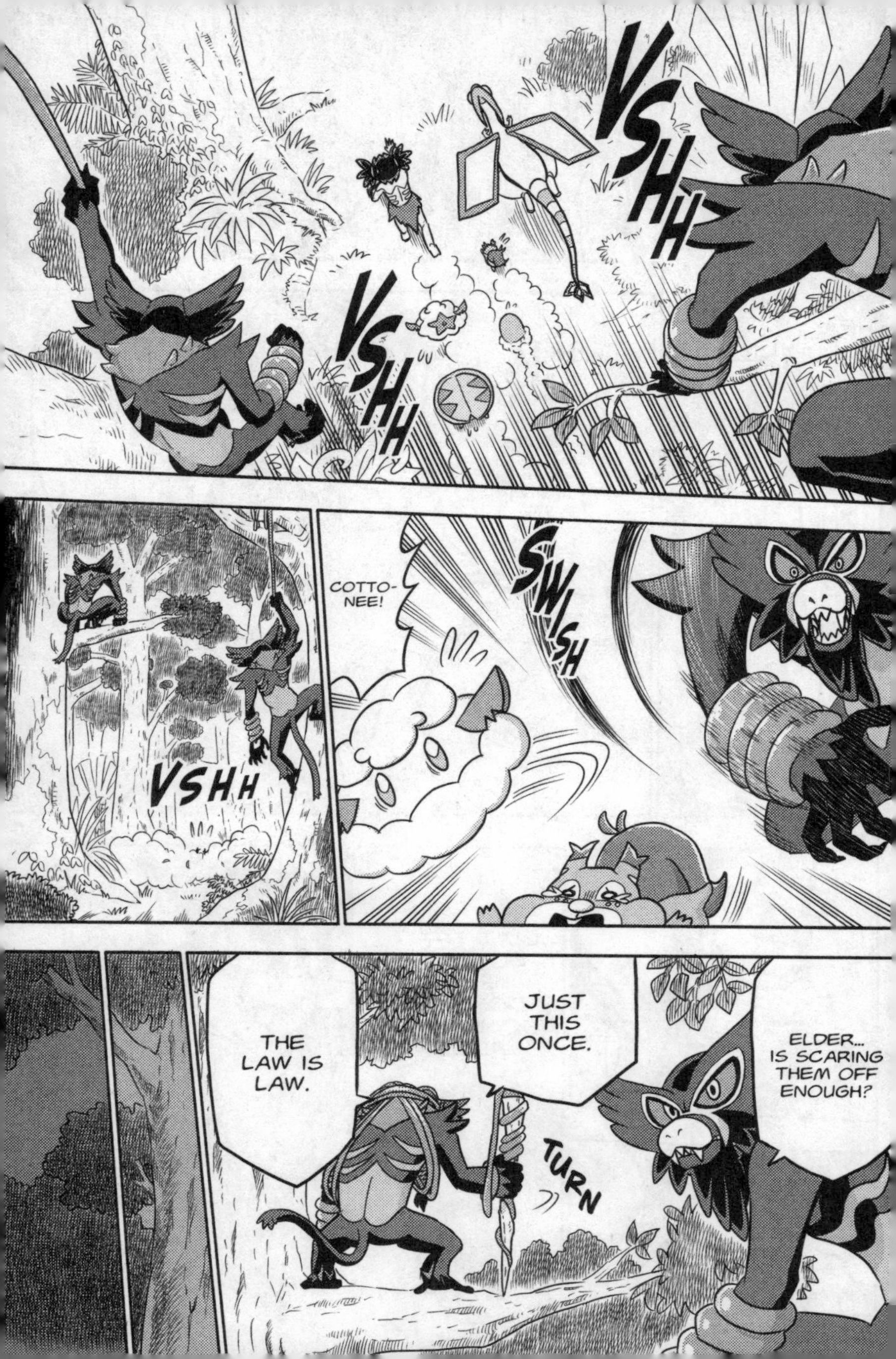
VSHH
VSHH
COTTO-NEE!
SWISH
VSHH
ELDER... IS SCARING THEM OFF ENOUGH?
TURN
JUST THIS ONCE.
THE LAW IS LAW.

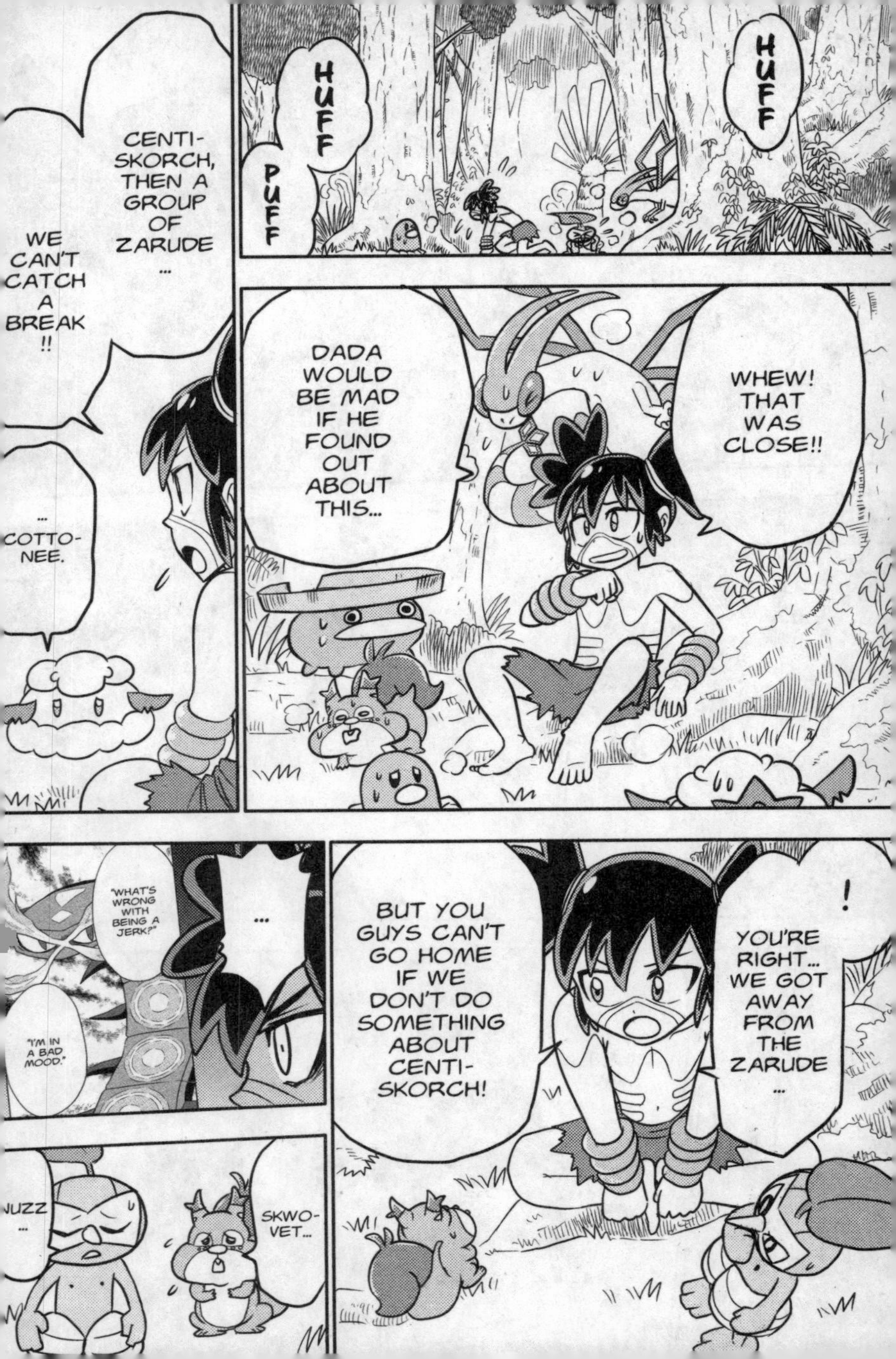
HUFF
HUFF PUFF
WHEW! THAT WAS CLOSE!!
DADA WOULD BE MAD IF HE FOUND OUT ABOUT THIS...
CENTI-SKORCH, THEN A GROUP OF ZARUDE ...
WE CAN'T CATCH A BREAK!!
... COTTO-NEE.
!
YOU'RE RIGHT... WE GOT AWAY FROM THE ZARUDE ...
BUT YOU GUYS CAN'T GO HOME IF WE DON'T DO SOMETHING ABOUT CENTI-SKORCH!
...
"WHAT'S WRONG WITH BEING A JERK?"
"I'M IN A BAD MOOD."
SKWO-VET...
NUZZ ...

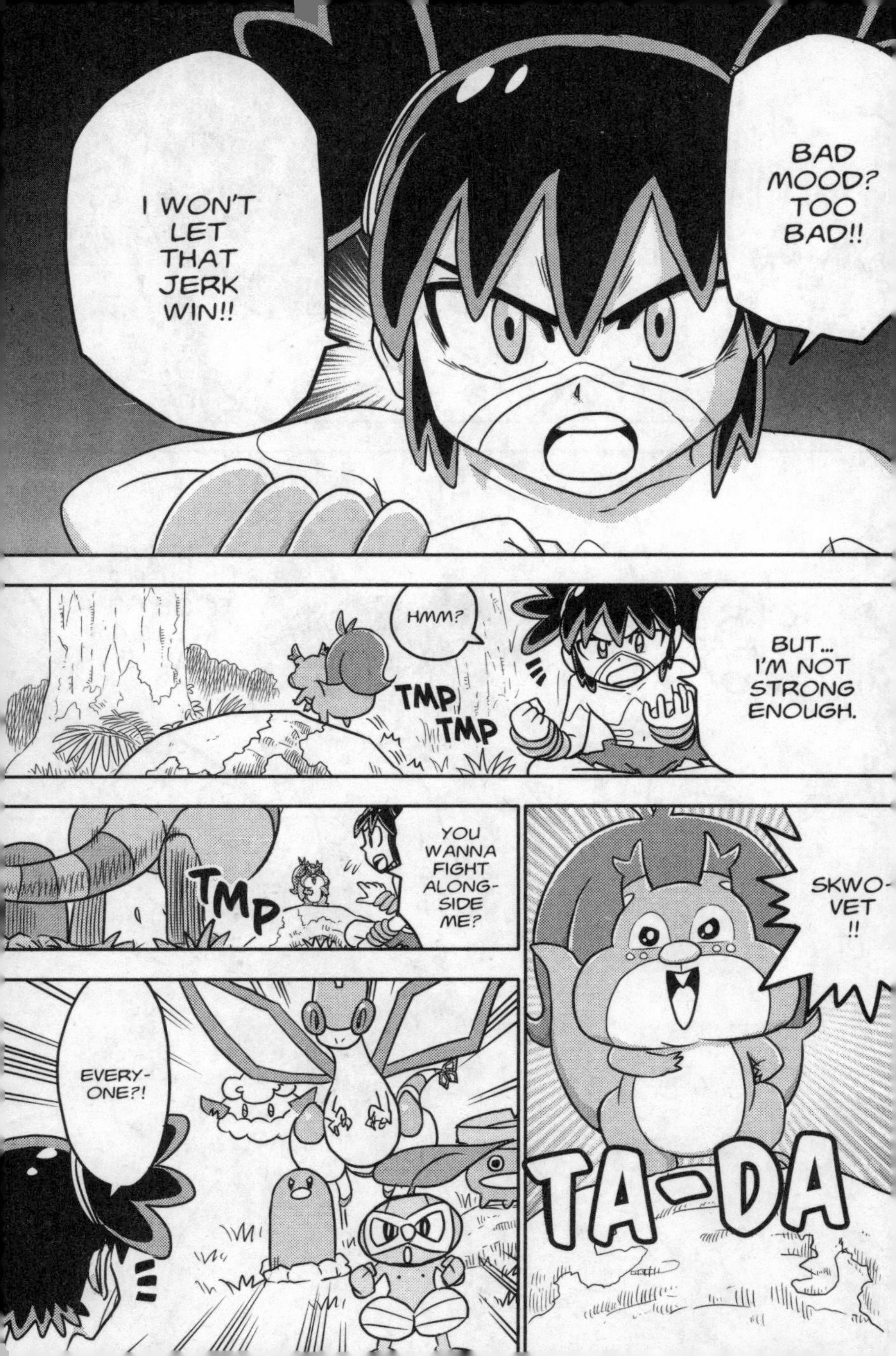
BAD MOOD? TOO BAD!!
I WON'T LET THAT JERK WIN!!
BUT... I'M NOT STRONG ENOUGH.
HMM?
TMP TMP
SKWO-VET!!
TA-DA
YOU WANNA FIGHT ALONG-SIDE ME?
TMP
EVERY-ONE?!

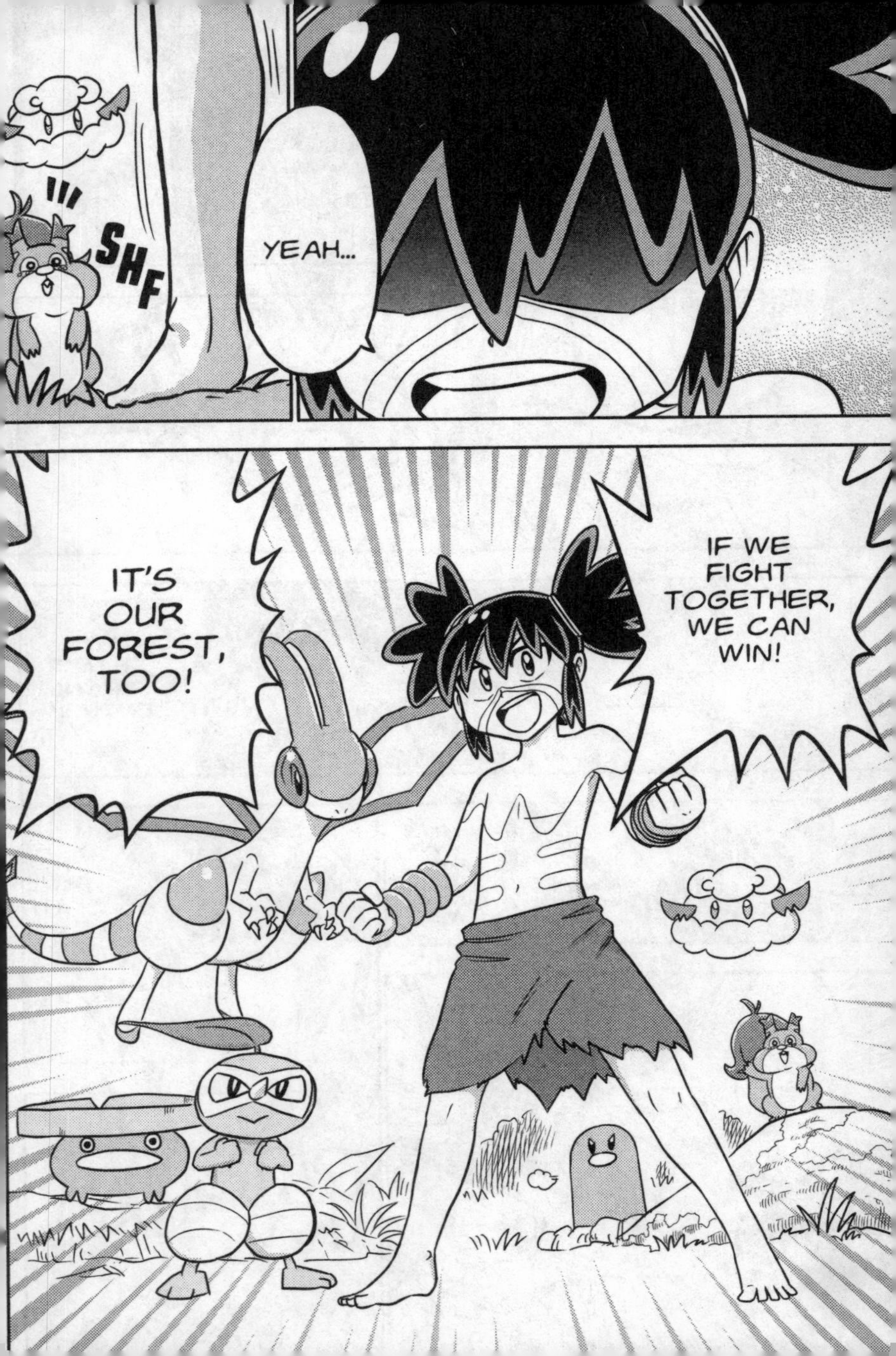
YEAH...
SHF
IF WE FIGHT TOGETHER, WE CAN WIN!
IT'S OUR FOREST, TOO!

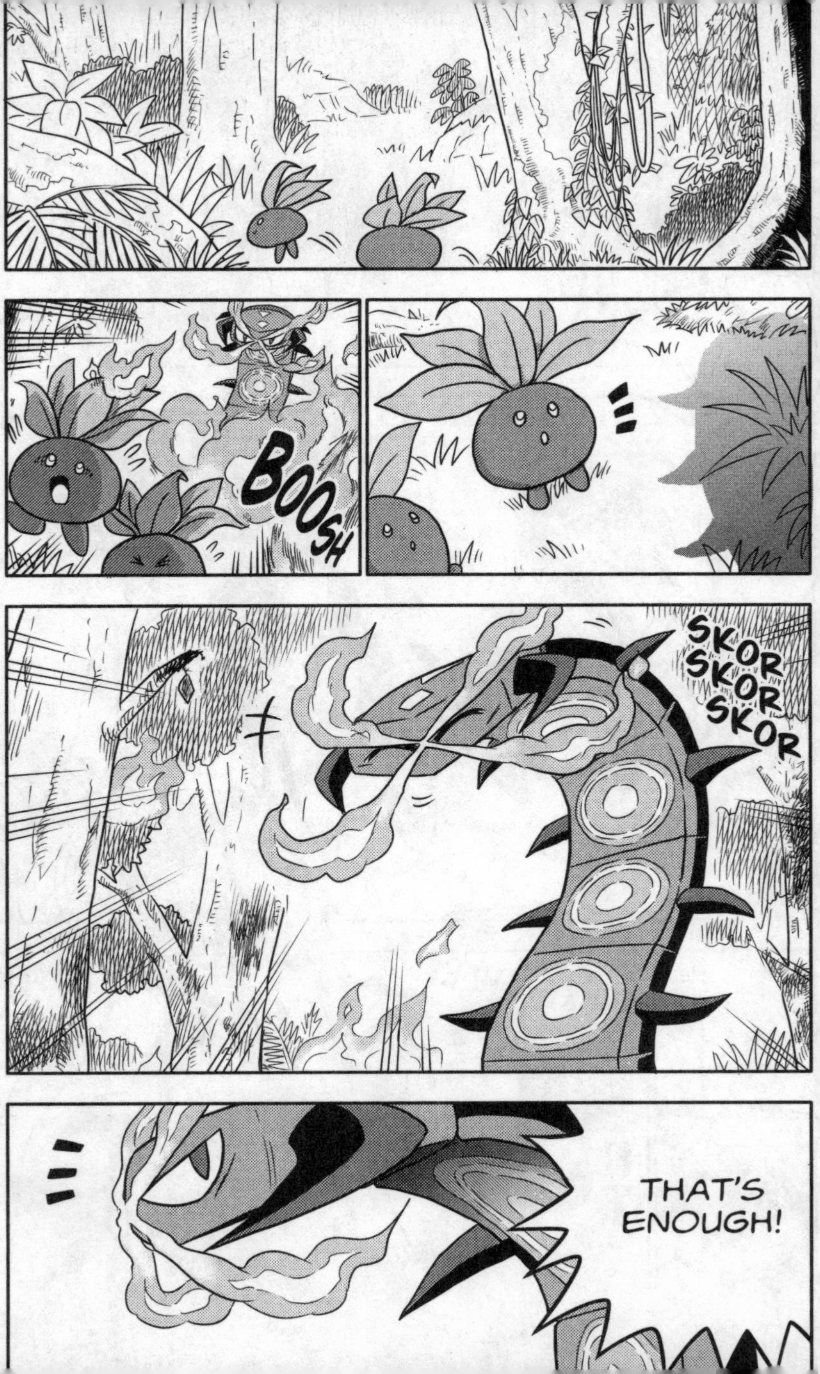
BOOSH
SKOR SKOR SKOR
THAT'S ENOUGH!

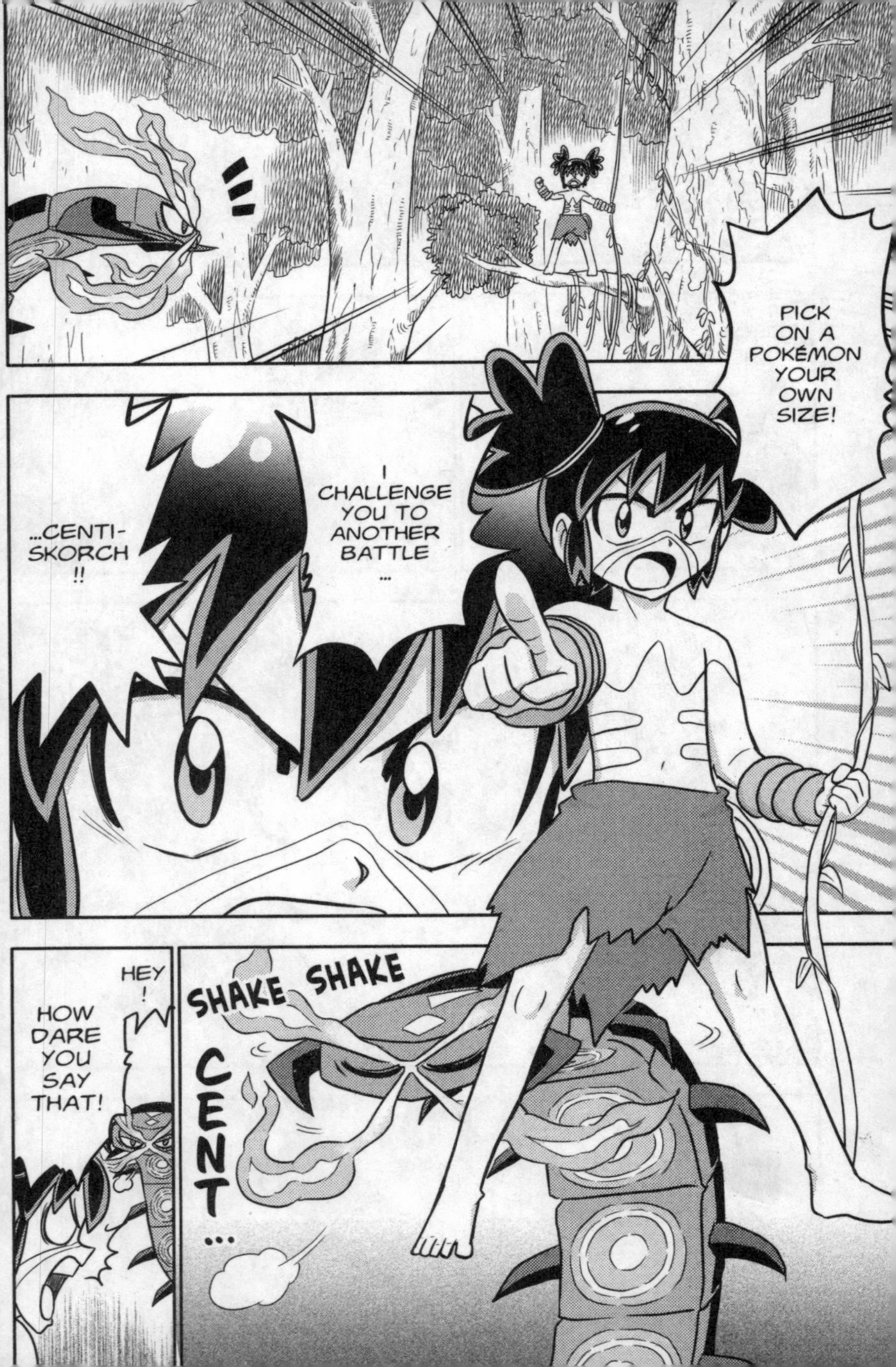
PICK ON A POKéMON YOUR OWN SIZE!
I CHALLENGE YOU TO ANOTHER BATTLE ...
...CENTI-SKORCH !!
SHAKE SHAKE
CENT ...
HEY !
HOW DARE YOU SAY THAT!

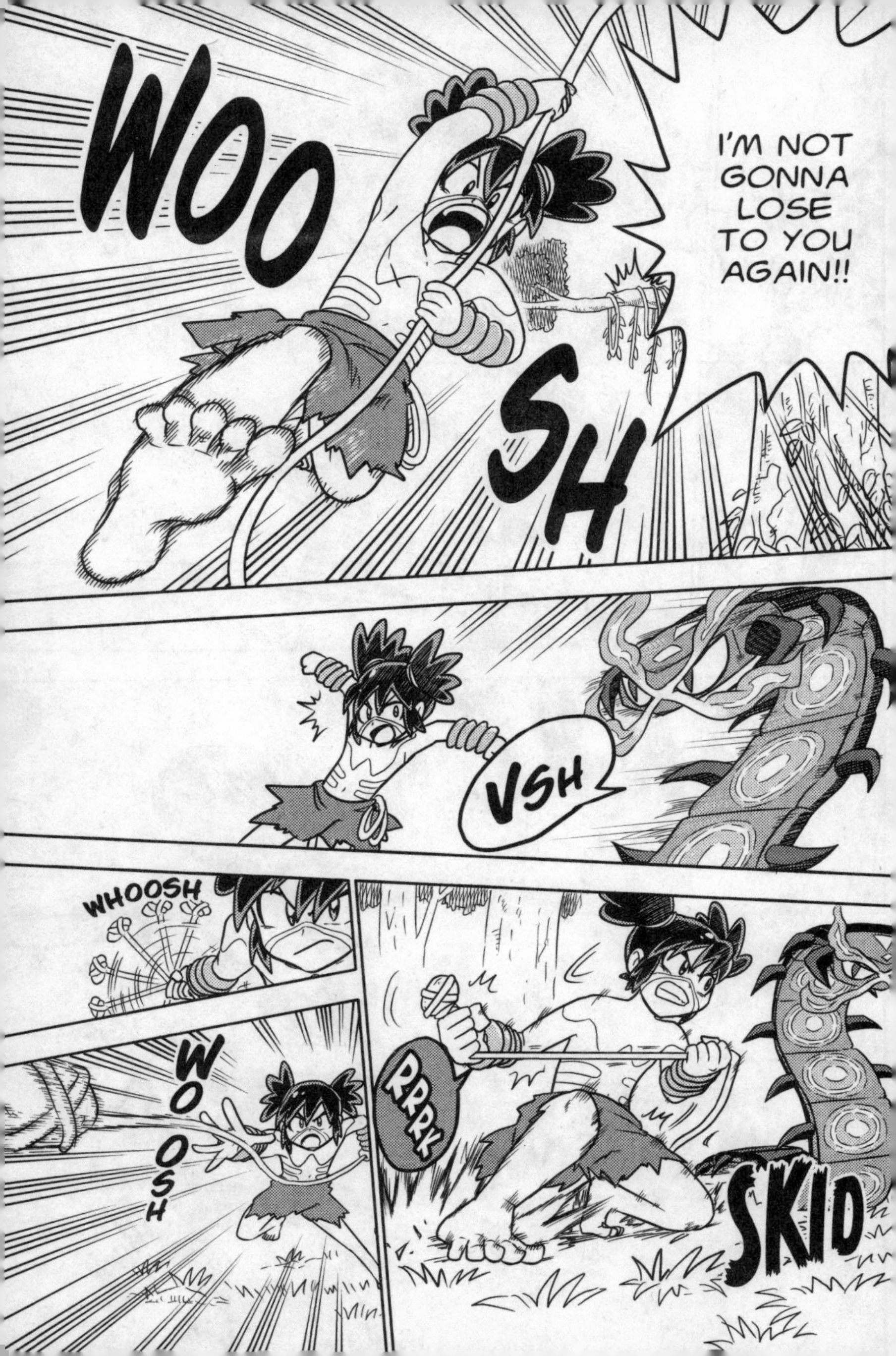
I'M NOT GONNA LOSE TO YOU AGAIN!!
WOOSH
VSH
RRRK
SKID
WHOOSH
WOOOSH

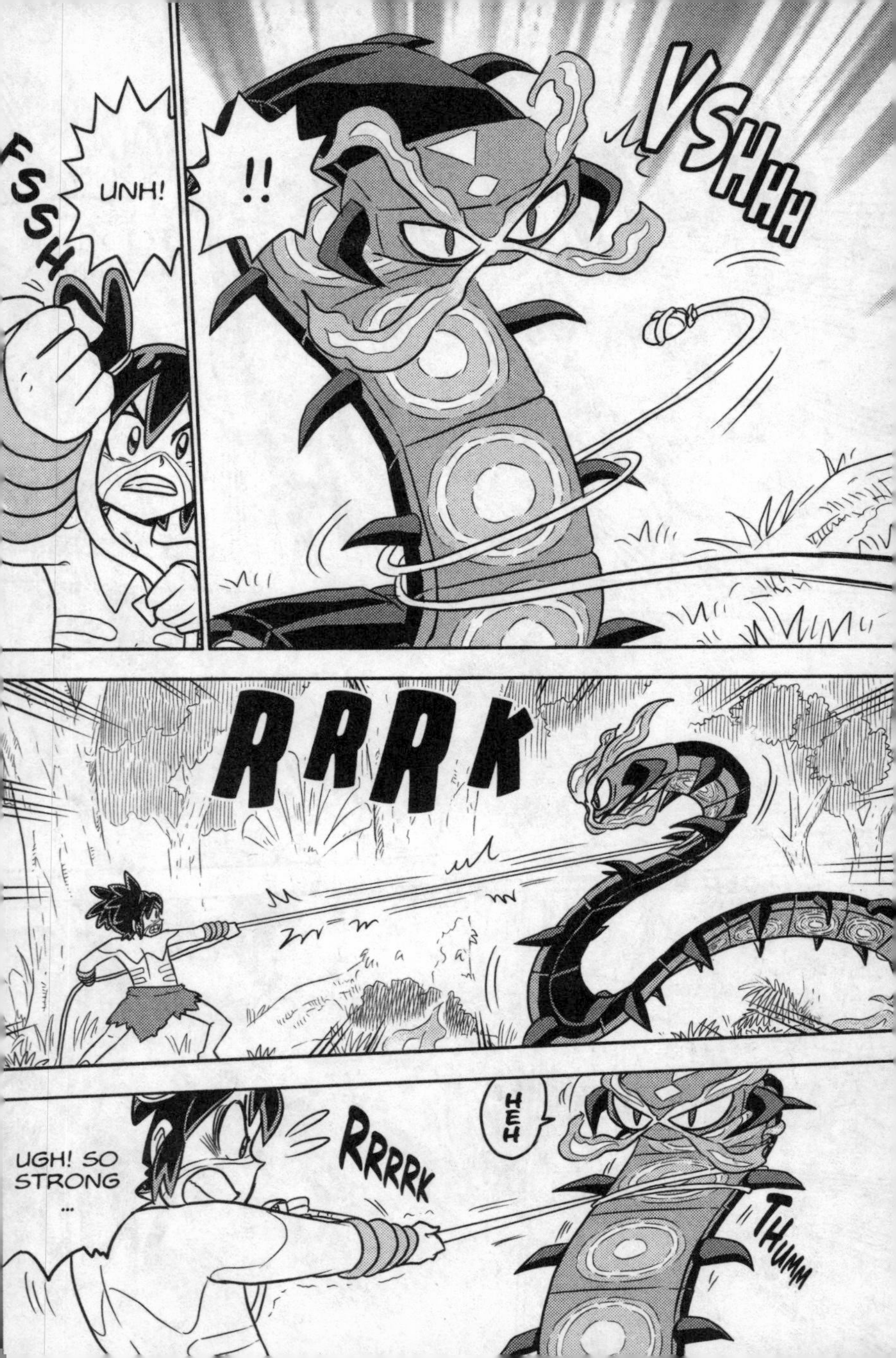
VSHHH
!!
UNH!
FSSH
RRRK
HEH
THUMM
RRRRK
UGH! SO STRONG ...

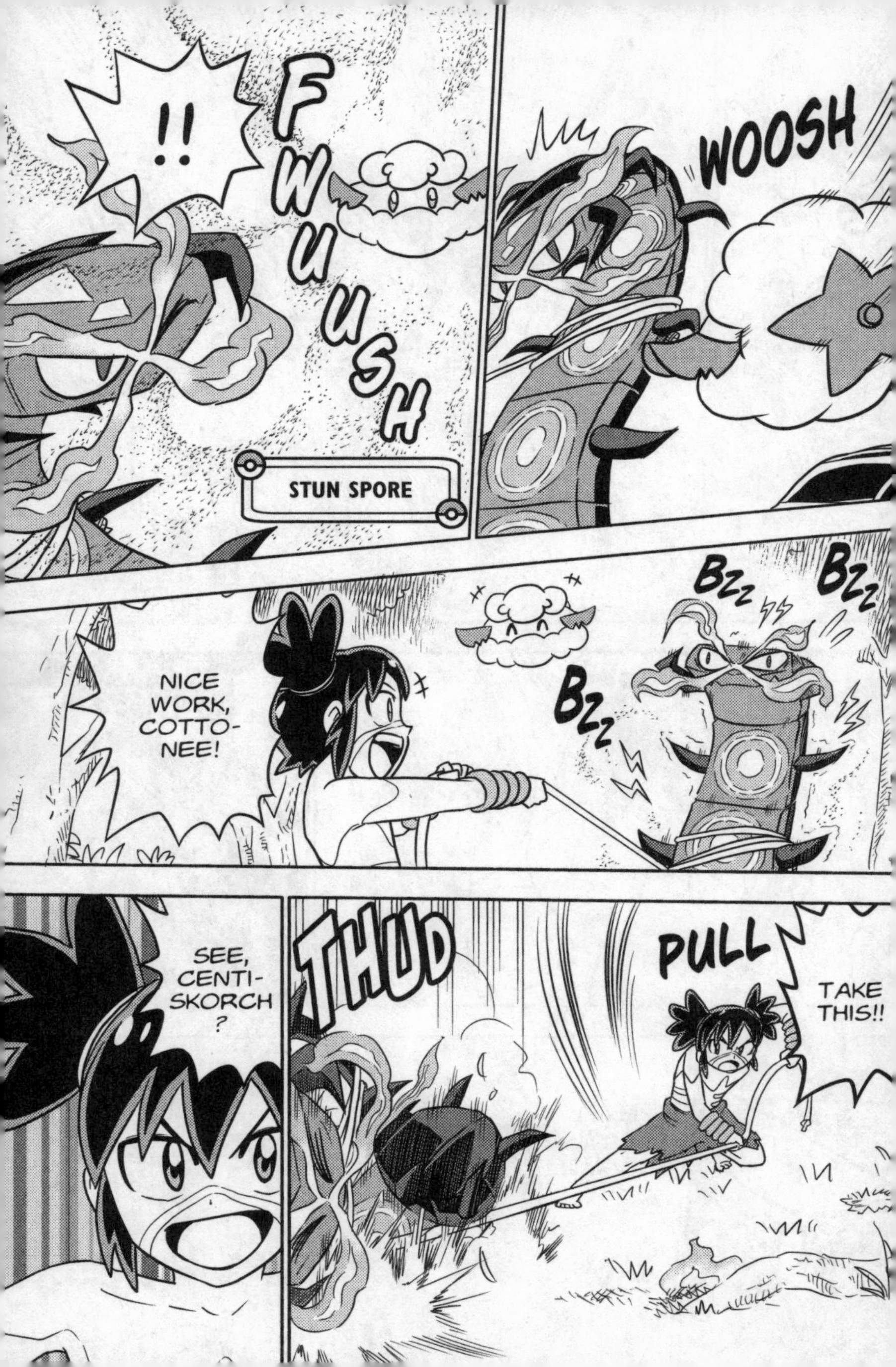
WOOSH
!!
FWUUSH
STUN SPORE
BZZ
BZZ
BZZ
NICE WORK, COTTO-NEE!
TAKE THIS!!
PULL
THUD
SEE, CENTI-SKORCH?

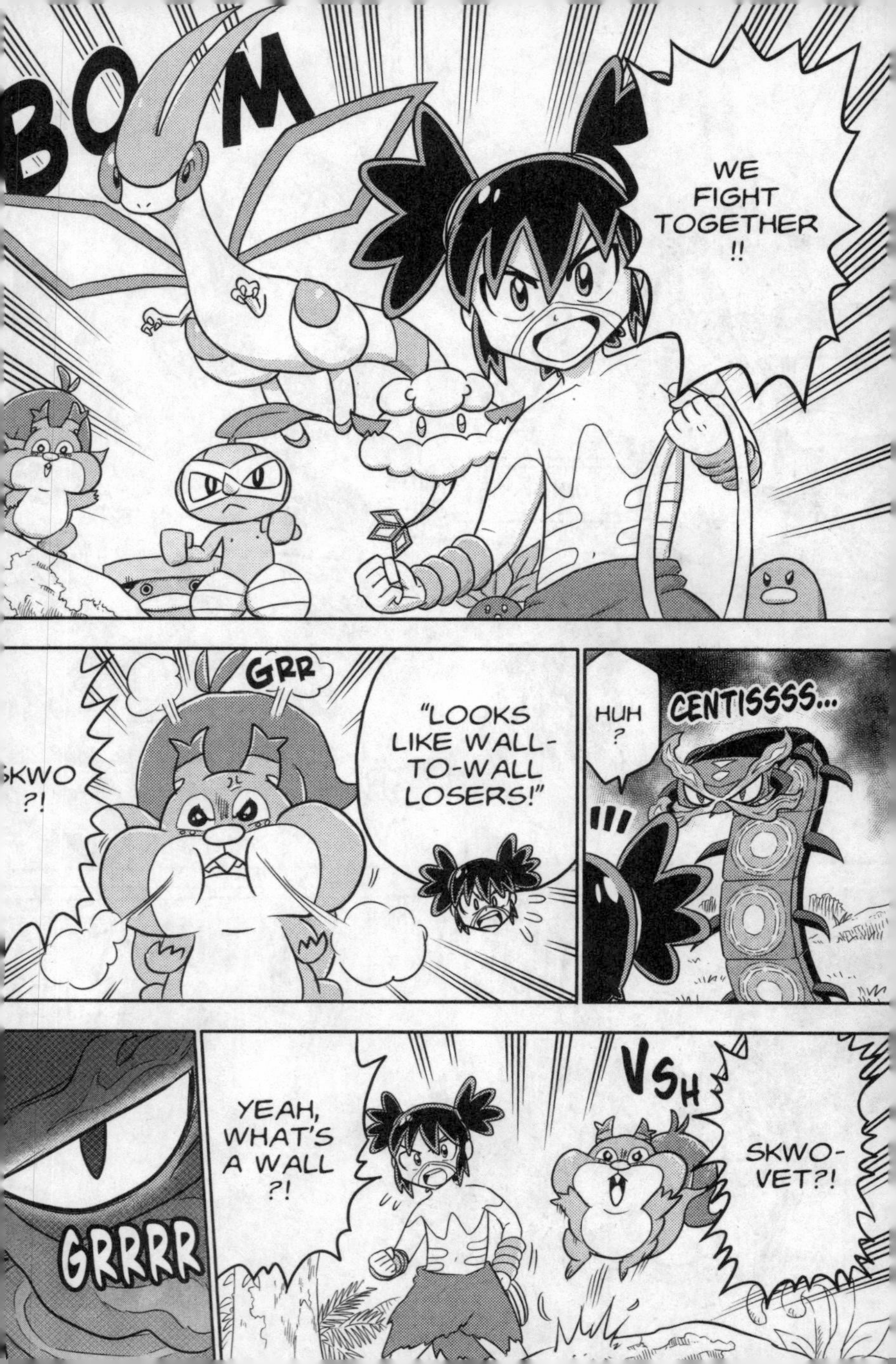
BOOM
WE FIGHT TOGETHER !!
HUH ?
CENTISSSS...
!!!
GRR
"LOOKS LIKE WALL-TO-WALL LOSERS!"
SKWO ?!
VSH
SKWO-VET?!
YEAH, WHAT'S A WALL ?!
GRRRR

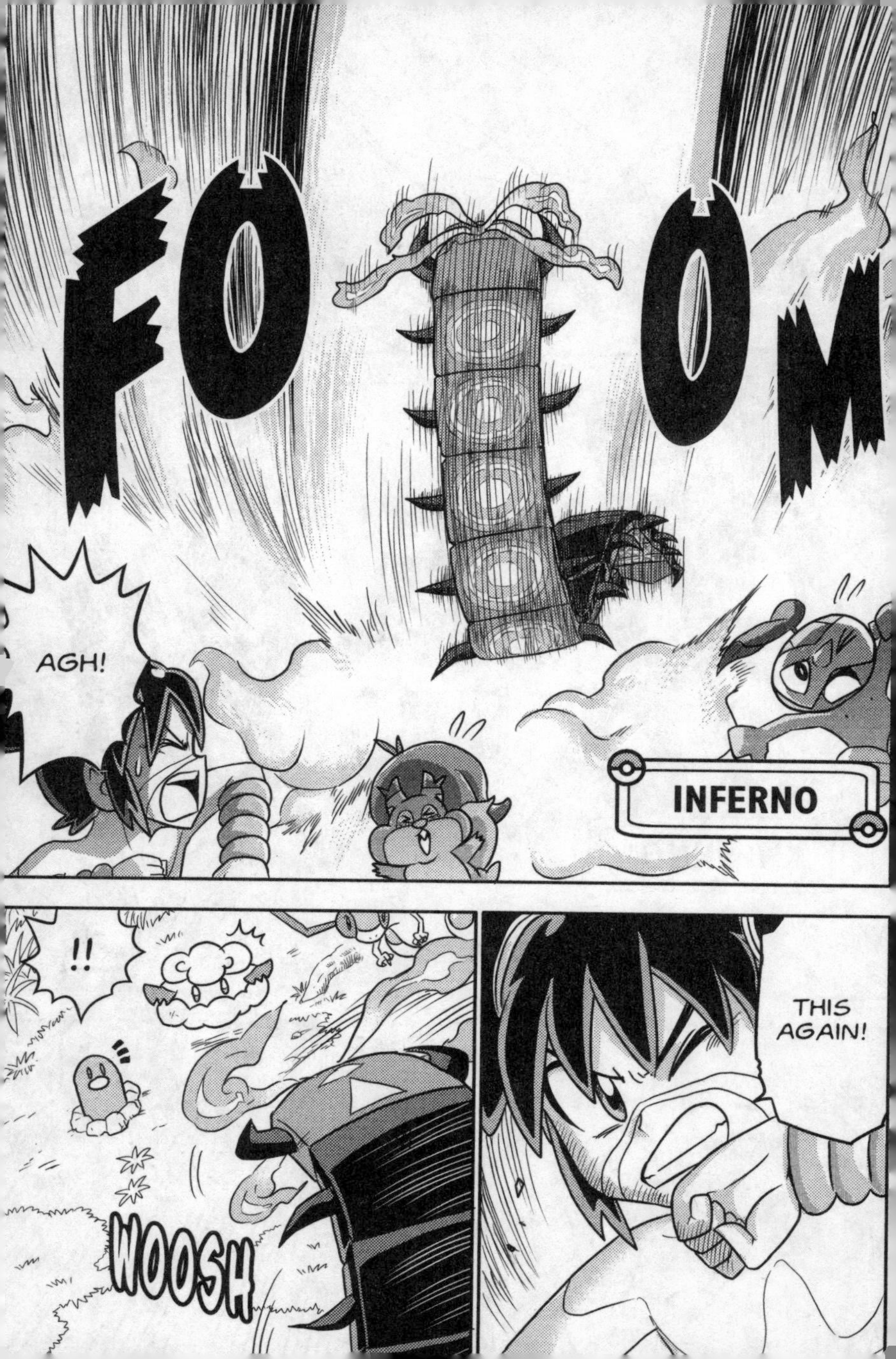

FOOM
INFERNO
AGH!
THIS AGAIN!
!!
WOOSH

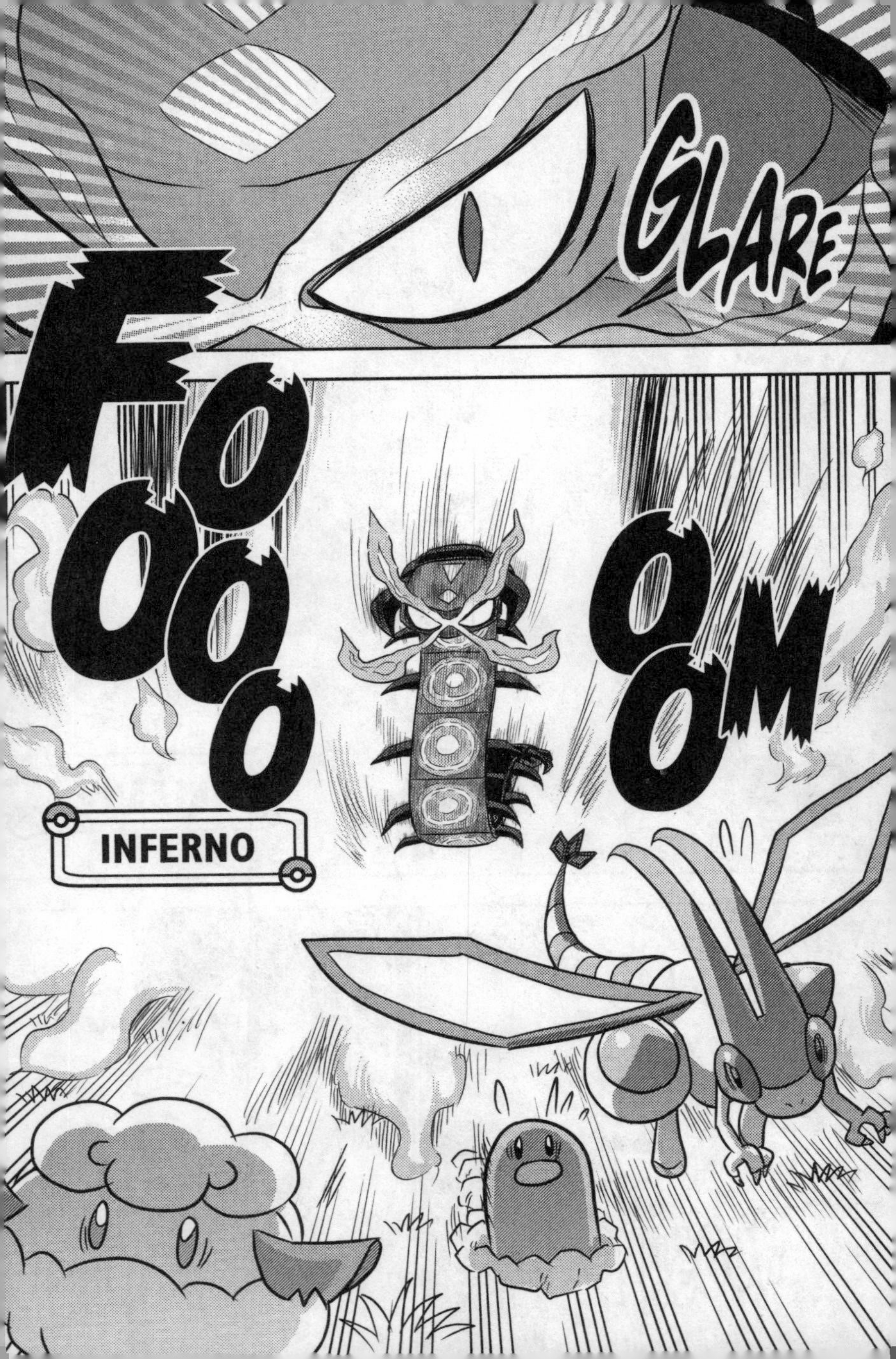
GLARE
FOOOOOOOM
INFERNO

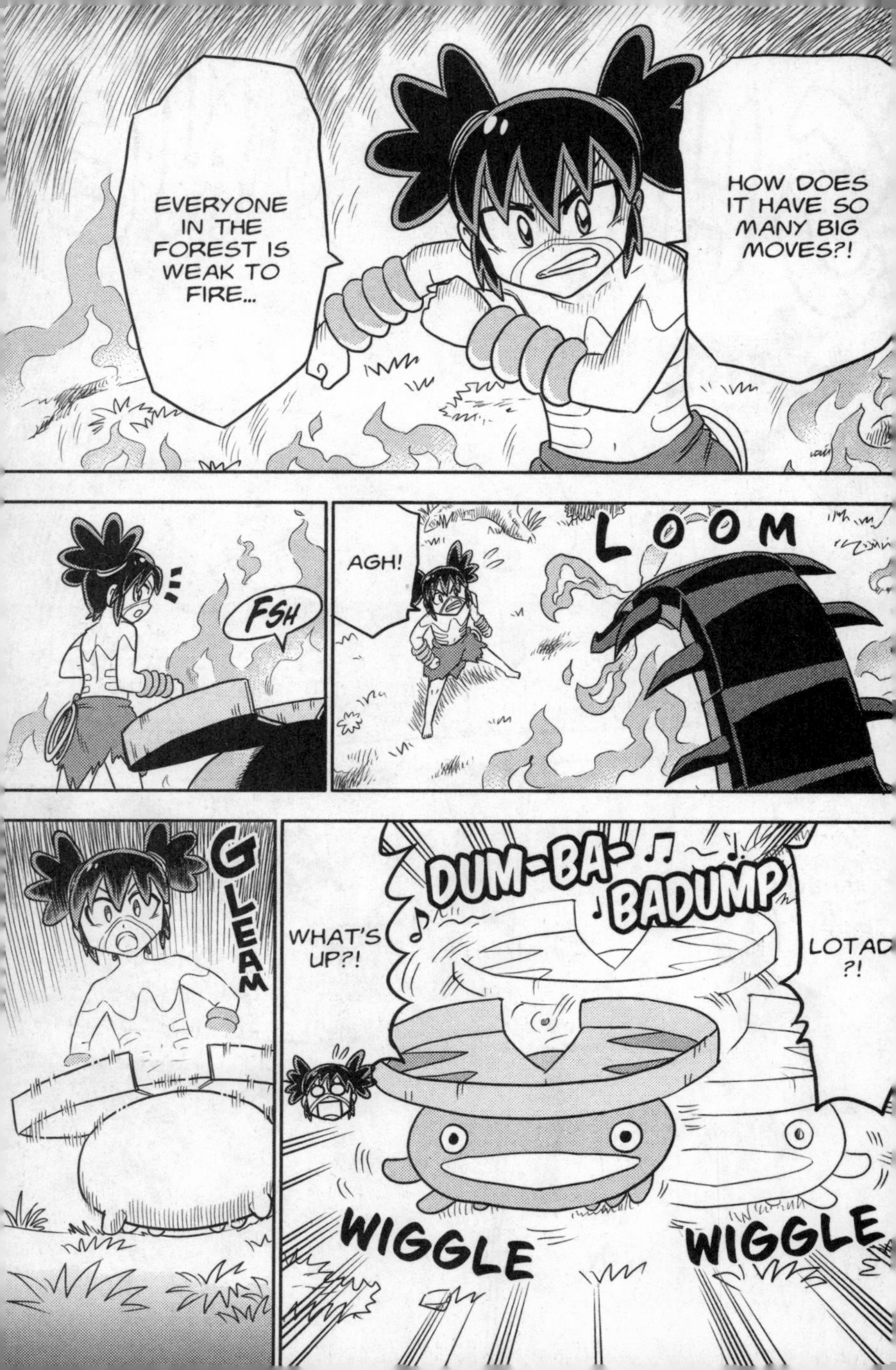
HOW DOES IT HAVE SO MANY BIG MOVES?!
EVERYONE IN THE FOREST IS WEAK TO FIRE...
LOOM
AGH!
FSH
DUM-BA-BADUMP
LOTAD?!
WHAT'S UP?!
WIGGLE
WIGGLE
GLEAM

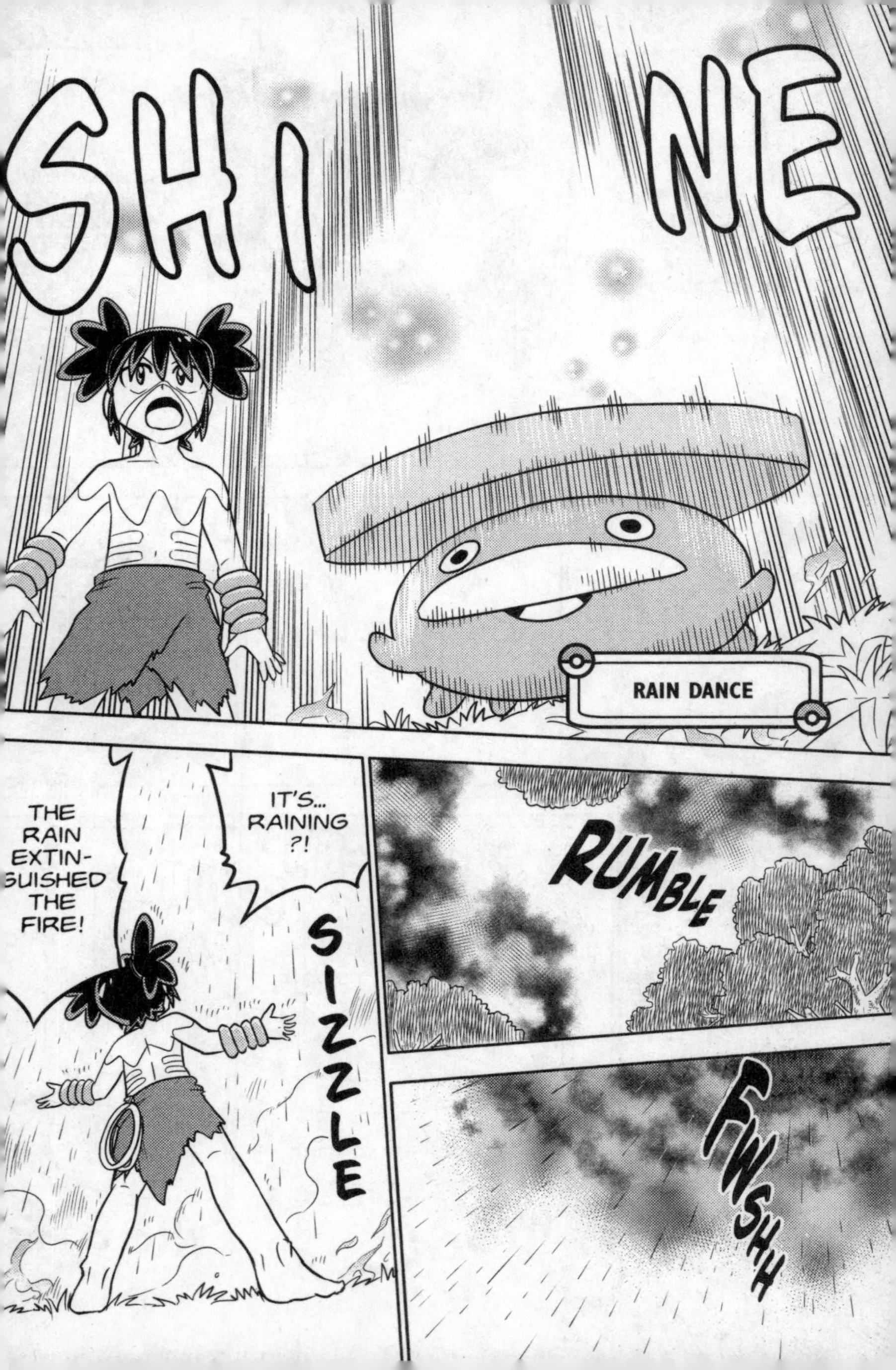
SHINE
RAIN DANCE
RUMBLE
FWSHH
IT'S... RAINING?!
THE RAIN EXTIN-GUISHED THE FIRE!
SIZZLE

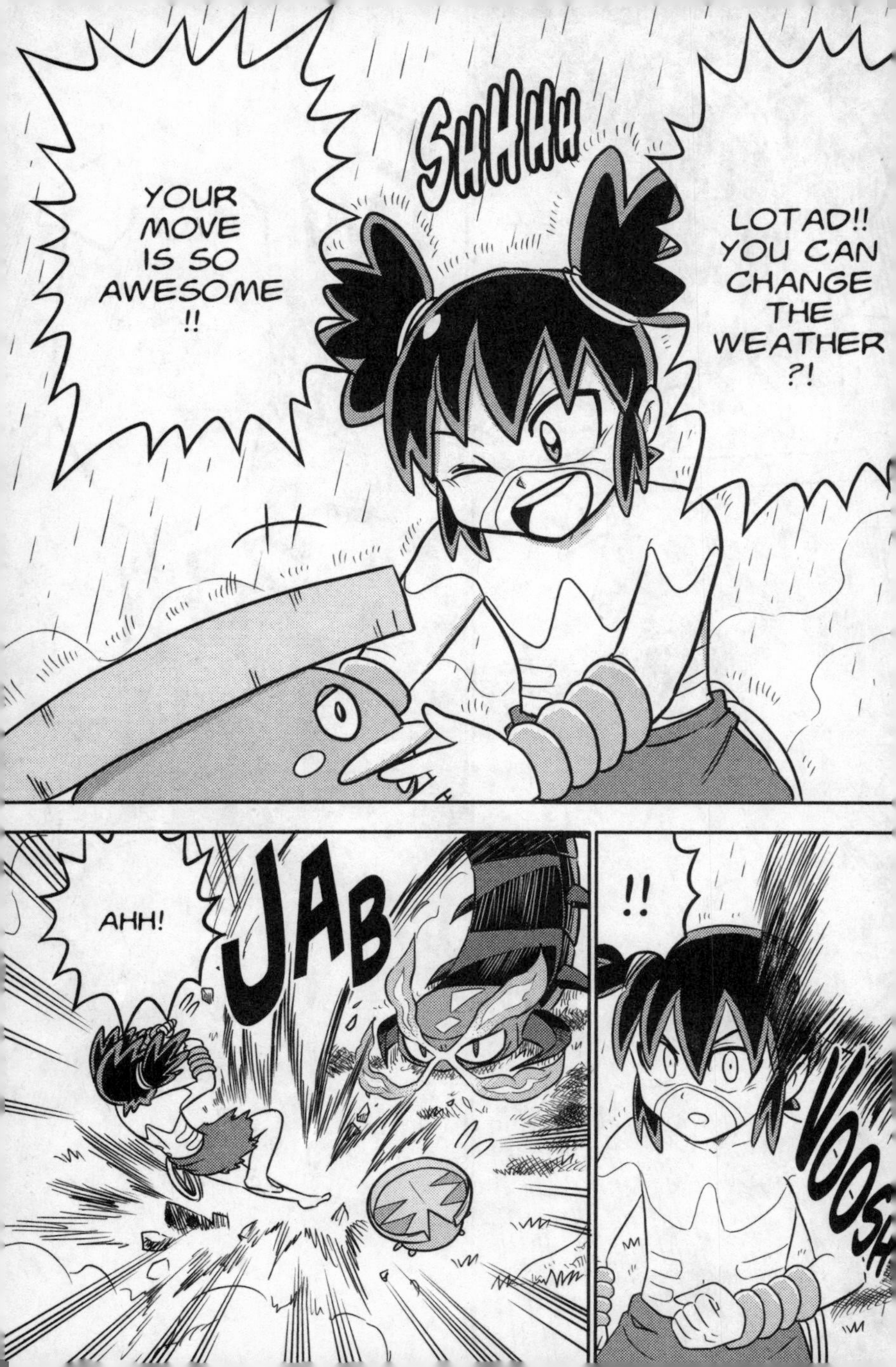
SHHHH
LOTAD!! YOU CAN CHANGE THE WEATHER ?!
YOUR MOVE IS SO AWESOME !!
!!
VOOSH
JAB
AHH!

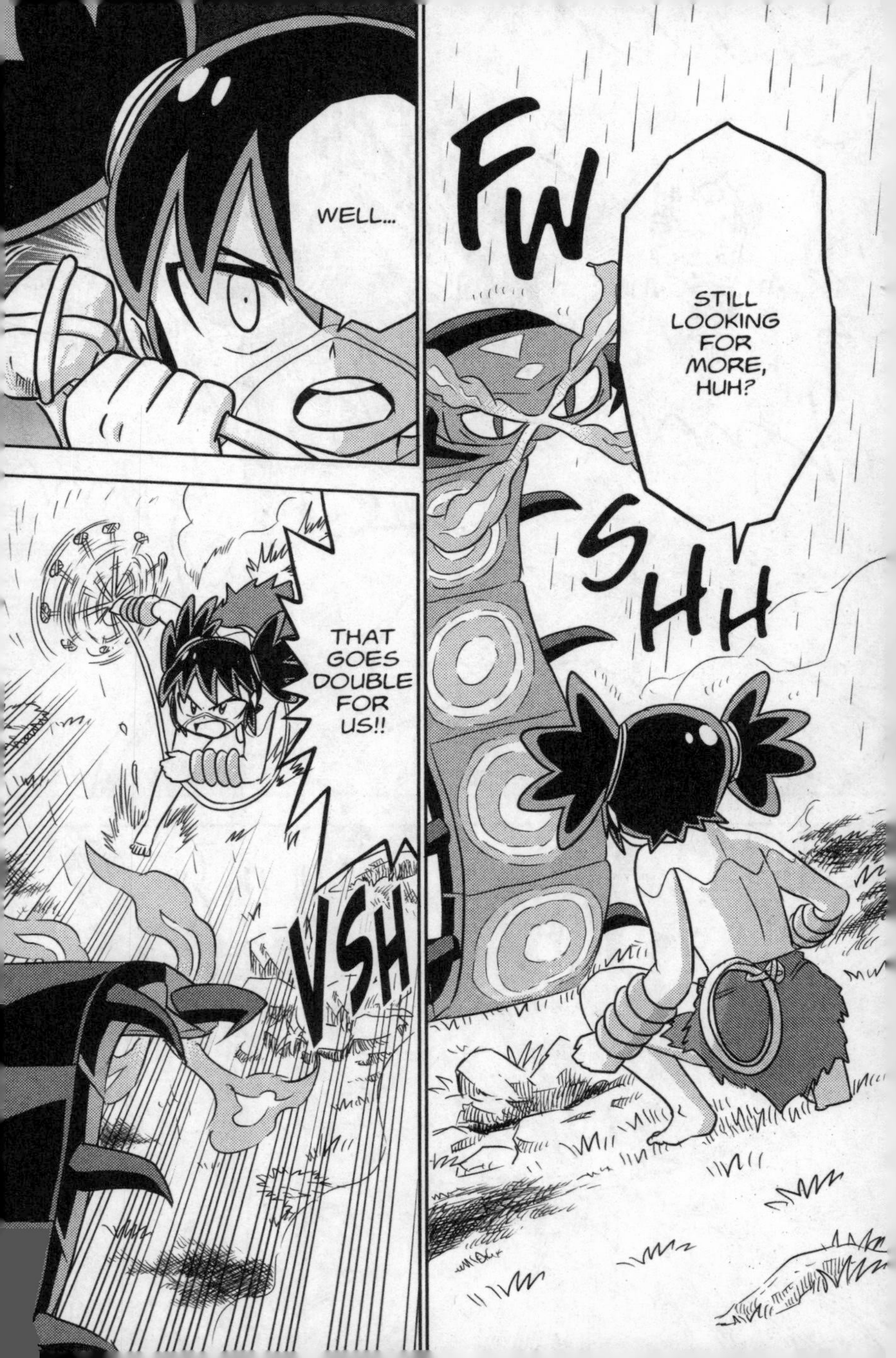
FW
STILL LOOKING FOR MORE, HUH?
SHHH
WELL...
THAT GOES DOUBLE FOR US!!
VSH

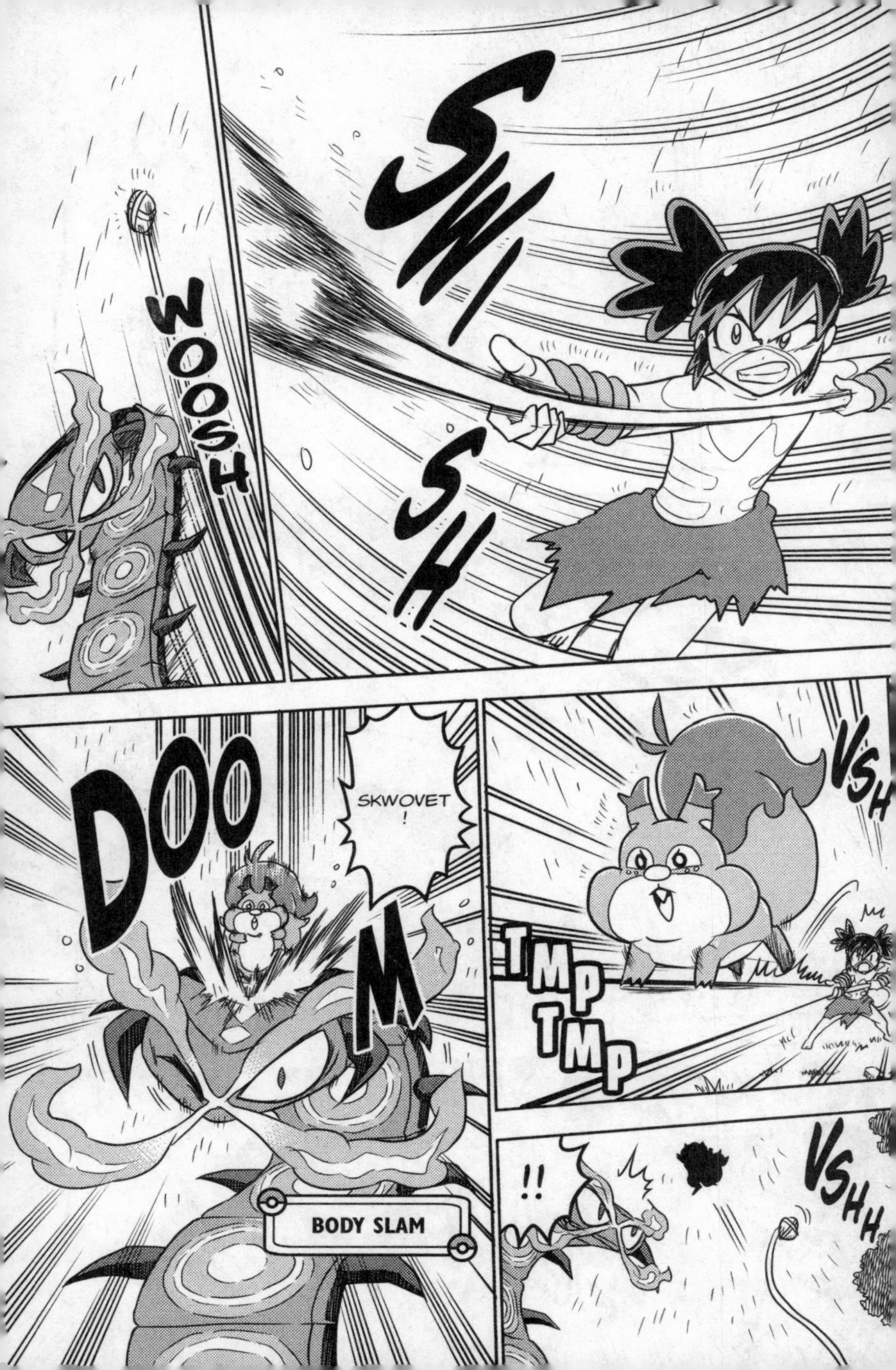
SWISH
WOOSH
VSH
TMP TMP
SKWOVET !
DOOM
BODY SLAM
VSHH
!!

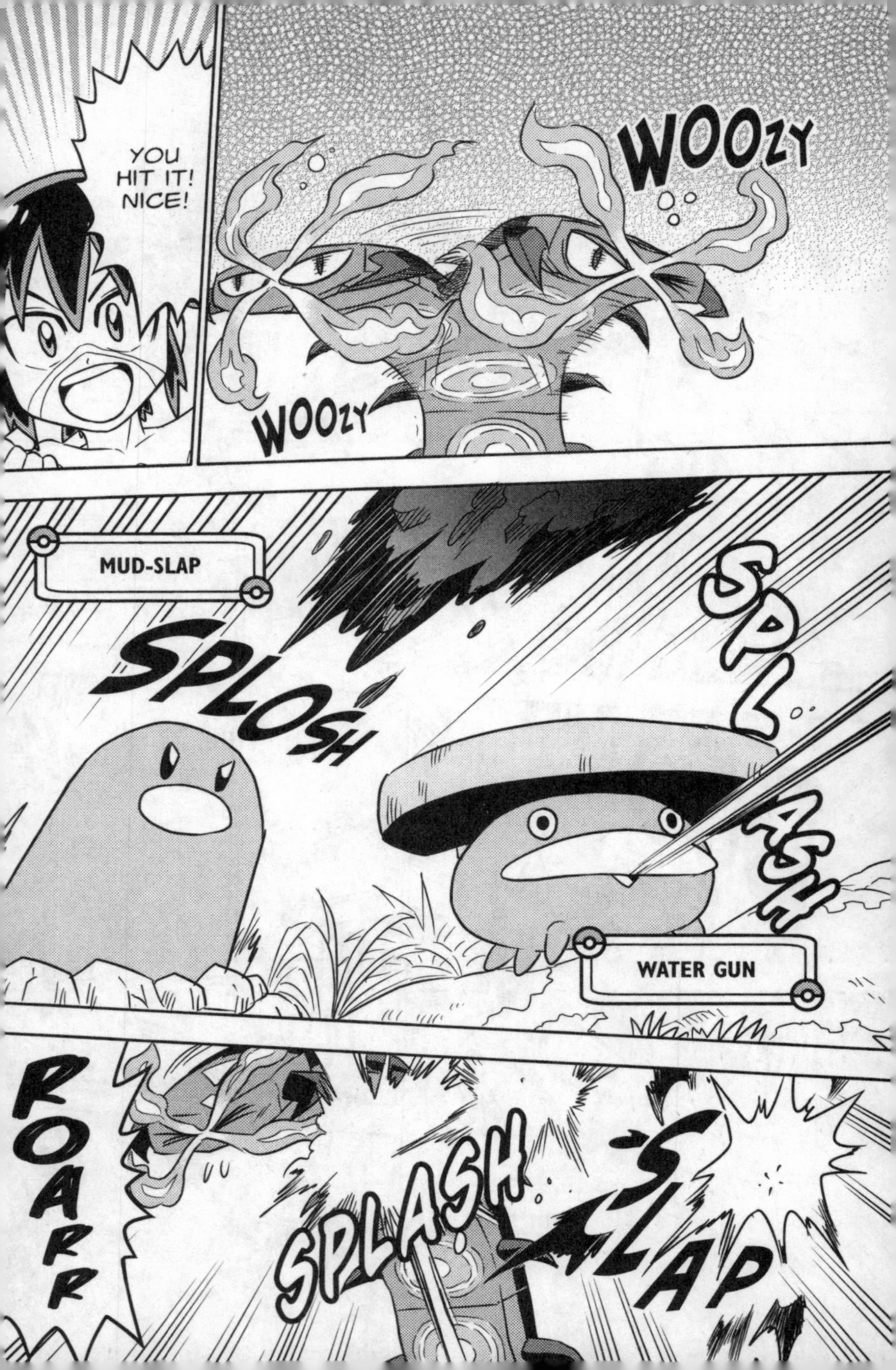

WOOZY
WOOZY
YOU HIT IT! NICE!
SPLASH
MUD-SLAP
SPLOSH
WATER GUN
SLAP
SPLASH
ROARR

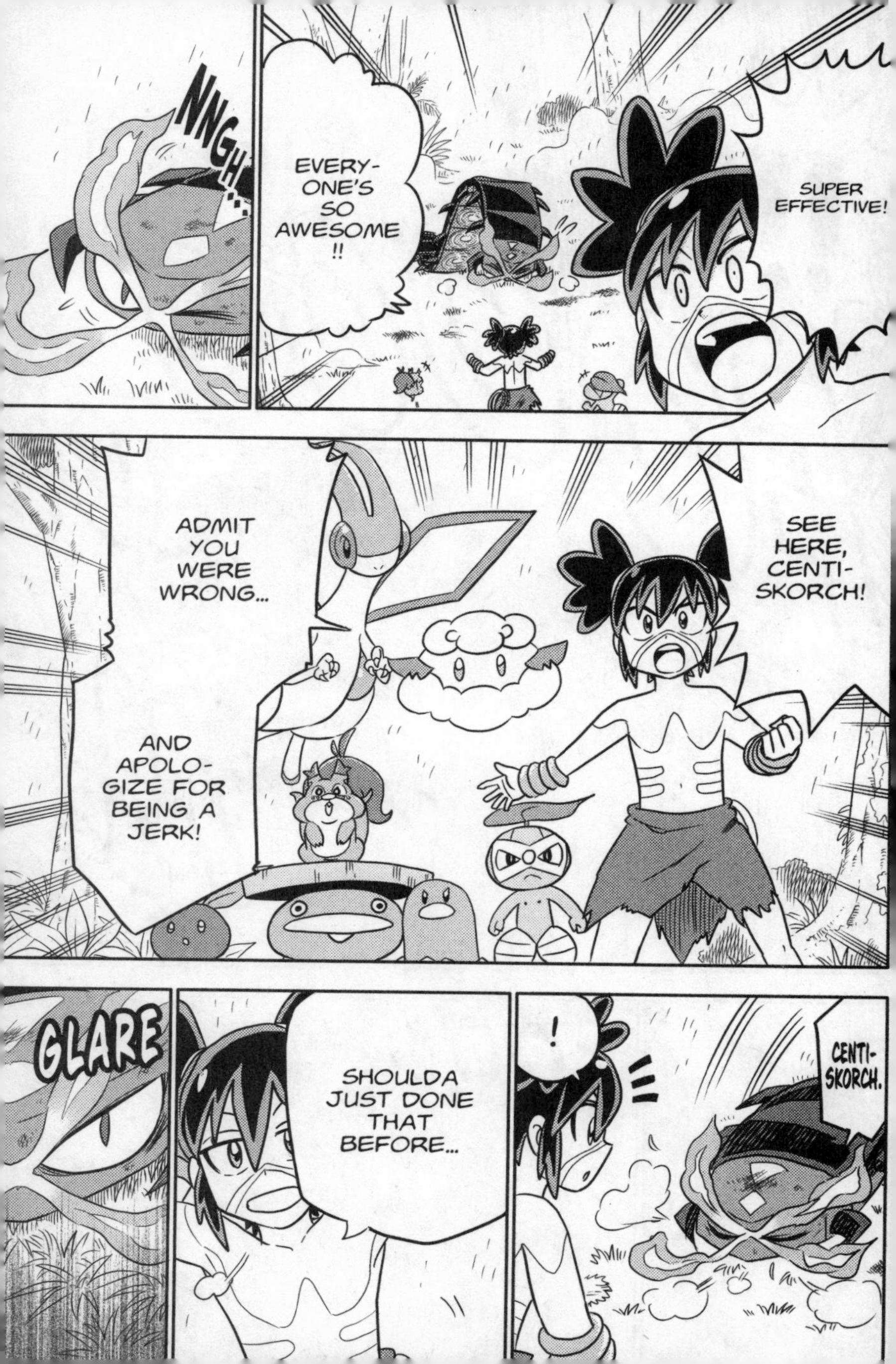
SUPER EFFECTIVE!
EVERY-ONE'S SO AWESOME !!
NNGH
SEE HERE, CENTI-SKORCH!
ADMIT YOU WERE WRONG...
AND APOLO-GIZE FOR BEING A JERK!
CENTI-SKORCH.
!
SHOULDA JUST DONE THAT BEFORE...
GLARE

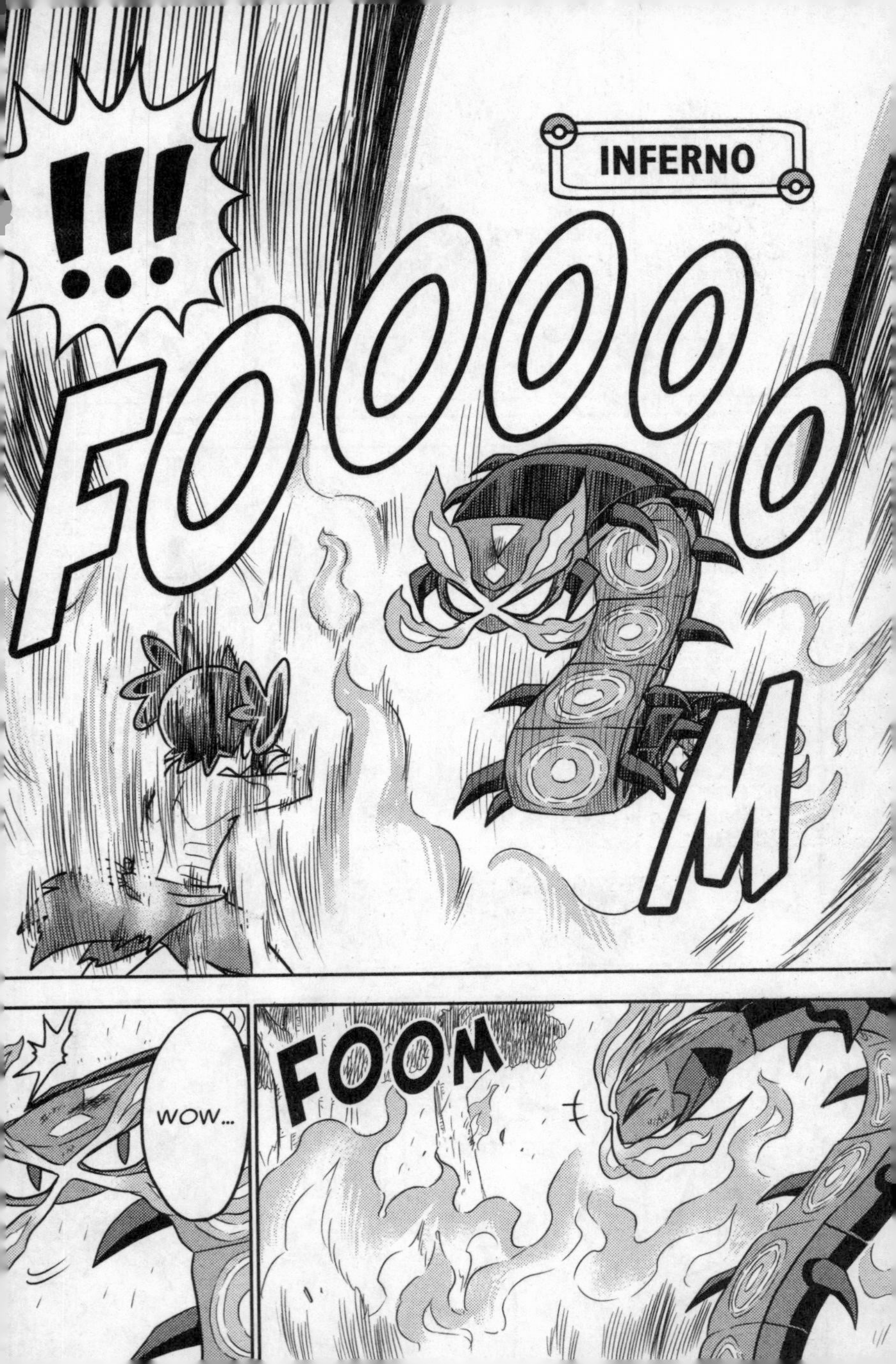
INFERNO
!!!
FOOOOOM
FOOM
WOW...

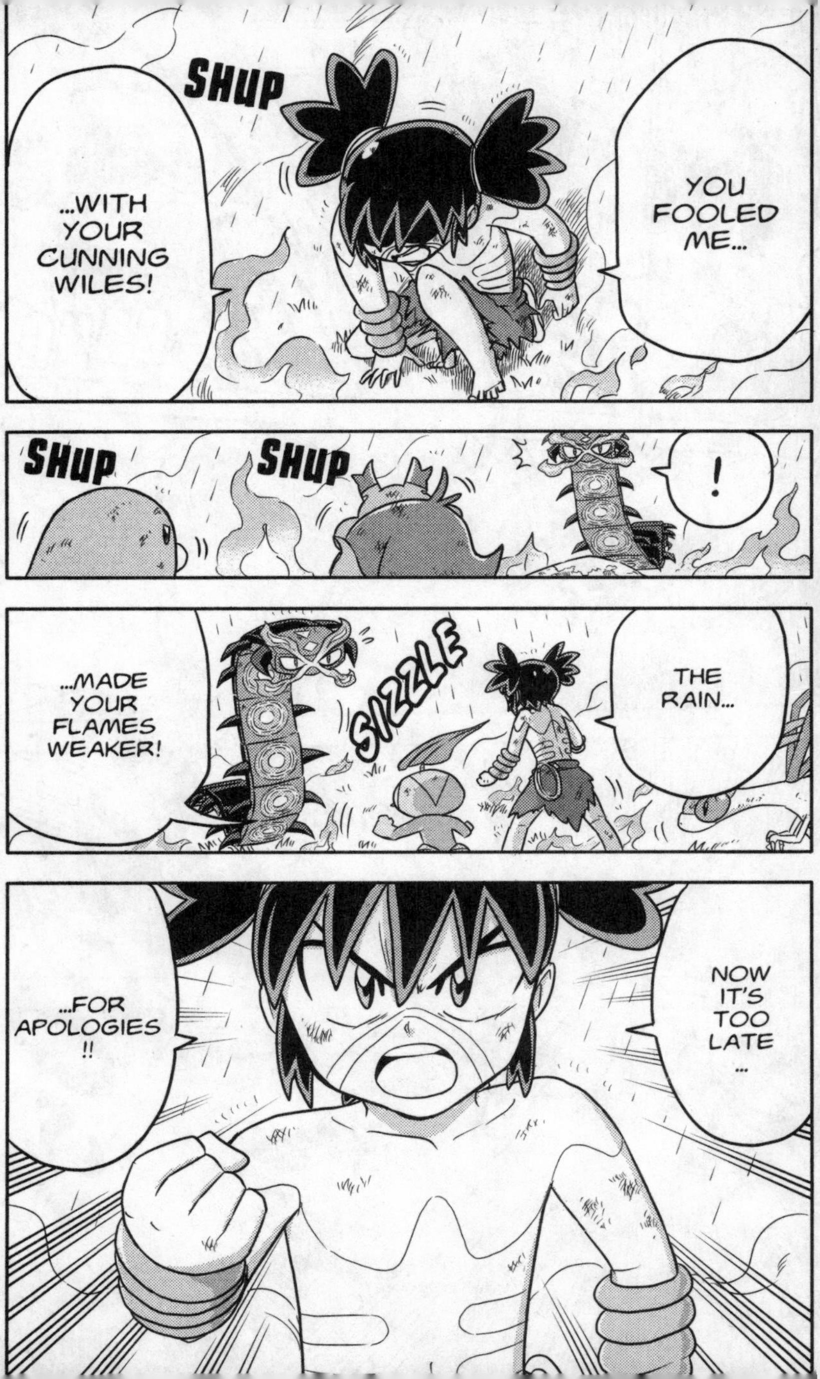
YOU FOOLED ME...
SHUP
...WITH YOUR CUNNING WILES!
!
SHUP
SHUP
THE RAIN...
SIZZLE
...MADE YOUR FLAMES WEAKER!
NOW IT'S TOO LATE ...
...FOR APOLOGIES !!

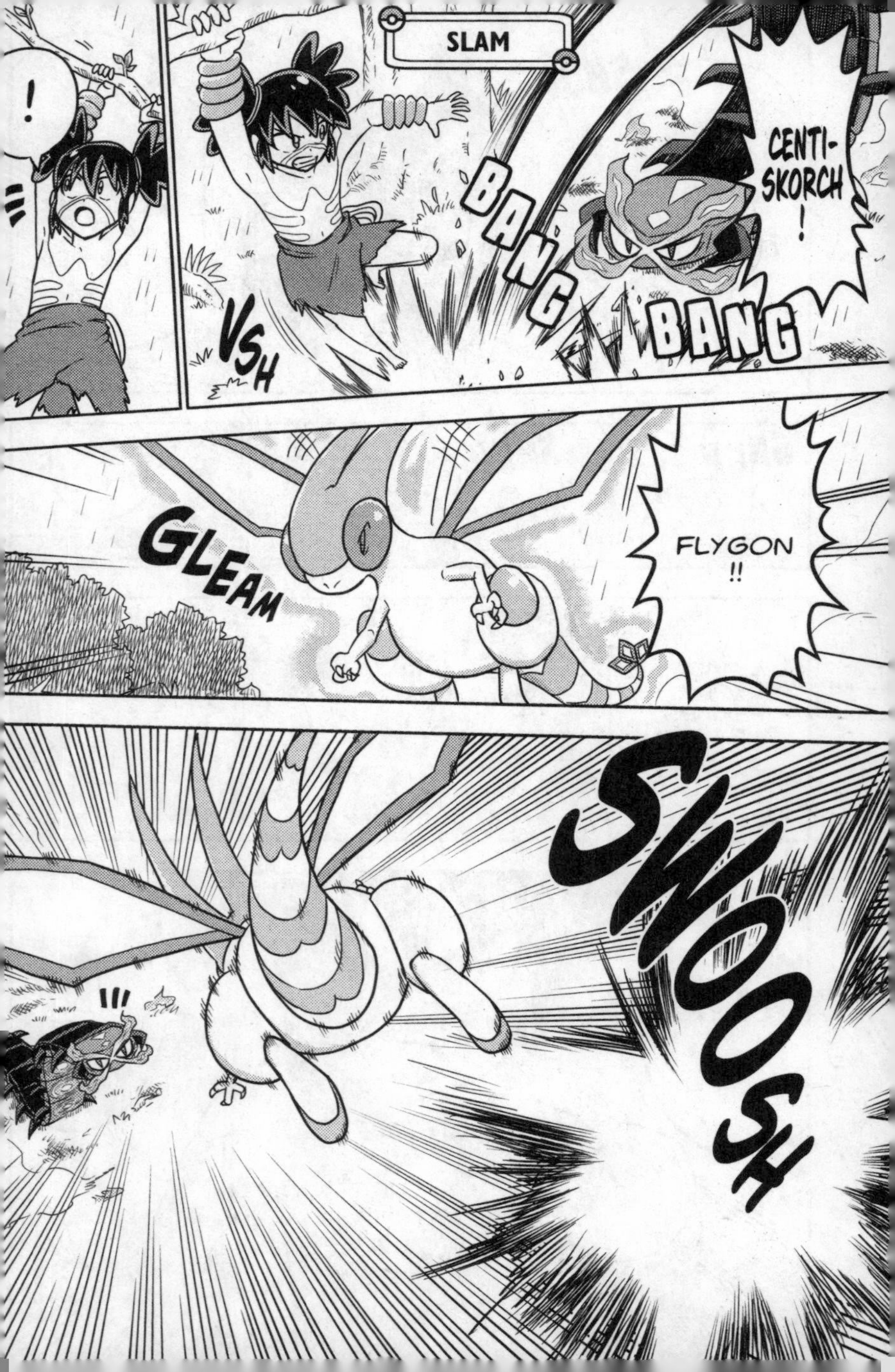
CENTI-SKORCH!
SLAM
BANG
BANG
VSH
!
FLYGON!!
GLEAM
SWOOSH
!!!

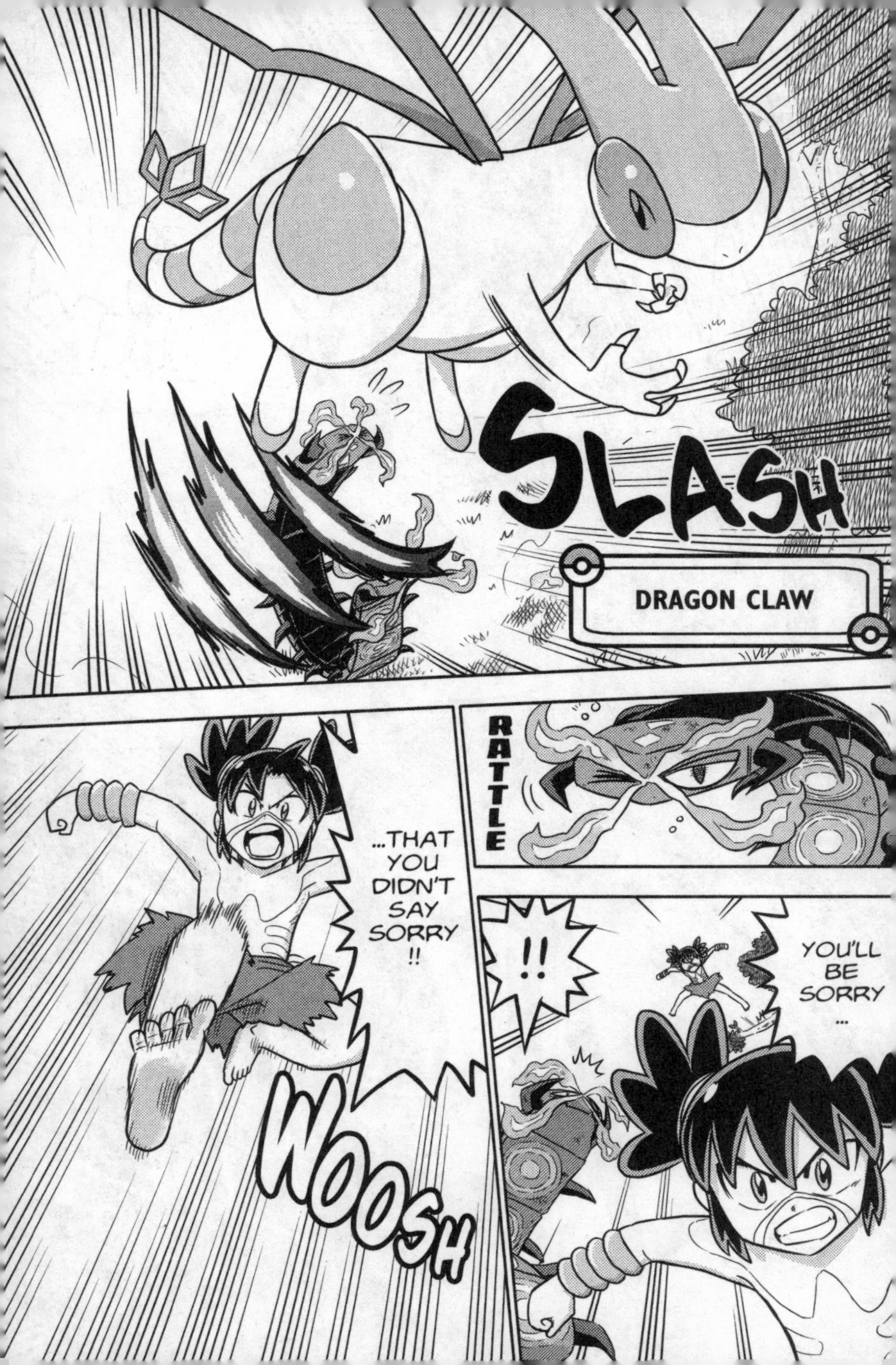
SLASH
DRAGON CLAW
RATTLE
YOU'LL BE SORRY ...
!!
...THAT YOU DIDN'T SAY SORRY !!
WOOSH

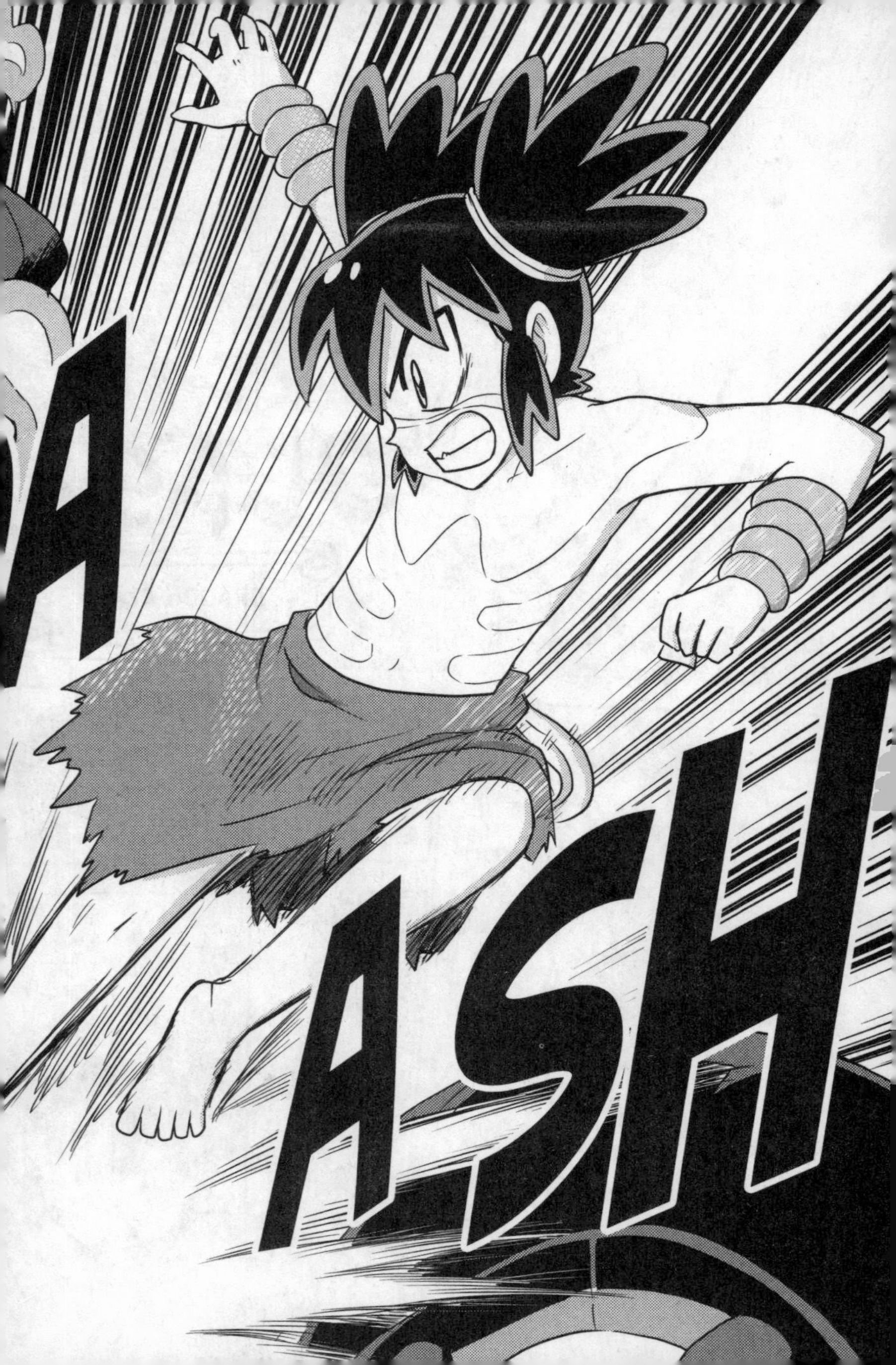

A
ASH

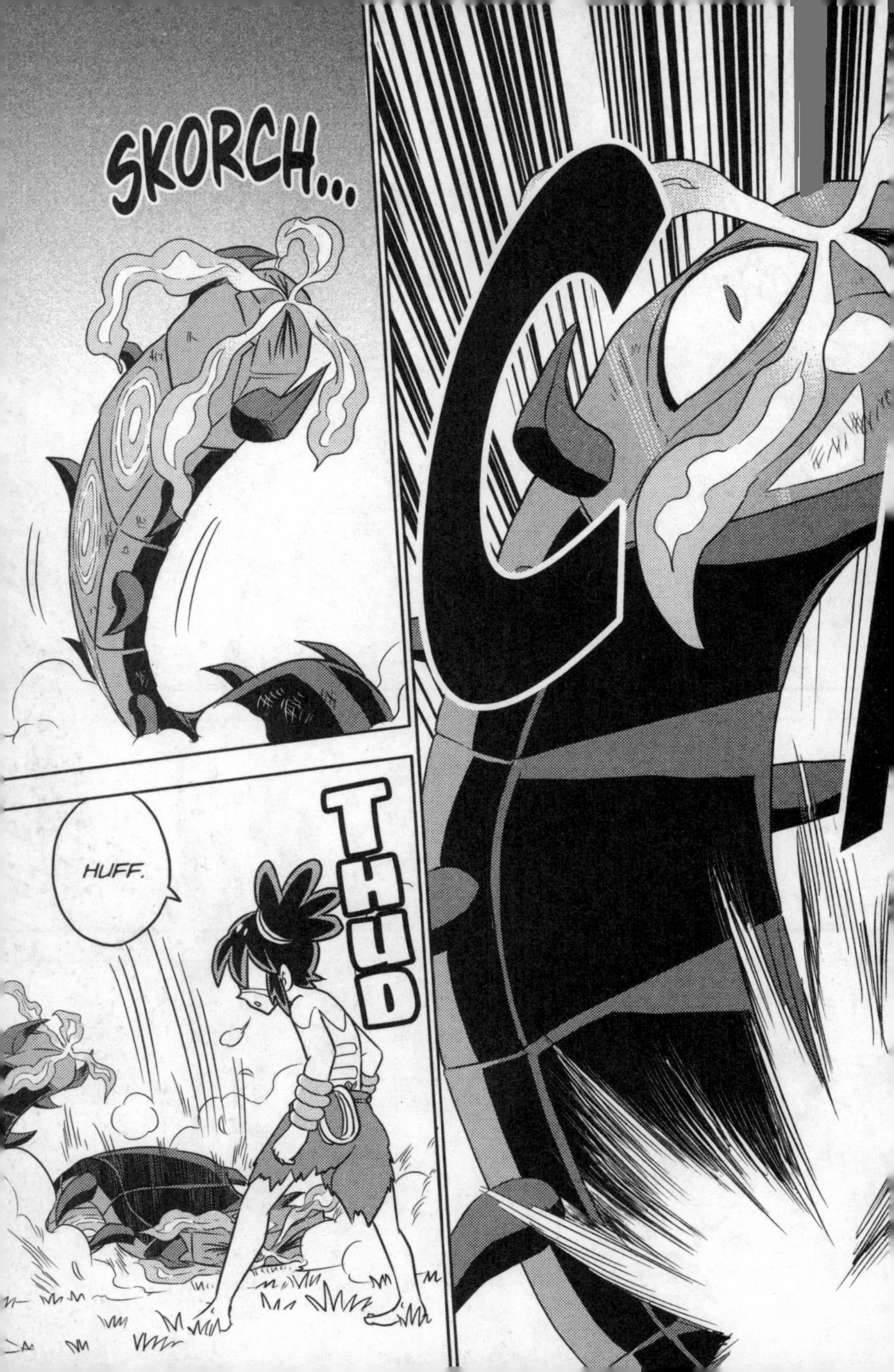
SKORCH...
THUD
HUFF.

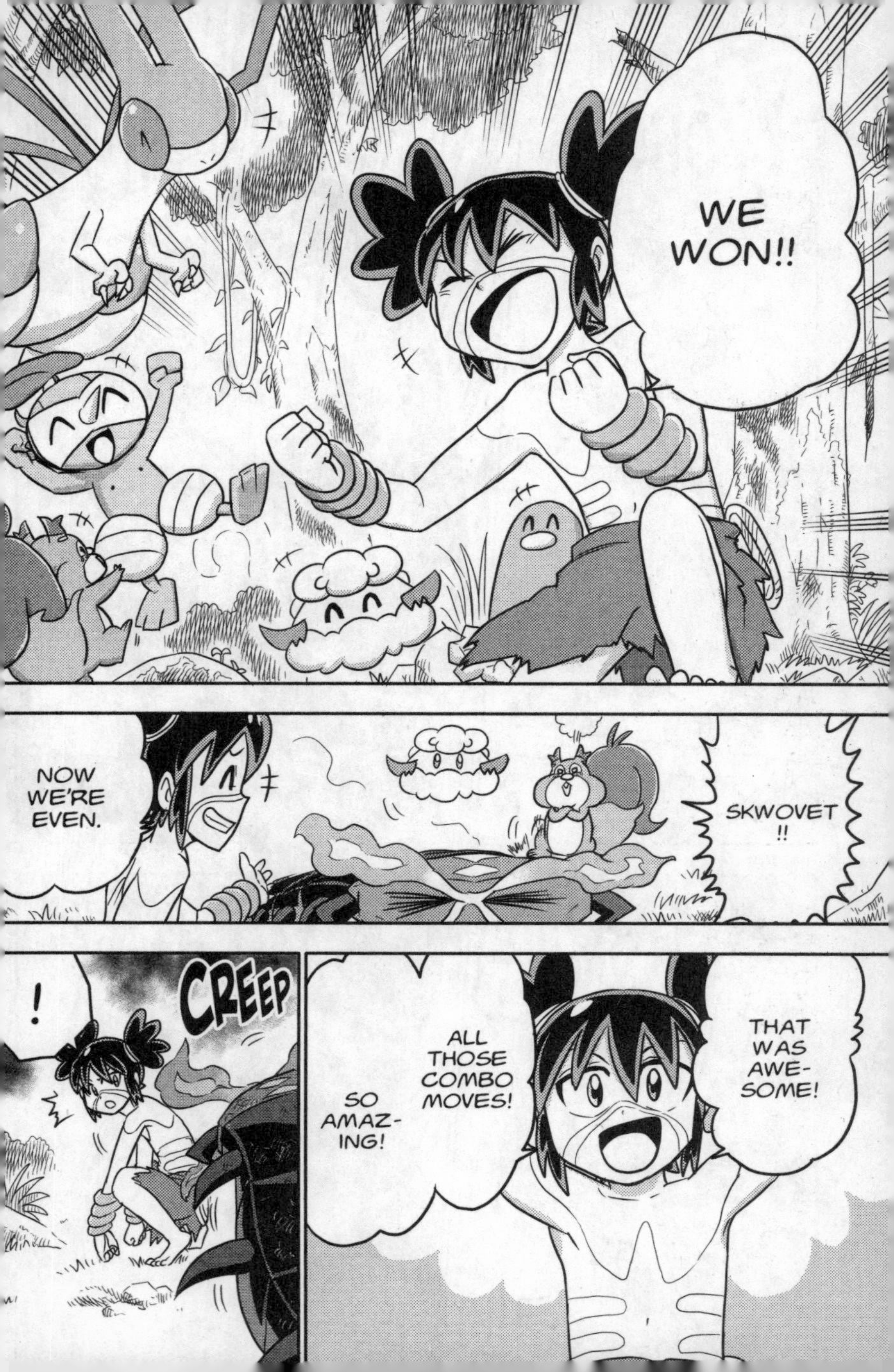
WE WON!!
SKWOVET !!
NOW WE'RE EVEN.
THAT WAS AWE-SOME!
ALL THOSE COMBO MOVES!
SO AMAZ-ING!
CREEP
!

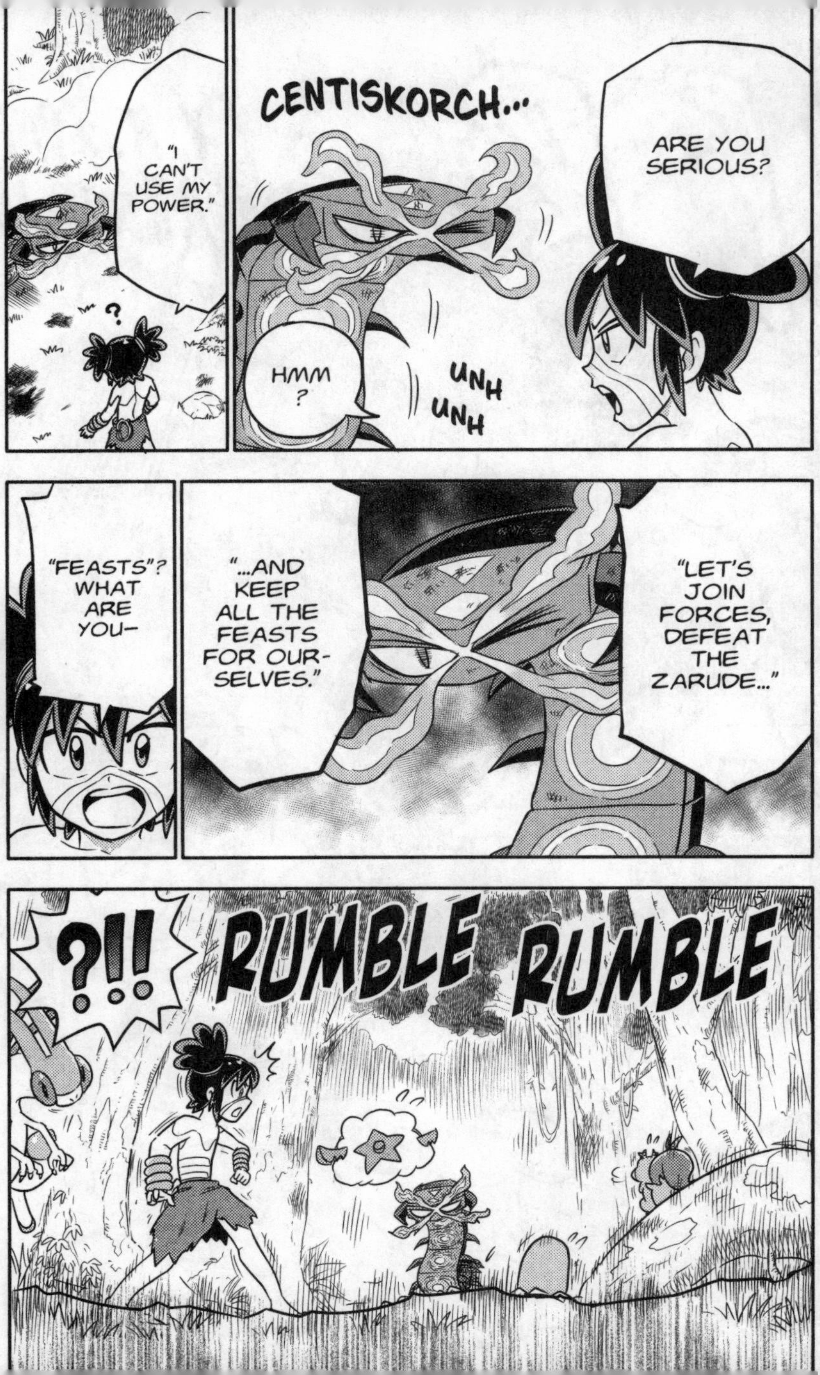
ARE YOU SERIOUS?
CENTISKORCH...
UNH UNH
HMM ?
"I CAN'T USE MY POWER."
?
"LET'S JOIN FORCES, DEFEAT THE ZARUDE..."
"...AND KEEP ALL THE FEASTS FOR OURSELVES."
"FEASTS"? WHAT ARE YOU-
RUMBLE RUMBLE
?!!

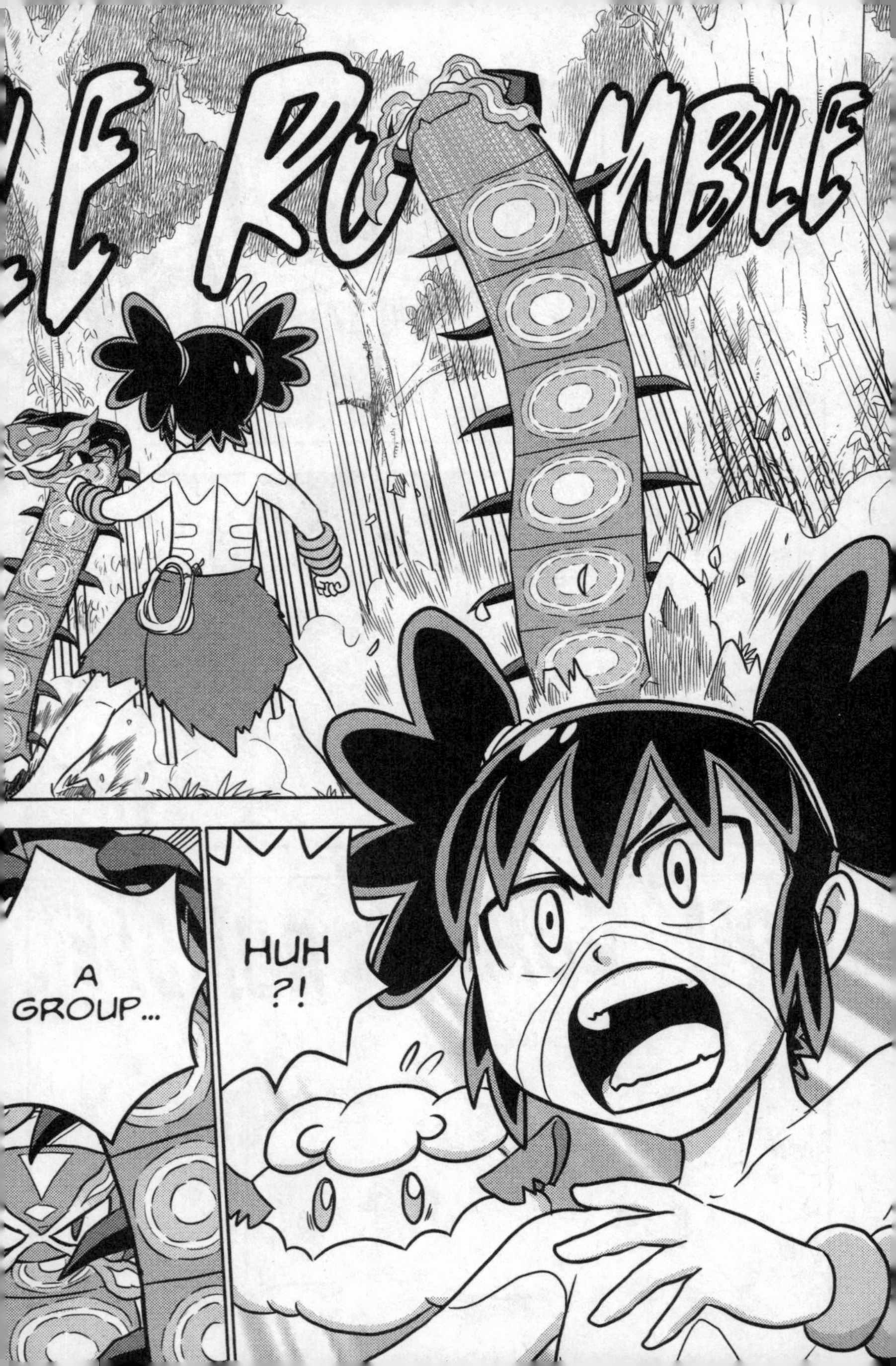
RUMBLE RUMBLE
HUH ?!
A GROUP...

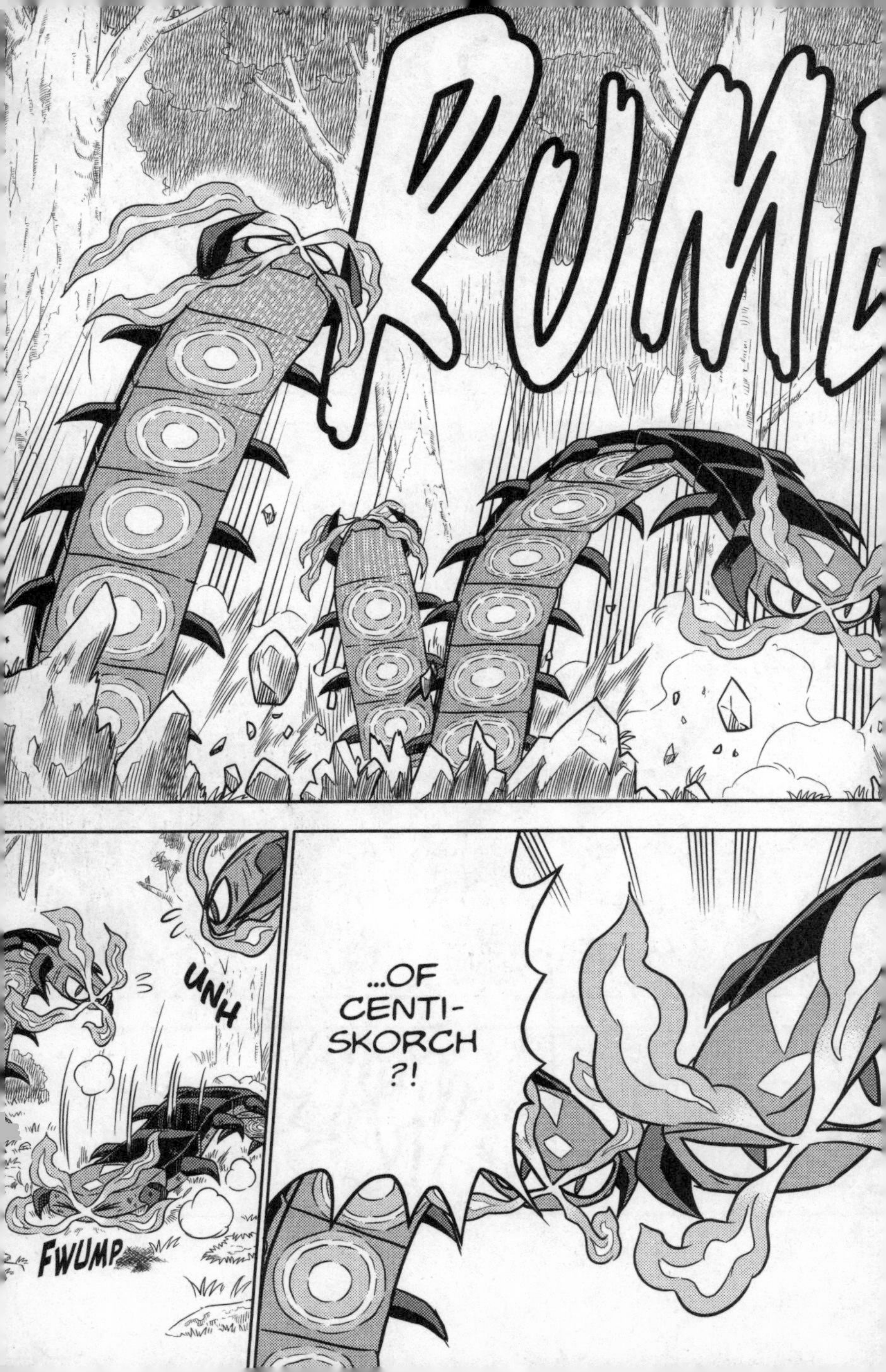
...OF CENTI-SKORCH ?!
UNH
FWUMP

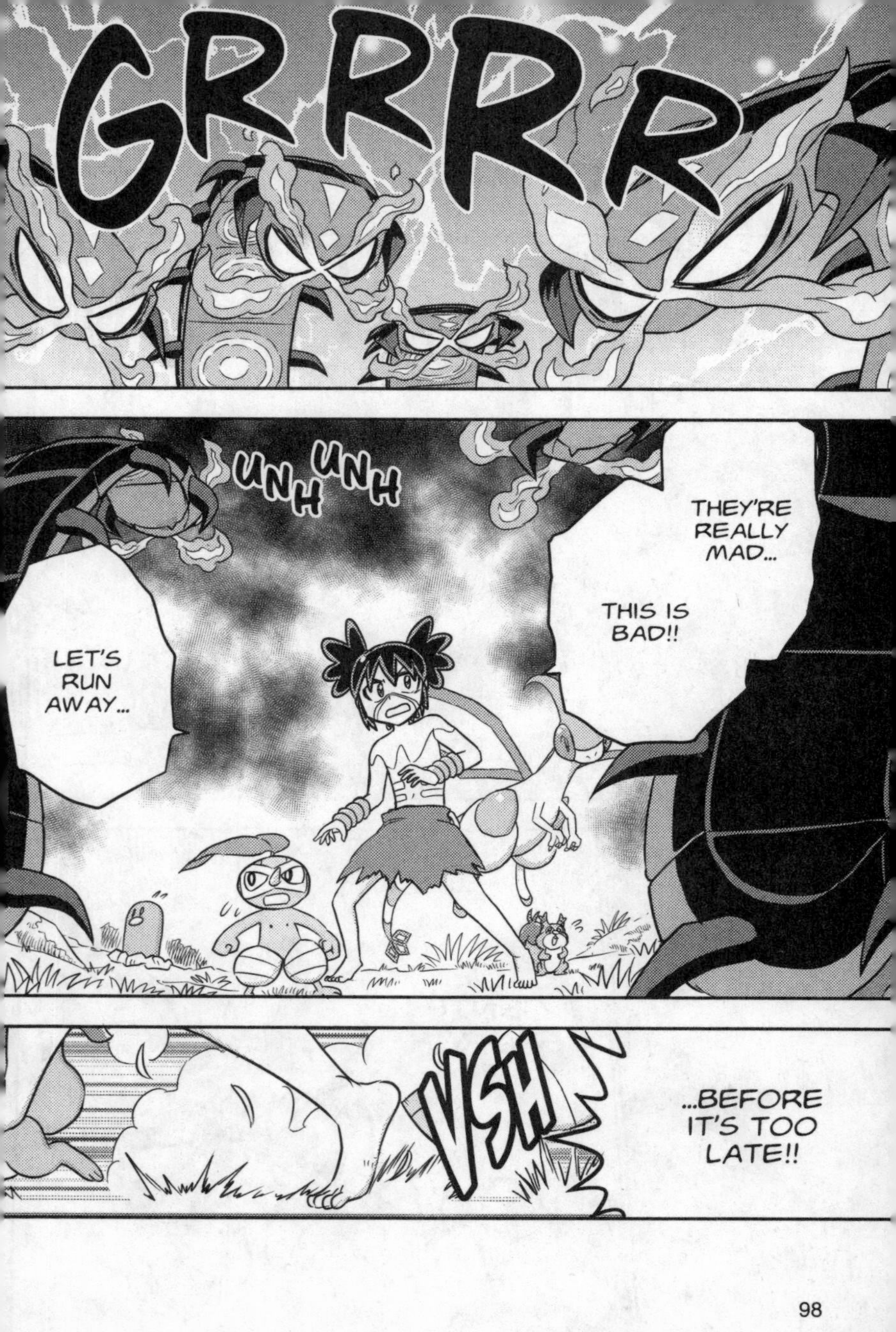
GRRRR
THEY'RE REALLY MAD...
UNH UNH
THIS IS BAD!!
LET'S RUN AWAY...
...BEFORE IT'S TOO LATE!!
VSH

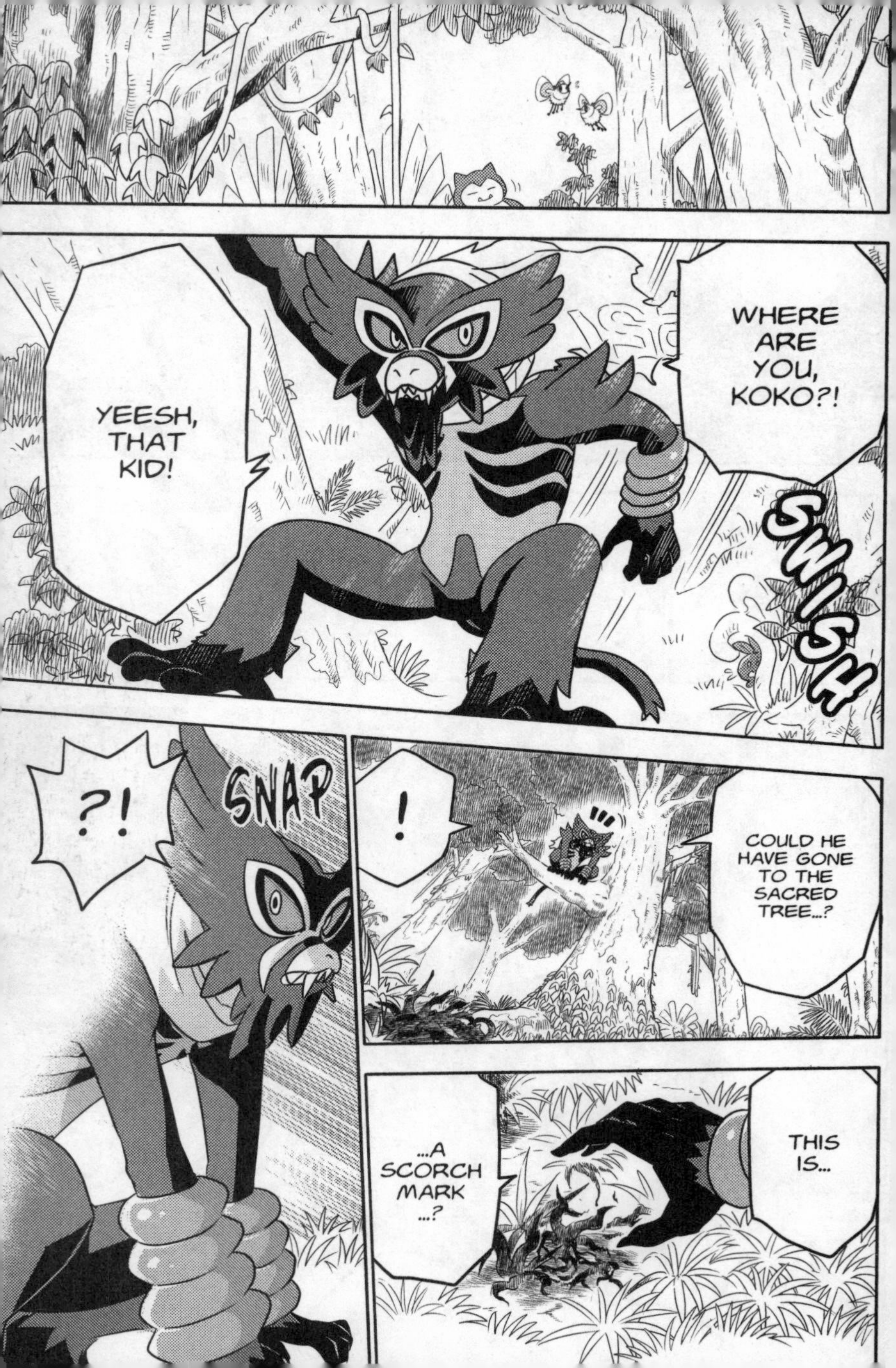
WHERE ARE YOU, KOKO?!
YEESH, THAT KID!
SWISH
COULD HE HAVE GONE TO THE SACRED TREE...?
!
THIS IS...
...A SCORCH MARK ...?
SNAP
?!

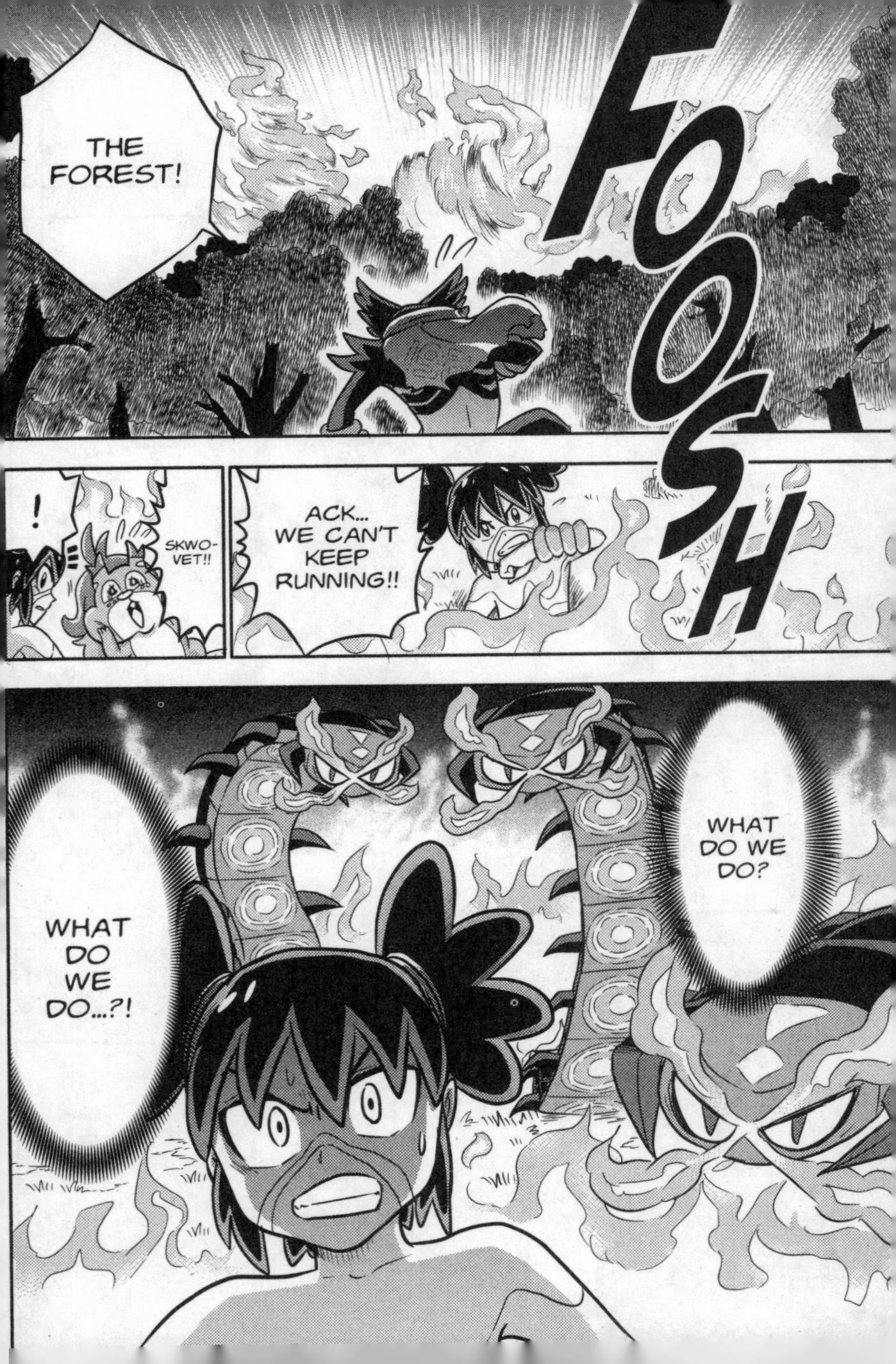
FOOSH
THE FOREST!
ACK... WE CAN'T KEEP RUNNING!!
!
SKWO-VET!!
WHAT DO WE DO?
WHAT DO WE DO...?!

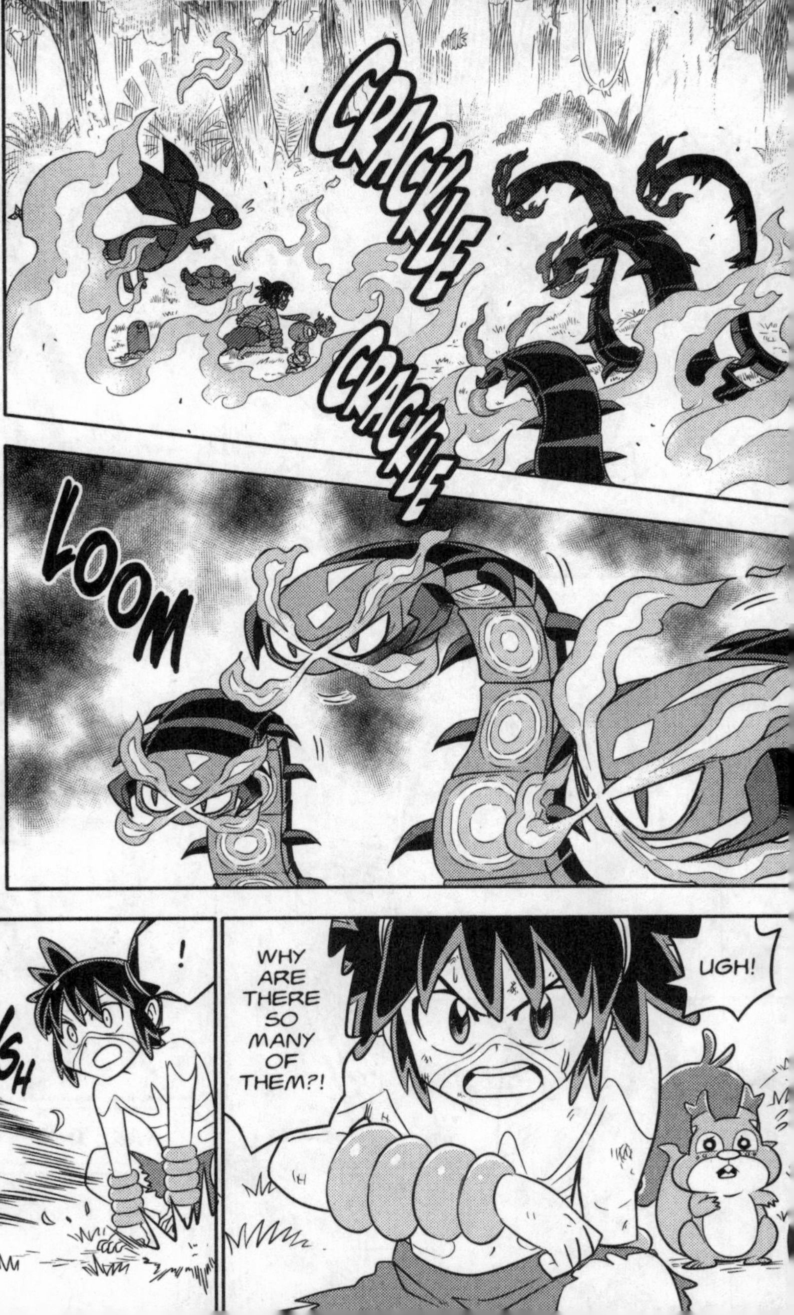
CRACKLE
CRACKLE
LOOM
UGH!
WHY ARE THERE SO MANY OF THEM?!
!
VSH

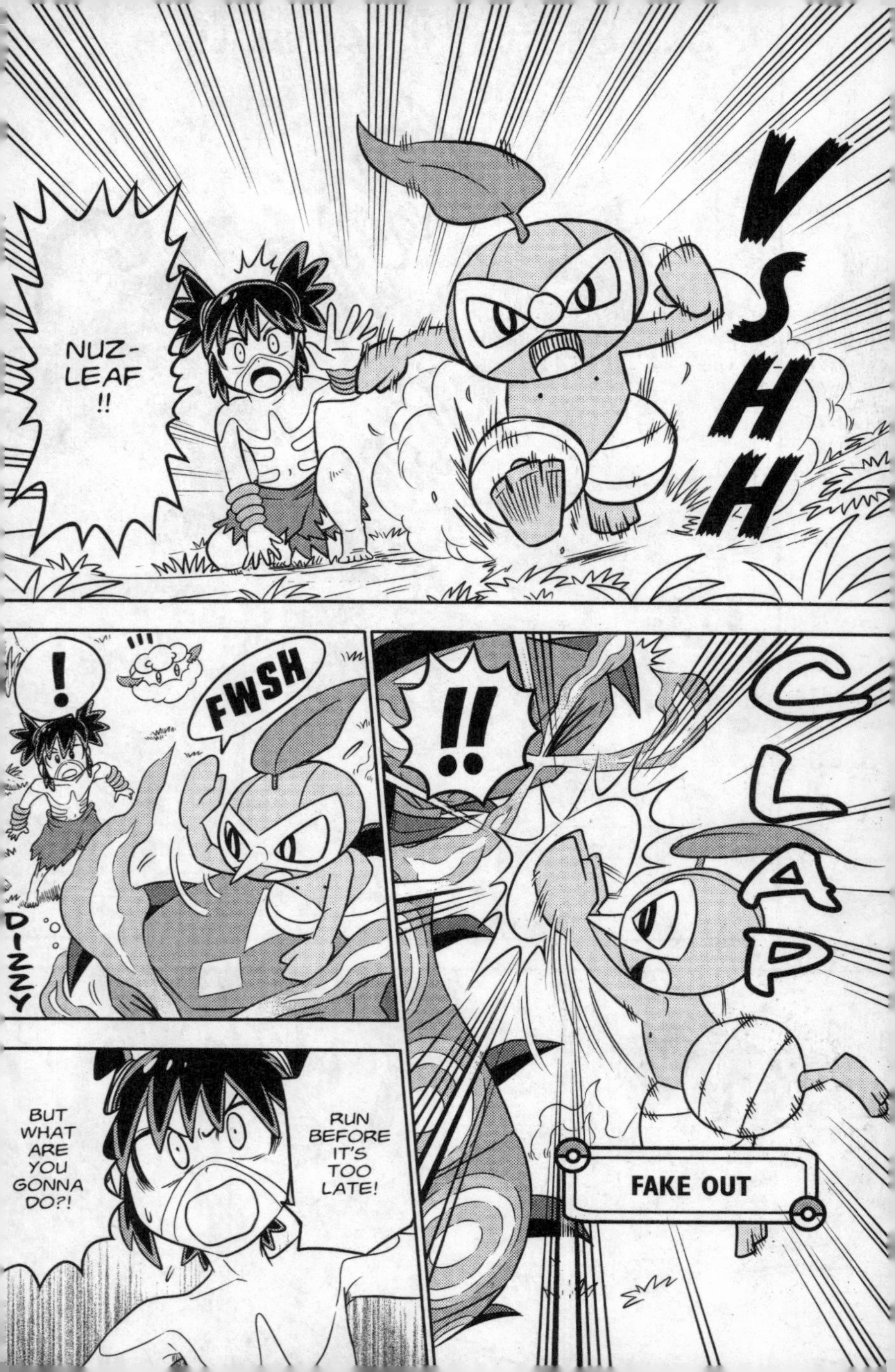
VSHHH
NUZ-LEAF!!
CLAP
!!
FAKE OUT
!
FWSH
DIZZY
RUN BEFORE IT'S TOO LATE!
BUT WHAT ARE YOU GONNA DO?!

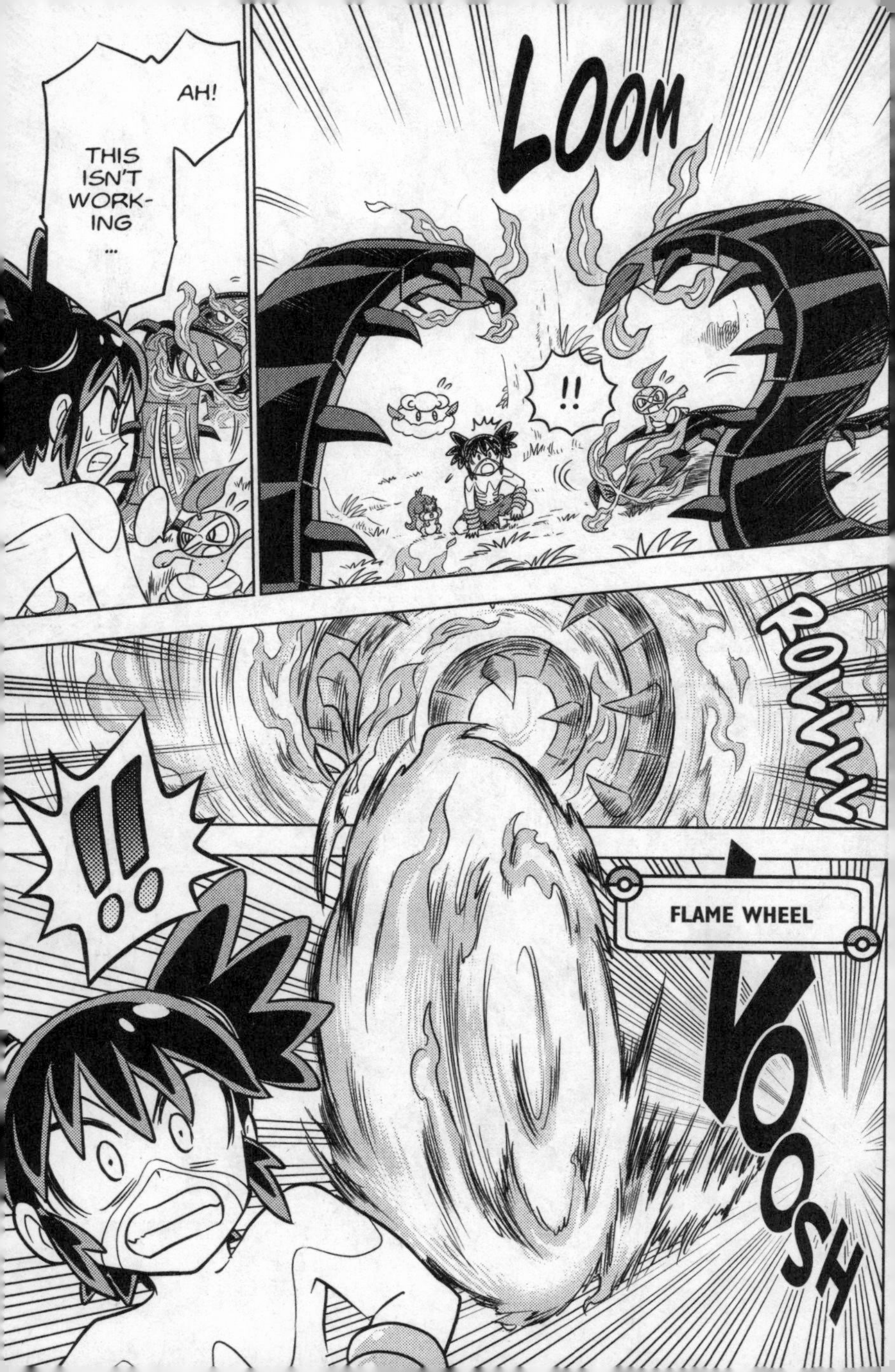
LOOM
!!
AH!
THIS ISN'T WORK-ING ...
ROLLLL
FLAME WHEEL
VOOSH
!!

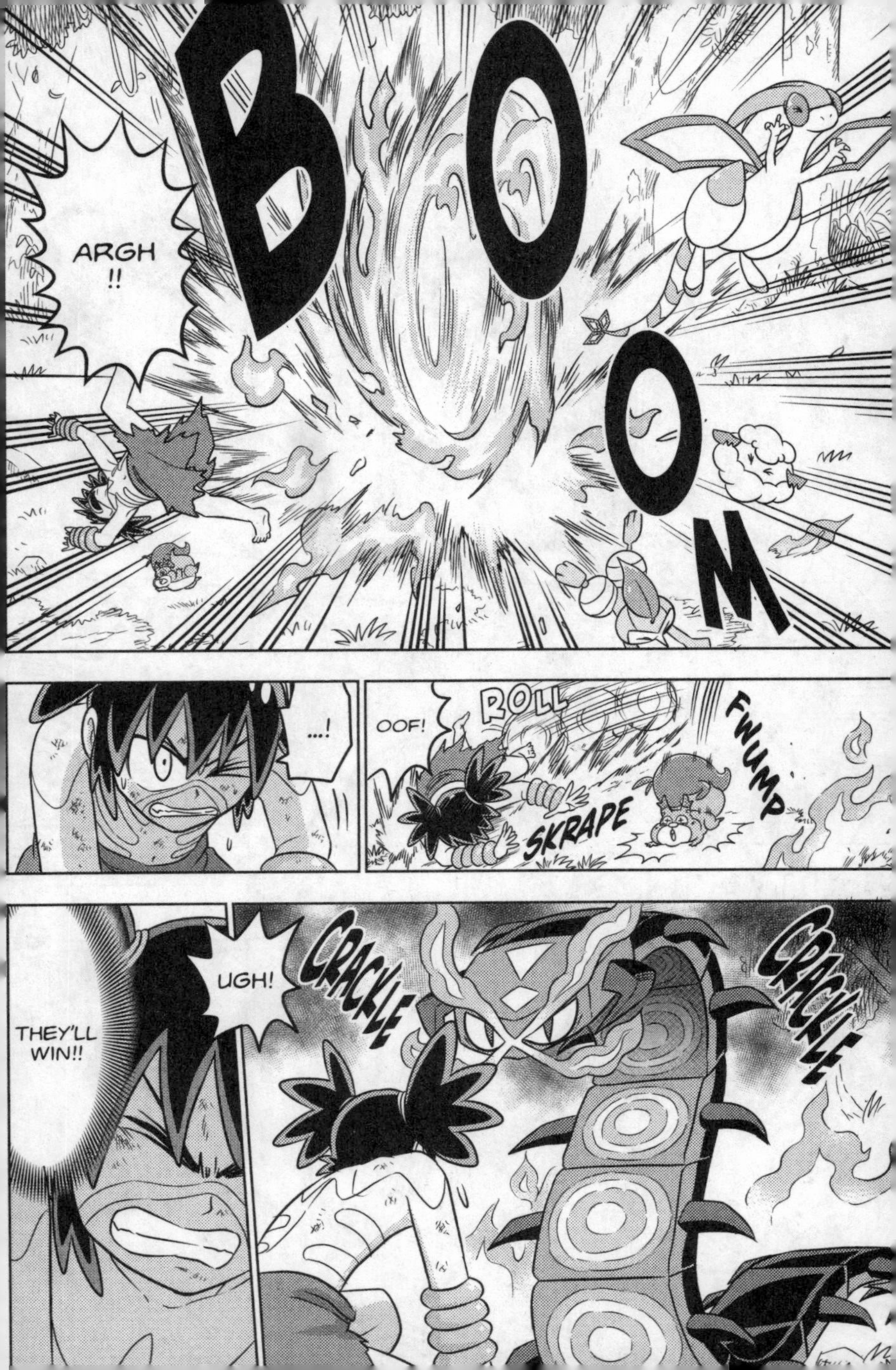
BOOOM
ARGH!!
ROLL
OOF!
FWUMP
SKRAPE
...!
CRACKLE
CRACKLE
UGH!
THEY'LL WIN!!

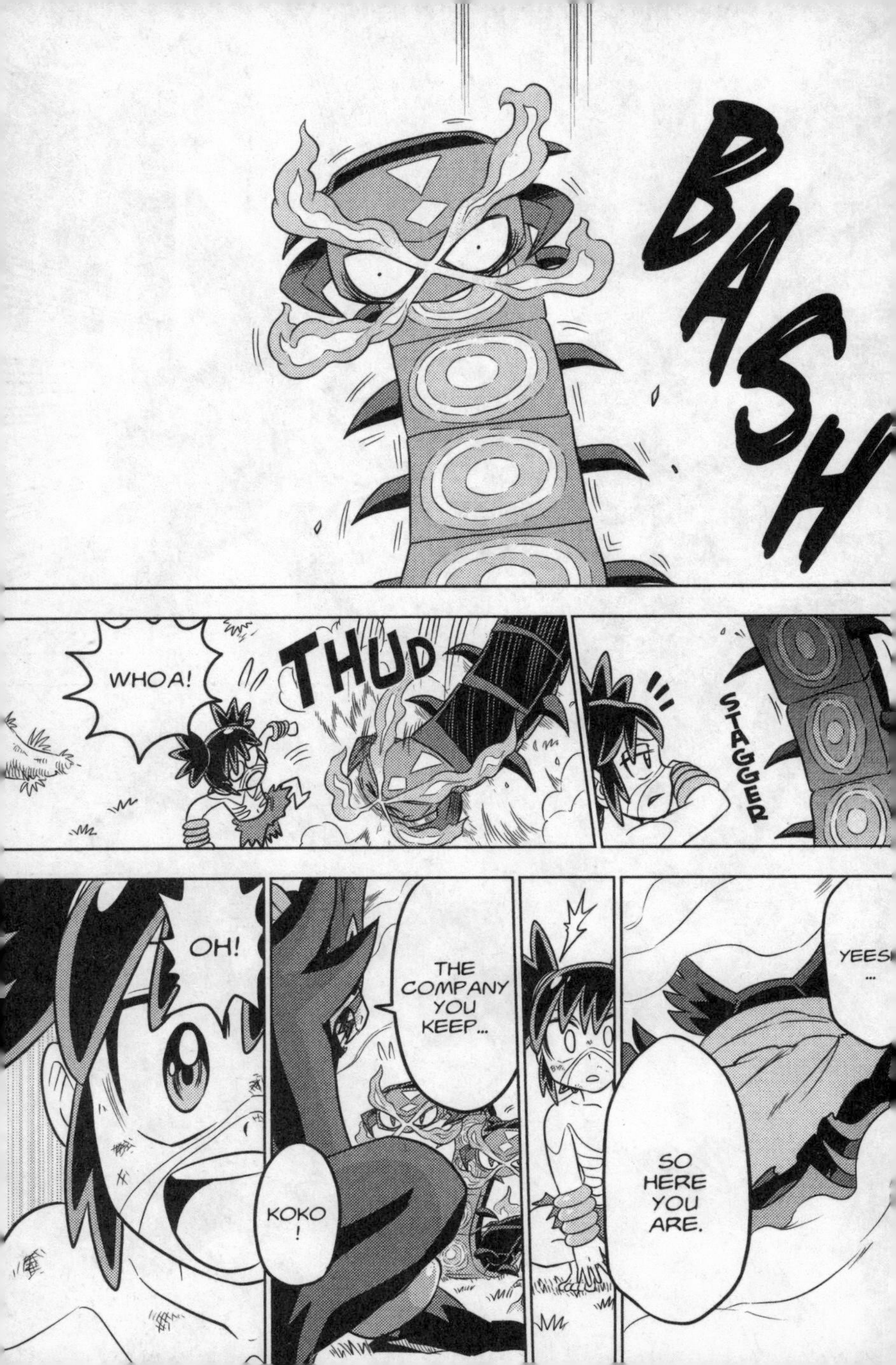
BASH
STAGGER
THUD
WHOA!
YEES...
SO HERE YOU ARE.
THE COMPANY YOU KEEP...
KOKO!
OH!

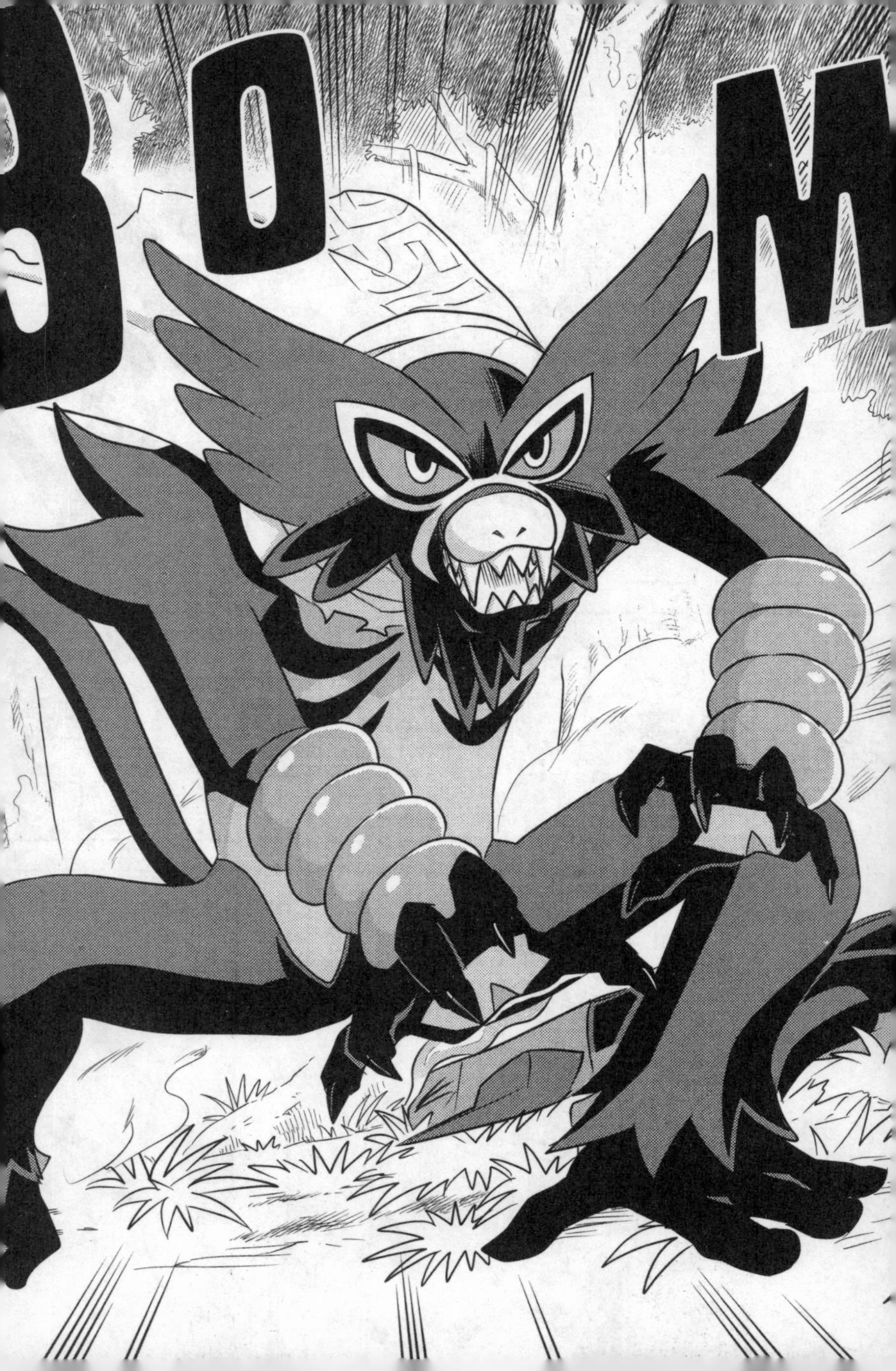
BOOM

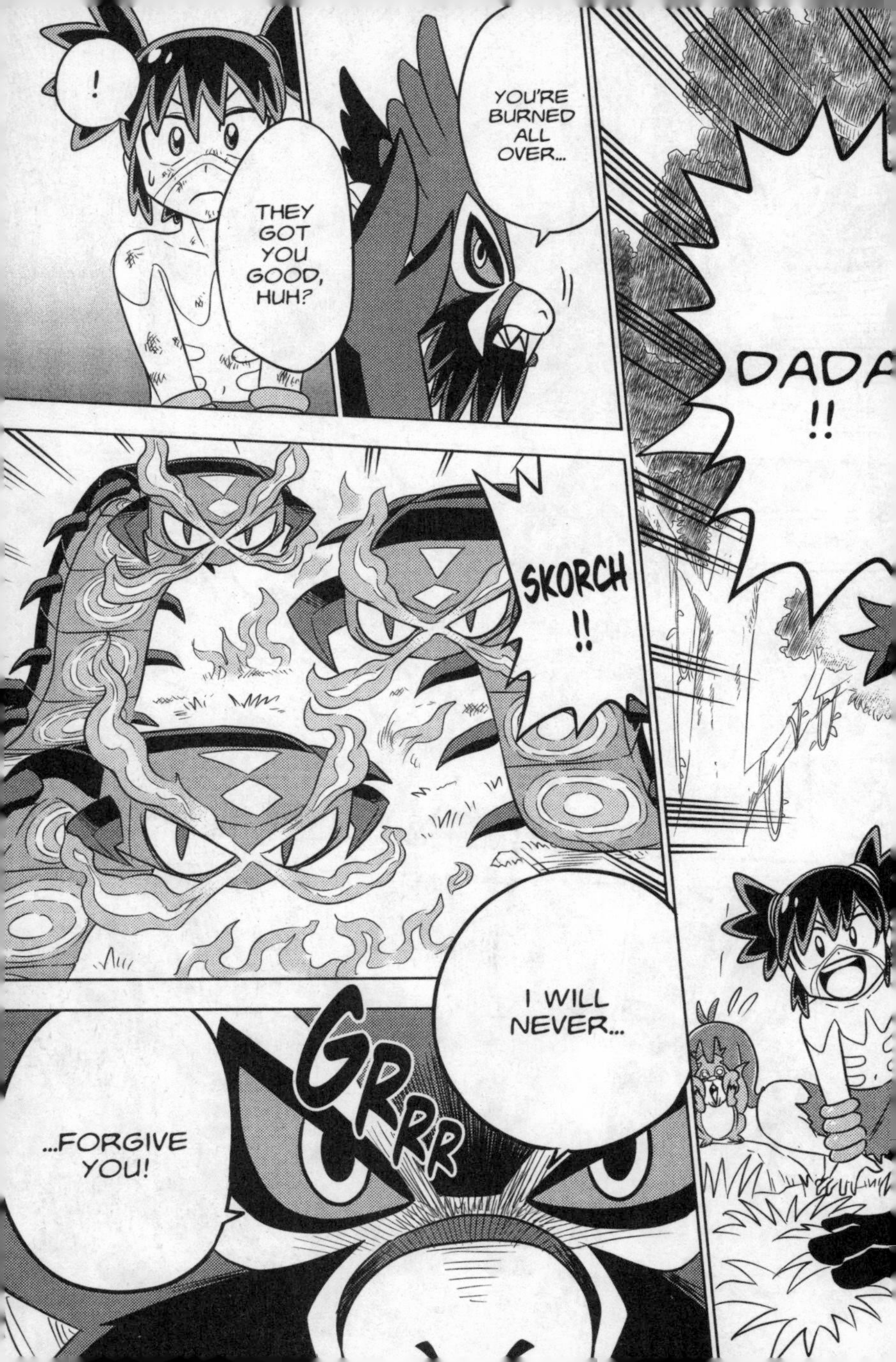
DADA
!!
YOU'RE BURNED ALL OVER...
THEY GOT YOU GOOD, HUH?
!
SKORCH
!!
I WILL NEVER...
GRRR
...FORGIVE YOU!

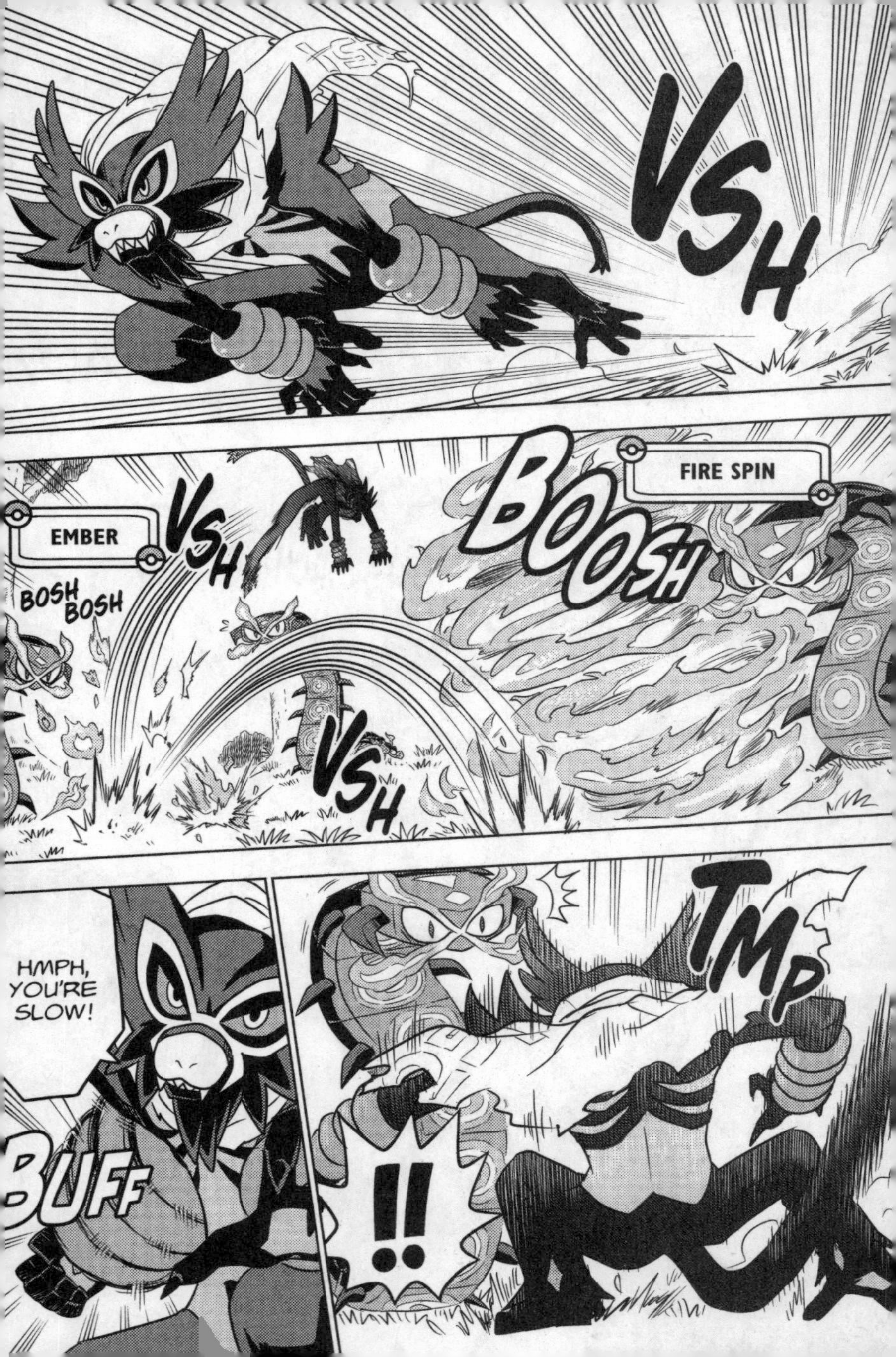
VSH
FIRE SPIN
BOOSH
VSH
EMBER
BOSH BOSH
VSH
TMP
!!
HMPH, YOU'RE SLOW!
BUFF

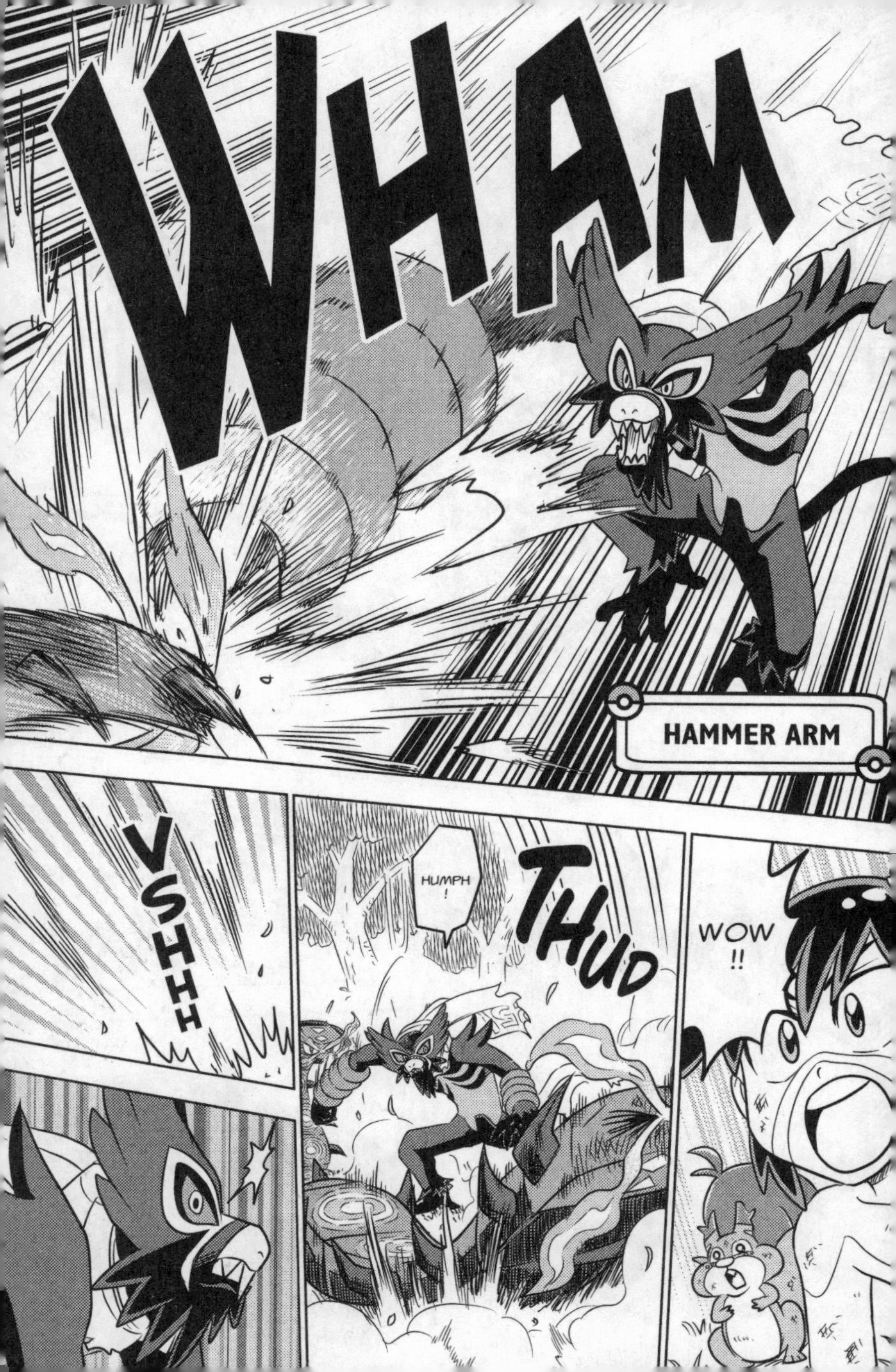
WHAM
HAMMER ARM
WOW !!
HUMPH !
THUD
VSHHH

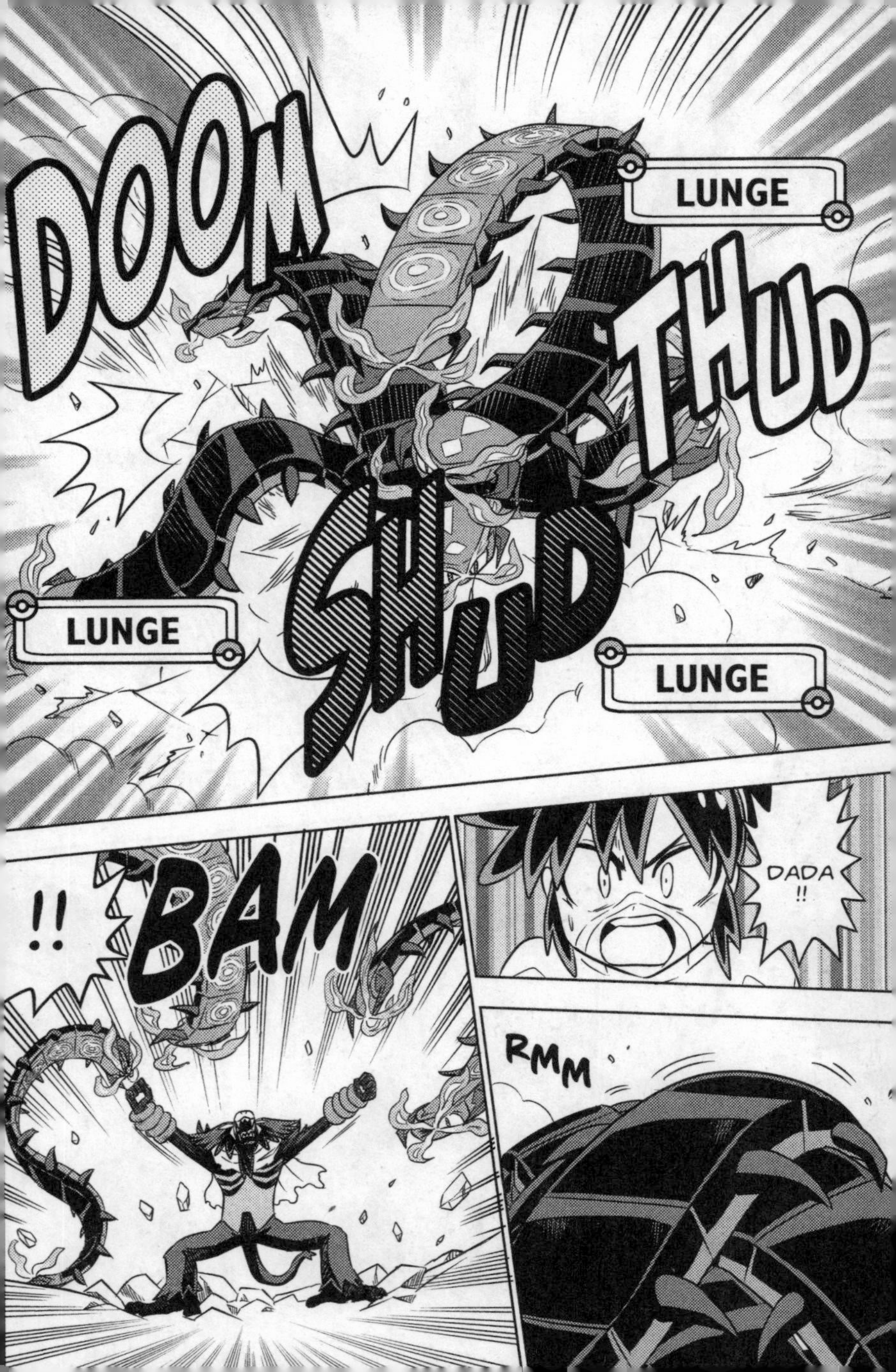
LUNGE
DOOM
THUD
SHUD
LUNGE
LUNGE
DADA!!
RMM
!!
BAM

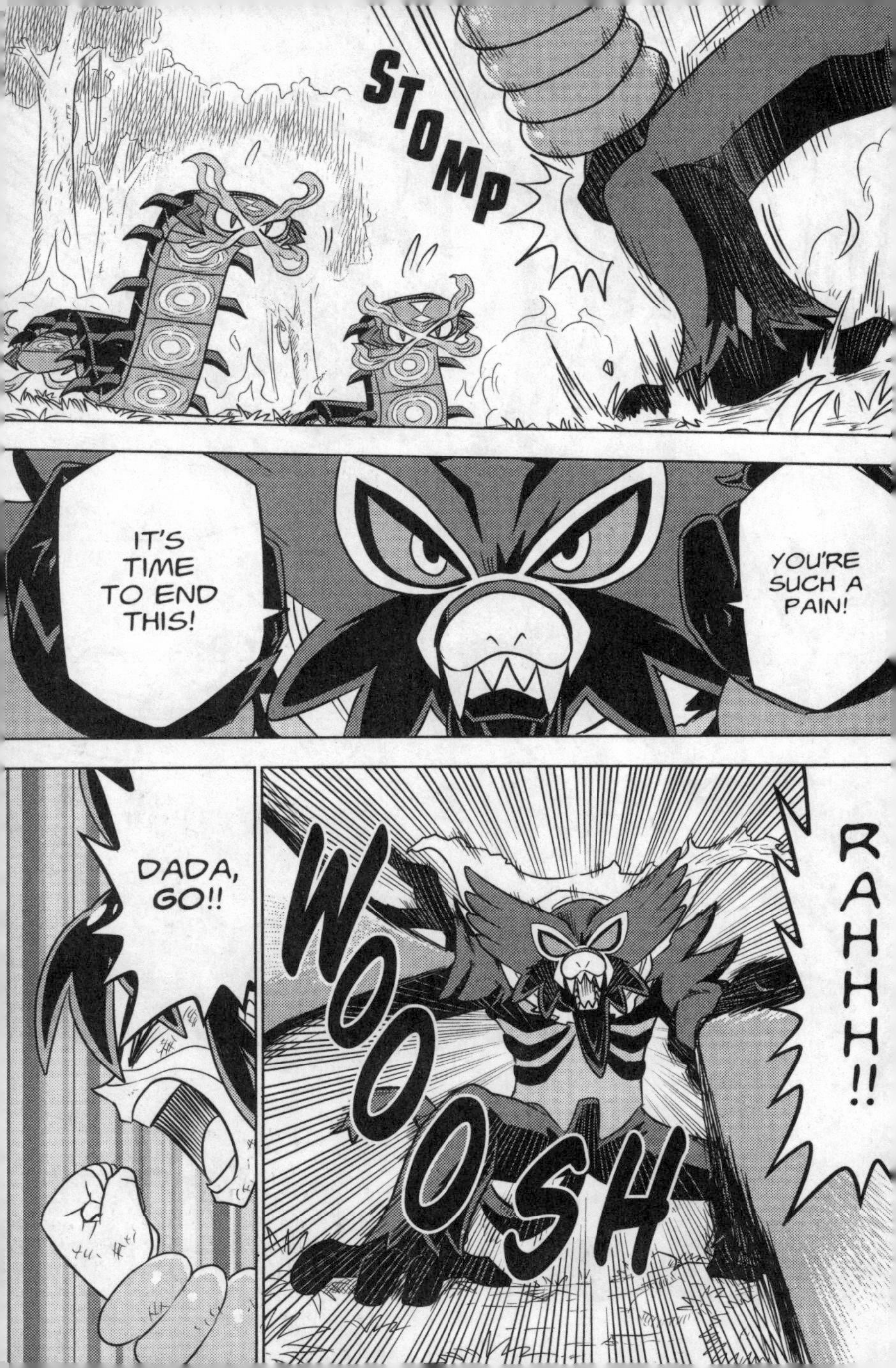
STOMP
YOU'RE SUCH A PAIN!
IT'S TIME TO END THIS!
RAHHH!!
WOOOSH
DADA, GO!!

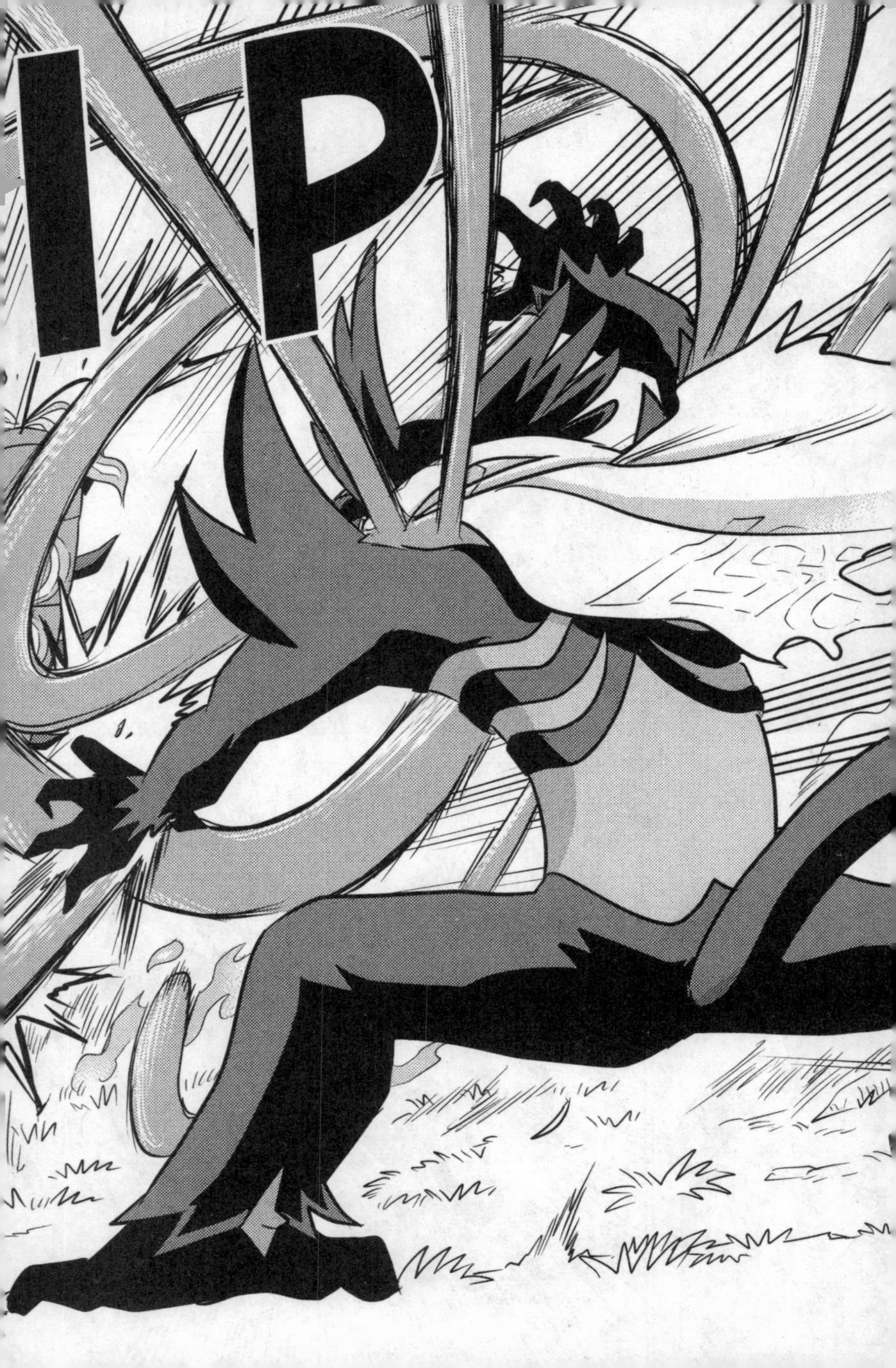
IP

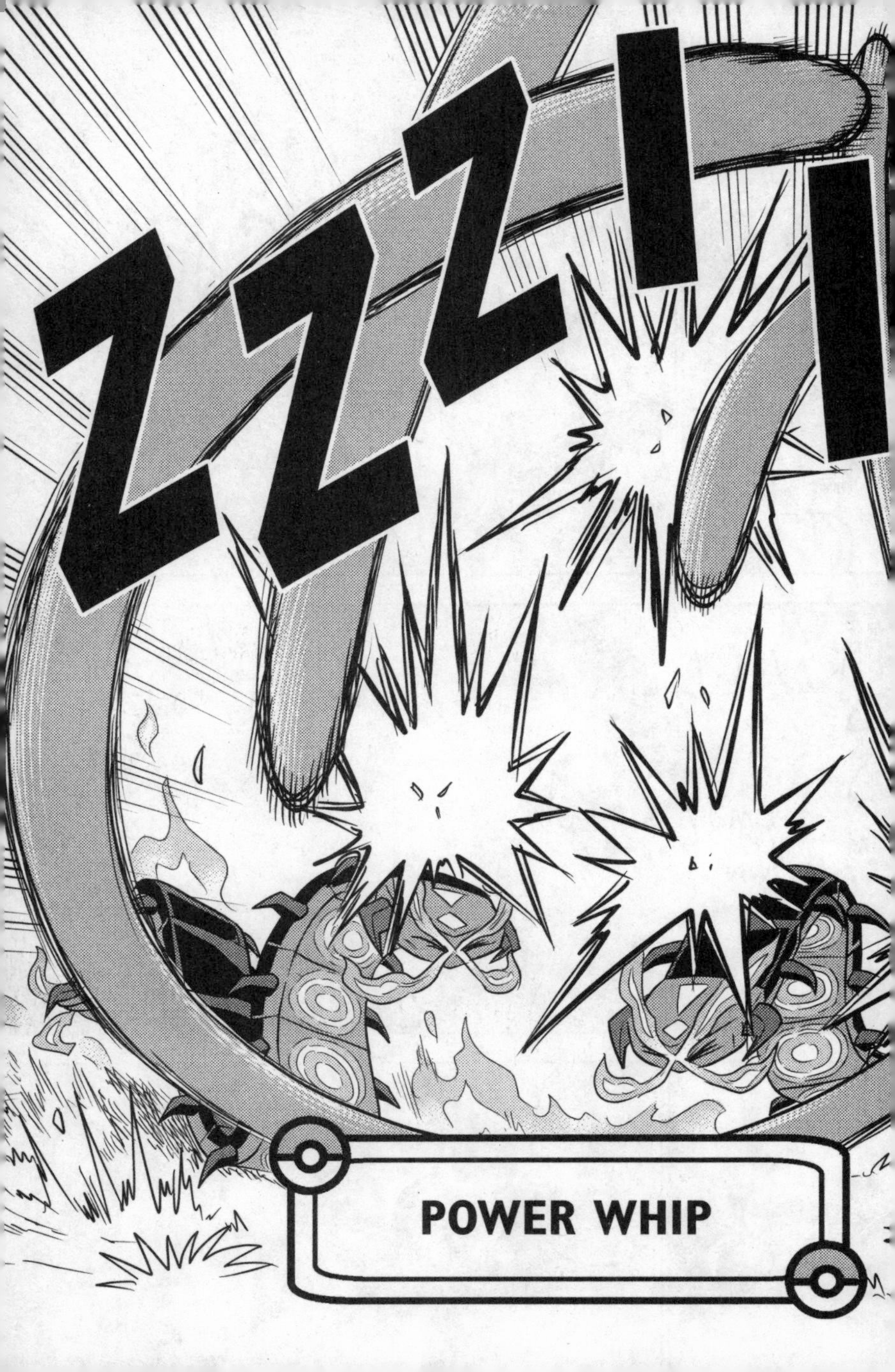
ZZZT
POWER WHIP

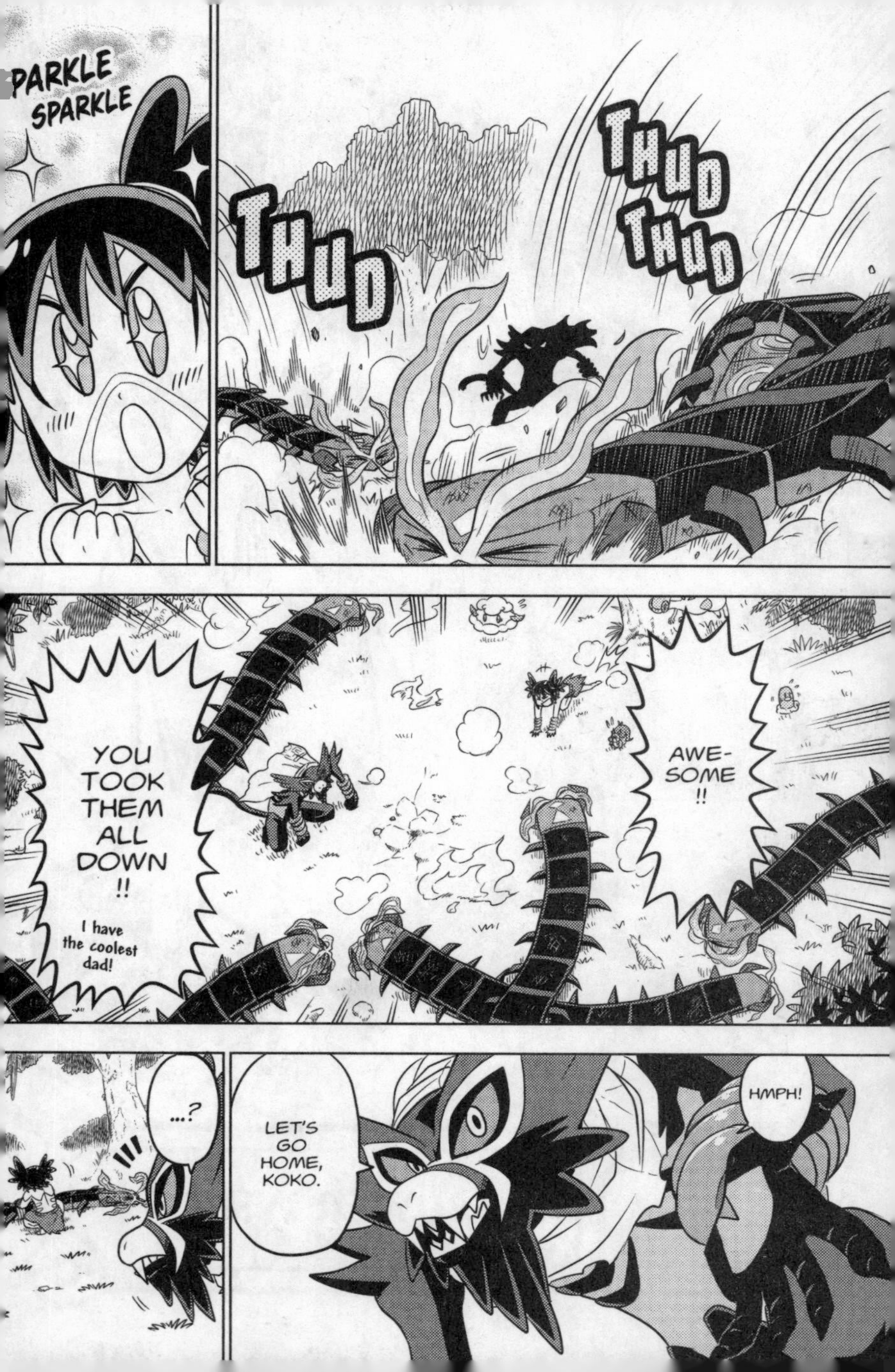

THUD THUD
THUD
PARKLE
SPARKLE
AWE-SOME !!
YOU TOOK THEM ALL DOWN !!
I have the coolest dad!
HMPH!
LET'S GO HOME, KOKO.
...?
!!!

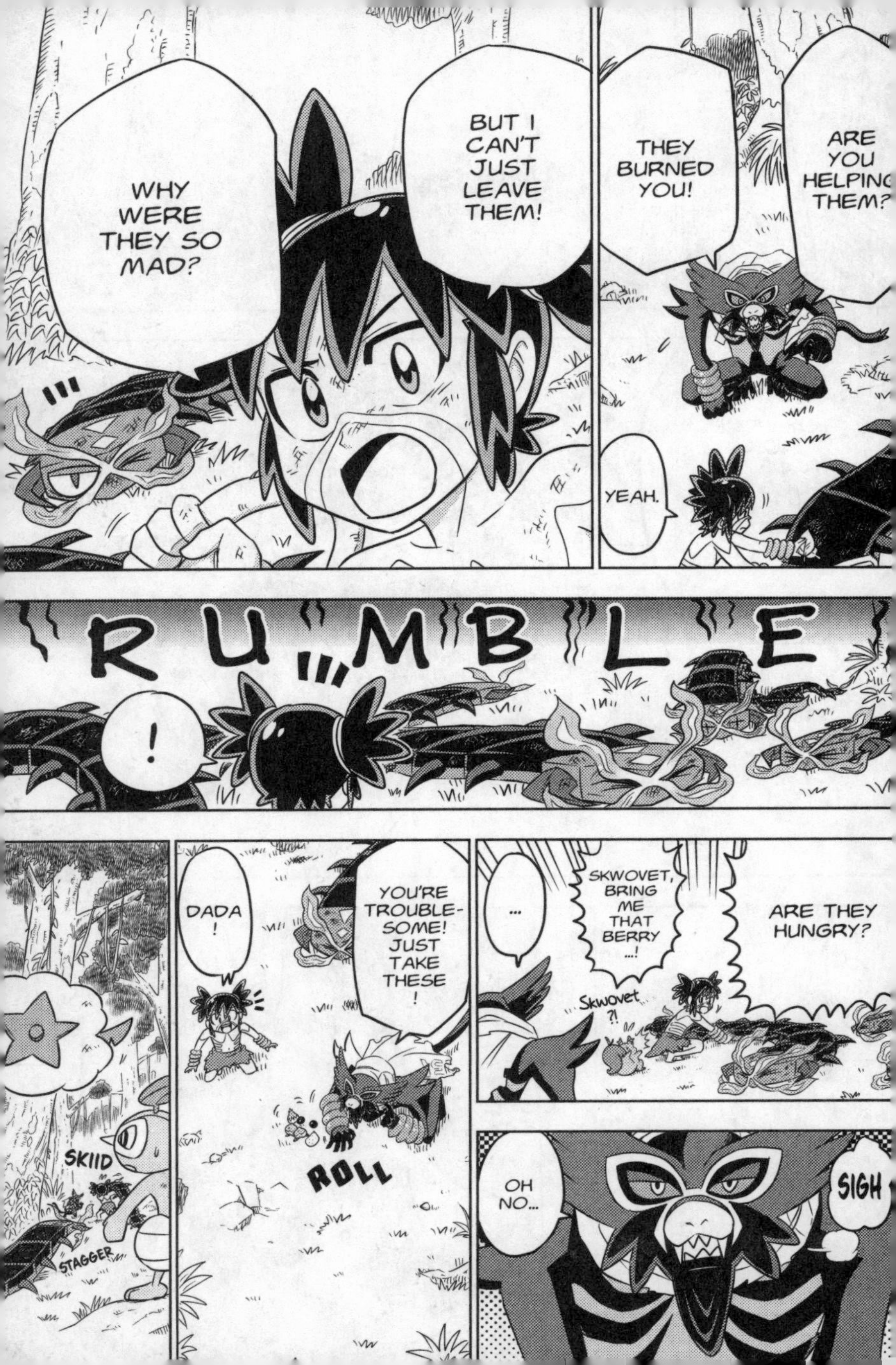
ARE YOU HELPING THEM?
THEY BURNED YOU!
YEAH.
BUT I CAN'T JUST LEAVE THEM!
WHY WERE THEY SO MAD?
RUMBLE
!
ARE THEY HUNGRY?
SKWOVET, BRING ME THAT BERRY ...!
...
Skwovet ?!
SIGH
OH NO...
YOU'RE TROUBLE-SOME! JUST TAKE THESE!
DADA!
ROLL
SKIID
STAGGER

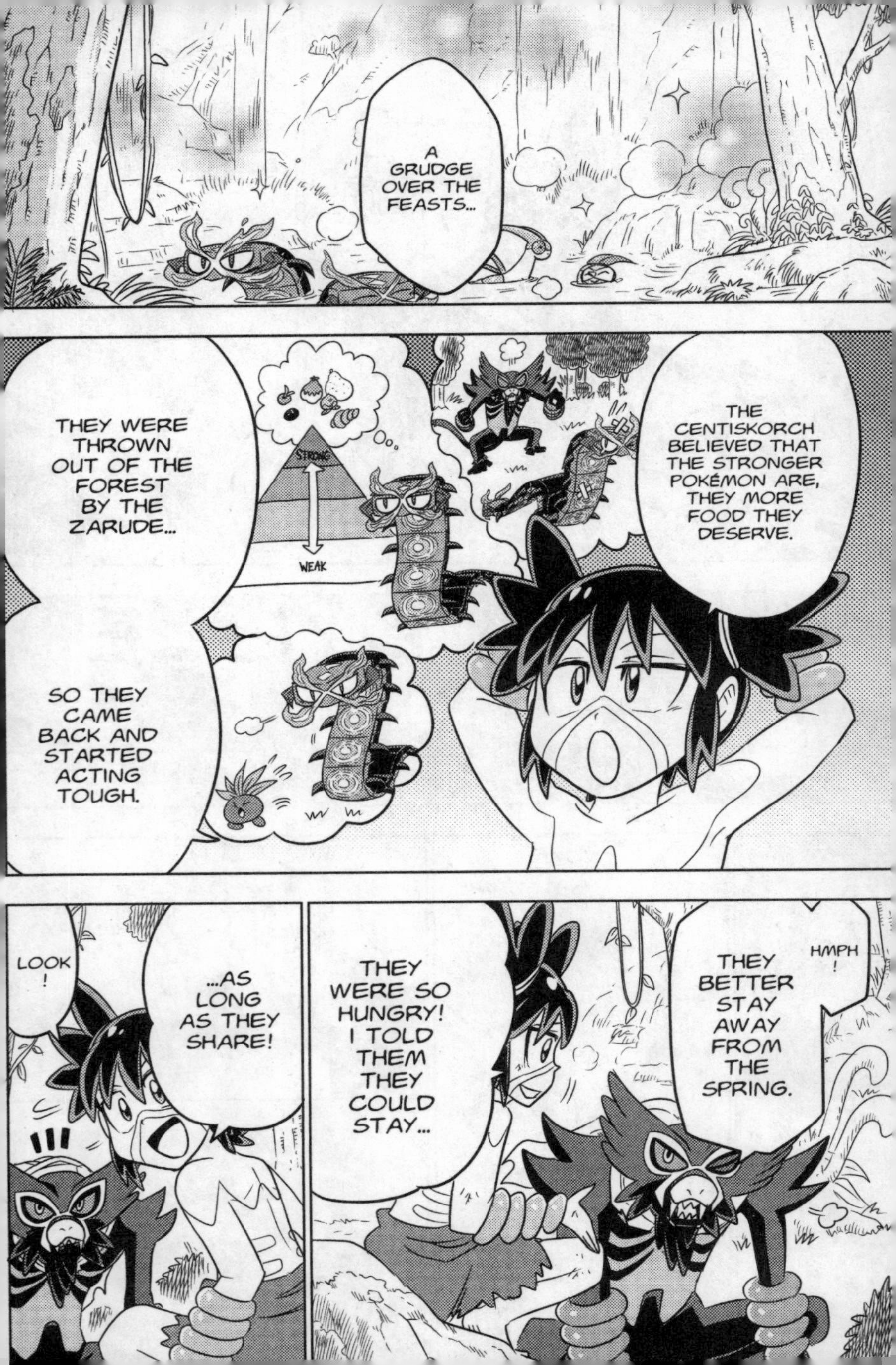
A GRUDGE OVER THE FEASTS...
THE CENTISKORCH BELIEVED THAT THE STRONGER POKÉMON ARE, THEY MORE FOOD THEY DESERVE.
STRONG
WEAK
THEY WERE THROWN OUT OF THE FOREST BY THE ZARUDE...
SO THEY CAME BACK AND STARTED ACTING TOUGH.
HMPH!
THEY BETTER STAY AWAY FROM THE SPRING.
THEY WERE SO HUNGRY! I TOLD THEM THEY COULD STAY...
...AS LONG AS THEY SHARE!
LOOK!

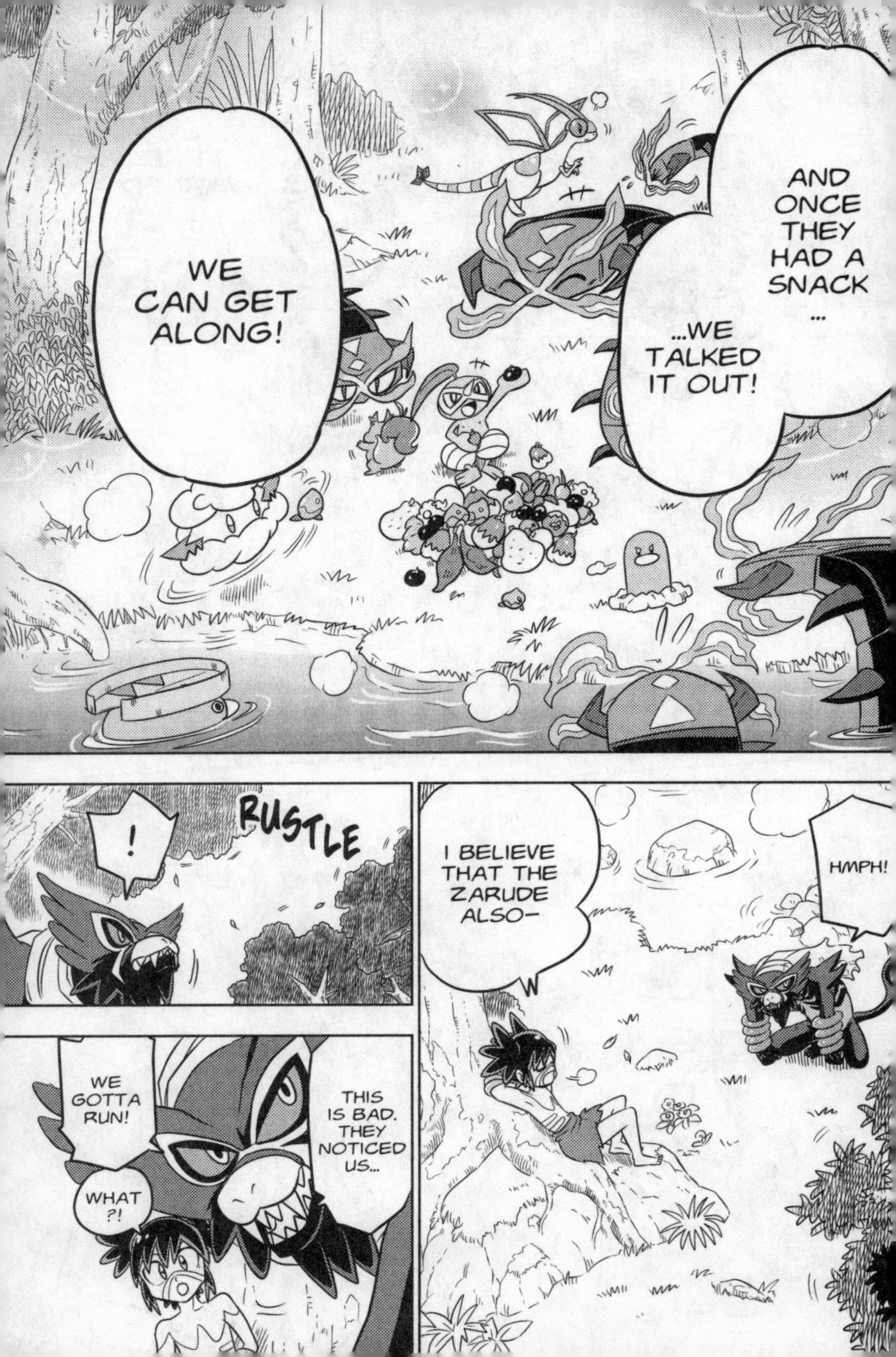
AND ONCE THEY HAD A SNACK ...
...WE TALKED IT OUT!
WE CAN GET ALONG!
I BELIEVE THAT THE ZARUDE ALSO–
HMPH!
!
RUSTLE
THIS IS BAD. THEY NOTICED US...
WE GOTTA RUN!
WHAT ?!

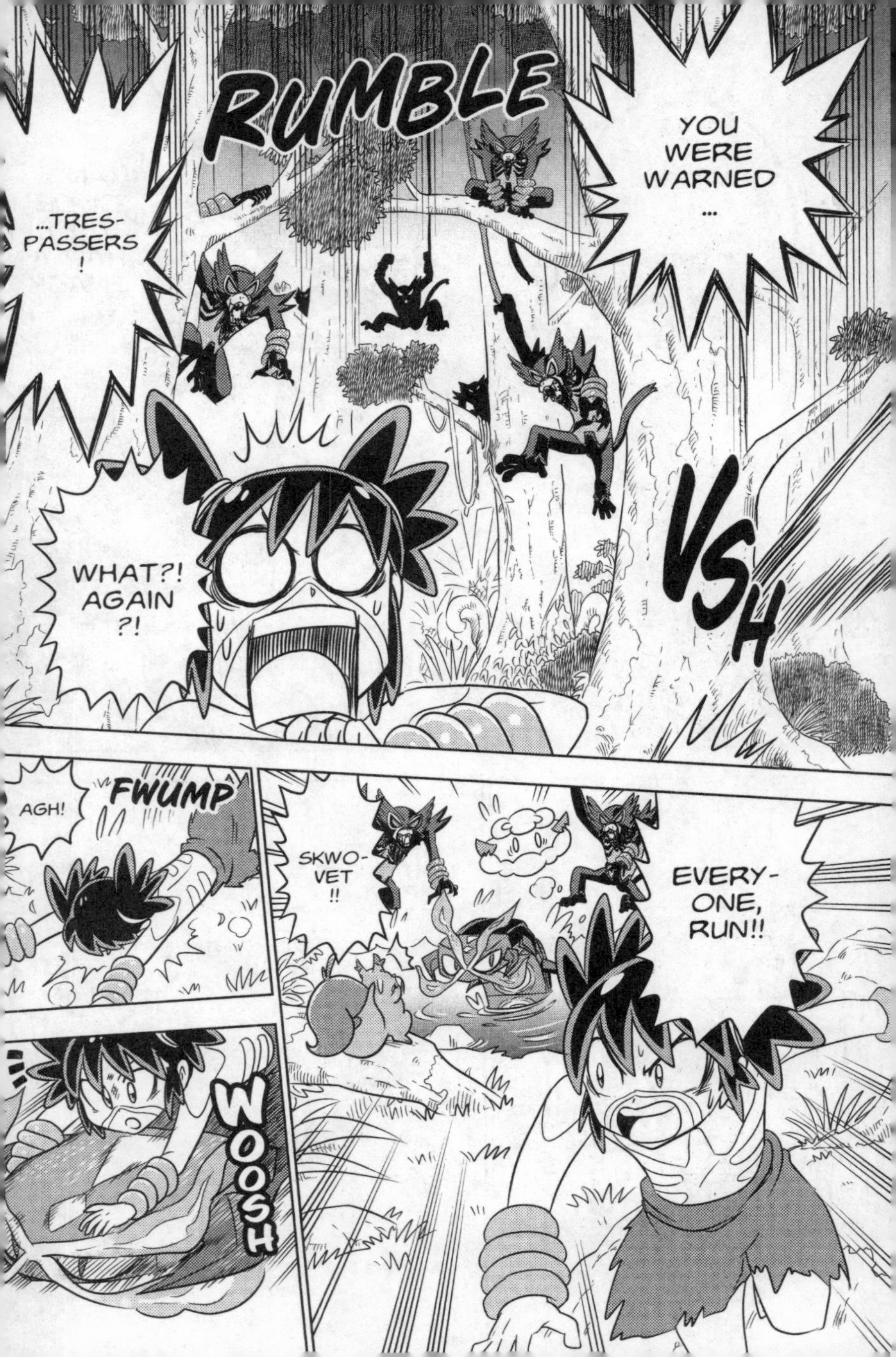
RUMBLE
YOU WERE WARNED ...
...TRES-PASSERS !
VSH
WHAT?! AGAIN ?!
EVERY-ONE, RUN!!
SKWO-VET !!
AGH!
FWUMP
WOOSH

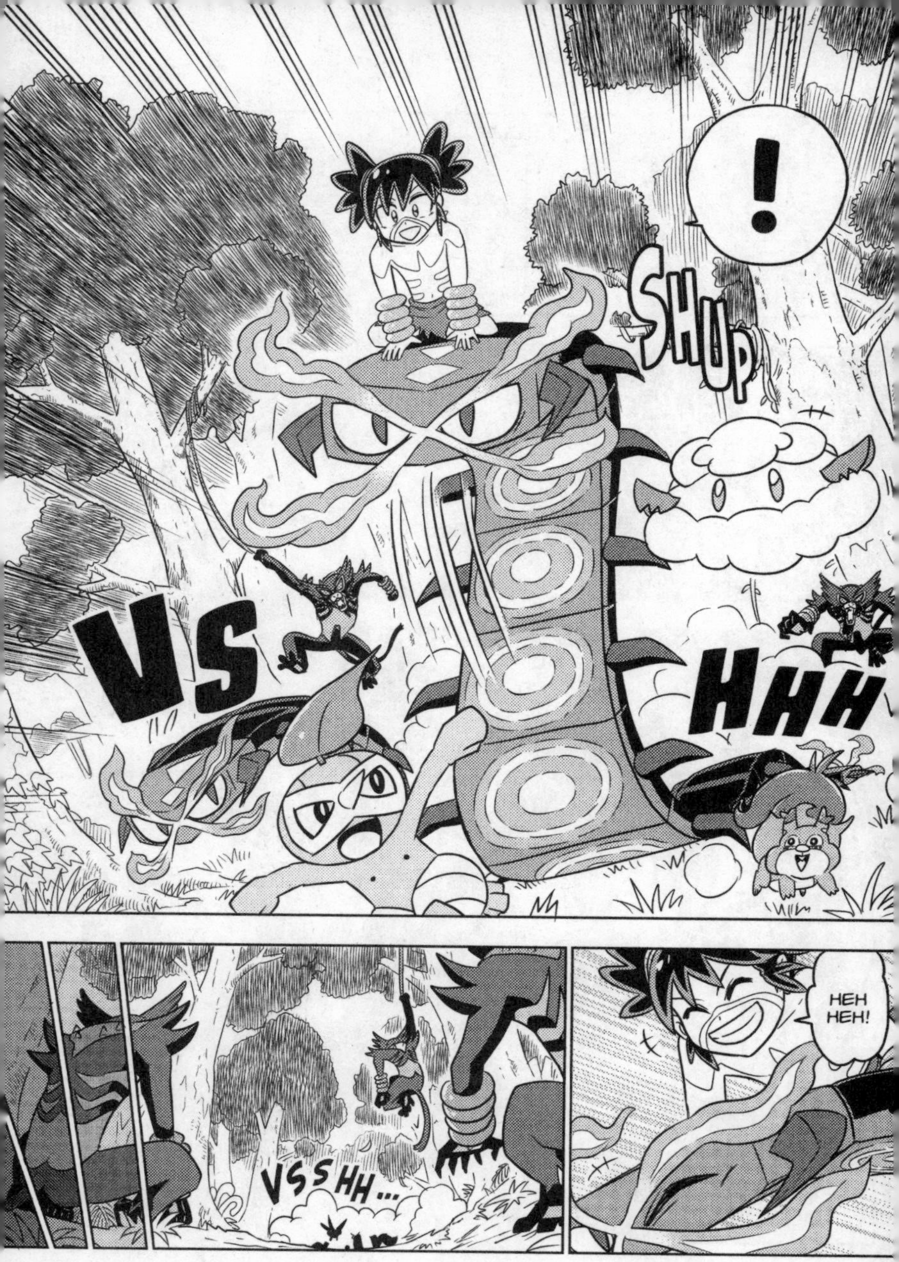
!
SHUP
VS
HHH
HEH HEH!
VSSHH...

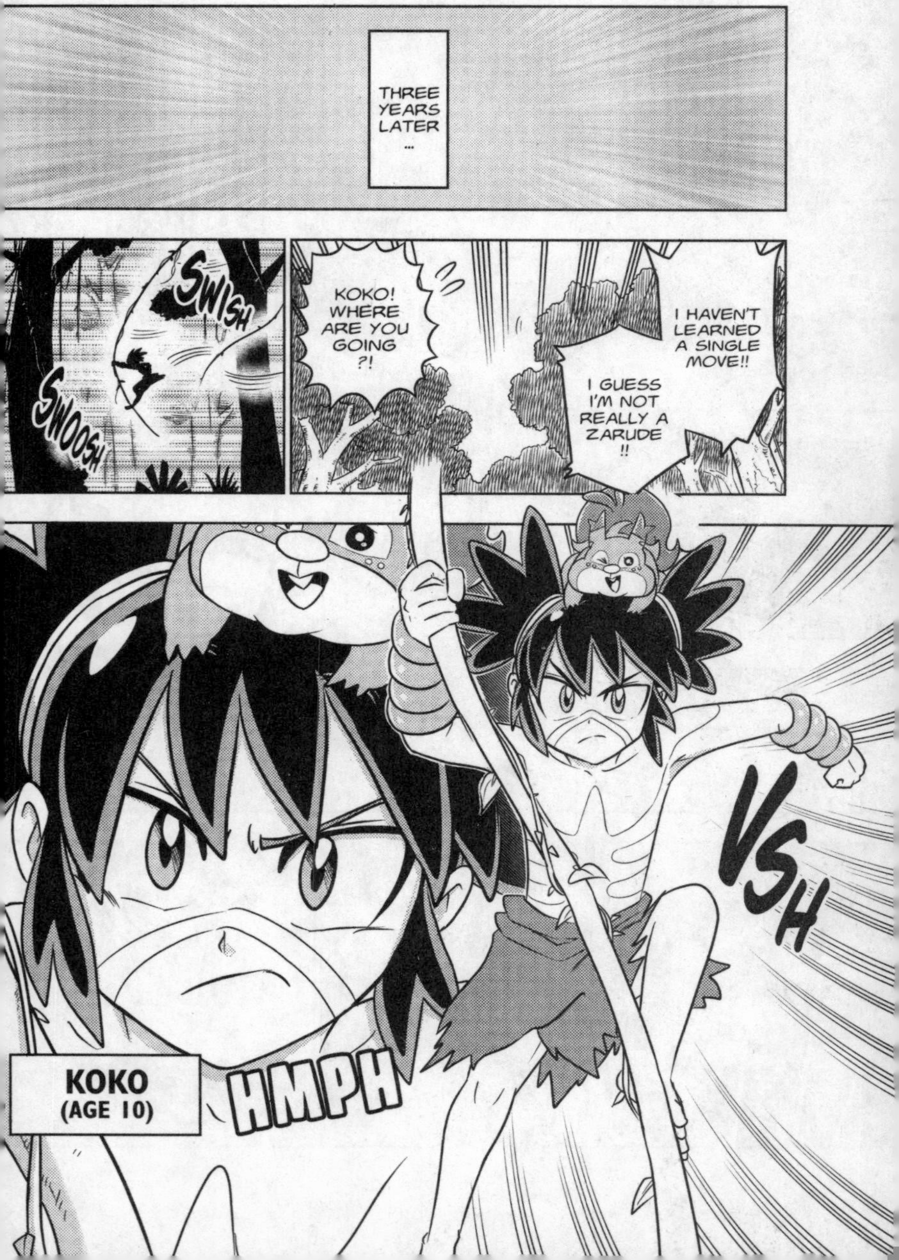
THREE YEARS LATER ...
KOKO! WHERE ARE YOU GOING ?!
I HAVEN'T LEARNED A SINGLE MOVE!!
I GUESS I'M NOT REALLY A ZARUDE !!
SWISH
SWOOSH
VSH
KOKO (AGE 10)
HMPH

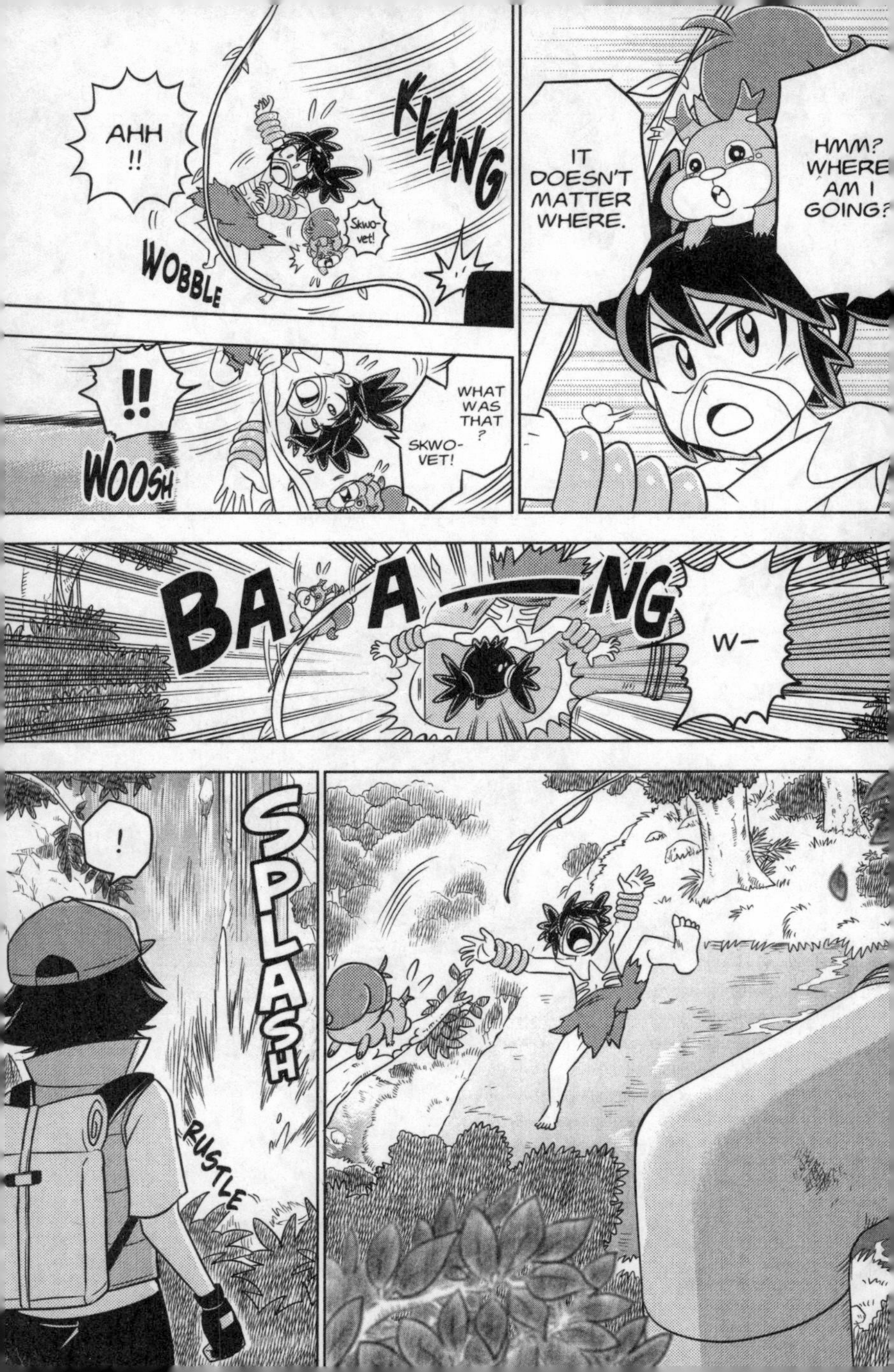
HMM? WHERE AM I GOING?
IT DOESN'T MATTER WHERE.
KLANG
AHH !!
Skwo-vet!
WOBBLE
WHAT WAS THAT?
SKWO-VET!
!!
WOOSH
W-
BA A——NG
SPLASH
!
RUSTLE

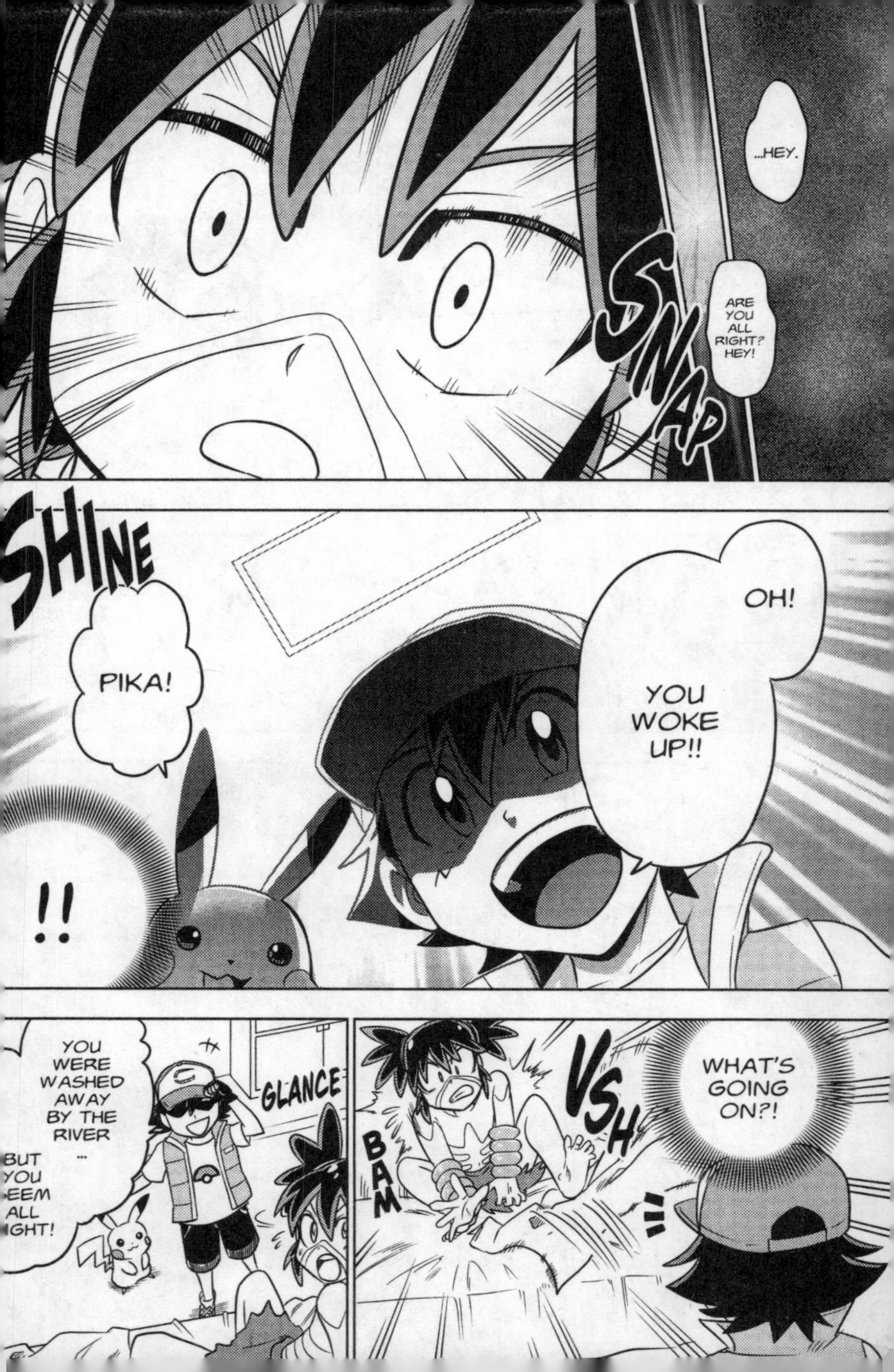
...HEY.
ARE YOU ALL RIGHT? HEY!
SNAP
OH!
YOU WOKE UP!!
SHINE
PIKA!
!!
WHAT'S GOING ON?!
VSH
BAM
GLANCE
YOU WERE WASHED AWAY BY THE RIVER ...
BUT YOU EEM ALL IGHT!

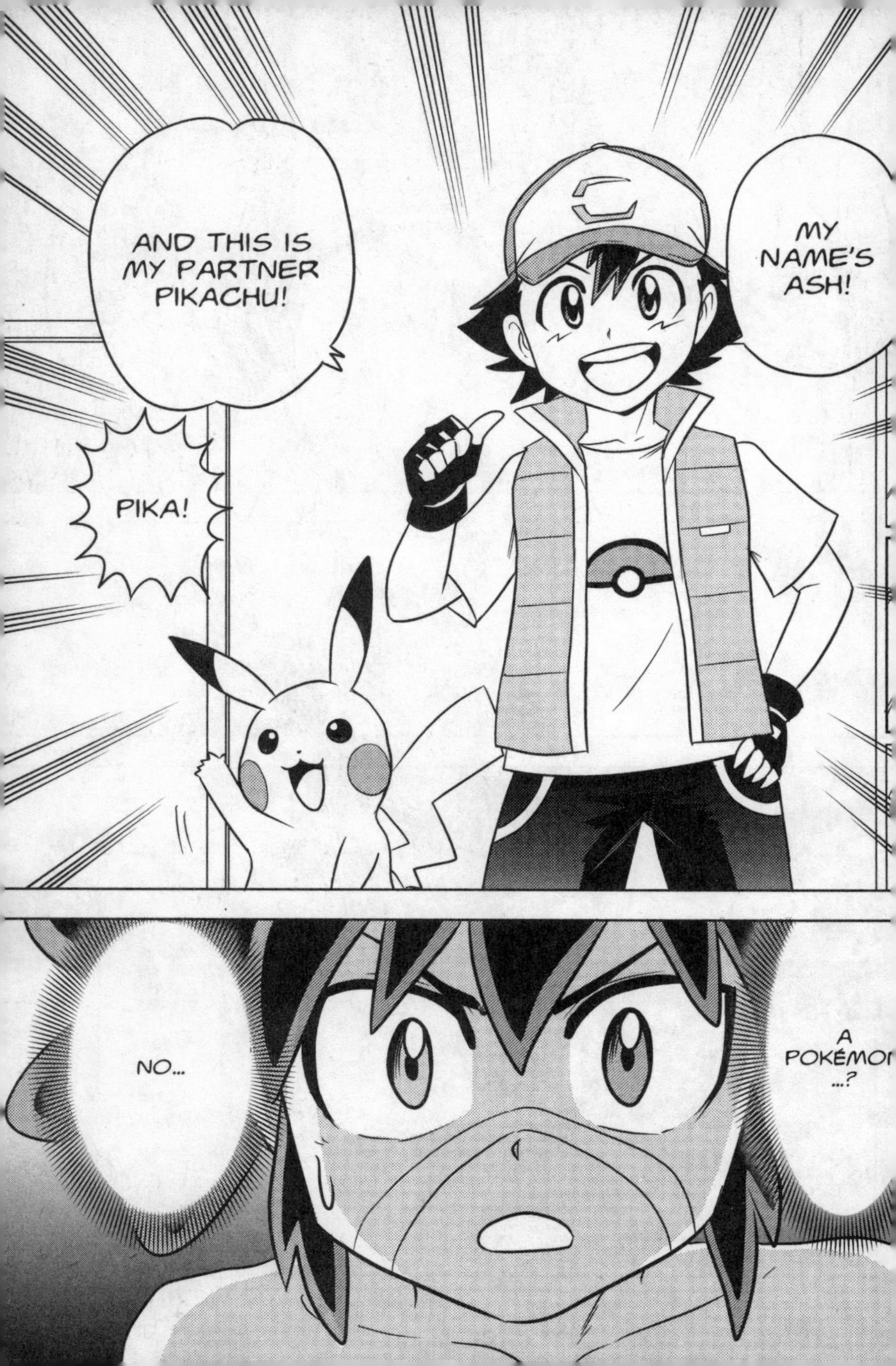
MY NAME'S ASH!
AND THIS IS MY PARTNER PIKACHU!
PIKA!
A POKÉMON ...?
NO...

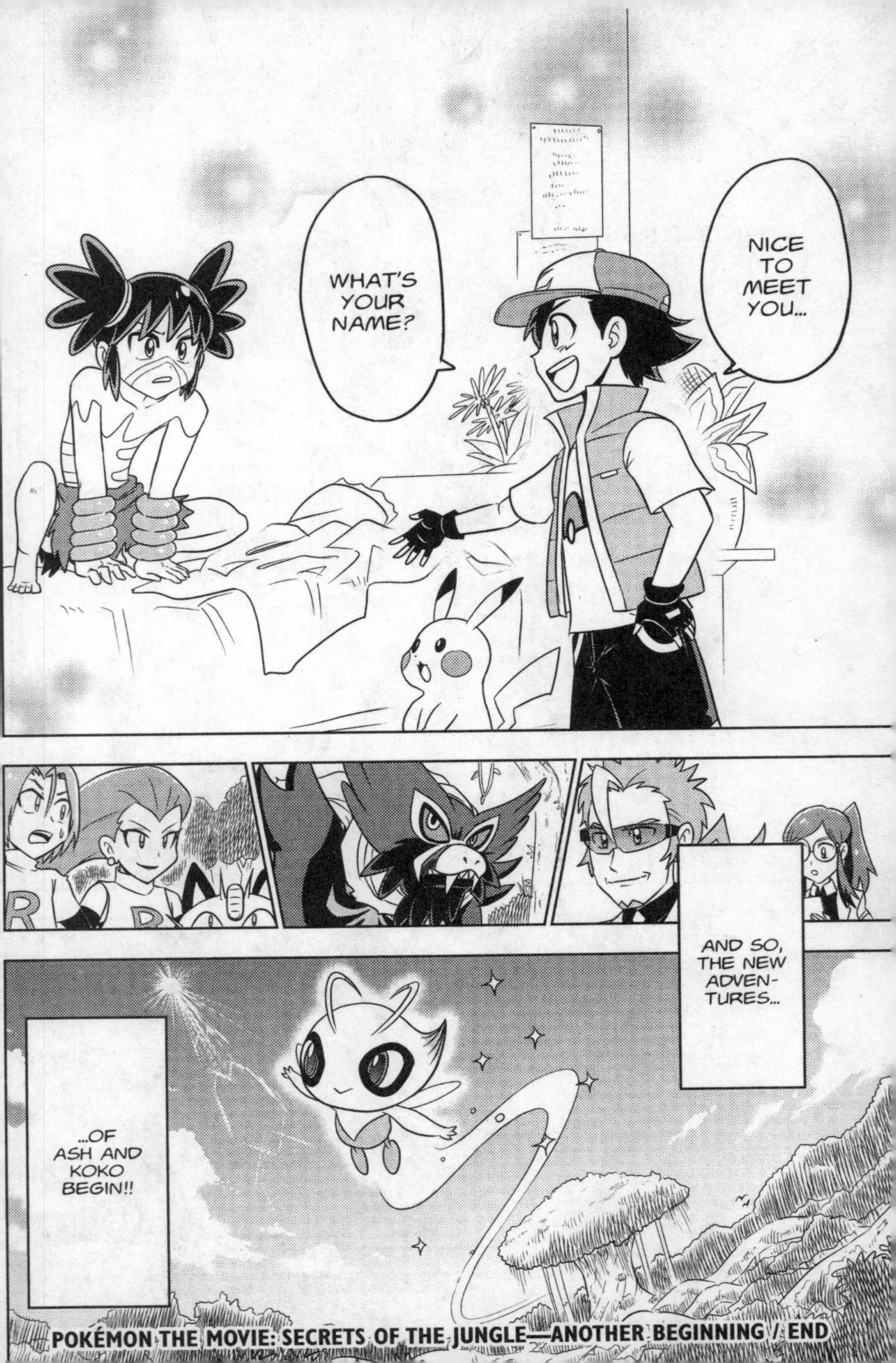
NICE TO MEET YOU...
WHAT'S YOUR NAME?
AND SO, THE NEW ADVEN- TURES...
...OF ASH AND KOKO BEGIN!!
POKÉMON THE MOVIE: SECRETS OF THE JUNGLE—ANOTHER BEGINNING / END

Teruaki Mizuno

I hope you enjoyed reading this prequel to *Pokémon the Movie: Secrets of the Jungle* as much as I had fun drawing wild Pokémon who are so full of life!

Teruaki Mizuno was born in Kanagawa, Japan. He is also the creator of *Metallica Metalluca, Chousoku Henkei Gyrozetter* (Super High-Speed Transforming Gyrozetter), and *Marvel's Future Avengers*.

POKÉMON THE MOVIE
SECRETS OF THE JUNGLE
ANOTHER BEGINNING

VIZ MEDIA EDITION
STORY AND ART BY Teruaki MIZUNO

Original Cover Design/Plus One

Translation/Misa 'Japanese Ammo'
English Adaptation/Molly Tanzer
Touch-Up & Lettering/Joanna Estep
Design/Julian [JR] Robinson
Editor/Joel Enos

Printed in Canada

Published by VIZ Media, LLC
P.O. Box 77010
San Francisco, CA 94107

10 9 8 7 6 5 4 3 2 1
First printing, February 2022

VIZ
viz.com

ratings.viz.com
RATED A ALL AGES

PARENTAL ADVISORY
POKÉMON THE MOVIE: SECRETS OF THE JUNGLE–ANOTHER BEGINNING is rated A and is suitable for readers of all ages.

POKÉMON™

MEWTWO STRIKES BACK
EVOLUTION

Story and Art by Machito Gomi

Original Concept by Satoshi Tajiri
Supervised by Tsunekazu Ishihara
Script by Takeshi Shudo

A manga adventure inspired by the hit Pokémon movie!

← READ THIS WAY!

1
2
1
3
4
2
5
6
3
7
8
4
9
5
142

Follow the action this way.

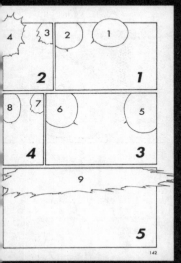

To properly enjoy this VIZ Media graphic novel, please turn it around and begin reading from right to left.

This book has been printed in the original Japanese format in order to keep the placement of the original artwork.

Have fun with it!